LEVEL GRIND

BOOKS I THROUGH IV

THE TWENTY-SIDED SORCERESS

VOLUME 1

LEVEL GRIND

BOOKS I THROUGH IV

ANNIE·BELLET

SAGA PRESS

LONDON SYDNEY **NEW YORK** TORONTO NEW DELHI

SAGA PRESS

AN IMPRINT OF SIMON & SCHUSTER, INC.

1230 AVENUE OF THE AMERICAS, NEW YORK, NEW YORK 10020

Justice Calling copyright © 2014 by Annemarie Buhl
Murder of Crows copyright © 2014 by Annemarie Buhl
Pack of Lies copyright © 2014 by Annemarie Buhl
Hunting Season copyright © 2014 by Annemarie Buhl
These titles have been previously published.
Cover illustrations copyright © 2016 by Chris McGrath

SAGA PRESS and colophon are registered trademarks of Simon & Schuster, Inc.
For information about special discounts for bulk purchases, please contact Simon & Schuster Special Sales at 1-866-506-1949 or business@simonandschuster.com.
The Simon & Schuster Speakers Bureau can bring authors to your live event. For more information or to book an event, contact the Simon & Schuster Speakers Bureau at 1-866-248-3049 or visit our website at www.simonspeakers.com.
Also available in a Saga Press hardcover edition.
The text for this book was set in ITC Galliard.
Manufactured in the United States of America
First Saga Press paperback edition October 2016
2 4 6 8 10 9 7 5 3 1
Library of Congress Cataloging-in-Publication Data
Names: Bellet, Annie, author.
Title: Level grind / Annie Bellet.
Description: First edition. | New York : Saga Press, 2016. | Series: The twenty-sided sorceress | Per publisher: omnibus editions issued without series enumeration.
Identifiers: LCCN 2016029801 | ISBN 9781481479400 (hardcover) | ISBN 9781481479394 (pbk)
Subjects: LCSH: Magic—Fiction. | Paranormal fiction. | BISAC: FICTION / Fantasy / Urban Life. | FICTION / Fantasy / Paranormal. | FICTION / Fantasy / Contemporary. | GSAFD: Fantasy fiction.
Classification: LCC PS3602.E6475 A6 2016 | DDC 813/.6—dc23
LC record available at https://lccn.loc.gov/2016029801

DEDICATED TO JEFF: 1969–2001
YOU MADE ME THE NERD I AM TODAY.
YOU WERE THE BEST BROTHER ANYONE COULD ASK FOR.
I MISS YOU LIKE HELL.

CONTENTS

JUSTICE CALLING

THE TWENTY SIDED SORCERESS: BOOK I

CHAPTER ONE ▶

Life-changing moments are sneaky little bastards. Often, we don't even know that nothing will ever be the same until long after, and only in hindsight can we look and say, "There! That was it! That changed everything."

Well, at least we could, if we're alive to do it.

For me, it was just another Thursday evening on a blustery spring day. I was finishing up a Japanese-to-English translation job and only somewhat pretending to mind the register in my comic and game shop. That's the benefit of being the owner, I suppose. No one was going to tell me to be cheerful and pay attention to customers.

There weren't any, anyway. Thursday nights are game night and we close early. I hadn't flipped the sign yet as I was waiting on Harper, my best friend of the last four years, to stop swearing at her game of *StarCraft*.

"No amount of Banelings in the world are going to save you here," I said, glancing over at her screen.

"Marines are overpowered," she growled.

"Sure," I said, trying not to laugh. It was an old gripe. Whatever race her opponent played in the game was always OP, according to the logic of Harper. "Maybe you should play with a mouse instead of just your trackpad?"

"I'm practicing my hotkeying," she said. "Shut up; you're distracting me."

The string of bells on the door tinkled and I turned away from my laptop to face the front of the store, figuring it was either a college student or a harried mother looking for *Pokémon* or *Magic: The Gathering* cards. Those types, beyond my regulars, are about all that trickle into my store on weekdays.

The man who came in was no college student, and he definitely wasn't a soccer mom. He walked through the door and paused, his head turning and his eyes wide from the change between daylight and the strategically placed lamps I keep in my shop. He took in the front display of the latest adventure releases and the wall rack of new-release comics, then stepped farther in, head turning as though searching for something or someone.

His uncertainty gave me a moment to look him over. He looked roughly thirty years old and somewhat like a Hollywood version of a Norse god. About six foot six with shaggy white-blond hair, features that a romance novel would call chiseled, and more lean muscle than a CrossFit junkie. He was also packing a handgun, mostly hidden beneath his custom-fitted leather jacket.

So, you know, not your average comic book or tabletop gaming enthusiast.

There was also the part where my wards hummed for moment, a sound only I could hear. Which meant he wasn't human, either.

Not that this was weird for the town of Wylde, Idaho. Most of the non-college-student population isn't wholly human. We're the shapeshifter capital of the West. Harper herself is a fox shifter; two of the other three in my game group are a wolverine and a coyote. Guy who owns the pawnshop next to me is a bona fide leprechaun, and the woman who runs the bakery on the other side is some kind of witch or maybe a druid.

The thick ley lines that run through the River of No Return Wilderness at the edge of town draw all kinds of supernaturals to the area.

It was what had drawn me here. I'd always heard the best place to hide a leaf is in a forest.

I was immediately on my guard. Wards aren't really my strong suit, so I didn't know what flavor of preternatural this giant was, but the gun didn't bode well. Nor did the way he looked at me like he recognized me, or the way he came over to the counter, moving with preternatural grace around the comic book displays. I gathered my power inside myself, preparing to send a bolt of pure energy into his chest if needed. I hadn't cast a real spell like that in years, but I figured I could get a single one off without knocking myself unconscious with the effort. Probably.

"Can I help you?" I asked, glad the counter was between us, even if the glass case full of dice and card boxes would be little more than a stutter step to clear for a shifter.

"Who are you?" he said. His voice was deep, with a slight accent. Russian, maybe. His eyes were the blue of glacier ice and his expression about as welcoming.

"Jade Crow," I said, teeth grinding with the effort of speaking and keeping control of my magic. "Who are you?"

"Hi, handsome," Harper said, climbing out of the overstuffed chair next to me that she'd been gaming in. She snapped her laptop shut and gave the newcomer a dazzling smile. She was angular and punky, with spiky brown hair and a way of making men forget what they were going to say when she smiled.

Then she stopped smiling and her eyes got huge, focusing in on the silver feather strung around his neck. "Oh, shit. Justice. Forgive me." And she bowed her head like she was addressing some kind of royalty.

"Justice? Like one of the shifter peacekeepers, right?" I said, my voice shaking a little with the effort of holding on to my powers for this long without letting loose. "The fuck is going on?" I glanced at Harper and then back at the intruder, keeping my eyes on the feather talisman. Yeah, it was better to look at his neck. Or his chin. His lips were way too kissable.

I shoved that thought away for later. Much, much later.

"I am Aleksei Kirov, a Justice of the Council of Nine. And you," he said, gesturing at me, "are a murderer."

"What?" Harper and I said at the same time. We shared a baffled glance. I hadn't killed anyone in my life, though not for lack of trying once. But still.

Behind the Justice, and invisible at the moment to anyone but myself, my spirit wolf guardian stirred, rising from where she'd been sleeping. Wolf didn't growl, though, just cocked her head and stared at Aleksei, ready for trouble but clearly not expecting it quite yet.

"I haven't killed anyone. Ever." I let go of the magic inside me before I accidentally lost control and unleashed. Wiping the sweat from my forehead, I ran my shaky hands over my hair and tugged my waist-length ponytail over my shoulder.

Aleksei relaxed as a confused look came over his face. "You tell the truth," he said. "But I saw you in a vision. The Nine sent me here. There are shifters in danger and you were at the center, at the crossroads between their lives and their deaths."

I opened my mouth. Closed it. A small chill went through me. The only way I could see shifters dying because of me was if *he* had found me. My psycho ex-mentor and ex-lover. I started to mentally pray to the powers of the Universe that *that* hadn't happened, or we were all in deep, deep shit.

"Nobody is in danger that we know of," Harper said. "Uh, Justice," she added, still trying to look respectful.

What I knew of the Council of Nine was practically legend, the shifter version of gods. They had Justices, powerful shifters appointed to keep the peace among shifter populations and to keep the secret of shifter existence from most of the human world. They were judge, jury, and executioner all in one. Shifters didn't get up to much crime, but if they did, the sentence was almost always death. Pretty good deterrent, I suppose.

"Besides, I'm not a shifter," I pointed out. "So, you have no power over me."

"Unless you pose a danger to shifters. What are you?" Aleksei asked, his ice-chip eyes narrowing. Subtlety was apparently not one of his charms.

"She's a hedge witch," Harper answered for me. I was glad, since this Justice guy seemed to have the ability to detect lies. Harper wasn't lying, because as far as she knew, that's what I was. She was just wrong.

Even though she was my best friend, I couldn't tell her the truth. I couldn't tell anyone that I was a sorceress. Because they'd all try to kill me or at least drive me away. Nobody likes sorcerers. Probably because most of us are assholes who kill and eat the hearts of supernatural beings for their power.

I was saved from having to verbally confirm or deny my witchiness by Ciaran. He pushed through my front door, all four foot nothing of him, his copper-and-silver hair neatly combed and his red coat clinging to his plump body. I looked at the clock on my computer monitor and muttered a curse. It was later than I'd thought.

"Harper," Ciaran said with a nod and barely a glance at Aleksei. "Jade," he addressed me in Irish, "I'd really like you to come have that look at my things before I die of old age."

"For a man who watched Saint Pat drive out the snakes, you're looking fine to me," I said, also in Irish.

That leprechaun neighbor of mine I mentioned? That's Ciaran. He'd picked up a load of things in an auction the day before, and as always with old things, he liked to have me check for magical auras and any hidden surprises. I didn't use my talents much out of fear of broadcasting my location, but minor magic like detection was as easy as breathing for me, so I did the neighborly thing and helped out when he needed.

"So, uh." I looked at Aleksei. "Since I haven't killed anyone and am not planning to, maybe you can just go Justice somewhere else? I'm closing shop."

"I will stay here. We will talk after. My visions are never wrong."

From how rigid he was and how intently he stared at me, I wondered if maybe he had a sword up his ass or something. "Okay, buddy. Just tone down the creepy before I get back. And you'll wait outside my store. I don't do strangers." Whoops. That came out weird. "In my store. I mean, alone. I mean I can't leave you here alone. So wait outside." Great. Now I was babbling.

"Fine," he said, and I swear to the Universe the bastard smirked at me.

Ciaran's shop is an antiquer's paradise and a neat freak's nightmare. Also probably a nightmare if you have allergies. He kept it tidy in its own cluttered way, but trying to keep dust off a few hundred old books, paintings, and curio cabinets full of knives, glassware, art plates, figurines, tools with unknown purpose, guns that last saw use during the Civil War, and other interesting items was a task even an immortal couldn't manage.

The shop had an almost smoky, magical feel that I loved. Above us, chandeliers of all kinds, from elk antlers to Waterford crystal, lit the place, casting shadows into the shadows until you felt as though you might come around a table piled with swords and find the wardrobe that leads to Narnia. The air wasn't musty; it was perfumed with orange and clove and some sort of citrus scent from whatever Ciaran used to wipe down the tables. The best part was that sometimes Ciaran really did have a magical item or two, though that was rare and he generally had me destroy them if we couldn't figure out what they did. Letting normals buy magical things was just asking for later trouble that nobody wanted.

"Hey," I whispered to Harper as we entered the shop, "what flavor is that Justice, anyway?"

"Flavor?" she whispered back. "Scary with a dollop of sexy?"

"No, like animal flavor," I said, whacking the back of her head with my palm.

"Oh. Tiger." She grinned and rubbed her head.

"Figures," I muttered. "Guess he wouldn't be, like, a rabbit or something." I'd bet a week of earnings he would be the biggest damn tiger ever. Shifter animals were usually larger than real-world ones anyway, but odds were that cocky bastard would be like the strongest, prettiest tiger ever to live. The universe was just like that.

"Most shifters are predators," Harper said, ducking in front of me. "Makes sense someone who has to hunt bad shifters and stuff would be a super predator, right?"

"You two done gossiping?" Ciaran called back to us. He was already halfway through the store.

Harper and I wound our way through the tables and cabinets toward the back office, where Ciaran kept any interesting purchases for me to go over, just in case, before putting them out on the floor.

"Was at an auction in Seattle last month," Ciaran explained, using English for Harper's benefit. "Just got the goods shipped in today. Some old pieces; might be worth checking out before I put a price on them. Even found some of those silver buttons your mum likes so much, Azalea."

Harper wrinkled her nose at him. He knew she hated being called by her name and preferred her gamer handle. She was about to reply when she stopped cold in front of me, forcing me to do a little dance sideways to avoid running into her. My arm whacked a cabinet, and it jingled and rocked but settled without breaking anything. Thank the universe. I figure if something ever fell in there, it would domino and the whole place would crash like a bad YouTube video.

"Where . . . How . . . No . . . I . . ." Harper couldn't get words out. She just pointed at a large stuffed fox that was perched on top of an oriental dresser.

"What about it, love? Are you all right?" Ciaran reached for Harper as she started to sink to the floor with horrible half-mewing, half-gulping cries.

I caught her first, wrapping my arms around her wiry body and finally seeing her face. Tears made her mascara run, and her shoulders shook in my arms.

"That's Rosie," she gasped. "That's my mom!"

CHAPTER TWO

Through the power of Irish hospitality or maybe some magical leprechaun mojo, Ciaran had Harper bundled in a sweater and holding a cup of mint tea before she even realized she'd finally stopped sobbing. Which was good, because Aleksei, who insisted Harper now call him Alek instead of Justice, was grilling her and Ciaran like a cop pushing a suspect.

To be fair, I don't think he intended it to come out that way. I'd known him for maybe half an hour now, and it seemed he only had one gear and it was stuck on one level: intense.

"I will go through my records, Jade, and see if I can get the ID of the man that sold this to me, all right?" Ciaran said. "It was a young man, on Tuesday; I remember that much."

"See it done." Alek turned his icy glare on Harper. His gaze seemed to soften, but it was hard to tell. "And why did no one notice her missing all this time? You said she's been gone since last weekend."

"Because she was out picking mushrooms," I said, stepping firmly between Alek and Harper. "Rose does that. She'll be gone in those woods a week or so. It's normal for her."

"How would a poacher get her?" Harper choked out. "She shouldn't have even been in fox form."

She was right about that. Rose, her mother, ran a bed-and-breakfast on a ranch that was grandfathered into the River of No Return Wilderness. She was an earthy, eccentric, and loving woman who took all sorts of shifter strays in. She liked to go camping in the wilderness every spring before the summer season brought in wildlife photographers, whitewater rafters, hikers, and all the other people the wilderness area attracted.

"I was sent here by the Council," Alek said, and he shook his head, eyes narrowing speculatively at me. "That means foul play."

"Hey, I was manning my shop. Plus I wouldn't touch a gun even if it snuggled and made me waffles." I glared at him. "Oh, Universe damn you. Now you are interrogating me. This is not cool."

"My vision says you are the key," he said, folding impressively muscled arms over his broad chest.

"Maybe you need your psychic eyes checked," I shot back.

"Guys," Harper said, sniffling. "Please. We need to find out how Mom . . . Oh, God, I can't say it. Just. Help me."

I turned to her, taking the tea from her hands and setting it aside. She collapsed into my arms, shaking with renewed sobs. I couldn't resist another glare at Alek, making it clear this was definitely his fault.

"Hey! Jade? Ciaran?" a male voice called out from within the shop.

Fuck. Game night.

"Ezee, Levi, we're back here," I yelled to them, then said to Alek as his hand reached for his gun, "Ease off there, Dirty Harry. They're furry friendlies."

"Is anyone human in this town?" he asked. He'd already sniffed at Ciaran and established he was safe since he wasn't a normal.

"Steve," Harper said, swallowing another sob and wiping her nose on the now-damp sleeve of Ciaran's sweater.

"Harper? You okay? What's going on?" The twins had made their way back to us.

Ezekiel and Levi Chapowits are Native American like myself, but

Nez Perce, not Crow. They're fraternal, not identical twins, but they share a lot of the same features. Strong bone structure, above-average height, thick black hair, dark eyes. Beyond that, and being giant nerds, they are nothing alike. Ezee is a coyote shifter and wears designer knockoff suits he sews himself. He teaches American history and Native studies up at Juniper College.

Levi is a wolverine who wears nothing but cargo pants, work boots, and tee shirts stained with the guts of the cars he works on in his shop. He wears his hair in a long Mohawk and has enough piercings in his face that I joke I could peel his skin and use it to strain pasta.

They both break the heart of every woman they meet, pretty much. Not just because they are handsome, smart, and awesome, but because Levi is happily married to a crazy hippie artist and owl shifter named Junebug, and Ezee is as gay as Neil Patrick Harris.

"Someone killed Mom," Harper blurted out.

"Frakking-A," Ezee said. "That why there's a Justice here?"

Trust Ezee to have noticed the tall, hot guy and taken in the feather talisman in a glance.

"What?" Levi said. "Oh, hello." He tipped his head to Alek.

Alek nodded back, finally seeming at a loss for words in the face of the twins. I was certain he'd start interrogating them soon enough, however.

"Where's Rose? What happened?" Levi asked.

"Behind you," I said softly.

A lot more curse words came from the twins as they looked Rose's dead body over.

"I don't see a wound," Ezee said finally.

"We should get an autopsy. That's what they do on TV." Harper pulled the sweater tight around herself and stood up.

"Is your medical examiner a shifter also?" Alek asked.

"No," Levi said. "He's with County. We aren't big enough to have our own." Levi also was a volunteer firefighter. That kind of multitasking happens when you live as long as shifters do and in a small town like Wylde.

I ran my hands over Rose's body, swallowing bile as nausea wormed through me. I was manhandling one of my favorite people in the world. My eyes felt too tight and hot in their sockets, and I realized I was about to cry. Shit. I never cry. Not in a couple decades. Not anymore.

I don't know much about taxidermy, but I figured there would be seams, staples, something. I felt nothing but her fur, its longer russet hairs rough and the lighter undercoat thick and soft on my fingers. I looked into her creepily realistic glass eyes and wished I could ask her what the hell she'd been doing in fox form and how she'd gotten caught. It was possible whoever had done this had no idea he'd killed and stuffed a person.

Which didn't make my desire to hunt him down and stuff him any less rage-filled and immediate.

"Vivian Lake can do it," I said. "She's the local vet. Wolf shifter," I added, seeing the look on Alek's face. I took a deep breath as I stepped away from Rose.

Time to put on my game master face and get shit done.

"Levi, call Steve. Tell him no game tonight, family emergency. Ezee, you take Harper up to my place." I pulled out my keys and tossed them to him. Harper looked as though she'd protest for a moment but then leaned into Ezee with another sob.

"Thank you, Jade," she whispered. "I don't think I can, I mean . . ."

"I know. It's okay. We'll figure this out. You have a car?" I said, turning back to Alek.

Ciaran came down the back stairs from his own apartment with a blanket, holding it out. I gave him a half-smile of thanks, glad he'd foreseen that we would want something to carry her in.

Before I could, Alek took the blanket and wrapped Rose up with a gentle carefulness that surprised me. As presumptuous as he was, I was kind of glad I didn't have to touch her again. He looked at me, apparently waiting for me to lead the way out. Another surprise. Maybe he wasn't always a macho asshole. Or maybe he just wanted to keep me in front of him so he could keep an eye on me. I shoved those thoughts away.

"Okay, Justice, since I'm betting you'll want to be there, let's go see Dr. Lake."

CHAPTER THREE

Alek didn't let me drive his truck. Guess the surprises had run out. It wasn't what Harper and I would joke was a "compensating for it" truck but a good-sized Ford with scratches and dents and a little dirt around the edges that let you know this guy used his truck for things, not just for driving around. The interior smelled of wet grass, damp earth, and a vanilla-laced musk that I was pretty sure came from Alek himself.

All my senses were aware of the huge, handsome man only inches away from me. Not a thing that boded well. The last time I'd been this instantly attracted to someone, he'd tried to fatten me up with magic, Hansel and Gretel style, and then eat my heart. I inched my ass as close to the door as possible, putting a bit more gap between us on the bench seat.

The drive to Dr. Lake's should have taken about five minutes, but we hit the single stoplight on Main and it was red. An old woman, someone I didn't recognize—which meant she was not a nerd and was probably part of the human half of Wylde—inched her way across the crosswalk.

"Where are you staying?" I asked, more out of a need to fill the silence and not think about what was inside the hand-sewn quilt on my lap. There were two tiny motels in town, mostly catering to the college for visiting family and to the summer tourists.

"I have a house trailer," he said. "It's at the Mikhail and Sons RV Park. You know it?"

Of course I knew it. Mikhail and his two sons were bear shifters. Vasili, the younger son, had a thing for *Magic: The Gathering* cards. His purchases paid my building rent every time a new expansion came out. They were good people. I could just imagine how they'd bent over backward to accommodate a Justice. I bet they hadn't charged him. I wasn't going to ask that aloud. I was more curious about this whole vision thing of his.

"So, how's that Justice thing work? Do you just get visions and know where to show up? And why didn't you see Rose in danger?" I hadn't meant that last part to sound so accusatory, but fuck it. What's the point of a supernatural system of law if they can't help people before someone gets killed?

"Is like a compass," he said, turning his head to look at me. His eyes were no longer ice chips but deep pools, and there was something sad in his gaze. "I know where to go; I know that I will be needed. The visions are what the Nine know, what they share with me in my dreams. I only know what they know. Is not my power but theirs."

I noticed his accent got stronger, and wondered if I'd upset him. It was hard to tell since his chiseled face gave little away.

"From what Harper has told me, the Nine are like gods. Can't they do a little better than vague visions?"

"They are not gods," Alek said. "And there is much in the world we cannot control." His tone and the sudden tightness in his jaw and shoulders warned me this was a dangerous subject.

"Hey, green light," I said, too brightly. The car behind us, clearly someone important and in a hurry, honked.

We rode the last couple minutes in silence. I wanted to ask him more about the vision of me, about me being somehow the crossroads between people living and dying. He seemed to think that meant I was killing people, but the most likely explanation was a lot scarier than that. If Samir, my ex, had found me, everyone I knew was in danger. Maybe his vision had nothing to do with whoever had killed Rose.

I took a deep breath and hugged the bundle, my eyes hot again with unshed tears.

"Left, into that parking lot," I said, pointing to Dr. Lake's practice. It was in a Victorian-style house—like a lot of us business owners in Wylde, Dr. Lake lived on the floor above her practice.

Alek came around and opened my door, taking Rose from me. I led the way into the office. Christie, a young wolf shifter who does reception for Dr. Lake, was the only one inside, and I sighed with relief.

"Hey, Christie; the doc in?" I asked.

"Yeah, she's doing paperwork," Christie said, eyeing the large bundle Alek carried. Or perhaps she was just eyeing Alek.

"Get her and tell her we'll be in the surgery room. Then you might want to close early. Just trust me, okay?" I really didn't want to show the body to Christie. She was barely out of her teens.

"Uh, okay." She didn't like it, but she got up and ran down the hall to Dr. Lake's office.

I led the way to the surgery room. The smell of alcohol tinged with an undertone of old blood make my skin goosebump. I knew the vet pretty well, since Harper was always rescuing hurt animals a sideswipe away from roadkill and begging me to take them to the vet for her. She couldn't stomach the times there was nothing to be done but easing the little critters into death, so I got the fun task of hearing Dr. Lake say there was nothing to do but help them cross over.

Dr. Lake came in directly after us. She was a tiny wolf shifter, short enough she would have legally needed a booster seat in the state of California, with a wiry, compact energy about her. She halted and tipped her chin up, her nostrils flaring as she sniffed the air. If I didn't hang out with shifters practically 24/7, it would have been creepy, but you get used to shifters sniffing people to recognize them or learn their mood or whatever.

"Another of Harper's creatures?" she asked.

"Not exactly," I said. I took the bundle from Alek and set Rose on the stainless-steel table, unfolding the blanket.

"That animal is dead," Dr. Lake said. "And has been stuffed. There's nothing I can do here."

"It's Rose Macnulty," I said softly. "We need to figure out how she died."

Dr. Lake's eyes widened and she took a half-step back, looking from Rose to me and finally to Alek. "Ah, Justice. This is a Council issue?"

"Shifter getting murdered is always a Council issue."

"Can you do an autopsy?" I asked. It wasn't really a question, since I bet she'd do whatever the big old Justice there told her to do, but no reason to ruffle more fur than Alek already was just by being himself.

Dr. Lake stepped up to the table and ran her hands expertly over Rose's body. She peeled back the fox's lips, felt along her belly, examined her paws. With a grunt, she nodded.

"I have no idea how they did it, but I'll open her and see if I can find out from the inside. No seams, no bullet wounds. It's an expert job." She shook her head. "Let me glove up. Get her on the table proper; no point getting that quilt icky."

I lifted Rose up so Alek could pull the blanket out. Nausea swept through me again, along with an electric tingle along my skin.

And I knew, with lightning clarity, where I'd felt that before.

It wasn't just revulsion at the body; I was touching foreign magic. There are lots of kinds of magic and lots of ways to draw power. I drew my power from myself, from something like a well inside of myself. It's unique to me. Any other kind of power—be it from a witch's ritual drawing on ley lines or natural forces, or another sorcerer—feels alien and weird to me. I can't use it or understand it, only sense it. Like being a native English speaker and finding all the books in your house suddenly written in Chinese. You know it says something, but the hell if you could tell anyone what that was.

"Wait," I said. I closed my eyes, reaching for a thread of my own power. I gritted my teeth and ran my hands along Rose's side. The wrongness resolved into a more solid impression. Black lines, dark on dark behind my eyelids, wrapped all around her body just beneath the skin before terminating in a complex knot in her chest.

And below that, the faint *bump-bump* of a heartbeat.

"Shit," I said, stumbling backward. "Don't cut. She's not dead. She's got a heartbeat."

"What?" Alek and Dr. Lake asked at the same time.

"It's magic. She's not dead. She's frozen somehow. Like stasis." I shivered. Dead might have been better. I couldn't imagine being frozen, unable to move or speak. Cut off from my human form.

"Can you do something about it?" Alek asked me. I didn't like the speculative way he was looking at me.

"No," I said. The truth, more or less. "This is way above my pay grade." Which was kind of a lie, but I hoped not enough of one that his apparent lie-detection abilities would notice. "It's not a kind of magic I can use. Whoever cast the spell has to undo it. If that's even possible." All that was the truth. Great universe, I hoped it was possible. If it wasn't, Rose would be trapped like this until the spell degraded enough to stop keeping her alive—and that could be years or even centuries, depending on how exactly this magic worked.

"So, I find who did this and make them undo it before I kill them. Good." Alek turned toward the door.

"Hold up there, Rambo. I need a ride back to my store." Not that I was looking forward to telling Harper what we'd found. I didn't know if not-quite-dead was worse. We had no answers, just more questions.

"I will keep Rose here, if you want, and see if I can figure out a way to monitor her vitals," Dr. Lake said, talking to Alek as much as to me. "If anything changes, I'll call you, Jade."

The light stayed green on the way back through town, and this time, we didn't talk at all.

CHAPTER FOUR

Ezee, Levi, and Harper were waiting for us in my apartment over the store.
I led Alek up the back steps. Three red-eyed faces greeted us as we came
into my small living room. The apartment is a long, narrow one-bed-
room unit with a single bathroom. The living area is dominated by my
purple velvet couch and a fifty-five-inch LED TV with about every con-
sole you can name set up under it. I mostly use my Xbox 360, but some
days nothing will do but to kill my thumbs playing *Armada* on my Sega
Dreamcast.

A girl needs options. To me, video games are like shoes. But with more
pixels and a plot.

Ezee and Levi had Harper, still bundled in Ciaran's red sweater,
between them. As we came in, they each took one of her hands and turned
their faces to us, expectant.

"So," I said with a weak smile. "You want the good news or the bad
news?"

"Mom's dead. There is no good news. Unless on the way to the vet, you
ran over the guy responsible." Harper glared at me, her green eyes puffy
and glittering with tears.

"Actually, she isn't dead. That's the good news. And kind of the bad news, too." I grimaced. That hadn't come out in the sympathetic, gentle way I'd rehearsed in my head.

"She's not dead? But I saw her. She was . . . How?" I could almost see the hope like will-o'-the-wisp lights turning on in Harper's eyes. I just prayed it wasn't a false hope I was giving her. How much worse would this get if Alek couldn't find the magic-user who did this and make him or her undo it?

"Magic," I said. "She's under some kind of spell holding her in her animal form and keeping her frozen like that."

"Why the hell would someone do that?" Levi said.

"Good fucking question." I shook my head and looked at Alek. He had come to loom beside me, standing too damn close for my comfort, but I wasn't about to inch away. It would have looked pretty obvious.

"I will ask when I find him," Alek said with a tiny smile that made me think about screaming rabbits and blood spraying on white walls. Not a nice smile, really.

"I don't care why," Harper yelled. "Just find him and make him undo it."

Ciaran knocked at the back door before entering the tense, now-quiet room. He was out of breath and excited. "I have the paperwork. Here." He held out a manila folder.

I took it and spread it open on the narrow black coffee table after clearing away the remotes and controllers. The photocopy of the ID said the guy who sold Rose was named Caleb Greer, age thirty-two, with an address in Boise, Idaho. Brown hair, brown eyes, five-foot-eight, one hundred and fifty pounds.

"He was thinner than that photo. If his ID hadn't put him at over thirty, I would have thought he was a college student," Ciaran said.

"He probably is," Ezee said. He leaned forward, looking at the paperwork upside down. "I mean, how likely is it that some middle-aged dude from Boise drove all the way out here to sell a stuffed fox? It's more likely a fake or stolen ID."

"I have his signature on the sale, and his fingerprints; there, see? I do everything aboveboard," Ciaran said. He folded his arms and pressed his lips into a line, muttering in Irish about idiot dogs.

"So, what, we just go start knocking on dorm room doors until Ciaran recognizes someone?" Levi asked.

"If that's what it takes," Harper said. The hope in her eyes had turned into anger.

I resisted making a comment about anger leading to hate and hate leading to the dark side, but the tension and level of predatory desire to kill were pretty palpable in the room. While it made a lot of sense in a "someone did something awful to someone I love" way, unleashing the hounds, so to speak, on the mostly normal population of Juniper College seemed like a pretty bad plan in actuality. For all we knew, some kid had found the bespelled Rose on the side of the road with a FREE sign on her and figured they could score a little extra cash.

"There's a better way," I said, mentally kicking myself even as my mouth kept moving. I shouldn't do magic. I shouldn't get involved. I felt like Sarah in *Labyrinth* when she falls down into the chute full of hands and chooses to keep going down. Too late now.

"I can do a spell," I continued. "There's enough with the signature and fingerprint that I can probably design a tracking thingy. If he or she is within twenty miles, it'll point right at them." There, that was more or less the truth. I carefully didn't look at Alek, though I could feel him looking intently at me. He didn't trust me anyway, so fuck him.

Hmm. Fucking Alek.

My brain hung up on that idea for a moment and I had to ask Harper to repeat herself once I realized she'd asked me something.

"What do you need?"

Technically, I didn't need anything. But I wasn't about to go along. This was clearly Justice business. If the kid was involved, nothing I could do would stop the death sentence on his head for messing with shifters.

Justices were judge, jury, and executioners. In most of the world outside the shifter-dense population of Wylde, shifters hid, maintaining a careful line between themselves and normals. Anyone stepping over the line risked humans finding out about the things that go bump in the night on a larger scale, and nobody wanted that. The Inquisition? The Nazis? Not just about persecuting humans. A lot of shifters, warlocks, and witches had gotten caught up in human madness over the centuries.

The Council of Nine and the system of Justices keeping peace and shifter law had come about sometime after the worst of the Inquisition, from what Ezee had told me. Compared to outright slaughter and experimentation, the inflexibility of shifter law was pretty understandable.

"A compass," I said. "I have the rest of what I need here."

"I will be right back," Ciaran said, turning and dashing back out my door.

He came back with a brass compass done up to look like an old-fashioned pocket watch.

"Perfect. Just give me a minute." I took the compass and the folder and went into my bedroom, locking the door behind me.

Deep breath. This wouldn't take a lot of magic. We'd still be safe. Wylde has so many ley lines, a full coven of witches, a couple thousand shifters, and probably a few other paranormals I didn't yet know about. One tiny spell wouldn't give me away. Probably.

Wolf materialized from thin air, like she does, and jumped up on my bed, watching me with her head cocked and ears perked. I couldn't tell if she approved or not.

I sank down onto my knees and put the compass on the floor on top of the thumbprint. Wrapping one hand around the large silver polyhedral die that hangs around my neck, I focused, bringing my magic up from the deep well inside.

This kind of magic isn't my specialty. In my old life, before I almost got killed and eaten, I was more of a fireball-throwing, showy sorceress.

Form a magic sword instantly out of ice that won't melt? No problem. Want to cause a localized earthquake or rain down acid? Again, I could do that, once upon a time. Samir and I used to train in an abandoned bunch of warehouses he'd bought up in Detroit, sometimes going out to lone islands in the Great Lakes to do the really spectacular stuff.

I'd grown up and honed my magic on Dungeons & Dragons manuals in the nineteen eighties, raised by an awesome bunch of programmers and gamers after my family kicked me out. Todd, Kayla, Sophie, and Ji-hoon had taken me in after I'd spent a hellish year on the streets of New York. They had been the closest thing to real family I'd ever had. Until Samir destroyed that, too.

Another deep breath. I let the past flow away from me and focused on the fingerprint, its ridges and whorls etched in black ink. There wasn't really a D&D spell precedent for what I wanted to do, but that was okay. Role-playing games are just that: games. They aren't any more real than Godzilla or He-Man. I'd used the spells as a sort of channel when I was growing up, a way of learning how to focus and impose my will on the power that flowed naturally within me.

I focused on the fingerprint, then on the idea of the hand that had formed the signature. My power flared into my amulet and poured down into the compass. The needle twitched, then spun, then stopped, pointing not north but now to the northwest. Toward Juniper College.

I sealed the spell with another focusing of my will, visualizing a thread of power like a monofilament line from the d20 around my neck to the compass. It would hold until I let it go or it got too far away, keeping the compass connected to my power.

"Wish that kid luck," I muttered to Wolf as I rose and took the compass back out into the living room.

"Here." I handed the compass to Alek. "This will point you right to the owner of that fingerprint. And, uh, be careful. Whoever did that to Rose isn't a nice person."

"I am not a nice person," Alek said with another killer-inside-me smile. "And I have certain defenses from magic that most do not have."

I almost asked but managed to close my mouth before it got him even more suspicious of me.

"Find him and make him undo the spell. Promise me, Justice." Harper's hands were curled into white fists in her lap as she spat the words out. I couldn't actually tell if she'd asked him to promise her justice or if she was using his title. Maybe both.

Alek started to shake his head as he said, "I will—" but I pinched the back of his thigh and twisted, hard, giving him my best don't-you-dare-crush-my-friend look.

"I will do my best," he amended, with only a slight twitch of a smile in reaction. Maybe he didn't completely hate me. Great.

He had really firm thighs. I shoved that thought away into the over-flowing paper bag in my head labeled "inappropriate thoughts about Alek."

After he left, another awkward silence descended. Harper finally broke it by standing up. "Where's Mom?"

"With Dr. Lake," I said. "She wanted to keep her under observation, monitor her vitals. She'll call me if there is any change." I tapped my jeans pocket where my phone was jammed. *Under observation and monitoring vitals* sounded good, clinical and nice, like Rose was just in the hospital after an accident instead of locked magically into her fox body, paralyzed and helpless.

Okay. My thoughts really weren't on the helpful train today.

"I want to go home," Harper said. "But I don't know if I can face Max. Oh, God." At the thought of her brother, her eyes started leaking again.

"We'll go with you," Levi said.

"Yeah, of course," Ezee and I agreed.

"Okay. But maybe we don't say anything. I don't know. I need to think." Harper took a deep breath and stood up.

"I'll be at my place, if you need me," Ciaran said, excusing himself.

"Thank you, Ciaran," I said, squeezing his arm as we all moved toward the door. "And Harper, we'll say or not say whatever you want. It's going to be okay."

I could have stabbed myself for saying that last part, but the look of hope she gave me made the lie worth it. Hell, for all I knew, maybe it wasn't a lie. Maybe the Justice was as badass as he thought and he'd kick in a door or drag the guy who did this back to Dr. Lake's, and we'd be having tea and cookies with Rose in her country-chic kitchen by moonrise.

After all, in a world full of shapeshifters, witches, gods, and sorcerers, maybe miracles can happen.

CHAPTER FIVE ▶

Dusk fell over us like a shroud as we drove out of the town proper and down the narrow two-lane road toward the Henhouse Bed and Breakfast, which Harper and her family called home. I rode in the back of Levi's Honda Civic with Harper, but we all rode in silence, each lost in our own thoughts, I guess.

The locals, like my friends in the car, call the River of No Return Wilderness "the Frank," after the prefix, since it's technically the Frank Church River of No Return Wilderness. I resisted calling it "the Frank," but in bleak moments like this, the full name fit. No return. Whatever happened after tonight, after finding Rose and whatever dark magic was trapping her like that, nothing would be exactly the same there. We were friends, sure, but we'd never faced any real adversity together. We sat around a table a couple times a week and pretended we were mages and bards and barbarians fighting dragons and evil lich kings.

I stared out the window so that I wouldn't be staring creepily at Harper and watched as the sun disappeared in a bloody smear behind the black spikes of the fir and pine trees.

Yeah. My brain wasn't feeling morbid and hopeless at all.

"Do you think she's awake? Conscious, I mean. Like, could she hear me?" Harper said softly. Her face was still pressed to the window, her eyes staring out into the darkening trees.

I knew what she meant. I'd been worrying over the same questions. I had no real answer, though. Harper had asked me what I thought, so I decided that would allow another small lie. It's almost funny how we destroy things by inches.

"I think she's sleeping. Magic like that takes a ritual. I bet she was asleep and still is. Big, blond, and scary out there will find the bastard that did it and stop him. Then she'll wake up, like Sleeping Beauty." I smiled at her in what I hoped was a reassuring way.

"But without the rape and having a baby after one hundred years thing," Ezee said over the back of his seat.

"Oh, God, what if he did things to her before the spell? Or after?" Harper started sobbing again.

"Not helping, dumbass." I leaned in and flicked Ezee's ear.

"Alek will find him," Levi said. "The Nine never fail to get some kind of justice."

"We should have gone with him," Harper said. "I should have."

"And what?" I said. "None of us have law enforcement backgrounds. None of us know shit about tracking down someone or how to deal with hostile magic." Wow, I was just full of lies tonight. Why quit when you're ahead, right? "We'd be in the way. Remember what you guys told me about the Justices? They are highly trained from, like, birth, and equipped to act as supernatural judge, jury, and executioner. I don't think any of us want to get in the way of that."

"I guess," Harper said, sitting up a little.

"We could always nerd the guy to death, I suppose," Levi said.

"Ooh, yeah, new torture technique. We'll make him watch nothing but *Highlander II* and *Star Trek V*!" Ezee twisted in his seat, reaching back to squeeze Harper's knee.

Harper giggled a little through her hiccupping sobs. "Anyone would give up their secrets to make that stop, huh?" Her smile was pretty weak sauce, but at least she wasn't staring blankly out the window and letting her mind run all kinds of horror scenarios.

My phone started playing the *Mega Man 2* theme, and I fumbled it out of my pocket. Ciaran.

"'Sup?"

"Two men, guns," Ciaran said quickly in Irish. In the background I heard someone, a male voice for sure, say something about speaking English, and Ciaran said it was just a greeting. Then he continued, and it sounded from the echo like he had me on speakerphone. "Jade, there's a problem with that stuffed fox I sold you. Sorry about the late hour, but could you bring it by the shop as soon as possible?"

"Sure thing. I've got it with me. I can be there in thirty?" It would only take us maybe fifteen to get back into town if Levi stepped on it.

"Sounds good. Come in the front; I'll leave it open for you."

"Cool. See you soon."

I made sure the phone call was disconnected and then growled at Levi. "Turn the car around. Two men with guns have Ciaran and are looking for Rose. We have to go back."

Levi hit the brakes and executed the quickest three-point turn I ever want to experience ever, or make that *never*, again. His car might look compact and reliable, but inside is a beast of an engine that probably isn't even street legal, and we felt the full g-force of it as he floored the gas and shot us back toward town.

"Call the sheriff?" Ezee asked.

"Not yet. We don't know what we're dealing with, and I don't want to get Ciaran killed. Let me go in and see. If I'm not out in a few, you guys can call then. I'll leave my phone line open to you so you can hear."

"How come you get to go in?" Harper said. "If they want my mom, they'll have to go through me. I don't fear bullets." She looked ready to go furry and get her serial killer on.

"They are expecting me. Going psycho on them might feel good, but it won't really solve anything. Also, we don't know yet what we are dealing with. They might be human, in which case killing them is kind of murder and even our cops might get mad about it," I said. The local sheriff was an elected position, so of course she was a shifter, but I think the last time our town saw an actual murder was back in the era of buggies and gunslingers in saloons wearing ten-gallon hats.

"Can you go faster?" Harper said.

"Maybe," Levi answered.

He could, it turns out. We got to Ciaran's store in less than fifteen minutes, slowing down to drive past it and not look like maniacs. The main street was almost abandoned after dark in our sleepy little town. Most people would be at the bars on the other end or over at the diner. All the shops were closed here and there was no foot traffic.

We pulled an emergency blanket out of the back of the Honda, and I shook it out and then crumpled it into a bundle in my arms. They were expecting someone to bring something in, after all. I figured, worst case, I could use the blanket as a lame distraction.

"Okay. Harper, stay out here by the car and keep an eye on the front." She started to protest and I gave her my best pleading look. "Trust me? I need you out here watching my back."

When she finally nodded and her shoulders slumped, I continued with my plan. "Levi and Ezee, head around back. If I'm not out in ten or if I say anything about my grandmother over the phone, call Sheriff Lee. I don't suppose anyone thought to get Alek's number?" I sure hadn't. I touched my amulet. The spell was still active, the link thick and strong. Alek likely wasn't far away if he still had the compass.

Headshakes met that last question. "Okay. It doesn't matter. Don't get shot."

Easy for me to say, I thought as I walked into Ciaran's Curios. The store was dark except for a light in the back hallway from the open office door.

The dimness only emphasized the odd shadows cast by various lamps, statues, cabinets, and other items. I'd never noticed this place was so creepy at night.

I'd never walked in here expecting armed men, either. Correlation is not causation, but I could make a pretty good case on this one.

I tried to quiet my random thoughts and come up with a real plan other than *don't get shot*. I thought about using magic to somehow subdue the men, but just upkeeping the tracking spell was making me more tired than I thought it would. A headache had viselike fingers around my temples.

Magic for a sorcerer is like a muscle: if you don't use it much, you won't completely lose it, but it will atrophy and not work the same later. I did exercise my power on weekends sometimes, lifting small rocks and holding them up in various patterns. Nothing big, nothing that would jiggle Samir's web of informants or sensors or however he tracked me, and bring him after me like a starving spider.

Maybe I could do something more coincidental, like more White Wolf mage than Dungeons & Dragons mage. Jam the guns. Knock a cabinet onto their heads.

Only, I had no idea how to jam a gun. Nor did I have a clue how much magic would get me noticed. The ley lines and supernatural population could hide only so much, especially from someone who knew my magic and what it looked and felt like.

So, I was down to just winging it. No magic. Maybe I should have gone to my place first and grabbed a knife. I recalled some saying about bringing a knife to a gunfight and it not being a good thing. Okay, we were down to hoping I could take out two men with only my wits and a scratchy wool blanket. Great plan.

"Ciaran? I've got the fox," I called out as I carefully wove my way through the shop. I didn't want to surprise anyone with a gun.

"In my office," Ciaran called out.

I saw a shadow move in the hallway beyond the office. It was way too big to be the leprechaun. One of the gunmen?

Then I caught a gleam of eyes, the way a cat's eyes pick up light and shine in the dark. Alek stepped forward just enough that I could make out his features, but he hung back so that he was still hidden from anyone inside the office itself. He raised a finger to his lips and then made a *get away* motion. I shook my head.

"Ciaran," I called out again. "It's really dark out here. Can you come turn on a light or something? I feel like I'm going to kill myself running into something, and this fox is super bulky."

There was muttering from the office. I crept forward, trying to be stealthy and not knock over anything. I let the blanket slide down my body to the floor and kicked it under a table, ready to follow it if bullets started flying.

"Be right there," Ciaran yelled.

He emerged from the office, a taller, thinner man standing directly behind him. I assumed that guy had the gun pointed at Ciaran's back.

"Drop the gun and tell your friend not to do anything stupid." Alek's voice was calm and deep. And cold enough to send chills down my spine.

"Fuck, man," said the guy behind Ciaran. He twisted his head and saw Alek's huge form in the shadows, pointing a big handgun at his head. "Jimmy, don't do anything stupid."

"There's a guy here with a gun," someone, I assumed Jimmy, said from inside the office. "What do we do? What? No, don't. Don't do that. We're sorry. We can fix this. Shit!"

The guy in the hallway turned slightly toward the door. "What's he doing?"

Ciaran chose that moment to sprint forward and then duck aside behind a large oriental cabinet. Panicking, the guy with the gun started shooting into the dark shop as he swung around toward Alek.

I dove for the floor as well, as something hot hit my hip. I felt as much as heard my phone shatter, and then lightning pain shot through my side and down my leg. I crawled with zero dignity under the table.

From my agonizing but safe-ish position, I saw Alek jumped by another man, this one shorter and bulkier than the first. They grappled and the first guy ran right at me, though I wasn't sure he could see me. In a brilliantly thought-out move, I shoved the wadded-up blanket next to me out in front of him and he sprawled into the table, knocking down the universe knows what around us.

The pain in my leg nearly blacked out my vision but I grabbed at the guy. He knew what had been done to Rose. He was the key; I couldn't let Harper down just because of a stupid wound.

"No. You. Don't," I hissed.

He stopped fighting me so suddenly, I actually lost my grip. For a moment he froze, and then he ripped at his neck, pulling out a medallion on a chain. I couldn't make out the details in the dim light, but nausea hit me and I felt the same kind of weird magic that had trapped Rose at work.

"No no no nononono." The man's voice became a litany as the medallion started to glow a sickly green.

In pain, bleeding, and out of options, I reached for my power almost on instinct, throwing my power into a giant silver circle around us both, trying to lock out the foreign magic. Whatever that thing was doing, it didn't seem good.

The other gunman was screaming, and I dimly heard Alek cursing. Then it stopped, the sickly green light winking out as though I'd imagined it. The man in front of me lay still, his chest slowly rising and falling, but by all appearances, he wasn't conscious.

"Jade!" Harper's voice.

Ciaran threw on the lights and I winced, blinking rapidly to try to adjust. Harper came up, kicking the gun farther from the man's hand. Boy, really, now that I had a look at him. I doubted he was over twenty-one.

"It's a trap," I said, waving at Harper to back off. "Get an ax."

"Trick, not trap. Geez." She poked him with her shoe.

Misquoting *Army of Darkness*. I really was hurt. I crawled forward, trying to keep my weight off my injured hip. I felt the bullet inside me, my body reacting to the unknown object and trying to heal it out. I needed to get out of here before I did fully heal or there would be some truly uncomfortable questions.

But I wanted the boy's medallion. I yanked it off his neck as I pretended to feel for a pulse and slid it into my bra as I curled my body to keep the bleeding side out of Harper's vision.

I failed.

"Did you get shot? You're bleeding." Harper yanked off her tee shirt and bent over me, trying to press it to my hip.

"My phone broke when I dove under the table," I said, taking her shirt and covering the bloody patch as best I could. I didn't want to look yet. If it looked anything like it felt, my side was a disaster. "Just cuts. I'll be fine."

"We called Sheriff Lee; she's on her way," Ezee said. "Bloody hell, did you get shot?"

I had to get out of there. Like, now.

"No, just cuts. I'm going to my place to clean up. This guy needs a medic or something. I don't know what happened." I tried to stand and regretted my life.

"This one is dead. I'm not sure how." Alek's voice.

Dead? Oh, that was bad. It was getting harder to think. I decided to worry about one thing at a time. Step one was figuring out how to walk out of there and up the stairs to my apartment, and if I could make it to the bathtub before I fainted from the pain. Be a lot easier to clean blood out of the bathroom than my living room carpet. I'd never get that security deposit back. Which was okay, since I owed it to myself, but still. I was a mean landlord.

"Harper, go with Jade. The less people messed up in this, the better, no?" Ciaran said.

"I've got to stay, since I called the sheriff," Levi said.

"And I do also, since she'll never believe only one of us was here," Ezee added.

"I've got her," Alek said. He moved with insane speed to my side, and then somehow I was in his arms. "Don't protest," he whispered in Russian, his breath warm on my hair. "Clearly, you don't want them to know you've been shot, so shut up and let me carry you."

Since the Zerg queen of white-hot pain and all her little pain-filled Broodlings were currently setting up a summer home in my hip, I decided to shut up and let him carry me.

CHAPTER SIX

Harper tried to follow us into my bathroom, but I shut the door in her face, muttering something about too many cooks in the kitchen. I hoped I made some kind of sense, but I was in too much pain and panic to care.

I'd used my magic—like, a lot of magic. Maybe too much. My head certainly thought I had used way too much. I was out of practice, and I felt like a former athlete who'd spent a couple years on the bench suddenly trying to beat Usain Bolt in the hundred-meter dash.

Plus the more passive side effects of not being human were taking a toll. My body was shoving shards of cell phone and what felt like a million pieces of bullet out of my hip, with what looked like a million gallons of blood.

Alek set me down as gently as he could in my bathtub and then pulled out a knife.

I flinched and held up my hands, but he just sighed and reached for my pants.

"I need to cut those away, take a look."

"Harper," I whispered, then switched to Russian. "She can hear us."

A weird warmth slid over the room, and I watched as the walls took on a slightly silvery sheen.

"No one outside this room can hear anything now," he said.

"Guess being a Justice comes with bonus features."

"First we take care of your wound. Then we'll talk."

I wasn't sure which part of that I looked forward to less. He cut my jeans away, and it wasn't anything like the fantasies I hadn't let myself have about him cutting my clothes off. I was too busy trying to seal my teeth to each other with my jaw muscles to tell him that, thank the universe.

With the wound washed off—which, let me tell you, was a peachy experience I never want to repeat—it didn't look so bad. Kind of like a steak after you take out your aggression on it with a hammer. And bonus, I now knew what my hip bone looked like, and I had a nice collection of metal fragments to show the grandkids. My phone seemed to have eaten the worst of the bullet, and it was super FUBAR.

I lay back in the tub once we got the wound clean, focusing on breathing and not passing out.

"The bleeding has stopped," Alek said. Helpful guy.

"Yeah. Give it a little while. I'll heal." I wished he would shut up and go away.

"You are no hedge witch."

"You are amazing at pointing out obvious things," I said, opening my eyes. "How did you know I'd understand Russian?"

"Call it a hunch."

He leaned against my bathroom counter, looking entirely out of place in the small room. I turned my head, choosing to look at the *Dragon Ball Z* poster I had on the bathroom door instead of into those speculating, piercing blue eyes.

"What happened back there? What kind of magic was that? And how did you save that boy?"

"That's way too many questions for my brain to handle right now," I said. All questions I didn't really want to answer. Some I didn't even have the answer to, anyway. Like what kind of magic this was. Human magic, I was pretty sure, so that meant ritual, most likely. But it wasn't like just anybody could use a ritual any more than a kid could open up the *Dungeons & Dragons Player's Guide* and cast Magic Missile. Magic was everywhere, in everything, but it was like sunlight or carbon molecules. If you don't have the tools to use it and the ability somehow to even tap in, there's no way you can make it work just by trying.

To work a ritual, you'd need knowledge, time, a power source you could access, the right ingredients, and foci, combined with a strong enough will to bind it all together. It wasn't those kids, not working alone. Jimmy, the dead one, he'd been on the phone with someone. Someone who had tried to kill both boys, using their medallions.

"You are thinking very hard for someone who pretends to know nothing," Alek said, interrupting my half-conscious train of thought.

"I don't know anything, not really. It's all speculation."

Cat quick, he bent over me and slid his large, warm hand into my shirt. When I'd pictured him groping my breasts, it wasn't exactly like that. He pulled the medallion out of my bra and dangled it over me. I made out a pattern of circles on its stained black surface, and it looked to be molded from clay.

"You pictured me groping your breasts?" he asked, and he had that smirk I'd seen a million years ago that afternoon, before everything went to hell on the handbasket express.

Clearly, I'd spoken aloud. "Blood loss talking," I said. I swiped at the medallion. "Give that back."

"Tell me what it is," he said, standing up out of my reach.

"I don't know." I gave him a smile to show that, hey, I could tell the truth sometimes.

"But you can find out." That wasn't even a question. No fair.

"I don't know," I said. "Maybe. Not tonight. I'm kind of in heal mode here. Why don't you go away? I'm rescinding your invitation."

"I am not a vampire." He cocked his head, those ice-chip eyes of his narrowing as he looked me over. "You can't order me out."

"Vampires don't exist," I muttered. I blushed and wondered if I had the blood left in my body for it. I was lying in a bathtub with half my pants missing and only a scrap of black panties covering my girl bits. I wished I'd worn nicer underwear. Or shaved in the last two days. He was a shifter, though, so maybe he preferred his women furry.

Ho-kay. That was definitely the blood loss talking.

I looked down at my hip. The wounds were mostly closed, looking a lot more like a bad abrasion than a bunch of stitch-worthy cuts. Time to get out of the bathtub and find if I had any Band-Aids.

"Still here?" I said. "Help me up."

He pulled me out of the tub as though I were no bigger than a kitten. I lost the scrap of panty but managed to yank a towel over myself as I leaned heavily on the bathroom counter.

"Okay, I need to clean up here, and you really need to leave. Maybe that kid will wake up and tell you what's going on."

He caught my chin in his hand and tilted my head toward him, leaning in close. He smelled like vanilla and sun-kissed hay. "I will come back tomorrow. And you will tell the truth, Jade Crow." All trace of smirk was gone from his face.

"Fuck you," I said, jerking my head away. Mistake, that. Red and black dots swam over my eyes and the headache vise tightened another notch.

"I thought you had revoked my invitation," he said, and just like a freakin' Dr. Jekyll and Mr. Hyde, he was smirking again.

"Do they train you to be this annoying at Justice Academy, or does it come naturally?" I said as I turned carefully around, deliberately not looking in the mirror, and pulled open the medicine cabinet. I did have Band-Aids. Score.

"It runs in my family." He set the medallion down on the counter and pulled the door open. The silvery shield he'd cast on the room dissolved. "I'll be back," he said over his shoulder.

Harper lurked near the door and ducked into the bathroom as soon as Alek left.

"He managed not to make that line sound ironic at all, wow," she said. "What were you guys doing in here?"

"Staring contest," I said. "And I don't think he was actually trying to quote *The Terminator.* You going to sleep over?"

"That okay?" She sounded so young and vulnerable. It was easy to forget sometimes that she was nearly twenty years younger than I was. I might look like I'm in my midtwenties, but I'm a lot closer to fifty than thirty.

"Of course," I said. "I don't really want to be alone, you know?"

Apparently, I wasn't done lying after all.

I didn't want to get up when my alarm blared to life, but the smell of waffles and bacon summoned me. I'd slept fitfully with weird dreams. The final dream ended with the sound of my alarm and the feel of Samir's hands around my throat as he whispered he would be here soon.

For a moment I wondered who was making bacon, but remembered that Harper had slept on my couch. At least she was earning her keep. I sat up too quickly and my hip pinged me with a reminder that I'd been shot the night before. I stumbled to the bathroom with a muttered good-morning to Harper and peeled up the Band-Aids.

There was a pretty amazing green, yellow, and purple bruise, but the cuts were all closed. A gaping wound would close within minutes. A bruise? That would stick around for days. Maybe it was my body's way of telling me I should really avoid taking damage.

I pulled on clothes, shared a somewhat awkward and quiet breakfast with Harper, and then went down to open my shop. Harper took her laptop and said she was going to go over to Dr. Lake's and sit with her mother, and then she planned to go home and talk to her brother Max about what was happening.

After the craziness of the day before, a quiet day in my shop seemed eerie. I kept waiting for something horrible to happen, but the hours went by without anyone ending up dead or frozen, without any other hot strangers with guns barging in.

Harper called the landline in the shop around four to tell me she was heading to the B&B to talk to Max. I felt weirdly isolated without my cell phone. I ordered a replacement online, but I wouldn't have it until the following Monday.

I had no word from Alek. Ciaran dropped by to say he'd solved everything with the cops, at least for the moment, and that the second kid was in a coma at the hospital. The sheriff was going to write it up as a robbery gone wrong. Nobody had any explanation for how Jimmy had died. It appeared his heart had stopped, just like that. I didn't envy Sheriff Lee her job explaining it to his parents or the admins at the college.

Ezee called the store as well, sometime after when I'd given up on doing inventory and was distracting myself by painting orc miniatures. He said he had recognized one of the kids from school and was going to ask around, see who they might have associated with. I told him to be careful and asked if he'd seen or heard from the Justice. He hadn't.

The medallion off the kid in the coma was upstairs. As the day faded, I thought about it more and more, trying to anticipate the questions Alek might have and how to answer them in a way that would make sense but not give away more about myself than I already had.

No good. I dropped a mini back onto the newspaper and gritted my teeth.

Thoughts of Samir flooded in. Had even the relatively small amounts of magic I'd used yesterday been too much? Was he even now on his way here to finally kill me? The tracking spell wouldn't register, I didn't think. Way too much ambient magic in this area for that to stand out. But the circle of protection I'd thrown up to fend off whatever killing ritual the shadowy man behind Rose's paralyzing was performing—that wasn't exactly minor magic. I mean, in the scale of things for me, it was minor. Or it would have been, once upon a time when I was in practice and in shape, magically speaking.

I looked around my shop. Pwned Comics and Games. It was home, the kind of place my teenage self had dreamed about all those years before, after my second family opened my eyes to the world of all that is nerd. I liked my life here. I didn't want things to change. I didn't want to have to run again.

Maybe I was still safe. No more magic, though. Not even my stone-floating exercises, at least not for a while. Whatever happened with Rose and the ritual mage who was behind all this was Alek's problem to handle. He was the one trained for this shit. I could provide emotional support to my friends, but I had to stop being involved.

I could stay for now. Keep my life there. Decision made, I relaxed a little.

Which was when, of course, the universe kicked me in the ass again.

Levi and Harper came through the front door in a rush. I knew it was trouble just from the energy they projected, before I even made out their upset faces and heard a peep from them.

"Ezee is missing," Levi said.

"What do you mean, *missing*?" I asked. My heart took up residence in my throat.

"He was supposed to meet me at work after his last class got out. He didn't show and he isn't answering either his cell or his office phone."

"Maybe he's at the library? Emergency student conference?" I tried to ignore my painful sense of foreboding.

"Did you talk to him today?" Harper asked.

Shit. "Shit," I said. "I did. He said he knew one of the perps from last night and was going to ask around, see who else might be connected to the guy."

"*Shit* is right," Levi muttered. "We're going over to Juniper to look for him. Come on."

How could I refuse that? He was my friend. This felt an awful lot like involvement, though.

"Where's the Justice?" I asked.

"I think he went to the hospital to see if that guy had woken up yet," Harper said. "He said something about it when he came to check on Mom earlier."

Which meant Alek was at least forty-five minutes away in another town. Wylde wasn't large enough to have a full hospital; we just had the emergency clinic and a couple doctors' offices.

"Okay, let me lock up," I said. What else could I do?

CHAPTER SEVEN

Juniper College is a private liberal arts university known for turning out a lot of serious students who go on to get PhDs and then work in low-level service jobs for the rest of their lives, trying to pay off massive student loans. Okay, so maybe not always that last part, but it was one of those elite small schools full of people who seemed more in love with learning than with practical life skills. I'd teased Ezee about it a lot, but in good fun.

I mean, I'd been raised by a bunch of professors and gone to a similar school. Once upon a time, I had thought I could be happy in academia for the rest of my life. Before Samir and my wild years as a sorceress in training, plotting to make the world my bitch.

The campus was just outside Wylde proper and butted up against the border of the River of No Return Wilderness. Ezee's office was in the oldest building on campus, a beautiful five-story timber and river-stone mansion that sat like a jewel in the middle of a grove of old-growth Douglas fir trees.

The sun was low in the sky when we arrived, the campus quiet in the spring chill. Here and there, students walked in packs, talking to each other or with heads buried in their phones, and no one gave us much of a glance.

Ezee's office was on the fourth floor. Levi had a key and let us in when knocking clearly showed his brother wasn't in residence.

Books filled one wall on shelves bending a little under their weight. Two overstuffed leather chairs with brass upholstery tacks decorating them in knotwork patters on the edges were positioned by the desk in a way that invited one in for a cozy chat over a cup of tea about the mysteries of the universe or, given Ezee's area of expertise, a lively talk about American history and treatment of Native peoples.

His desk was orderly, his laptop sitting in sleep mode and plugged into the spike bar on one side. A pile of papers sat waiting to be graded or handed back. There was a pink pen, uncapped, lying on the open area of the desk, as though Ezee had just set it down and was about to return to whatever he'd been writing. Even his desk chair was rotated toward the door, as though he'd only stepped out for a moment, and the Armani aftershave he used still hung in the air.

"Maybe he's in the bathroom? Or we could check the library," I said.

"It feels like he's here. Somehow." Levi shook his head and sniffed the air. "I think he's close. I can't tell. It's like something is blocking my connection to him."

The twins might be fraternal, but shifter twins were an almost unheard-of phenomenon. It wasn't a surprise that they were bonded in a magical way. We often joked that if you pinched one, the other would flinch. Or at least glare at you, if it was Levi. Flinching wasn't manly enough for him.

"Do you know his computer password?" Harper asked.

"Is the Pope Catholic?"

"Okay, yeah, stupid question."

Levi sat at the desk and unlocked the laptop. "Nothing immediate that I can see. Let me check his calendar. He writes down everything."

"Can I help you?" A man's voice from right behind me made me jump. Nausea twisted in my gut, and I took a step back into the office as I turned and looked the guy over.

He was about my height, maybe five eight, pudgy, close to forty, with thinning brown hair and glasses that exaggerated the bulge of his blue eyes. He wore a brown sweater and a pair of faded khakis and looked utterly unassuming. Yet he set off my creep alert instantly. Maybe it was the nausea. Maybe it was the events of the last day.

"Hi, we're looking for Professor Chapowits," I said. Despite my no-magic vow, I summoned a little of my power and tried to detect if this guy had any magic on him. Nothing. Damn. Maybe I was paranoid.

"He's not here," the man said. "How did you get into his office?" He seemed weirdly nervous, his eyes darting from me to Harper to Levi and the computer.

"I'm his brother," Levi said, swinging the chair around. "You are?"

"I'm Bernie, uh, Barnes. I work here. That's my office." He jerked a thumb over his shoulder. "Ezekiel is gone for the day. You shouldn't be going through his things."

"He wouldn't have left his laptop, and he'd be answering his phone," Levi said. "Did you see him? What did he say?"

"I just saw him leave a little while ago. Maybe he was getting coffee. He likes to get coffee at the student café. You should try there." Bernie Barnes, whose name sounded like a bad Stan Lee villain, smiled weakly at us, nodding as though he'd thought of something brilliant.

I really didn't like this guy. He seemed desperate to convince us that Ezee wasn't here and everything was fine. I studied him more with my magic-enhanced vision. It wasn't that I was getting nothing, I realized. I was seeing not just an absence of magic but an actual void. He should have registered as a human, with the little ticks and flurries of ambient power that flowed around all life forms. But to my vision, it was like he wasn't there at all.

"Why don't you come with us?" I said. "Show us where it is."

"Okay," Bernie said, surprising me. "Let me lock up my office." He turned and walked down the hall.

"That guy seem weird to you?" Harper asked.

"Hella weird," Levi said.

I stepped out of the office and saw Bernie disappearing not into one of the offices in the hall but through the stairwell doors.

"Shit, he's running," I said.

We bolted after him, Harper and Levi leaving me in their dust as we raced for the stairs. Bernie Barnes flew down those steps ahead of them, outpacing even shifter speed with his lead. Of course, even with super speed, they could charge down four flights of stairs only so quickly.

Make that five flights. Bernie headed for the basement, and there we lost him.

The bottom-floor stairway opened into a cramped hall with three doors leading off. No sign of Bernie. The hum of a furnace room greeted me as I slid to a stop beside Harper.

"Which door?" Harper said. She sniffed the air. "I can't smell him. Just dampness."

The air was humid and clammy. I assumed the door with the vents in it was to the mechanical room, so that left two others. Levi pulled open one and revealed a janitorial closet. Not that way. The other door opened to a set of iron stairs that led even farther down. We listened at the top of those steps but heard nothing from below over the noise from the old furnace.

"I think that might lead to the steam tunnels. I vote that way." Harper started down the steps.

"Unless he's hiding in the mechanical room, waiting for us to go away. Maybe we should split up," Levi said.

"Because splitting the party always leads to win, right?" I said. "Oh, wait, no, it usually leads to death."

"This isn't a game," Levi hissed at me. "My brother could be down there. That guy knows something. He could be the evil behind all this."

"That guy?" Harper said. "But he's so chubby and . . . nerdy."

"Oh, right, so evil can't look like a dopey professor? Do you even read comic books?"

"You trying to accuse me of being a fake nerd girl? Seriously?"

"Hey, you two, stop it." I stepped between them. They were both irritated, their shoulders thrown back, heads forward, posturing like they wanted a fight. Sure, Harper and Levi arguing wasn't unusual, but they didn't generally do it in a way that looked like they were about to shift and tear each other apart.

Levi's lips peeled back and his eyes went from dark brown to golden as he gathered his power. He was about to shift.

That was when I sensed the trap. Magic, the same shadowy magic that was binding Rose, coiled around the room like a snake waiting to strike. Waiting for the two shifters to reach into that other world, where their animal selves waited, and shift. I had no idea what the trap would do to them. I doubted it would freeze them like Rose—it would take a lot more power than I felt in that room to do something that complicated— but I'd put money on at least knocking them out. It was a pretty hefty spell gathering there.

"*Stop!*" I yelled at Levi as Harper growled behind me and Levi tensed to spring.

The trap sprang as he went from man to wolverine in less then a heartbeat. I threw as much power as I could yank up from within myself into another silver circle around all three of us and threw myself into Levi's furry body.

Shadowy power swirled around my circle and then dissipated with a discordant chime that rang inside my head as I held on to the image of a silver protecting circle even as I tried to hold back a wolverine almost as big as I was. Levi's claws ripped into my back, and then he was a man again, holding on to me instead of me holding him.

"Shit. Jade. Shit. I'm so sorry." Levi's body shook as he pulled away and then reached out again, his hands bloody.

"It's okay. It was a trap," I managed to say.

"Jade. Your back," Harper said. She knelt behind me and reached for the shreds of my shirt.

"It's not so bad," I said, though it felt pretty unfun. The pain was not the white-hot stab of the bullet wound the night before but a more twisting ache. I'd already used too much magic warding off and diffusing the trap. What was a little more? I called on more power and it came even easier than the day before, my sorceress skills apparently not as rusty as I'd thought. I sealed myself off from the pain, pushing power at the wounds and imagining I was a cleric casting a Cure Moderate Wounds spell.

"Shit," Harper said. "How did you do that?"

"You aren't a hedge witch," Levi said softly, staring at me with a mix of awe and fear on his face.

"No. I'll explain later," I said. I wouldn't. I had to leave Wylde, like, yesterday. It wasn't safe there anymore.

But first I'd go down into those steam tunnels with them and see if we could find Ezee. If there were more traps, well, what was a little extra magic? Samir wouldn't be there in the next hour.

I hoped.

"Come on. Let's go see what's down those steps," I said, getting to my feet.

Levi unzipped his hoodie and handed it to me. I pulled it on over my ruined shirt and felt like crying. My friends were good people. I was going to miss them like crazy. But I'd rather miss them than get them killed.

"Gamers in steam tunnels. This always ends well," I said, trying to smile.

Neither of them smiled back.

The steps led down into a tight corridor. The clamminess increased, and as we moved carefully forward, the air took on the faint scent of decay.

The corridor branched. Levi sniffed and motioned to the right. Even I could tell the smell of dead things was stronger that way. We didn't speak. My head started pounding, and it was difficult to breathe as the stench escalated.

The tunnel terminated in a round room that had probably held more mechanical devices for moving warm air around the place fifty or a hundred years ago. Now it just held a room out of a B-movie horror flick.

A huge pentagram was drawn on the floor in what looked like brownish paint but was probably dried blood. On a metal shelf to one side were an assortment of dried herbs, a couple ritual daggers straight out of a Kit Rae catalog complete with gem skulls and extraneous spiked bits, and a few books about magic. The books were bunk, new age and totally harmless. Yet somehow, this guy and his flunkies had managed to raise a lot of power. On the other side of the pentagram was a desk with a few papers strewn across it, and beyond that, another door.

"Oh, God," Harper moaned. She'd walked over to the desk and stood with her arms wrapped protectively around herself.

I moved to where I could see past her and the desk and found the source of the dead animal smell.

Two wolves were crouched there, both frozen like Rose, snarls on their faces. They were far too large to be real wolves, I realized. They had been shifters. One was rotted away, bones clearly sticking out in yellowed contrast to the grey fur. Its eyes were gone; only dark, gunky sockets remained.

The other wolf was in slightly better shape. Its body was emaciated, looking like a creature out of a Humane Society commercial but even worse. Patches of its fur had come off, and I could count its ribs and just about every other bone in its body. Its dark brown eyes were still there, staring up at us.

"I think Ezee was here," Levi whispered, coming up beside Harper and me. "I can faintly smell him."

"They are dead, right? Not like Mom," Harper said. I wasn't sure she was talking to me, but I put my hand gently on her shoulder anyway.

"That smell certainly says so," I said. I looked down at the desk. "Hey, is that a map?" Maybe we'd finally caught a break there.

"Yeah. That's a map of the Frank near the Wylde river region here." Levi bent over the map, tracing the lines. "Guess he got out in too much of a hurry to take it. Wonder what this writing is."

I studied the writing. "Sanskrit?" I guessed. "It's notes about the full moon hitting zenith and some kind of conjunction with Jupiter. Those lines there that look random? Those are ley lines, I think. He's mapped out a node of power there. That can't be good."

"How many languages do you speak?" Levi was staring at me again.

"All of them."

"No, seriously," he said.

See? Even when I tell the truth, no one believes me. What's the point?

"Is Mom going to end up like that?" Harper said. Her eyes were locked on the wolves.

"No, Harper, geez. Don't even think like that. We've uncovered a huge lead for Alek, right?" I gave her shoulder a little shake.

"The full moon is tonight," Levi said.

"We have to find Alek," I said. "Come on, that guy is long gone and I don't want us lost down here. We know where he will be. Bring the map and stuff."

"Are you sure they are dead?" Harper said, refusing to be pulled away as Levi gathered up the papers on the desk.

Oh, for fuck's sake. I swallowed the words and walked around the desk, breathing only through my mouth as my eyes watered under the assault of the bodies' acrid smell. I bent and put my hand on the head of the wolf that was less rotted out and summoned up my magic again.

The same twisting dark bonds that had locked Rose up were present in the wolf. Same pattern, same flow toward an intricate knot I could sense but not unravel.

Same faint heartbeat beneath it.

I stumbled back too quickly and ended up on my ass against the wall. I knew what Bernie Barnes was up to. I knew where all his power was coming from. The emaciated bodies filled in the final puzzle piece.

It shouldn't have been possible, but somehow, he had found a way to paralyze shifters and then cannibalize their innate power for his own spells.

"He's not dead, is he? He's like Mom. That's what Mom is gonna be. No, no," Harper cried out, and started to come around the desk.

"Get her out of here, Levi," I said, shoving myself to my feet. "I'll meet you guys at the car. Go!"

Levi's eyes met mine and he nodded gravely, understanding what I meant to do. He grabbed Harper's arm and yanked her toward the door we'd come in. "Come on, kid. We need to get out of here."

Tears streaming down her face, she looked at me and then nodded bleakly.

I waited until they were through the door and out of sight before I walked over to the shelf and picked up one of the daggers. I wanted to cuss Alek and his stupid fucking visions right out, but it wasn't him who had done this. His vision was about to come true, in a way, but it was my choice. I'm good at lying and at running, but I try not to lie to myself too much. It's a bad habit.

I stood over the wolf, my hand shaking as I held the dagger. I knew I should drive it into the wolf's heart. Which would make me a killer.

Warmth spread through me as a furry head butted into my side, rocking me on my feet. Wolf, my guardian, materialized beside me and nudged my arm again. I looked at her through blurred vision. The tears I'd been trying to shed in the last two days were there finally, stinging as they ran down my cheeks.

"Okay," I whispered. "Message received."

I knelt and drove the dagger into the wolf's chest.

CHAPTER EIGHT ▶

We didn't have to track Alek down. He was waiting for us outside the game shop when we arrived after a silent and tense car ride.

"We know who it is."

"He has Ezee."

"He has my brother."

All three of us spoke on top of each other, and Alek held up a hand.

"One at a time, and maybe not out here?" He looked at me and frowned. "I smell blood."

"I'm fine," I said. I pulled out my keys, bumping my bruised hip as I did so. Another painful reminder that I wasn't fine. Nothing was. Again I felt irrational anger at Alek for coming into my world and wrecking everything. Two days before, everything had been normal. Now, my life was ruined. Again.

Inside the shop, Levi and I quickly explained what had happened at the school. I pushed the miniatures to the side and Levi laid out the map we'd found. Harper sat heavily in my chair behind the desk and booted up my computer.

"Think he actually works there? We can find out who he really is on the faculty page, I think," she said. Her face was too calm, her eyes puffy but clear. She had the hollow look of someone who had suffered too much pain too quickly and burned down to an empty core of rage.

I knew that feeling. I knew that look. Intimately. I was halfway there myself. The other half? Sheer terror.

"I'm going upstairs to get a new shirt," I said.

Alek followed me. I wasn't really surprised.

"If we are going to talk," I said, "then you better do that silence-ward thingy you did last night." Fuck. Only, the last night, I'd been bleeding in my bathtub. Two nights before, I'd been plotting how to sucker my players into their latest adventure and rolling up stats on a lich lord.

Silvery magic slipped over the walls of my bedroom. I pulled out a Batman tee shirt and pulled off the bloody hoodie and my torn-up shirt. I kept my back to Alek, and he waited until I was clothed again before speaking.

"This Bernie Barnes, he's a sorcerer like you?" he asked.

So, he had figured out what I was. Guess that wasn't really a surprise.

"No. He's using rituals, which I guess makes him a warlock. The magic isn't inside him; he's stealing it. I think that's what the ley-line map and his notes are about." I sat heavily on my bed and looked down at my hands. There was dried blood under my nails. Awesome. Tears threatened again. Twenty-plus years without crying, and now I was about to do it twice in a day. More awesome.

"Stealing power from shifters," Alek prompted. "Like a sorcerer."

"Stop saying that. You're wrong. We can't steal power, not like that." I glared at him. "I have power because I was born with it. It's like this well inside me. A witch or warlock or whatever you call a human magic-user has only the ability to use power, not the actual power itself inside them. They have to do special rituals or tap power sources like ley lines, bodies of water, or plots of land, Gods, that kind of thing, to actually work magic. Shifters are different. You guys are one-trick ponies. Well, you might not be." I stopped for a steadying breath and waved my hand at my shimmering walls. "But most shifters just have that one connection to their animal. You guys *are* magic instead of using it. And it isn't a magic that is accessible to anyone else. If I ate your heart, nothing would happen but a bad stomachache."

"You eat hearts? I thought that was legend." He ran a hand through his hair. Some fell over his forehead and I wanted to get up and go to him, brush it away. Lean into his vanilla-and-musk warmth and pretend he was just a hot guy in my bedroom and that I wasn't sitting there on borrowed time while the world went to ruin around me.

"I don't," I said. "But I could. If, say, I ate the heart of this Bernie guy, I'd have his knowledge, his ability to use the kind of power he's wielding." I saw Alek's expression at that and realized I really shouldn't have used this situation as an example. "Anyway, that's a sorcerer thing. Bernie can't do that. I think—and again, I'm making educated but pretty crazy guesses with the stuff we already know—he's not using shifter powers so much as using their life force as a source. He's doing it with shifters probably for a couple reasons. One, no one is going to be that alarmed if they come across a guy with a bunch of stuffed animals lying around. Two, you guys have a lot of life source. What makes you hard to kill is what makes you perfect as a sort of magical battery for this guy."

Now that I was saying it all aloud, it made even more sense than it had in my head as I ran through my ideas on the drive back to my shop.

"The full moon, the ley-line node, and a fresh, healthy shifter to power whatever he's doing out there tonight . . . Well, put it together and you've got really bad news. He might be able to tap into the node from there and create some kind of permanent conduit. After that, and considering how he views your kind as walking batteries, you'll have a serious problem."

"Yes," Alek said. "But we can stop him tonight, before the moon rises. Make him undo what he has done. And then I'll kill him."

"Wait, what's this *we*, white man?" I said. "I am not going with you.

And don't you dare drag Levi and Harper along, either. They nearly got caught in one of this guy's traps today. You have training, experience. They don't. Right now, this guy is pretty much just a human. You should be able to handle that." Though we had no idea how many minions he had left. Two were out of commission. Were there more? I shoved the thought into the *not my problem* file.

"Why not come with me? You have power and you can help stop him—do your protection thing and tell me if he's undoing his magic."

"No. I'm leaving town before I get us all killed." He'd been right when he told me the night before that I would tell him the truth. He already knew what I was. What did it matter if he knew the rest? "I'm here in Wylde because I thought the ley lines and the abundance of shifters and other magic users would hide me. But it was only going to work as long as I didn't use my own magic. All those horror stories you hear about sorcerers? They aren't really about the rest of us, few as we are. They are about one man and he's probably on his way here right now to destroy me and anyone I care about."

"Then I will fight him with you in exchange for your help on this current matter." Alek looked skeptical, and his shrug was overly casual.

I laughed, the sound raw and ugly. I could have left it at that; he didn't need to understand, after all. I didn't need to change his mind. But I wanted him to know the truth—it was weirdly important to me that he see I was right, that I couldn't stay, how badly I had to run. It wasn't only terror making me go; it was the only way anyone would survive.

"Wolf, show him," I said softly, looking over at where my guardian was flopped on the floor by my dresser. Alek gave me a strange look, which was fair, since as far as he could see, I was talking to an empty patch of carpet.

Then he gasped and his hand slid to his gun as Wolf chose to become visible. She was all black, the size of a pony, with a wolf's head and ears, a body like a tiger's, giant paws with retractable claws like a lynx's, and the long, thick tail of a snow leopard. Her eyes were the black of a perfect night sky with no moon, their depths endless and full of tiny stars.

"Undying," he murmured, and for a moment I thought he might bow or something. "She is with you?" He looked at me with something like awe on his face.

Wolf was a spirit guardian, what some called the Undying. The legend went that they were the guards of the beings that had become the humans' gods. I don't really know about that, since Wolf doesn't talk to me and certainly doesn't share any secrets of the universe with me.

"I guess so. My cousins dropped me down a mine shaft as a bad joke when I was four. I was hurt and terrified, but then Wolf showed up. She stopped the pain and carried me out. Been with me ever since." I stood up and went to her. "But that isn't what I wanted you to see." I touched her belly where a stark white line of scar tissue broke up the perfect darkness of her fur.

"Samir, the sorcerer after me, he did that to her last time I ran from him."

"He scarred an Undying?" Alek gave a low whistle.

"He's been gathering power and eating the hearts of any rivals since back when a guy named Jesus told the meek they'd inherit the earth," I said. "Now do you see? You want me to help you stop the magical equivalent of a drunk driver while I'm telling you I need to get the hell out of here before I bring down a world-ending meteor on our heads."

Wolf butted me with her head and then disappeared. No idea what she meant by that gesture, as usual. I chose to ignore the feeling of unhappiness I got from it.

"So, you will keep running from him." Alek's tone made it clear that wasn't a question. "Until when?" That was probably rhetorical.

I ignored his tone. "Until I'm strong enough to fight him."

"And you grow stronger while you run away?" Alek said in a tone I was starting to really hate.

"I don't know. He's evil, Alek, and he hates me with an obsessive rage.

He hunted me down after I failed to kill him the first time, used my family to lure me out. He would have killed all of us if I hadn't run." Tears sprang to my eyes and I curled my hands into fists. "He killed them. Because of me."

Technically, they'd killed themselves after he'd captured and tortured them and then hooked them up to a bomb. I could still hear Ji-hoon's last words telling me not to come, telling me to flee as far and as fast as I could. Could hear the sound of the bomb as the four of them decided they would rather give their lives by setting the device off than let Samir take me as well.

"You tried to kill him?"

"Damnit. Yes. I found out he wasn't really my lover or my friend. He was using me, fattening up my magic by training me and helping me be more powerful so he could make a tastier meal of me later. So, yeah, I tried to kill him. I failed, okay? Twice. And now this is my life. I run away so that I can live. So that my friends here can live."

"I understand," he said. His voice had gone cold and quiet. "I will go stop this warlock myself."

He turned and walked to the door, throwing it open as he dropped his soundproofing ward. Then he hesitated and looked back at me.

"You survive," he said. "Not live. You are not living, Jade Crow."

"Fuck you," I yelled after him. I didn't need his judgment. Anger would have been better than the disappointment in his face. Better than those words, words so close to the ones my own heart whispered to me in the dead hours of the night sometimes.

I stumbled into the bathroom and saw the medallion sitting on the counter, where I'd apparently forgotten it the night before. I shoved it into a drawer. I turned the water on as hot as I could stand and scrubbed at my hands until no more blood stained them. Then I splashed water on my face until I could look into the mirror and pretend I didn't look like a mess.

Levi and Harper were still in the shop, alone. I let out my breath with a huff of relief. At least Alek had made them stay here.

"That guy told us the truth," Levi said. "His name really is Bernard Barnes and he's a professor of religious studies at Juniper."

"Well, I guess that's good," I said. My brain was already inventorying the place, trying to decide what I would take with me and what I would leave. I'd have to leave most of it.

"He said you weren't going to help," Harper said. She came around from behind the counter and stood, hands on her hips, looking at me with accusing green eyes.

"I'd get in the way," I said.

"That's what he said about us." Harper shook her head.

"He's right, Harper. He's a Justice. They are like super-shifters, right? That's what you guys told me. Your Council of Nine sent him here to fix things. So, let him do his job."

"She's right," Levi said, his voice rough but soft. "Let's go, Harper."

I was glad to have support from his quarter, but it surprised me. I squinted at him. "Where are you going?"

"To see Mom at Dr. Lake's. Max is with her. If that's okay with you?" Harper said the last part with an exaggerated sneer.

Fuck. My last conversation with my best friend was going to be a fight. Totally awesomesauce. Not.

"Yeah, of course," I said. I went to her and tried to give her a hug.

She stepped back. "See you later," she said. Levi was already half out the door.

"Bye, guys," I whispered as the door chimes rang.

CHAPTER NINE

How do you leave a home? If the third time was supposed to be the charm, one would think I'd have this down by now.

I locked up my shop and went back upstairs. A couple pairs of jeans, the few tee shirts I hadn't bled on and destroyed in the last couple days, socks, underclothes, my Pikachu footie pajamas. I didn't take any of my posters or figurines, but I did pack my dice bag. I knew wherever I went, I could probably find gamers. We are legion, after all.

I did my dishes and vacuumed all the floors. I was walking out on my lease, so I figured the least I could do was clean up the place a bit. I looked around. This was my life. And now it was over. Again.

I walked down into the shop and flicked on a light. My orc miniatures sat on the counter, primed and ready for paint to bring them to life. I could almost hear the echo of my friends' laughter from the back room where the game table stood empty, could smell the traces of a hundred pizza deliveries and spilled soda pop. The concrete floors were scuffed around the counter where Harper's combat boots always left marks when she stood there for hours on end chatting away with me while playing *Hearthstone* on her laptop.

I walked behind the counter and took a single framed picture off the wall. It was the only thing I still had from my last real home, twenty years before.

It was just a pen sketch. Four figures done up comic-book style and a small Korean signature in red ink at the bottom. Ji-hoon, one of my surrogate parents, had been an illustrator for Marvel back in the Comics Bronze Age of the late seventies and eighties. He'd done a family portrait for me as a high school graduation present.

There was Kayla with her usual side ponytail and giant smile. Sophie with her 1980s punk-band Mohawk and one hand flipping off the artist. Todd with his hair over his forehead, his oversized glasses, and his favorite Pi tee shirt on. Ji-hoon with his carefully cut black hair and slight stature that he always exaggerated in self-portraits. And an awkward girl named Jessica Carter with waist-length black hair, big cheekbones, and a huge glowing d20 pendant around her neck.

That had been me. I'd been Jade Crow when I was born. Then Jessica Carter to my second family. Jade Crow again to my third.

I didn't know who I would be next. I just wanted to be myself, whoever that was. But I'd chosen the wrong boyfriend in college, and any normal life after that was game over for me. Alek had been right about that. I had to be in survival mode, always. I'd forgotten that truth the last few years, making a home here in Wylde.

I'd been stupid.

"And this, kids, is why we can't have nice things," I said to the picture before tucking it into my duffle bag.

I looked around again. Damnit. I didn't want to leave. Maybe my car wouldn't start and I'd be stuck. Maybe Samir had given up on me. The last time he'd gotten anywhere near me that I knew of was over a decade before. Maybe he wasn't still looking for my magical signature, waiting to trap me. Maybe he was dead.

Fat fucking chance.

I had to leave. Tonight. Putting it off would make leaving tougher.

My friends were pissed at me. I was pissed at me. Would using more magic to help Alek have been so awful?

I wasn't sure. I didn't trust what I might do if faced with a choice between saving Rose and Ezee and letting them die.

Alek had said his vision showed me standing at a crossroads between shifters dying and living. I'd killed one shifter, a man whose name I might never know. It didn't matter it that it was a mercy killing. I didn't want to kill anyone.

Lies. I wanted to kill Samir. Sometimes, I dreamed terrible and explicit revenge fantasies when I couldn't sleep on the worst nights. I wanted to rain hell upon him in the worst way. And yet. He had a couple thousand years of practice on me, and only in my deepest nightmares did I even speculate how many sorcerers and human mages he'd eaten over the millennia. There was no way I'd ever be strong enough to face him.

And you grow stronger while you run away? Alek's words ran through my mind.

I hadn't grown stronger. The magic I had used in the last two days felt pretty weak to me. My power was still there, but I'd grown out of shape, out of practice. I was getting weaker.

"All the more reason you can't stay," I said aloud to the accusing silence. Maybe I was a coward, but I'd be an *alive* coward. And my friends would be safe. I was doing the right thing.

I sighed and wondered whom I was trying to convince, standing here arguing with myself in my head about a decision that only had one good answer where everyone got to go on living.

You are not living, Jade Crow. Alek's words in my head again.

Footsteps raced up the street outside, distracting me from my stupid inner turmoil, and I was already turning toward the door when Max, Harper's little brother, ran into it and started yelling my name.

I unlocked the door and Max nearly fell into my arms as he burst through, talking rapidly.

"Whoa there, buddy. Slow down. Who took Rose?" I tried to parse his rushed sentences.

"Harper and Levi," he said. "They came by a while ago, said I should go get some coffee. I went out, and when I got back, nobody was there. They took Mom. I thought I should run to you 'cause your phone just goes to voicemail and no one is picking up and I don't know where they are."

"I do," I muttered, thinking hard. Levi had definitely given in too easily. "Idiot."

"Me?"

"No, not you. Me. I should have known they'd go after Alek. They're going to try to fight the guy who did that to your mom and force him to undo it."

"Good," Max said.

"What? No. Not good." They were going to get in the way at best, and at worst get Alek killed if he was distracted trying to protect them. They'd get everyone killed, or enslaved and paralyzed, and universe knew what else. Fucking toast on a stick.

I had to stop them. Or save them. I couldn't just leave now.

Besides, I really *did* want to fight something. Bernard Barnes wasn't Samir, but he was a start.

Maybe this was the universe's way of telling me it was time to stop running.

"All right, Universe," I said, glaring up at the ceiling. "Message received."

"What are you going to do?" Max said as he followed me up the steps and into my apartment.

"I know sort of where they were going, but we don't have the map. So, I have to cast a spell on this medallion I took off one of the evil minions so we can track the person who made it, who I bet is the guy your sister and Levi went after, and so we can stop him from killing everyone before the moon hits zenith."

"Cool," Max said.

Oh, to be fifteen again.

The medallion was still in the bathroom drawer. I looked it over, find-ing little imperfections and dents in the clay that I hoped meant it was handmade. The stain on it reminded me of dried blood, and I tried not to think about that too hard as I held it in both hands and called on my magic.

It was a variation of the spell I'd done for Alek, only I needed no compass this time. The medallion would act as my guide. I felt it pulling northwest.

"You have your permit, right?" I asked Max as we descended the stairs to my car. The moon was already peeking up over the buildings.

"Yeah?"

"Good." I tossed him my keys. "I need to focus on this spell. You're driving. Try not to kill us."

For the record, my car started up just fine.

"Pull over here," I told Max after about half an hour of driving on the narrow highway along the border of the River of No Return Wilderness. "This is where I have to go on foot."

"The moon is over the trees," he said as we got out of the car. "How far is it? How long do we have?"

I almost said, "Who is this *we*, white man?" but I'd used that line once today and I figured there was some kind of cosmic limit.

"Me. I'm going. You are staying here with my car and making sure it doesn't get stolen."

"Stolen. Right." His shoulders slumped.

"I mean it, Max. Please?" I softened my tone and gave him my best desperate-female gaze.

"Okay," he muttered.

I followed the medallion's pull into the trees, shoving my way through the undergrowth. It was goddamned dark in there. I used more magic, feeding it into my talisman until the d20 glowed enough that I could see a few feet ahead. The ferns and weeds grew fewer as I moved into the more mature forest away from the road, but I was still moving too slowly. My lungs hurt and my leg muscles burned as I half-stumbled, half-ran through the dark woods.

This wasn't working. At this rate, I'd get there about dawn if they were really deep into the wilderness. There might have been an access road or old logging path that provided a better way, but my tracking spell wasn't Google Maps. It could only tell me direction, not the best route by car.

How long had it been since Alek and company stormed out of my store? Two hours? Three? Maybe they'd won and were on their way back to rub my face in how I'd missed all the action.

"Stop talking yourself out of doing shit," I said aloud as I stopped moving for a moment and leaned against a tree. I wasn't sure about lovely, but the woods were dark and deep. Robert Frost had gotten that part right. I guess two of three ain't bad. Wind rustled in the branches high over my head as I gasped in the cool, damp air.

Wolf materialized beside me and cocked her head at me.

"You going to help?" I asked her, not expecting an answer.

She bent low and twisted her head toward her back.

"Guess that's a yes," I said, smiling at her. "Thank you." I jumped up onto her back, digging my free hand into her thick, warm fur and clinging with my sore legs. I hadn't ridden on Wolf's back since she'd dragged us both bleeding and half-dead out of the burning rubble where my family had chosen death and where I'd made my second and most disastrous stand against Samir.

This ride was a lot more fun. She sprang forward, gliding just over the ground in large, smooth bounds. I kept my grip on her fur and on the medallion, holding the tracking spell as best I could, but she seemed to know where to go. We soared through the woods, covering miles in a rush. I finally gave up on the spell and used that hand to grip my braid, keeping my head down as branches whipped by and threatened to tear off all my hair. Long hair can be a bitch.

After an eternity that wasn't long enough, Wolf slowed and dropped into a crouch. As my ears adjusted to the sudden lack of movement and wind, I heard chanting coming from up ahead. I blinked tears from my eyes and peered into the darkness. There seemed to be more light in front of us than a full moon on a clear night could account for.

Wolf crept forward until she reached the edge of a giant clearing where the trees stopped abruptly and the land sloped downward. In the moonlight I saw a field at the bottom of the hill. Tiki torches were set in a loose ring, providing enough light to make out what was going on.

There were no triumphant friends or even a raging battle. As far as I could tell, my side had already pretty much lost whatever fight had happened.

Within the ring of light were two circles drawn with what I guessed was loose chalk. The smaller circle held a huge white tiger. Alek, I guessed. He was caught within a holding spell, I assumed, since he should have been able to just step out of the thing but instead was turning and growling as though he were caught in an iron cage.

The second, larger circle contained Bernie Barnes in a ridiculous black hooded robe with silver runes sewn onto it. He knelt over a reddish-brown dog. No, not a dog. A coyote. Ezee. Barnes was chanting in Sanskrit, the words much less relevant than the twisting shadow lines of power swirling like ghosts above him.

For a moment, I didn't see Harper or Levi. Maybe Max had been wrong. I scanned the ground inside the ring of torches, and two dark shapes on the edge caught my eye. A fox and a wolverine, red and fawn fur bright against the dark grass. I couldn't tell from there if they were alive, but they definitely weren't conscious.

Rage swelled in me, white-hot, and with it came more of my magic. I fed my frustration into it and gathered power in my hands.

"All right, Wolf," I whispered to my companion, "the plan is we charge down there and wreck that motherfucker's night."

I couldn't kill him, since we needed him to undo his spells, but I could make him hurt. Make him regret ever even thinking about using magic. I could show him what a real goddamn mage could do.

Wolf charged. We burst down the hill and into the ring of torches, and I brought my hands up, aiming balls of force right at Bernie's hooded head.

I totally would have saved the night if the evil minion I hadn't spotted had waited just another few seconds.

But he didn't.

Instead, he shot me in the back.

CHAPTER TEN

The shot was loud. The bullet ripped through me and the pain wiped my grip on my magic. That whole thing with the bullet in the hip? A flesh wound compared to the tearing pain that spiked through my chest. I think I stopped breathing.

I tumbled off Wolf's back and stopped my fall with my face. My arms and legs didn't seem to want to respond. I didn't think a bullet could kill a sorceress, but this one felt like it was giving an A-plus effort.

The pain turned from lightning strikes to a deep, terrifying chill. I heard the chanting continue, and beside me Wolf growled. She might look scary as fuck, but she can't actually do anything to a human. Or stop a bullet.

My eyes didn't seem to want to open, either. The grass was wet and cool on my cheek. Maybe I'd just stay there. It smelled good. Clean. Nothing like blood or dying animals. I don't like blood. It's so sticky.

"I got her!" a man's voice called out near me.

Wolf licked my back, her tongue molten hot, and I screamed. The pain faded back enough that I could think again, and when I moved my hands to get them underneath me and pry my face off the dirt, they sluggishly obeyed.

I raised my head, spitting out blood and dirt. My mouth was gritty, but at least my eyes were working now, and I seemed to be able to breathe again. A young man in a black robe stood about ten feet from me, pointing a gun and grinning.

I reached for my magic, and this time I didn't try to really control the flow of it. I tore open the dams on my power and let it fill me to the brim. The pain gave up, turning off like a switch had been flipped. I knew somewhere in my subconscious that I was going to really regret this tomorrow, but I wanted to live until tomorrow.

I wrapped one hand around my talisman and struggled to my knees. I thrust my magic down into my left arm and used it to extend my fist, slapping the gun out of the evil minion's hand. He yelled in surprise, but I didn't stop there. I swung my arm back, using the same force to punch him in the face.

He went down and stayed down. Guess no one had ever told him not to bring a gun to a mage fight.

I laughed, though the sound came out as more of a hiccupping cough. The chanting grew quicker, more frantic. I twisted and looked at Bernie. The moonlight shone on the huge silver dagger in his hands as he raised it over Ezee's body. He was twenty feet away from me at least. I tried to rise and my vision swam with red and black dots.

Tiger-Alek roared, drawing my gaze to him. He was closer. I remembered how quickly he could move. He just needed out of that circle.

That, I could do.

I let go of my talisman and slammed both fists into the ground, channeling the raging tide of my magic into the surface of the earth. I visualized it charging just under the roots of the grass like a tunneling Arrakis sandworm. The grass rippled and the earth buckled in a straight line from my hands to the circle trapping Alek.

When the ripple hit the circle, I yanked my fists up and threw them wide in a breaking motion.

The circle flew apart, dark shards of power shooting into the air and chalk exploding in a white cloud. Tiger-Alek sprang free and took two great leaping bounds before he crashed through the circle surrounding Bernie.

"Don't kill him!" I yelled. My magical tide was receding. I was definitely hitting a limit. I pushed myself to my feet.

Tiger-Alek slammed into Bernie, knocking him to the side. Then he was just Alek again. He grabbed the chubby warlock by his robe and twisted his wrist in a crazy Bruce Lee kind of move until Bernie screamed and dropped the knife. Even stumbling forward and still fifteen feet away, I heard Bernie's arm break.

"Is the spell broken?" Alek called to me.

I looked around. No more shadows flew around the broken circle, and though I could still sense Bernie's weird, nauseating magic, it wasn't strong anymore.

"I think so," I said. "Harper? Levi?"

"Alive. I can hear them breathing."

Super senses must be nice. I sagged with relief.

"Good. So, Bernie Barnes, we meet again." I looked down at the whimpering man. He looked so pathetic that I almost felt sorry for him. Almost.

"You don't understand," he whined. "You don't know what you've done. I was so close."

"I. Don't. Fucking. Care," I said. "Save the Bond-villain explanation for whatever god greets you in hell. Unless, of course, you want to live."

There was zero way he was going to live. Shifter justice isn't very nice. But he didn't need to know that yet.

"Yes," he said, his bug-like blue eyes filled with desperation.

"All you have to do is undo your spells, the ones that suck power from my friends. Very simple." I smiled at him.

From his reaction, it wasn't a very pleasant smile.

"I, uh," he stuttered, and then looked up at Alek and then back at me. "I can't."

"You worked the spell. How?"

"I found an old book. Bought it on eBay. Most of it was gibberish, but then some of the spells worked. But I couldn't get enough power, not from people. They kept dying, you see. Then I discovered one of them." He looked back up at Alek. "Werepeople. The book described using magical creatures as vessels."

"Where is this book?" And what fucking idiot warlock had written down such dangerous spells? Rage trickled back through me, giving me a second wind, and I glared down at the shaking man.

"I burnt it. I didn't want my disciples to steal it. Jimmy and Collin were always lifting things, trying to find ways to gain power like I did. Then they sold that damn fox for weed money. This is their fault!"

"Oh, yeah, your problem was that you hired bad help. Sure." I looked at Alek. His eyes were flame and ice in the flickering torchlight.

"He's telling the truth," Alek said softly.

"So, you can't undo your spells? You really don't know how?"

"No, I'm telling you. The book didn't tell me that. Why would I want to? Before now, I mean. Those two," he said, motioning toward Harper and Levi, "they aren't tapped. They are just unconscious. They'll wake up. See? It's only that one."

"Not just him," I said. "What about the fox? What about those wolves under your office?"

"I can't do anything about it now. Don't let that thing kill me. I won't do it again. I'm sorry," Bernie said, his voice rising into a high screech.

I sank to my knees and reached out for Ezee's body beside me, sliding my hand into his soft brown fur. Shadow bonds wrapped around him in the same twisting pattern they did on Rose. I found his heartbeat, faint but there.

"This is the crossroads," I whispered, looking up at Alek. "This is what you saw."

He just stared down at me, not moving, his face giving nothing away. I knew somehow that he would let me decide. That if I said the word, he'd become the Justice once more and execute the sentence of death on Bernie Barnes.

That was one path, one road leading away from the junction I now metaphorically stood at. Down that path, Bernie died. Rose and Ezee also died. Slowly and horribly, or else they would have to be put down by friends. By me, or maybe Alek. I wasn't going to ask Harper or Levi to do it.

On that path, they died.

There was another path.

"No, Bernie," I said, the words falling like stones from my mouth. "You won't do it again." I summoned my magic, fighting the pounding exhaustion that threatened to stem the flow.

Then I plunged my hand, cloaked in raw power, into Bernie's chest and ripped out his heart.

I didn't let myself think about what I was doing. I just acted, shoving the bleeding hunk of muscle into my mouth and biting down hard. I didn't know if I had to eat the whole thing or not. I hoped not. It was hot and tough, like trying to chew a raw steak. I ripped off the biggest piece I could and swallowed it without chewing more than once, half-choking, and I fought to not immediately vomit it back up.

Shadowy power exploded in my chest as I swallowed, and a flood of images and impressions overloaded my mind. Ugly, jock-type boys gathered around me, taunting me for my glasses, my weird name. Learning Sanskrit. Stabbing a shadowy knife into a screaming man's chest. Cinnamon rolls. Shadow power welling inside me as young men sat at my feet, eager to learn. I think I passed out as Bernie's life and mine collided.

Then the sensory overload stopped, and just like that, I was awake.

My head was clear and this strange new knowledge was there, as though I'd downloaded a new file to the desktop of my brain.

I reached for Ezee, the shadow bonds inside him clear as lines on a map to me now. I knew what they were for, how they leached his life force and transmuted it into an energy I now knew how to use.

I was relieved that the very idea of this still nauseated the fuck out of me.

I unraveled the bonds. I didn't need a book to understand how this magic worked. Now that I could touch it, control it, my sorceress abilities took over and bent it to my will. I snapped the bonds, unwinding the knot around his heart.

He came alive with a yelp and sprang up. Then he shifted, turning instantly from coyote back to a man.

"Jade," he said, and then looked past me and ran for his twin's inert form.

I didn't take it personally. He could thank me later. All I wanted to do now was pass out and sleep for maybe a couple million years. The rush of new power was fading, leaving me hollow. The pain in my chest came back with an insistent throb, and spots danced in my vision again. Not enough spots, though, to keep me from turning and seeing Bernie's dead body lying in a black heap on the bloody grass. I felt nothing but a faint sadness for the man he could have been if he'd chosen another path.

I decided I could process later. It was definitely past time to be unconscious. On cue, Alek lifted me into his impossibly strong arms.

"Max," I said. "He's out there, at the highway. Someone should call him."

"Shh," he murmured. "I'll handle it from here."

He was warm, so warm. My skin felt rimed with ice in comparison. I nuzzled my head into his shoulder, pressing my bruised nose to his chest.

"You smell good," I said.

And then, because the Universe can sometimes be a merciful bitch, I passed the fuck out.

CHAPTER ELEVEN

It took me three days before I could do more than stumble to the bathroom and sip orange juice. I managed to pull up enough power at some point after I woke up the first day to free Rose from Bernie's spell. Doing so knocked me out again right afterward.

I don't know what Alek said to the evil minion who'd shot me. I decided I wouldn't ask. He'd shot me, after all. I also had no idea what happened to Bernie's body, but I was willing to bet it would never be found. The boy in the coma woke up after I killed Bernie and fled town. Without the book and without Bernie to teach them, I figured he was probably harmless now.

Unfortunately, the spell that had bound Rose and Ezee didn't put them to sleep. They'd both been awake and aware the entire time. Rose told us how she'd been approached by two young men who had said they were lost while hiking and how they'd lured her into one of Bernie's magical traps. The boy in the coma had stolen her from Bernie and sold her to Ciaran after he and Bernie argued about how they weren't learning useful magic yet.

While I was sleeping off my magical hangover and healing from a shot in the chest, Ezee had told Levi, Max, Rose, and Harper a pretty sensational account of my daring rescue. Harper and Levi were convinced I had a dire wolf familiar who could turn invisible at will now. I didn't correct them.

He left out the part where I nommed down on a man's heart. I was grateful for that. I still didn't know how I felt about it.

When I mercy-killed the wolf in Bernie's lair, I had felt so much pain and regret and revulsion for what I had to do. My heart had felt like it was going to crawl out of my chest, and I wanted to scrub my hands clean of blood like Lady Macbeth every time I thought about him. It had been merciful. The right thing to do. I still felt awful and sick about it. Bernie's memories hadn't even provided names for his victims. He hadn't cared enough to learn them.

But when I thought about Bernie, about thrusting my power into his chest and the hot, chewy taste of his heart between my teeth, I felt nothing. Empty. And I knew I would make the same choice again if I had to. I could run the scene through my mind a hundred times and I knew I would always choose his death and my friend's lives. Always.

After three days, I made Max drive me home in my car. Levi followed us and took him back to the B&B. I wanted to be alone. To process. The twins and Harper told me they understood, but I could see a million questions in their eyes. Questions I'd have to find answers for eventually if I was going to stick around.

My duffle bag was still sitting on the floor of my shop. Waiting for me to run. I picked it up and took it into my apartment. I dropped it on the coffee table and slumped onto my couch.

Stay? Or go?

Things weren't different. Samir was still going to come for me. I wasn't ready. I was more powerful than I had been a week before, thanks to Bernie's donation, but I was magically flabby. I couldn't even put up a fight half as good as the one I'd given him twenty years before. Not yet.

Someone tapped lightly on my door. I hadn't heard footsteps, so I knew instantly who it was. One giant blond pain in the ass coming right up.

"It's open," I called out. I actually wanted to talk to Alek. He'd been in and out of the B&B over the weekend, but we'd never had a chance to be alone.

He closed the door behind him and smiled at me before detouring into my kitchen and setting down a bag on the counter. Garlic and soy sauce wafted over to me. It smelled like heaven.

"Is that Chinese I smell?" I asked, even though the bag that read LEE'S MAGIC KITCHEN on the front was kind of a dead giveaway. "You are a god among men."

"That's a much nicer greeting than you gave me the first time we met," he said. He came over and sat down on the couch beside me, close enough that his thigh touched mine. I didn't move away.

"Yeah, well, you weren't exactly nice either. I believe you called me a murderer." I frowned as I said it. I hadn't been one that day. I was definitely one now.

He studied me for a moment and then looked at my duffle bag. "Are you still leaving?"

"I don't know," I said. "I'm tired of running. And as much as it really, really kills me to admit you were right . . . well . . . you were right."

"What's that? I'm sorry; I think I dozed off for a moment." He was smirking again.

"My ex is still going to come for me," I said, ignoring his teasing. "I'm not ready."

He shrugged. "So, get ready."

"It's not that simple. I'll have to start using my magic. A lot. Training. I don't even know where to begin. I should probably learn to use a gun, or how to fight, or maybe kung fu. I'm not cut out for this, and I probably don't have enough time before he shows up. He could be here tomorrow. Or in a year. I don't know. It's not simple," I repeated.

"Yes," he said, flipping to serious mode. "It is. I have been assigned to this region. The Nine want a Justice around here for a while. I can help you, if you'll let me."

"Even knowing what I am? Seeing what I did?" I bit my lower lip and held my breath. This was the conversation I wanted to have, but I dreaded it anyway.

"Two weeks ago, I was sent a dream by the Nine. In that dream I saw a beautiful woman with hair like smoke and eyes full of fire. A giant crow soared above her, and on one side of her was a pile of corpses shrouded in shadows as far as my eye could see. On the other side, there was a sea of woodland creatures who laughed and danced in a sunny meadow."

"I think the humans have psychotherapy that can help with that," I said, trying to diffuse the awkwardness I felt at his intense recounting.

"Hush," he said. "That woman was you, Jade Crow. But she was not you, also. That night, in the circle beneath the full moon, I saw you choose the sunlight, choose life. That is a strength I am happy to encourage. A woman I want to know."

Tears burned in my eyes. I was going to have to magically cauterize my tear ducts or something at this rate if I kept crying all the time.

"But I killed him," I said, curling my hands into fists in my lap. "And I don't feel bad about it. At all. I'd do it again. I *want* to do it again. To Samir. I want to rip his heart out and destroy him forever."

"Good." Alek wrapped his hands around mine and gently pried my fingers open, rubbing his thumbs over my palms. "Some people need killing. Not everyone deserves life. This is something they taught me at Justice Academy."

I squinted at him. "Wait, there's really a Justice Academy?"

He laughed, the sound deep and beautiful and clean. "No."

"Fucker," I muttered.

Then he kissed me. His lips were firm against mine and liquid desire raced from my mouth straight into my lady bits. I moaned as his tongue slid into my mouth, and I crawled into his lap as his hands wrapped around my back and tangled in my hair. After what felt like much too short a time, he pulled away. Looking into his eyes, I saw only a warm summer-sky shade of blue—none of the glacial ice I'd always compared them to.

"The food will get cold," he murmured. "Do you care?"

"Yes," I said as my stomach growled in a very unsexy manner. "To be continued, okay?"

"If you are staying," he said, and I knew he meant more than just here, in this moment.

"Yes," I said. I could almost say it without feeling terrified.

"I like when you tell the truth," he said.

"I'm a work in progress." I pried myself off his lap. "Now we're gonna eat. And then you, mister, are going to play a video game with me."

"Oh?" He stood up and pulled me back against him, nuzzling my hair.

I could definitely get used to that. "Yep. I can't date a nongamer. It's just not done. So, we're going to have to shoot some bandits and save the Borderlands."

"I've never played a video game," he said.

"Don't worry," I teased. "I'll be gentle."

He bent down and bit my earlobe before whispering in Russian, "I won't."

His words turned my legs into Gumby imitations, but I managed to stagger away from him toward the kitchen, ducking my head so my hair fell in a curtain and covered my blushing face. I might have brown skin, but I was sure I was scarlet at that moment. This thing between Alek and me, whatever this was, it was new to me. I hadn't dated in years, choosing to keep my relationships in Wylde strictly friendship-based. After all, I really hadn't shown great judgment in choosing boyfriends before.

But there I was, about to share a meal with a sexy tiger shifter who knew what I was, knew the dangers I posed, and was still here. In my home. Not running.

I knew then that Alek was right, damn him. I was done just surviving. It was time to live.

MURDER OF CROWS

THE TWENTY-SIDED SORCERESS: BOOK II

CHAPTER ONE ▶

The battlefield was quiet in the summer sunlight. I heard only the hum of insects and a light shushing of wind. My back was sweaty where I pressed it against the bark of an oak, using the tree as cover from the enemy I couldn't see or hear but knew was out there across the meadow. The pile of ammo at my feet had dwindled down to a double handful. In the shade of the trees to my right, Harper's brother, Max, lay prone, red dripping down his chest and staining the dead leaves beneath him.

To the other side of me, Alek crouched among slender aspen trees, his arm useless, his leg oozing colors, his gun on the ground. He gave me a Gallic shrug and slight smile, the afternoon breeze lifting his white-blond hair off his forehead, his ice-blue eyes glinting with dark humor.

A paintball burst on a tree trunk just over his head.

"So," he said. "We're outmanned and outgunned."

"Maybe you should untie my hands," I said.

"That's not the point of the game," Max pointed out.

"For a corpse, you are doing a lot of talking." I glared at the kid, but he just grinned.

Peeking around the tree, I surveyed the meadow. Ezee's body was a dark lump in the grass. He was the only one I'd brought down so far, no thanks to the "help" on my team. I was pretty damn sure Alek and Max had gotten shot on purpose so that I'd have to figure out how to take down Harper and Ezee's twin, Levi, on my own.

We were gathered on this lovely summer Sunday out at the Henhouse Bed and Breakfast, where Harper and Max's mother Rosie was letting us train. Three months before, I'd saved her from an evil warlock but exposed myself to an old rival. A man who would come after me.

Kind of surprising he hadn't already, really. Samir, my psycho killer ex, had restrained himself to sending cryptic postcards and had yet to show his face. I knew he would tire of sending messages and show up eventually.

I needed to get my sorceress powers stronger before that happened. Much, much stronger.

Hence the paintball game of ultimate unfairness. Ezee, Harper, and Levi were all accomplished paintballers as well as shapeshifters, which meant they got super speed, strength, extraordinary senses, and great reaction time to go with their crack-shot abilities, and they were on the opposing side. That left me with Alek, who should have been good at paintball since he could shoot real guns just fine, and Max, who was more enthusiastic than skilled. Sure, my team was shifters also, and yet here they were, out of the game already without more than a couple shots fired.

Leaving me, with my hands literally tied behind my back, to somehow win this thing. Magically. No gun. No hands. Just power. But the rules said I had to win by hitting my opponents with paintballs, so I couldn't just wrap a shield around myself and go hunt them down that way. No shields allowed today, either.

They'd taken away all my fun. By "fun," I do mean crutches. Bastards.

A green ball splattered on the tree trunk behind me.

"Best two out of three?" I yelled.

Another paintball, this one orange, smacked into the tree, misting paint onto my nose.

"Guess that's a no," I muttered as I wiped my nose on my shoulder as best I could.

"Perhaps if you sit here all day, they will get bored and come to you," Alek said. He pulled a knife from his boot, using its point to pick at his fingernails.

I considered telling him where to stick that knife but decided to concentrate on how I was going to win this thing. I looked around the tree again. The meadow sloped slightly downhill toward the thicket of saplings and brush where Harper and Levi were holed up. They couldn't cross the meadow, as Ezee's suspiciously snoring body demonstrated, but neither could I go to them. I couldn't even see them down there, and I knew they'd be able to see me much clearer with their supernaturally enhanced senses.

If only my spirit guardian, the wolflike creature I creatively called Wolf, were useful for this shit. She was lounging in the shade deeper into the trees in which I was currently hiding, her tufted ears perked as I glared at her, and she swished her long and thick black tail. Wolf could help me with only magical attacks and problems. Not that she would help here, anyway. She seemed to understand this was all play and was content to watch. Traitor.

I twisted my arms a bit, testing the orange baling twine's knots. They weren't tied that tight—the purpose wasn't to really restrain me but to keep me from using gestures to help me cast spells. I was much better at casting when I could use my hands to direct energy. It was another crutch. Truly great magic shouldn't need hands. I needed my brain to be able to think outside the normal physical limitations of the world.

It's easy to pick up a couple rocks or paintballs with magic when you can just extend it as a gesture your body and mind are already used to. But visualizing having three or four or five hands? Tougher. The human brain isn't used to being able to lift five things at once in all directions. In order to get my brain to do it, I had to break reality a little, starting in my thoughts.

Break reality. I clung to that thought. I had been flinging paintballs at them like I was the gun, but there was really no need to do so. I didn't need to conform to the physics of a gun when I threw. I could be like that one cheesy movie where they bent bullets and stuff.

Theoretically.

"You aren't dead," I whispered to Alek, "so get ready to help." I didn't have super senses, but I had someone who did.

Alek's leg and arm had been hit, but he wasn't technically out, though he couldn't shoot anymore. That was okay; I didn't need his gun. I needed the tiger in him, his keen hunter's senses and instincts. He was a freakin' Justice, the shifter equivalent of Robocop, basically. Judge, jury, and sometimes executioner. He should be able to handle a little long-distance reconnaissance.

"What do you need?" he whispered back.

I told him. He started to laugh but choked it back and nodded.

I dropped down carefully to make room by the oak trunk for Alek, keeping my profile as low as possible. I closed my eyes and visualized the thicket Harper and Levi were hiding in. I heard the slight shift of clothing as Alek crept up to the tree I'd been hiding behind, felt his warmth as he crouched against my body. I was almost sad Max was lying right there, because suddenly I could think of a lot more interesting things to be doing in the woods on a warm summer day.

Okay, focus. Paintball. Not licking Alek's chin and begging for kisses. Yeah.

I opened my eyes, keeping the image of the thicket in my mind as I looked down at the small pile of paintballs. One of the exercises I did regularly, the only one I kept doing in my twenty-five years of running and hiding from Samir, was to lift multiple stones into the air and form patterns. The paintballs weren't much different from the stones. About the same size, a little lighter.

Usually, however, I had my hands to help me visualize things. I couldn't even grab my talisman, the silver twenty-sided die around my neck, for a focus.

I summoned my power, letting it stream through me in a shivering rush, and lifted one paintball, then another, and another, until all eight remaining were in the air. I sent them up through the trees, as high as I could without losing my thin tether of magic and control. I just hoped I could stretch my magic across the meadow. Too late now to back out of the plan. If this didn't work, I'd have to surrender. No more ammo.

"Ready?" Alek whispered.

I nodded, not trusting speech.

Alek whipped his head out from behind the tree, squinting down the field, his eyes probably picking out details in the shifting shadows of the thicket that I would never know.

A paintball burst on the tree by his head; another whizzed by and splattered on the next tree in.

"Send the balls; I know where they are," he whispered.

I sent my paintballs, still high up in the air, down the left of the field, hoping they would be far out of Harper and Levi's lines of sight. Alek looked around the tree again, this time from the other side.

"Harper is behind that bush with the dark green and white leaves. Levi is crouched behind those two saplings with the twinned trunks."

I peeked around the tree, picking out where he'd said they were. I saw nothing but slight movement in the leaves of the bush, which could have been wind. If Alek was wrong, we'd lose.

Fortunately, in the three months I'd been sharing my bed with him, I'd learned that Alek wasn't wrong very often. And he hated losing almost as much as I did.

In my mind, I gathered the paintballs into two groups of four, pushing on my magic to send one group over the bush, where Harper was and the other group around behind the saplings. Their foliage wasn't thick, the trees too young to have many branches. I guess Harper and Levi hadn't thought about cover from above.

Rule number one of horror movies? No one ever looks up.

My magic was holding, though it felt like I had dragged hot wires out of my brain, and my power was slippery in my mental grasp. I could see the thin tethers holding the balls in the air, which meant another sorcerer would be able to as well. I filed that information away.

"Geronimo," I said under my breath as I pooled more magic around the balls and shoved them downward as hard as my weakening control would allow.

"Fuck!"

"Holy shitballs!"

The exclamations from the thicket were music to my ears.

Harper and Levi stood up from their spots, their heads and shoulders running with a rainbow of paint colors. In the meadow, Ezee sat up and started laughing.

"You two look like a unicorn took a shit on you," Max yelled, getting to his feet.

"Frag the weak! Hurdle the dead!" I yelled, heaving to my feet and running out into the meadow. I used a bit of power to burn away the baling twine on my wrists and thrust my sore arms out, making airplane noises as I ran in a circle through the grass.

"What are you, an Argentinean soccer player?" Ezee said, still laughing. He brushed at his khaki shorts, though there was nothing to be done about the splatters of paint. Somehow, he made them look artsy and cool. Ezee could make any outfit look nice.

"*Fútbol*, not soccer. Geez," I said, grinning.

Paint exploded onto my chest, the balls stinging madly as they burst. I fell backward into the grass.

"Hey," I said as Harper stalked toward me. "I won; no fair."

"Mom has tea ready. Let's go get cleaned up." Harper stuck her tongue out at me and walked toward the large house in the distance.

"Sorry," Levi called out. "Can't trust a fox, eh? Good job with dropping those balls on us, by the way." He offered a hand to his brother and they followed after Harper.

"If only Harper felt the same way," I muttered. "Somebody is a sore loser."

Alek swept me up into his arms and kissed my forehead. "Takes one to know one, eh?"

Laughing, covered in paint and tired as hell, I pushed him away and followed the others to the house. Another lesson learned, I guess.

I wasn't laughing later when we got back to my place. Alek was still mostly living in his little trailer, which he'd parked out at the B&B at Rosie's invitation, but we spent a lot of nights at my apartment above my game-and-comics store.

My mail was stuffed in the box by my back door, and I saw the postcard even as I picked up the slim pile. Another missive from Samir. Awesome.

"Want me to burn it?" Alek asked as I set the mail on my kitchen table and picked up the postcard.

"No, safer to keep them in the iron box behind wards," I said. Alek was the only one I had told about the postcards, mostly because he'd been there when the first arrived in the mail a mere week after the mess with the warlock.

This one was like the others, only my address and name on it, no message. Just a stylized *S*. Creepy fucker. The first had been of the Eiffel Tower in Paris. The next showed up a couple weeks later and had a picture of a canal in Venice. The third was another three weeks after that with a bunch of castle ruins from some place in Scotland.

This was the fourth. It was just a photo of a bunch of trees, no small text on the back telling me where it was taken. It looked weirdly familiar, however. I pushed away the shiver that crept over my skin. There were conifer forests like that all over the world. No reason to think it was from around here.

"Sometimes, I wish he'd just show up and get this over with," I muttered. I didn't really. Samir would crush me. I was getting stronger, but I had no illusions that I could beat a sorcerer who'd been around since the days when Brutus stabbed a guy named Caesar.

"Every minute he doesn't is good for you," Alek said. "You did well today; you are getting stronger, learning new ways to control your powers."

I smiled up at him. He always somehow knew the right thing to say, even if sometimes I wanted to punch him in the face for saying uncomfortable truths. It was Alek who had postulated that Samir hadn't shown up yet because he was uncertain of me. Alek had a point. I had gone dark for twenty-five years, running and hiding and barely using magic. Samir had almost caught up to me a couple times, but I'd slipped away from him and stayed hidden.

Until three months before. Then I'd blazed onto the magical map. Alek pointed out that I'd appeared there, near the River of No Return wilderness, which had one of the strongest networks of ley lines running beneath its millions of unbroken wild acreage, and living in a town full of shapeshifters and other magical beings. From Samir's perspective, this whole thing probably looked like some kind of trap. Why else would I stop hiding if I weren't ready for him, right?

Alek's logic made a certain kind of sense. Samir was arrogant enough to believe his calculated approach to life was the way anyone would approach things. He wasn't the type to risk his life for anyone, so he would never understand or conceive of the choice I'd made three months before. I could have stayed hidden, but friends would have died, and I would have had to leave the life I'd built there.

I was done running. Hence the whole training to use my powers and pretending that if I did, I could win against Samir.

I knew I couldn't. But I didn't have the heart to tell Alek or Harper or the twins that. They believed in me; the least I could do was try to go down fighting when the time came.

"I'm taking a shower," I said. "Joining me?"

"No," Alek said with regret in his voice. "I'm going to try calling Carlos again." His handsome brow creased in worry. It was Sunday, which meant he usually called and talked to his mentor and friend, a fellow Justice named Carlos. It had been two weeks since Carlos and he had talked, however, and Alek was worried. I hoped he would reach him tonight. A Justice going silent was probably not a good sign.

I came out into the living room after showering the last of the paint out of my waist-length black hair and cuddled up to Alek on the couch. I knew from the worry in his blue eyes even before I asked that he hadn't reached Carlos.

"Nothing?"

"No," he said, sliding an arm around my shoulders. "Nothing."

"Wouldn't the Council tell you if there was something to worry about?" I leaned into him, tucking my head against his broad chest, and breathed in his vanilla-musk scent.

"Perhaps," he said softly. He shook his head and took a steadying breath. "I called for pizza while you were in the shower. Half all meat, half pepperoni and pineapple."

It was a sign of how comfortable we were getting with each other that he knew what to get me, especially considering he thought fruit on pizza was an abomination. I wasn't sure how I felt about that—the comfort level or the whole aversion to delicious pineapple.

"You still coming to game on Thursday? You aren't going to dodge it again, right? We're down a man 'cause Steve has that family thing." We'd been trying to get Alek to game with us for months. I'd broken him in to video games, but we'd yet to get dice into his hands.

He sighed. "I'll be there," he said, nuzzling my hair and sliding his hands under my tee shirt.

Which was when someone knocked on the door.

"Pizza!" Alek said, grinning as I pushed my tee shirt back down.

"I'm gonna kill that guy for his timing," I muttered.

Alek opened the door, but it wasn't the pizza man. Instead a tall, wiry man stood there, his eyes sunken and tired-looking in his nut-brown face, but his irises were still the moss green I remembered, and his thick black hair was still cropped close to his skull. Just as it had been when I'd last seen him, over thirty years before.

When he told me I was dead to the tribe. When he kicked me out of my home for good.

"Jade," the man said, looking uncertainly past Alek.

"Alek," I said. "Would you kindly slam the door in my father's face?"

CHAPTER TWO ▶

Alek didn't end up slamming the door. The pizza guy chose that moment to show up, causing a shuffle of people as we paid him and sent him away, which ended up with all of us standing awkwardly in my kitchen.

"What are you doing here, Jasper?" I asked, emphasizing his name. He didn't get to be called Dad anymore. "How did you even find me?"

My anger wasn't pretty. It burned through me, threatening to boil over, and my magic sang in my veins as I struggled not to do something regrettable. I had thought my resentment, anger, and grief long dead. Guess I was wrong about that. I didn't think Alek would let me blast my father out of existence, however, even if I had truly wanted to. Alek was a Justice and supposed to protect shifters. Dear old Dad was a crow shifter. QED and all that jazz.

"I hired a private investigator," Jasper said. He glanced at Alek, who was wisely standing by my side and keeping his mouth shut for the moment. "I didn't expect to find you so close to home."

"This is my home." My father looked smaller and older than I remembered, but I knew it was likely time and memory playing tricks on me. I'd been all of fourteen and just a kid the last time I saw him. He was still taller than I, his face mostly unlined in that ageless way older shifters had, where he could be anywhere from thirty-five to fifty, depending on expression and lighting.

"Jade," he said, softly this time, his green eyes full of a desperate fire. "I need your help."

I laughed. I couldn't stop it from coming out, the hysterical giggles turning into full-blown gasping laughter.

"Go fuck yourself," I said. "And get the fuck out of my house."

"Jade," Alek said, placing a hand on my shoulder. His touch was steadying, even if it pissed me off a little more.

"You stay out of this." I looked up at him as I gained control of my laughter. "That man kicked me out; they all did. Sent me away to live with a woman who was little better than a slave master and her rapist husband. You know the last words that man spoke to me?" I pointed at Jasper. "'You are dead to the People. You must go away from here and never return.' So, don't you go feeling sorry for him."

I hadn't discussed that part of my life with Alek. He knew I'd been on the street, knew about my real family, the four nerds who took me in when I was a teenager and raised me until Samir killed them. I hadn't told Alek about the People. They were a dead part of my life.

"Does Granddaddy Crow know you are here?" I asked Jasper. I figured the old bastard who led the cult that was my former tribe would know. No one did anything without Sky Heart's say-so.

"Sky Heart does not know," Jasper said. "I have come to you on my own. We are desperate."

That surprised me. The Crow who were my former people weren't anything like the Crow tribe, the Apsáalooke who lived in Montana and were mostly human. Jasper's Crow were crow shifters exclusively. Back in the early seventeen hundreds, Sky Heart, a crow shifter and warrior of the actual Crow people, decided crow shifters were special and should live apart. He took a group of them gathered from many tribes and went west to finally settle in what became northern Washington state, at a thousand-acre forested parcel of land he named Three Feathers. To guard the people and shore up his own power, Sky Heart summoned a powerful spirit, who called itself Shishishiel, the Crow, and from there on out gathered only crow shifters to him. Which involved some fairly underhanded shit like stealing crow shifters from other places, killing those who didn't want to come live with the People, and, oh yeah, kicking out any children who didn't turn into crows.

So, you know, typical cult. I hadn't realized it when I'd been in it, of course. It wasn't until years later when I talked it over with my adopted family that I had seen how dysfunctional they really were. Before that, all I knew was that I was different and had to leave.

"The pizza is getting cold," Alek said. His stomach rumbled.

"So, eat it," I said. "Jasper is leaving."

"I cannot leave," Jasper said. "Just please hear me out."

"It cannot hurt to hear him out." Alek turned those big blue eyes of his on me and I sighed.

So, we ended up sitting around the kitchen table, Alek eating his pizza, me picking at a slice of mine, and Jasper clutching the glass of water Alek had offered him like it was the last piece of floating wood in a shipwreck.

Part of me wanted to break the ice and ask how Pearl, my mother, was. But I resisted. This man didn't deserve a lifeline like that, nor did either he or my mother deserve my interest or concern.

Finally, after long enough that the awkwardness in the air was as congealed at the cheese on my pizza, Jasper spoke.

"Someone, or something, is killing off the People," he said. "Sky Heart promises he and Shishishiel can stop it, but I think he lies. He says that it is because we have grown too weak, too easy on our young, our blood too diluted with crows who are not Natives. I do not believe this is so."

"You are half white," I pointed out. "Wasn't it Sky Heart who brought in your mother? He is the one who tracks down crow shifters from all over North America and forces them to join you, so he'd be the one to blame if your so-called blood is getting too impure." The whole thing disgusted me. Ruby, my grandmother, had died before I was born, sometime back around World War Two, but my mother had told me about her, about how Sky Heart kept her imprisoned in his home until she bore him a son who changed into a crow. She was where my father got his green eyes.

"Yes," he said, not meeting my gaze. "This is a reason I do not believe. There is magic at work. These murders are not natural. Someone is killing us off and no one will act."

Magic. Samir. No, that would be too easy. If he was killing off my former family to get to me, he'd be gloating more about it. And my father wouldn't be standing here talking to me. He'd be dead.

"Is Pearl alive?" I asked.

"Yes, your mother is fine. But without magic of our own to stop the killing . . ." He trailed off, eyes still fixed on the water droplets condensing on his glass.

So, not Samir. I took a deep breath. It wouldn't—shouldn't—matter if it were. I wasn't going to help the people who had declared me dead and cast me out.

"What makes you think I have magic that can help you?" I kept staring at him, hard. When I had left, my powers were barely anything. I could occasionally move things with my mind when I was really upset, but that was about it. It wasn't until a couple years later, with the help of my new family and some Dungeons & Dragons manuals to act as focuses, that I'd begun to really work magic.

Jasper raised his head. "Because of what you are," he said. "Because of who your father is."

My chair hit the floor as I jerked to my feet. This was like a bad parody of *Star Wars*. "My . . . father? You were my father." I made sure, even in my shock, to keep to the past tense. My chest hurt, as though bands were tightening inside my ribs, making it hard to breathe. Alek rose and picked up my chair, gently pushing on my shoulders until I sat again.

"No. Your mother left us for a while, many years ago." Jasper took a few deep breaths and continued. "After Ruby died, she was unhappy with the People."

"So, she escaped," I said. I shrugged Alek's hands off my shoulders. I wished he would leave in the same moment that I was glad he was there. Someone needed to witness the total crazy, I guess.

"Yes." Jasper said the word like it pained him. "She was pregnant when she came back. With you."

Came back? "Dragged back by Sky Heart and my father" was probably more accurate, if I had to guess, but there was no point asking.

"So, who is my father?"

"I do not know," Jasper said. He held up a hand to stall my exasperated exclamation. "Your mother says he was a powerful sorcerer. She was sure you inherited his powers. Even as a baby when you were angry, we saw things shift and move. Do you not have powers?"

I didn't know if I was relieved by this news. Not being related to the asshole in front of me was sort of nice, but it left me with more questions. And a horrible fear.

"Did Pearl say what this man looked like? Was he Native American at least?" I prayed Jasper would say yes. *Universe, please, let him say yes.*

"Yes," he said, and the lump in my throat lessened. "She has said that much. You are full-blood, if that worried you." There was bitterness in his tone.

I almost explained. It wasn't that I cared if I had white or whatever blood in me. It was that Samir wasn't Native and, for a terrible moment, I'd feared that I'd been lovers with my own father. It would have made a horrible kind of sense and be just the sort of twisted, fucked-up shit Samir would pull.

I didn't owe Jasper any explanations, so I kept quiet about why I'd asked. Alek's considering stare told me he had guessed my reasoning behind the question. I figured there were some awkward conversations we'd have to have later. Much, much later. After I got Jasper out of my house.

"Shifters are dying?" Alek asked, turning his piercing gaze on Jasper. "Has the Council sent someone?" The Council of Nine was a guardian and governing body for shifters, though no one really knew much about them, not even Alek, who worked for them. The Nine were practically shifter gods, there but not exactly reachable by phone.

"They did, though Sky Heart does not recognize the Nine. A man showed up after the third murder. Our leader had words with him, then the Justice left."

I watched Alek's face as he seemed to do some mental math, and that sinking feeling started up again in my stomach.

"This Justice, was he a white man?" Alek asked.

"No, black. A huge man, I think a lion shifter from how he smelled. Sky Heart was very angry with him."

Alek moved from the side of the table to loom over Jasper. "When did you see the Justice last?" His tone was intense as he bit off each syllable, his hands clenched into fists at his sides.

"A week ago? No, a little more. It was Friday, I think, so eight or nine days. Why?"

Alek pulled his silver feather talisman that marked him as a Justice out from under his shirt. Jasper's eyes widened but an excited expression came over him.

"Good, you can help as well. We need both of you. Shifters being murdered is Council business, no? No matter what Sky Heart says." His eyes flicked between us.

"The Justice who showed up," Alek said, "his name is Carlos." He looked at me. "I have to go contact the Council."

"What about Jasper?" I said. I knew that this might be Justice business, now that Carlos was involved, but no way was this man staying in my home a minute longer than necessary.

"He will come with me," Alek said after a moment. He smiled, his face sympathetic, and I couldn't decide if I wanted to punch him or kiss him. That happens to me a lot with Alek.

"You will consider helping, Jade?" Jasper rose as Alek stepped back, giving him space again.

"No," I said, and pretended that the look of despair on his face didn't tug any heartstrings. "This is Justice business. They can deal with it."

It was a lie. I knew that if Alek asked me instead of Jasper, I'd go help. Maybe. My wounds weren't healed even after thirty-three years, and I wasn't sure I wanted to rip off the bandages. My past was better left in the past.

Alek and Jasper moved toward the door.

"I'll call you or come by tomorrow, yes?" Alek said.

"Okay," I said, leaning up to give him a kiss. I made sure to put tongue in it, hoping it would make Jasper uncomfortable. Guess I'm petty like that.

"Wait," I called after them as they were halfway down the stairs. "How many murders?" I asked Jasper.

"Eleven," he said, his lips pressing into a white line and his expression going flat in a way I remembered from when I was a kid, a flatness that said there was too much emotion beneath for him to handle.

Eleven. When I'd left Three Feathers, there had been about a hundred Crow living there. I closed the door and slid down it to the floor.

Guess it was a good thing I'm a Band-Aid-fast kind of girl, because I knew in my heart that no matter what Alek found out or what his Council said, I was going back to Three Feathers and the People.

CHAPTER THREE

Alek showed up at Pwned Comics and Games, my store, late the next afternoon. I was grateful he didn't have Jasper in tow, but any hope I had of his talk with the Council going well died when I saw the expression on his face. I wasn't sure I'd ever seen him so grim, not even when he'd been pissed at me for trying to run away three months before instead of facing the evil warlock hurting my friends.

"Bad news?" I asked.

"No," he said. "No news. The Council showed up in a dream last night and told me to stay."

"They showed up? I thought they just spoke through weird visions and feelings and stuff?"

"Usually," he said, running a hand through his white-blond hair until pieces of it stuck out at odd angles. "Last night, they spoke directly to me."

"So, you are staying," I said. It wasn't really a question. Alek was a Justice. He wouldn't go against his gods.

"No. I'm going. Only question is if you are coming with me."

Apparently, I could still be surprised by people. I came around the counter and slid my arms around his waist. He smelled good, as always. Solid, warm. He was worth risking things for, worth keeping safe.

"Oh," I said. "Uh, okay." There wasn't much else to say. I had already decided the night before that I would go if the Council wasn't going to take care of things. The People had thrown me out, but they were still people and I couldn't stand by and let them all die at the hands of some crazy murderer. Nor could I let Alek walk into the situation alone.

Especially since I had a niggling feeling that murderer might be Samir, or at least instigated by my psycho ex.

"Good," he murmured into my hair. "I'll be glad for your company."

Yep. Definitely worth risking life, limb, and heart for.

We decided to leave in the morning, early. Three Feathers in Washington state was a ten- to twelve-hour drive from Wylde, Idaho. Jasper had left ahead of us, as soon as Alek assured him that he, at least, was coming to help.

Alek and I took his truck and his little gypsy-style trailer. I left an annoyed Harper in charge of the store with a promise to call her with updates.

On the ride, Alek filled me in on what Jasper had been able to tell him about the murders. The killer (or killers) was somehow hiding from the expert hunters, and was also somehow able to leave the bodies spectacularly displayed where they would be found immediately. Not an easy task in over a thousand acres of old-growth forest on the side of the Cascade Mountains.

The method of death? Something a Hannibal Lecter fan would approve of, I guess. "Removal of the organs" was all Jasper would tell Alek. He said we would have to talk to Sky Heart if we wanted to know more.

I had packed light, wishing I had more magical gizmos to bring. Over the last few months, I'd been trying to craft some items, but apparently my player hadn't gotten the Craft Magic Item feat at char gen. So far, my attempts to store magical energy in things had resulted in some impressive pockmarks in my kitchen floor and little else.

I hadn't tapped into the memories that Bernard Barnes, the former evil warlock whose heart and power I'd consumed, had left inside me. It was too gross, too disturbing to see his life laid out in my head and to pick through the madness and murderating for the potential gems of useful knowledge.

For now, I was just trying to work with what I had. Too bad I was a lot better at slinging fireballs than more finessed, useful magic.

I just hoped that whoever this killer was, he wasn't immune to fire.

"What am I walking into?" Alek said after I don't know how many hours of driving had gone by. He had refused to let me drive his truck, so I had been staring out the window, trying not to think about anything at all, until his question pulled me back.

"What do you mean? With the People?" I shifted on the bench seat and stared at his handsome profile.

He nodded, his eyes flicking to me and then back to the road.

"Fuck if I know," I said. "I haven't been there in thirty-three years. I assume a lot of the people are the same, since Sky Heart doesn't let his people go. It's like a cult. Everybody with the same last name, half the people related somehow to the other half except a few people who got dragged in at some point. Mostly Native Americans, few whites, few Hispanics. Sky Heart is the one who picks people, ordains if they are good enough to be there. And every damn one will be a crow shifter; you can bet on that."

"That's it?"

"What? You want a biography of all hundred or more people at Three Feathers? How old are you, really?"

His eyes flicked to me again. "Sixty-one."

"How much of your childhood do you remember? Can you name what the adults were doing and how they thought about things when you were ten? I was fourteen when I was kicked out. I remember a couple of my cousins, people close in age to me, and I remember my parents. But mostly, I've spent all these years *not* remembering."

Alek took a deep breath, then nodded slowly. "All right. I see your point."

"You look good for your age," I said, trying on a smile. I shouldn't have asked his age. It wasn't something us long-lifers did much. Time wasn't the same for us, and age wasn't either.

"You too," he said, his eyes crinkling as he returned my smile. "Veritable spring chicken."

"Cradle-robber," I muttered. The chuckle we shared felt forced, but at least it was something.

We lapsed back into silence and I went back to staring out the window, watching dirt and trees slide by until they blurred, one patch of road the same as another, me trying to not remember as hard as I knew how.

Jasper had given Alek directions, but we didn't need them. Somehow, even thirty-three years later, I knew the turnoff, knew the shape of the trees, and recognized the gravel road leading into Three Feathers.

Of course, all the NO TRESPASSING signs with obligatory shotgun holes in them would have tipped off anyone. Sky Heart pretended his land was an official Indian reservation, though it was no such thing. The locals in the nearest town figured it was, however, and he also kept people paid off in the local government to look the other way. The humans must have figured it was just a big patch of woods full of crazy Indians and left it at that. The People kept to themselves, homeschooling their kids, living on whatever investments Sky Heart had made and whatever they crafted to sell. Woodworking, pottery, weaving, and game meat had all been popular choices when I was a kid, and I doubt Sky Heart had changed much since.

I guess when you are over three hundred years old and an egomaniacal cult leader, change doesn't really come easy.

I swallowed my bitter thoughts along with the nerves in my stomach as we drove up the main road and approached the group of buildings that formed the core of Three Feathers. The sun was sinking in the sky, its rays limning the treetops and casting long shadows over the huge clearing the road dead-ended into.

The big log house was Sky Heart's, though he often shared it with whomever he was sleeping with, and one of its rooms had been the dedicated schoolroom when I was little. Two large pole barns flanked the house, their sheet metal siding stained with rivulets of rust, like old blood. The roofs were new, as were the solar panels decorating them. The People preferred to live as off the grid as they could, so that development didn't surprise me at all.

Dotted farther out in the clearing and along paths through the trees were more small cabins and clusters of trailers. Three Feathers could almost be mistaken for a campground. Trucks and a few cars were parked in neat lines beside the pole barns.

Everywhere, there were the People. They came out of the shaded forest and houses, gathering in stiff clusters around the edge of the gravel turnabout where Alek brought his truck to a stop. Most were Native, at least in part. Most were related to each other and, I guess, to me. Inbreeding wasn't exactly uncommon, what with Sky Heart's obsession with the purity of his crow shifters. I recognized many of the faces, though names flitted through my mind like angry birds, refusing to be caught.

The air was thick with tension and I could almost taste the anxiety I read on the faces around me. Lines etched in skin that shouldn't have seen signs of age for centuries, mouth after mouth pressed into pale lines, dark eyes wide and haunted. Knives and small-caliber pistols tucked into belts, hands close by, hovering like disturbed insects. Fear reigned here.

Then one face trapped my gaze. Pearl, my mother, was still tall and beautiful, her back ramrod straight and her long black hair pulled tight into two braids, the ends wrapped in red leather. She was near two hundred years old but looked in her early forties, only the tightness around her eyes and small wrinkles at her mouth disturbing her smooth brown skin.

I had a lot of questions for her. I just hoped she had answers that weren't more lies or that didn't only lead to more questions.

"Time's up," I muttered. "Let's do this."

Alek raised an eyebrow at me. He didn't get the Leroy Jenkins reference, but that was okay. It was mostly for me, to remind myself who I was. Not the girl they'd forced out decades before; that was for sure.

I opened my door and stepped out as Alek did the same. The sound of a pump-action shotgun being racked drew my immediate attention, and I reached inside for my magic even as I turned toward the porch of the big house.

"This is tribal land," the man descending the steps called out, the shotgun in his hands pointed right at Alek. "Go away, or else." He punctuated the *or else* by lifting the shotgun and poking the air with the barrel as though it had a bayonet on it.

Sky Heart was the same as I remembered, though not quite the boogeyman of my nightmares anymore, not after knowing Samir. He was a big slab of a man with red-brown skin and light blue eyes that were his namesake. His black hair was down to his knees, woven through with crow feathers and brightly colored threads until it looked more like a Plains Indian headdress than a man's hair. He wore a western-style shirt with mother of pearl buttons and jeans with cowboy boots, and had the physical and charismatic presence of John Wayne and Charles Manson all rolled into one.

Alek held up one hand and made sure his silver feather necklace was visible. "I am a Justice of the Council of Nine," he said in a tone I remembered from the time we met and he accused me of being a murderer. It's not a tone you want directed at you; that's for damn certain. "I am here to investigate the murders of your people."

"And her?" Sky Heart swung the gun down to point at me, and I think I burned a couple permanent willpower points not blasting him off his feet.

"Hello, Granddad," I said instead. Technically, he wasn't my grandfather, something I hadn't known until Jasper did the whole reverse Darth Vader thing on me, but it still felt satisfying to see Sky Heart's face tense and then squeeze into an unattractive expression of disgust.

"You are an exile," he said.

"She's with me," Alek said at the same time. "We have questions for you, if you'd prefer to answer them inside." He motioned at the house after casting a pointed glance around at the growing crowd.

"You, I will talk to," Sky Heart said. "Not her."

"It's fine," I said to Alek. "I'll talk to people out here."

He looked unhappy about it but nodded, seeing the logic, and followed the already-retreating Sky Heart into the house. The people around us started moving again, and a hum of low conversation buzzed in my ears, the words blending together but the sounds giving off impressions of hope and fear mixing like oil and water.

"Go on, all of you," my mother said to the crowd, making a shooing motion with her hands. "You've got better things to do than gawk."

I recognized my two cousins standing near Jasper, John and Connor. The infamous two who had led me into an abandoned mine when I was very small and left me there, lost and alone. I'd gotten Wolf out of the deal, so it wasn't all bad. They looked like men now, not the gangly boys they had been when I had left. They didn't meet my gaze, turning away at Pearl's shooing and fading back into the trees with most of the rest of the People.

One girl didn't. She hovered at the edge of the nearest pole barn, her face somehow familiar to me even though she couldn't have been older than her early teens. Shifters can live for hundreds of years, but until about twenty or so, they age at the same pace as humans. The girl had chin-length black hair and deep green eyes, the only anomaly on her otherwise perfectly Native American face. Her lips were wide, her nose straight, her cheekbones high and sharp.

She looked a bit, well, like me.

"Fuck," I muttered. I looked at Pearl. "Tell me that's not your daughter?"

Pearl stepped forward, her dark eyes inscrutable. "Emerald," she said, waving at the girl, "come meet your sister."

In the last two days, I'd learned that my father wasn't my father, and now I had a sister. Awesomesauce. And someone was kind of literally decimating these people. Double awesomesauce.

"I'm Jade," I said.

"She's not my sister," said Emerald, who was clearly the latest victim of our family's rock-centric naming scheme.

"Half, I guess," I said, dishing out a glare for Jasper.

"You told her?" Pearl said, her lips pressing into a line.

"She needed to know. Where have the lies gotten us?"

"Yeah, about that," I said.

"Not here." Pearl turned and walked away.

Emerald gave me a searing once-over with all the scorn a teenager could muster and stomped after our mother.

I had little choice but to follow.

They say you can never go home again, but I think that's more for poetic value. That or it should be changed to *You really shouldn't go home again*, which applied a lot harder in my case.

Our home was a three-bedroom log cabin, and the kitchen and bathroom were about the only things that had been updated since the seventies. The eighteen seventies. The walls were logs decorated with woven blankets that had been there when I was a kid. The couch was different; our old one had been dark blue, but this had the same heavy

Victorian style that looked opulent and sucked to sit on. I chose a hand-crafted kitchen chair instead.

"Who was my father?" I asked. No point in small talk. I didn't care how they were doing. Besides, I could see how that conversation would go. *Hi, how are you? Oh, in danger of being horribly killed, and yourself?* Yeah. No.

"Is she really my sister?" Emerald said.

"Go to your room, Em," Jasper told her.

"Why? Who is she? She's not Crow."

"No," I said, forming a small ball of purple fire in one palm. "I'm something much, much cooler." It was more prestidigitation than real magic, but flashy. The stress was getting to me and I felt the need to be petty and push back a little. To remind these people I wasn't just a kid anymore.

"Shit," Em said, her green eyes going wide.

"Em, language! Jade, please," Pearl said in a perfect *cut it out* mother voice.

"Let the kid stay. She should learn how fucked-up we really are, eh?" I looked at Em and offered her a wry smile. She couldn't have been much older than fourteen or fifteen, but I wasn't sure if she had changed yet, had found her inner shifter animal. Just because her parents were crow shifters didn't mean she would be. I hoped for her sake that she was.

Em flopped down onto the couch and gave her parents a stubborn look. Jasper sighed, and Pearl sank down onto one of the other kitchen chairs. Their movements had the feel of habit, of set pieces shifting on a stage.

"He gave his name as Ash. He was maybe Shoshone or Blackfoot," Pearl said, wiping her hands on her sundress and leaving sweaty streaks behind on the green cotton. "I don't have answers for you, Jade. I'm sorry."

Sorry? Fuck this. I rose from my chair and paced the short distance to the kitchen window. The view was as I remembered, too, from all those evenings doing dishes standing in this very spot. My life seemed layered onto itself, past and present swirling into an unreality. I had never thought to be back there, so I'd never mentally prepared for this moment. I turned back to them.

"You just ran off, slept with some random Indian dude, and then came home?"

"I was confused, lost, and he gave me a lift. It was a strange time for me after Ruby died." She shrugged. "I didn't know I was pregnant until Sky Heart brought me back. I had no way to contact your father anyway, and I hoped, well . . ." She trailed off but it was clear what she had hoped. She had hoped I was a crow shifter, not whatever my father had been.

"He was a sorcerer?" I asked. It wasn't like there were a lot of sorcerers in the world. We tended to kill each other off or get hunted down and killed by other people. Gaining power by eating the hearts of other magic-users doesn't exactly make us a popular bunch.

She nodded. "He could do things, like light a fire with just his will. No words, no rituals. He was . . . special." The wistfulness in her face was there and gone again like a shooting star, but I didn't think I'd imagined it.

For a long moment, no one spoke. Em stared at her sneakers, chewing on her lower lip. Jasper slipped his hand into Pearl's and she pressed imagined creases out of her dress, not meeting my eye.

What was there to say? So, Jasper wasn't my dad. Oh, well. He hadn't been my dad for over thirty years. This family wasn't mine anymore; they'd given up that claim pretty spectacularly by kicking me out and dumping me with an awful woman and her rapist husband.

Yet here I was. *So*, I wanted to say, *how 'bout them murders?* I repressed a nervous giggle.

"Thank you," Jasper said, looking over at me finally. "For coming. Sky Heart won't admit it, but he has grown old and tired. I am not sure he can keep us safe this time."

Em looked up at him with a gasp. "Dad," she said. I guessed she didn't hear him talk negatively about the supreme leader very often.

"Wait," I said. "What do you mean, *this time*? Has this happened before?" That would have been, you know, good to know. My frakking family and their frakking secrets. It was getting old.

He and Pearl exchanged a look, then both glanced at Em, then turned their gazes back to me. Again, it felt like players on a stage, moving from cue to cue for an audience, only now it seemed the play was hitting the climax but the actors couldn't remember their lines. Jasper's thin shoulders hunched, and he looked a decade older as he opened his mouth to answer, though his eyes told me what his words would say before he spoke.

He didn't get a chance to speak.

Screams tore through the quiet clearing, and a woman ran toward the big house, crying out for Sky Heart.

We bolted from the cabin and across the gravel drive. My family's house was close to Sky Heart's, given their direct blood ties as well as status in the tribe. Close enough that I had made it onto the big house's porch by the time Alek and Sky Heart came through the door.

Close enough to hear the woman's first coherent words.

"He's dead. It's happened again. He's dead. Dead."

CHAPTER FOUR ▶

The body was staged just beyond the farthest-out trailer in a recently cleared area at the edge of the older trees. There were a couple of large rocks and a tree stump that had been dug around but not cut from the ground and hauled away yet. It was next to that stump that the man's body was staked out.

I felt an odd tingle on my skin as we crossed into the clearing, and filed away the sensation for examining later. The air was eerily still and the sinking sun shot weak red-tinged light through the trees, spearing the corpse.

"Back," snarled Sky Heart as other people tried to follow him closer. Jasper and two other men turned and held out their arms, pushing away the growing crowd.

Alek and I ignored them all and approached the body. He was middle-aged, which meant he was one of the older residents. His face seemed familiar, but I couldn't place a name to it. His eyes were open, clouded and reflecting only sky. There was a tiny trickle of blood dried at the corner of his pale lips.

The air was thick with the sweet smell of blood underpinned with feces and dirt. The man's plaid shirt was ripped, his hands staked through with large iron nails, but there wasn't much blood on them. His nails were dirty and broken. My brain took in details, eyes looking everywhere but at the mess of his chest. Until his chest moved.

"Fuck," I yelled, jumping back.

Alek, cool as always, didn't even flinch, just gave me a sideways look before bending over the body. I moved back up beside him and forced myself to look, to really see.

His chest had been ripped open, like something from a B-grade horror movie, his ribs grey and brownish with drying blood, broken and protruding into the open air. Pinned inside his chest, where his heart and lungs should have been, was a live crow. Its beak was wired shut and its wings were stuck through with crude iron nails, but the poor thing still struggled, its feathers soaked and sticky with blood.

Alek reached into that nightmare and broke the crow's neck.

"Were they all like this?" he asked Sky Heart.

Sky Heart nodded, fingering a small leather-and-bead bag that hung around his neck. "Yes," he said. He looked in that moment as Jasper had described. Old. Tired.

"Is this how it happened before? Years ago?" I asked. It was a guess, going off what my parents had been talking about before this new murder interrupted us.

He jerked as though struck and looked at me, hate creeping into his pale eyes.

"Before?" Alek asked, rising to his feet.

"This is Crow business. Shishishiel will protect us. This is not for outsiders to interfere."

"Yeah, 'cause Shishishiel the great crow spirit dude is really doing a bang-up job so far, right?" I glared at him, refusing to be intimidated anymore. Jasper had been right about more than one thing. Something unnatural was at work here.

Killing a shifter isn't as hard as killing a sorcerer. You don't have to eat their heart, for example. Decapitation will do the trick, or just a large amount of physical damage all at once. Like exploding someone's chest and removing their heart and lungs and stuff. That seemed pretty effective. Not an easy thing to do, however, to a man who could turn instantly into a bird and fly away. A man who would have hundreds of years of experience, be stronger and faster than a human, and who could tank a lot of damage.

"You will be gone from this place by nightfall," Sky Heart said to Alek, pitching his voice loudly enough that I'm pretty sure the whole camp could hear him. "And you will take that woman with you."

"Shifters are dying," Alek said. "I will be going nowhere until that stops. You can either help or get out of my way. I obey the Council, not you." He was standing up to his full six-foot-six height and had turned on his alpha power, as I liked to think of it. Waves of it radiated off him like heat on asphalt, and for a moment, it was as though the huge white tiger that was his alternate shape lived just beneath his skin, his ice-blue eyes the eyes of an apex predator, his muscles tensed and ready to make the kill.

Sky Heart seemed to shrink under that power, but he clutched the beaded bag around his neck and pressed his lips into a line. "I must discuss with Shishishiel," he said loudly, and then added so quietly that I barely heard him, "Please, give me tonight to think on this."

I couldn't recall a time in my childhood that Sky Heart had ever said *please*. Score one for Alek, I suppose. Or score one for how dire this situation was. That was a pretty uncomfortable thought. Shishishiel was a powerful spirit, but these murders weren't stopping without additional help; that much was clear.

I turned from the staring contest as Alek nodded, and forced myself to look more closely at the body.

"Who was he?" I asked.

"Mark, my husband," the woman who had broken the news said. I hadn't heard her approach but she stood, thick shoulders shaking and eyes runny with tears, not ten feet away.

Most of the People are given pretty generic names. It keeps it easy for records when they have to pretend to be further-on generations of who they really are. There are a lot of biblical disciples in there: Matthews, Marks, Lukes, and Johns. For the women, flower names are pretty usual. Except in my family, of course. We all get rocks. The way the People often differentiated one John or Luke or Rose from another was using nick-names.

"Redtail," I said, half question, half vague recollection from decades before.

"Yes," she sniffled. That made her Mary or Marigold, I thought. Some things from childhood were so clear, other things faded away and lost. Sadly, the clear things were pretty much all the awful, hurtful parts.

I looked away from the grieving woman and tried to look at Redtail in a clinical way. *CSI: Magic Edition*, right? I could do this. I concentrated, bringing up a little power, trying to figure out what I wanted to know, to see. There wasn't a Dungeons & Dragons spell for figuring out how someone was murdered, was there? Nothing came to my mind.

I thought about how I could see my own sorcery, about how Samir used to demonstrate things to me and I could see and feel his power, familiar but different. Like how warm water and cold water are both water, but not the same to the touch.

So. Detect Magic. That was what I needed, for the moment. I pushed on my power as I closed my eyes, visualizing it in my head as coating my sight and giving me the ability to see what I should be able to only sense.

In D&D, Detect Magic can be dangerous. If there is too much magic or the spells used around you are too high of a level, you'll knock yourself out. I hoped that real life wasn't like that. With the warlock who had tried to kill my friends, I'd been able to sense his magic as a wrongness, like smelling rot or mold even if you can't see it.

I opened my eyes and looked at the body. Nothing. Maybe I was failing to do what I wanted to do magically. There were no other sorcerers around to cast a spell so I could see if it was working. I hadn't been able to sense the warlock's magic until I touched his victim. I really didn't want to do that, but if it would help, if it would save lives, well . . . Part of being an adult is doing things you don't want to do, right?

I swallowed bile and tried to not breathe as I bent down over the body and laid my hand on his arm. Fuck adulthood. His skin was cold. Very cold. Like he'd been frozen. A deep shiver twisted my spine, locking up my muscles for a moment, and darkness crept in at the corners of my vision. Then the world turned white, trees and sky and ripped-up body disappearing under a blanket of freezing white light.

"Jade." Alek's voice and warm hands brought me back. I wasn't touching the body anymore—instead, I was feet away, Alek holding me in his arms as I lay half-prone on the churned-up ground.

"Rage," I muttered. My tongue felt too thick, my mouth full of sourness, and an unnaturally cold, deep hatred still rang inside me. "Something is really angry, and it isn't normal." I wasn't sure I was making much sense.

Alek lifted me up. "You're freezing," he muttered. "I'm taking her to my trailer. We will talk later, after you have spoken to your crow spirit," he said to Sky Heart.

I let Alek carry me like a damsel in distress all the way back to his little home on wheels, my mind slowly unfracturing as I tried to parse what had happened. There was magic at work, which I guess was pretty obvious from the whole exploded-chest thing. It wasn't sorcery, though, not my brand of it. It wasn't anything I had any experience with—which wasn't saying much, alas. I'd spent the better part of twenty-five years running away from Samir and avoiding magic and magical things at all costs. I didn't exactly have a talking skull or a giant library of musty tomes to research this stuff. Just impressions and guesses.

I pressed my face against Alek's chest, his shifter warmth seeping slowly into my body. I was supposed to be at home with my friends, leveling up in anticipation of all of us getting killed by my psycho ex, not back reliving childhood trauma and playing amateur detective. It wasn't fair. Sky Heart and the People had cast me out. They deserved whatever they got. It wasn't my problem.

Whining about my lot in life and blaming the victims of terrible crimes? Weird.

I called up my magic again, letting it flow through me, this time for warmth and to purge all feeling of whatever it was I'd sensed on Redtail's corpse. I'm not a stranger to self-pity parties, but the anger rising in me felt off, unnatural. My power shoved it back, pushing away the cold and the resentment until I felt more like myself.

Rage. Resentment. Hatred. All lingering strongly on the body of a man who had probably felt none of those things. I doubted it was his ghost or spirit.

I didn't know much about spirits, but I knew some. Samir had been interested in all that stuff. He had multiple giant libraries full of musty tomes, though I'd only ever seen one in person. He had kept me away from the book learning, being uninterested in my gaining real knowledge. He had only wanted me to gain power, the way the witch in fairy tales fattens the kids before nomming down on them. There were sort of such a thing as ghosts, but they were more impressions than really the dead still somehow living on. Strong emotions, big events that were usually traumatic, powerful people dying, that kind of thing—all that could create a spirit. How powerful the spirit was and what it could do depended on how powerful the event or person creating it was.

Alek set me down to unlock his door, and I managed to stay on my feet. My body felt like I'd been punched repeatedly, but my magic had warmed me and cleared the cobwebs from my head. I was able to mount the handful of steps and enter the little cabin under my own power.

The trailer he lives in is very small, about a hundred and ten square feet. It's efficient, with a kitchenette on one side, a small gas heater and fold-out table and seats on the other, a bathroom at the back, and a ladder, leading to a sleeping loft, built up against the inner wall. Books were piled on cubby-like shelves built into the walls, alongside jars of tea and dry goods. The whole place smelled of cedar, beeswax, and bay oil. Cozy, especially given Alek's size, but he moved about the tiny space with the ease of long familiarity.

I sank into one of the padded seats as soon as he'd unfolded it and leaned against the wall. Alek held up a hand and his face grew flat with concentration. A shimmering layer of power slipped up the walls, warding off the trailer. I knew no one would be able to overhear anything we said. Smart. That's why they pay him the big bucks, I guess.

"It's not Samir," I said. "Not a sorcerer; that I'm pretty sure of. But we are dealing with magic."

"You should warn me before you do things," he said with a shake of his shaggy blond head.

"You were busy with your who-is-the-alpha staring contest. I didn't want to interrupt. Besides, why else would I touch a corpse? The whole doing-magic-now thing was pretty obvious, I'd think."

"I'm going to get you a shirt that says DOES NOT PLAY WELL WITH OTHERS," he muttered.

"I think I own that shirt," I said, trying to smile. "Get Sky Heart one instead. Then we can be twinsies." That got me a wry grin before he turned around and turned on the gas stove.

"So, what are we dealing with?" he asked as he filled a kettle for tea.

"Besides a narcissistic cult leader?"

"Jade . . ."

"A spirit, I think. All I felt was this horrible freezing rage. Not like a hot anger, the kind that flares and burns out. This was real hatred, true rage." I knew, because I'd felt something similar once.

Listening to your family die horribly while you could do nothing to stop it? Yeah. That'll cause a feeling like the one I'd just touched.

"Could a spirit affect the physical world like this without an inter-mediary?" Alek took the other seat and unfolded the table between us.

I tipped my head back against the wall and shut my eyes, trying to recall everything I could about spirits and the way they worked. I sort of had one following me around, after all, so you'd think I would know more. But Wolf was special, a creature outside of reality in many ways. She would probably know all sorts of things about spirits, but if she could speak, she certainly hadn't demonstrated it in the last forty years. I thought about my guardian more and sighed.

"I don't know," I said. "I don't think so. Wolf can't do much about corporeal threats, only help with magic stuff, as far as I can tell. I don't know what rules the Undying follow, if any, but it seems likely that something or someone is enabling this spirit or using its power."

"Not Sky Heart," Alek said with certainty. "He is terrified, but he will not tell me anything. He speaks in half-truths. Carlos went away, but I do not think he went far."

The kettle whistled and Alek prepared tea. I closed my eyes again and made myself remember the feelings I'd touched, the look of the scene, how the body had been cold, how it had smelled. Blood. But there hadn't been that much blood on the ground. Killed elsewhere? I thought so. Redtail was a large man, weighed two-twenty easily. Not easy to move. And how did the killer stake the body and put a live crow into the chest so close to the trailers without someone hearing them? In daylight?

I could see why Jasper was convinced there was magic at work there. It was pretty obvious no normal human was doing this. Too many ways a human could fuck it up, and they wouldn't be strong enough to manage it on their own. Even more than one human would have left a trace, might have caught attention.

"What did you smell?" I asked as Alek set down an earthen mug steam-ing with jasmine tea on the table and pushed it at me.

"Blood," he said. "Like in a slaughterhouse. Earth. Feces, I think from the body. I sensed no power, saw no obvious drag marks. It is odd."

"And the body was cold. Too cold. How did it get there? We know nothing." I wrapped my hands around my mug, willing the steam and warm ceramic to push away the last of the chill clinging to me. "But the pageantry," I said after a moment. "That feels human to me. It's a statement."

"But what is the killer trying to say?" Alek sipped his tea and a line formed between his blond brows.

"Hi, I'm totally bug-fucking crazy?" I resisted the urge to take my thumbs and smooth the line away.

"But not all-powerful, or the killer or killers would strike more often, no?"

"Unsub," I said. "We should call him or her the unsub. That's what they do on TV. Didn't they teach you that at Justice Academy?"

"Unknown subject," he said, the corners of his mouth turning up in a faint smile. "Sure, along with how to use a toothpick and some gum to build a nuke, how to run countersurveillance maneuvers, make crispy bacon, and kill someone with the five-finger death punch."

I grinned at him. My friends and I were clearly rubbing off on him if he could make jokes like that in a situation like this. My grin died quickly, however, as I remembered something else.

"I don't think Sky Heart can talk to Shishishiel anymore," I said. "When I was little, I remember I could sense the spirit with him, like vast wings unfurling at the edges of my vision. Something has changed, and I don't think it is just that I'm older now."

"I know," Alek said. "He was lying about consulting the Crow spirit."

"What else did he lie about?" I asked. Alek had powers beyond just normal shifter powers, though I didn't know what all of them were. He could do wards, like the one protecting us from eavesdroppers, and he was a walking lie detector. That latter part was a little annoying in a relationship, but it came in handy other times. Like now.

Scratch, scratch, scritch. Our heads whipped toward the door. I summoned my power, preparing a nice bolt of welcome as Alek rose and moved into position. I stood up on the seat, wincing as it creaked under my weight, but keeping my eye and the summoned magic in my hand at the door over Alek's broad shoulders.

One hand drawing his sidearm and holding it at his thigh, Alek swung the door open and turned sideways to make sure we both had clear shots.

It was Emerald, my half sister. She held a towel that looked to be wrapped around something and looked up at us with huge, scared green eyes.

"Please," she whispered, then she cast a furtive look over her shoulder. "The kids. You have to find them."

CHAPTER FIVE ▶

After we ushered her inside, Alek offered Em the seat he'd been in, but she shook her head, setting the bundle down on the table and unfolding it. Inside were three items. A teddy bear—hand-sewn from the look of it. A hairbrush with dark hairs still caught in it. A braided friendship bracelet.

"These belonged to the kids. So you can find them." Em looked at me, her green eyes wary.

"What kids?" I asked, forcing my breathing to normalize and my hands to stop shaking after the adrenaline hit I'd just given myself.

"This is where you live?" She looked around the trailer as though she hadn't heard me.

"Phenomenal cosmic power," I said. "Itty-bitty living space."

Em gave me a blank look and then glanced toward Alek where he leaned on the kitchen counter, with an expression that asked if I'd always been nuts or not. I guess the reference was lost on her. Probably one of the few kids in the entire United States who hadn't been raised on Disney movies.

"What kids?" Alek repeated, gifting me with a slight shake of his head.

"The fledglings. Like me. There are three others. They've all gone missing," Em whispered, glancing around again.

"The trailer is warded; no one can hear us," I said.

She hunched her shoulders, the news not relaxing her like I thought it would, and cast another look toward the door.

"Should we go invite Pearl inside?" I asked. I wasn't sure how I felt about her using Emerald to talk to us, but maybe she thought we'd be more sympathetic to a kid. Or maybe she worried that I wouldn't listen to her after what they'd done to me. Or she was a coward. I mentally filled in the bubble for option D: all of the above.

"No," Em said, her hands coming up like a suspect surrendering to the police. "Please. Grandfather is already angry with Dad over him leaving and bringing you here. I can't get Mom in trouble, too. I'm a fledgling; nobody will be too mad at me for being curious about you."

"The kids are missing?" Alek said, his voice taking on a slight growl now.

Right, the kids. Probably more important than family politics. I swallowed my opinions on my mother and tried to look attentive and open.

"Grandfather says they are dead, that the evil spirit got them because they didn't obey, but Mom thinks they are alive. She said that your magic could find them with these things if they are. Can you?" She put that last question out there with a defiant jut of her chin.

Pearl was right, but I wondered how she knew that. She had clearly spent more than just a night or two with my biological father if she knew things that sorcerers were capable of and how our magic might work.

"Yes," I said. "I probably can. You said they are fledglings, so they haven't shifted yet?" She'd said *other* fledglings, which meant she hadn't either. It made me a little sad and a lot angry. Her fate in the Tribe was unknown, then.

"No, they are too little. I will be Crow any day now; Dad said so."

"I hope he is right," I said softly.

"When did the children go missing?" Alek asked.

"Thomas and Primrose disappeared two weeks ago, after Night Singer got killed. Peter," she said, then stopped and took a quick gulping breath.

"He went beyond the boundary stones a couple days ago. Said he could hear Thomas calling to him. They are cousins and almost the same age. That's Peter's hairbrush."

"Boundary stones?" I thought of the tingle I'd felt when approaching Redtail's body.

"Grandfather set them to protect us from the evil."

"Bang-up job he's doing, too," I muttered.

"Grandfather and Shishishiel will protect us," she said. She spoke the words with the strength of a zealot, but the quiver in her chin and the desperation in her eyes turned them from conviction into prayer.

I hurriedly asked another question, not wanting an argument. "Your parents said something about this happening before—do you know when? And what happened?"

Em shook her head and wrapped her arms around herself. "I've heard some of the elders talk about it, but they always shut up when they notice me. It was a long time ago, like a hundred years or something, I think."

A hundred years. Long before my time as well. I sighed and looked at Alek. "Without more answers from Sky Heart, I don't see how we can help."

"You can't find them?" Em asked. Her face closed off again, eyes narrowing, lips pressing together into a pale line.

"I can try," I said. "But we don't know what we are facing out there."

"We will look for them," Alek said. I raised an eyebrow at him and he shrugged as if to say, *What else can we do?*

"Okay," Em said, edging toward the door. "Can I go now?"

"Yes," Alek said, cutting me off before my mouth was half-open to ask more questions. He pressed himself to the side and let her squeeze by him.

"She was our best source of information," I said.

"She's a kid and she's terrified. We have a direction to go in now.

Perhaps if we find these children, Sky Heart will allow us to help."

Fat fucking chance of that. I didn't say so; there was no point. Alek was right. Finding the kids was something I could help with, something tangible to do besides sit around and wait until more people got killed.

If the children were alive. Visions of little bodies gutted and splayed with crows struggling in their bloody chest cavities swarmed my mind. I shoved them away. The evil spirit, as Em had called it, liked to be dramatic. If the children had been murdered, they would have been left where the tribe could find them, wouldn't they? I hoped that wasn't my brain engaging in wishful thinking and trying to put order and sense where there was none.

"Fine," I said, looking at the three sad items that represented three lost and probably dead kids. "Let me finish my tea and then we can go look for them."

"No," Alek said, sinking down into the seat across from me. "Not tonight. First light. We should not go wandering around unknown woods in the dark. Alive or not, one night should make little difference, no?"

I hated that he was right, but he was right. I had known these woods well over thirty years before. But forests are not static; they live and breathe and change. Stumbling around half-familiar land in the middle of the night was a good way to get hurt, even without an evil spirit that could incapacitate a shifter running around.

The woods weren't the only thing around me that was half-familiar and yet irrevocably changed. It took me a long time to fall asleep, even with Alek's familiar warmth and his musky vanilla-and-clove smell making me feel safer. His calm presence didn't banish my resentment, my old anger. Lying there in the dark, I wasn't sure anything could.

We slipped out of the trailer as soon as the sky lightened. It would get warmer later, but the morning air was crisp and cool, and dew dampened the grass and ferns, glittering like tears in the early-morning sunlight. My hair was in a tight braid down my back, and I put on a kerchief over my head to protect from branches and brambles. Jeans, a *Half-Life* tee shirt, and sturdy hiking boots rounded out my outfit.

I had pulled hairs from the brush and twisted them into a knot so I could tuck them into a rubber band on my wrist and have my hands free in case I needed them. We had decided to use Peter's hair, since it was the most personal thing, being a former part of the boy's body, and because he was the most recently missing, which we hoped meant we'd find him alive. The plan was to cast the spell, follow it to Peter, and if he wasn't with the others, to return and do it again until we found them all.

We didn't really have much of a plan for dealing with the spirit if we found it beyond *kill it with fire* or something similar. I wasn't sure how we'd accomplish that. Not that I was bad with fire, Fireball being one of my magical specialties, but using it in the woods seemed like a terrible idea. I looked around for Wolf, but my guardian was nowhere to be seen. She came and went as she pleased, but her absence made me uneasy. She was probably the best defense I had against a spirit. I hoped she'd show up sooner rather than later, but had to trust if I got in real trouble, she'd appear. She always had before.

Alek and I had agreed to play it by ear and hope our combined strengths could deal with it. I wished I had time to figure out how to make a knife or something "ghost touch" like in the D&D manuals, but enchanting items hadn't ever been one of my fortes. It was possible, however. Anything was possible with sorcery, provided you could focus the power and summon enough of it.

I pushed away the thoughts of what we couldn't do or deal with, grabbed my d20 talisman with one hand, and focused on the knot of hair strapped to my other wrist. My magic flowed through me and I pushed it into the knot, casting the tracking spell. The spell was pretty crude, telling me only direction. The knot pulled on me, pointing the way, leading us into the woods.

We moved cautiously for a while, passing through the warded boundary of the camp. I spotted one of the boundary stones, now that I knew to look for it, and made a mental note to come back and examine the hunk of white granite when I didn't need my focus to keep the tracking spell going.

The woods were quiet. No insect or bird sounds. Even the brush didn't seem to shift or rustle except where we disturbed it, and there was no wind. The spell pulled us north and a little west from the houses, into older woods, the underbrush falling away as the canopy above grew denser. It was easier to move here but dimmer. The dead lower branches of the coniferous trees stuck out like accusing fingers, jabbing at us and obstructing longer-distance vision.

We'd been walking carefully along for at least an hour, not speaking, just following the spell. Alek drew up beside me and held up his hand. I stopped and looked around, keeping my concentration on the knot of hair but trying to peer into the dim forest. I heard nothing for a moment, and then the sound of footsteps, the crunching of dead pine needles and the snap of little sticks.

"Carlos?" Alek called out, his ice-blue eyes focusing on something I couldn't yet see. "Wait!"

The footsteps sped up, retreating. Alek took off after them. I started to follow, but a flash of red caught my eye. Emerald, in a red sweatshirt, moving parallel through the woods with us. What the fuck was she doing there? I had to get her to go back before she ended up missing or worse.

"Em, damnit! Come here." I turned and waved at her. She shook her head and ran off in a different direction from where Alek had gone.

I didn't even think about what I was doing and charged after her. She was only twenty or thirty feet away. I could catch her.

I stumbled through the trees, following the elusive red sweatshirt, muttering curses and calling out to her to come back. A broken-off spear of dead branch swiped my arm, cutting into my skin and drawing blood.

The sudden pain cleared my mind for a moment and I jerked to a stop as the girl in the sweatshirt disappeared. I summoned my power, using it the way I had the night before, pushing it through my body and mind like cleansing fire. It took a lot more energy this time, and I felt an intense ball of rage and resentment and confusion push back. It was almost tangible. The spirit.

"Oh fuck toast on a stick," I muttered, looking around. No Alek. No Em, though I suspected she had never been real. The spirit was here and it was royally fucking with us. We'd broken the cardinal rule of adventuring.

Never. Split. The. Party.

I gripped my talisman and kept my power going through me, though I knew between that and holding the tracking spell, I was going to tire sooner rather than later. It was eating more concentration and power than I liked to just hold off whatever that thing was. Better exhausted than dead, I guess. I had to find Alek before the spirit did. No, I wasn't going to think about Alek splayed and dead and bloody and *Oh, fuck.*

For a moment, I panicked, my heart pounding and blood rushing to my head. I forced the panic down with careful, steady breaths. I could track Alek if I went back to camp and got something of his. I turned and started retracing my steps, eyeing what little I could see of the sky to get my bearings.

The spirit was smart, separating us. Using illusions and deception. I should have expected it from what Em said, but with so little information, it was hard to know what it was capable of.

I was learning, though. Boy, was I learning.

"Why can't my life be more like a porno than a horror movie?" I muttered as I walked. I forced a chuckle at that. If this was a porn movie, with my luck, Maid Marian and her Merry Men would show up. I could almost hear Harper quipping, "Time for the mandatory girl-on-girl scene."

I smiled and shook my head. What was I even thinking about? I almost walked into a huge tree as a giant black beast appeared beside me and slammed into my hip, knocking me on my ass. It was a huge beast, the size of a pony, with the head of a wolf, the body of a tiger, tufted ears like a lynx, and, I swear to the Universe, an amused expression in its fathomless, starry night-black eyes.

Wolf. My guardian and one of the fabled Undying. *Fucking finally*. I glared at her, but her furry black face and unfathomable eyes just kept laughing at me. My head cleared again and I swore some more, mostly to make myself feel better as I got to my feet and brushed pine needles off my ass.

I'd lost my grip on my magic, and I snatched it back, dragging on the well of power inside. It was so easy to become distracted. More spirit shenanigans. This was getting really frustrating.

"Where have you been?" I said to Wolf. Spirits are something she's supposed to be able to help with, being all magical and shit.

She whined and pawed at the tree I'd almost run into. It looked familiar. It was really two trees that had grown too close together, their trunks twisting and combining as they strained for the sunlight. The kissing tree, we used to call it.

Which meant the old mine entrance was close by. I shivered. Though I'd only been four when my cousins John and Connor got me lost down there on purpose, I still vividly remembered the dank air, the dirty walls pressing in, and the feeling of being buried alive, trapped in a labyrinth and all alone in the dark. If it hadn't been for Wolf, I might never have come out of there.

The mine. It would make a good hideout if one were a terrible person who didn't mind darkness. It had been boarded up after I'd been lost in it, but still, it might be worth checking. I pushed power back into the tracking spell, recasting it on a hunch. The knot of hair pulled me back to the north, toward the mine. The pull was strong. Peter wasn't far.

Turn back and try to find Alek? Or find the kid? I didn't want to go back into the mine, and the spirit was fucking with me pretty hard, despite my magic. I had Wolf with me now, however. And I knew what Alek would want. He'd say to go after the kid. No question.

"This is a terrible idea," I muttered.

Then, one hand on Wolf's thick fur and one pointing out in front of me to guide the way, we went north.

CHAPTER SIX

The entrance to the mine was no longer boarded up. The entrance had been cleared recently; brush was cut back and the old boards were piled off to one side. The opening yawned in the sunlight like a beast, damp air slightly cooler than the air in the clearing around it seeping out and making me shiver.

At least, I told myself the goose bumps on my arms were from the air.

I called on more magic, focusing it on my outstretched hand and bringing up a brightly glowing ball of golden light. I sent the light ball floating into the entrance. The floor in the opening was scuffed and furrowed, the dirt having long since clogged the tracks that used to run down there. I saw fresh footprints and went to examine them.

A man had come this way. Alek? No, the feet were too small for that. Alek had giant Viking-boat feet. It was too much to hope he'd come this way.

The spirit wouldn't have left prints. Wolf didn't, anyway. Perhaps the intermediary we'd speculated about? Gah. I hated that all the things I found just led to more questions. The tracking spell pulled downward. So, Peter was in there. Or Peter's corpse.

I looked down at Wolf and took a deep breath. My magic flowed through me and my mind felt clear, so I hoped I was making this probably incredibly stupid decision of my own free will.

"Wolf," I said. "I need you to find Alek. You have to protect him from the spirit or whatever is doing this, okay?"

She whined a little and turned her head east, her nose lifting as she scented the air. She looked back at me as though wondering if I was serious.

"I'm serious," I said. "Please go protect Alek."

With another whine, she vanished. I pulled my light ball back and made my talisman glow instead. Keeping that going while I kept the tracking spell up and my head clear of spirit interference was going to suck, but I didn't have a choice. I told myself to just think of this as more practice. If I couldn't handle running a few concurrent spells and finding a lost kid, I had no hope against Samir.

With that cheery thought, I faced the gaping mine entrance.

"I ain't afraid of no ghost," I muttered. It almost made me smile. Almost. Cautiously, I stepped inside, following the pull of Peter's knotted hair down the main tunnel.

The walls changed from earth to stone as I descended. The mine had been active back a century or more before, but while the shaft dropped at a sharp angle, it was clear of most debris. I thought it would have fallen in after all this time, but the thick timbers reinforcing it held. The ground layer had built up, especially once the tunnel leveled off after a few hundred feet and the first split came.

The tracking spell tugged left, so I took the left channel. Water dripped somewhere ahead. Or maybe behind. It was impossible for me to tell. The glow from my talisman illuminated only a few feet around me. Had Peter just wandered in here and gotten lost? I doubted it. The kids I grew up with used to dare each other about how far we could go in. I'd gone with John and Connor, trusting them and their flashlights, feeling like a really important person that they would let me go along when they normally shut me out of all activities.

The mine had felt like a horrible maze then. It seemed smaller, less ominous now in some ways and even more terrifying in others. Smaller because I had magic now, a way to defend myself, to get myself out of here. More terrifying because there was a spirit possibly down here waiting to fuck with me. I kept my magic flowing, ignoring the headache that was starting to tighten a vise around my skull. I couldn't afford to get distracted or lost down there, not if I wanted to find the kid and get out again.

Besides, I kinda wanted to encounter the intermediary and kick the unsub's ass. That way, I would know they weren't doing something awful to Alek.

I don't know how far underground I went. The tunnel dropped again, branched twice more, and dropped deeper. The walls were all rock now, timbers in the ceiling obscured by darkness, though the height wasn't much and I had to duck. No roots nudged through down there—I was too deep for that, I guess, somewhere into the rocky soil or perhaps even the bedrock.

Then the tunnel opened up, the walls no longer close beside me. The smell of crushed pine needles and cooked meat flooded my nose. The hell?

I pushed more power into my talisman, making more light. The shaft had ended in a cavern, the ceiling somewhere overhead and out of range of my limited sight. I could make out furniture to my left, a table of some kind in the dim edge of my vision. I moved toward it, my glowing d20 casting crazy shadows in the space.

One of the shadows moved oddly in the corner of my eye and I spun to the right, gathering power into a shield. I was too tired, too slow.

I made out the shape of a man before the baseball bat he was wielding smashed into my head. I felt pain, tasted blood, but I didn't see stars. Only darkness.

I came to with the mother of all headaches. I hate getting knocked out, and this was the second time in as many days. It's disorienting as fuck. Most knockouts are pretty quick, not like in the movies where the person goes down and stays down for a convenient amount of time. I had a feeling more time had passed, however. I remembered the hit first, that explosion of pain, then the where and what next.

It was pitch-black when I opened my eyes, and I couldn't make out a thing. I hoped that meant I was still underground rather than blind.

I took stock of my body, flexing fingers and toes. I was still dressed, but there were restraints of some kind on my wrists and ankles. My arms were pulled back behind and half under me as I lay on my side, and my fingers felt swollen, though they wiggled, so they weren't totally asleep. With the painful tingling in them, I found myself wishing they were. I tried to push my legs apart, but they were stuck together with whatever was binding me. Something clanked and I guessed I was chained up. The bindings felt rigid enough to be metal. Shit.

I listened, hearing breathing near me. All I could smell were dirt and the faint scent of cooked meat. I figured I had to be in the cavern still or near it. Pushing through the pounding pain in my head, I tried to call up my magic and bring light into my talisman.

The magic flowed into me grudgingly, and hanging on to it hurt so much that I whimpered. Something moved near me, and I froze as the breathing noise grew closer, almost drowned out by the clack of metal on stone. My talisman didn't light up. I realized I couldn't feel the chain around my neck, couldn't sense the residual power that I stored in it. My d20 necklace was missing.

"Hey," said a soft male voice. "You awake?"

Was it a trap? Probably a trap. I decided I didn't care.

"Yeah," I whispered. "Are we alone?"

"The kids are sleeping, I believe. And I haven't heard the man in a little while," the voice said. He had an accent, very slight, but almost

Hispanic in how he accented some syllables and not others. He was near me now. I felt the warmth coming off him, felt his breath as he talked. A hand touched my arm and I tried not to flinch. "You were very beat up. I did not think you would wake. You are not a shifter."

"Carlos?" I guessed, going with the most obvious explanation.

"Yes," he said, a little louder now, excited. "Who are you?"

"Jade, a friend of Aleksei Kirov's," I said, knowing that he and Alek talked all the time. He might know who I was, if Alek had mentioned me. I hadn't ever been brave enough to ask. "Alek is here somewhere, in the woods. He didn't come into the mine. Are we still in the mine?"

"Yes, I think so. There's a huge cavern off this area. I heard Not Afraid pacing in there, talking to himself earlier. He is gone now."

"Not Afraid? He told you his name? Is he a shifter?" I tried to remember if I had ever heard of a Crow by that nickname. It rang no bells.

"He and I have talked a little. When he brings food and the bucket. He is not a shifter. I don't know what he is. He smells of dead things, old bones, old blood."

I remembered that Alek had told me Carlos was a lion shifter. His hands seemed free; he had touched me after all. "Can you untie me? Can you shift?"

"No," he said, and I could hear the head shake that came with it. "We've all got manacles on, hooked into the stone floor. I have a collar on that is also chained down. If I shift, it'll kill me, since I can't shift out of it."

"Okay," I said. "Close your eyes. I'm going to make a light."

"Make a light?"

I focused, trying to ignore the headache and my own fear, shoving it all away and focusing on my magic. No hands. No talisman. Well, I'd been practicing for this, right? I summoned a ball of light, just as I had out in front of the mine, though I kept this one small and blue-tinted. By choice, not because I was exhausted and out of my element with no hands and no tools. That's what I told myself.

I squinted against the light and looked around me. Carlos knelt next to me, a large black man, heavyset, though it looked to be mostly muscle, with dreads that fell below his shoulders, and golden brown eyes squinting back at me. His hair was a mess of pine needles and dirt, and his clothes were streaked with dirt and dried blood. I guessed he hadn't come very quietly. A metal collar with nasty spikes pointing inward decorated his throat, and a thick manacle was bound to his leg, both tying him into a heavy ring in the middle of the small chamber with large chains.

Twisting my head to see beyond Carlos, I made out three small shapes huddled against the far wall, a camo-patterned blanket covering all three. A large chain connected to the ring disappeared under the blanket, and I guessed they all must be tied to it somehow. One set of eyes blinked against the light—a boy, I thought, though it was hard to tell in the near darkness.

"Peter, Thomas, and Primrose?" I asked quietly as I twisted more, trying to sit upright.

"Yes," Carlos said. He moved as best he could with the thick chain restraining him and helped to prop me up against the cold, damp wall.

"Why are we alive?" I said even more quietly. He was a shifter; I barely had to speak aloud for him to hear me, and I didn't want the kids to overhear us if I could help it.

"This I don't know. I think because we are not crow shifters. He told me I am not a part of things and I would be able to go once he was done." Carlos shook his head. "The kids, I think he is waiting to see if they will change into crow or not."

"That could be a few years," I said. They were pretty young from what I could tell, years younger than Emerald. The knowledge that he had gone out of his way to keep Carlos and the children alive was somewhat comforting. Alek wasn't a crow shifter, so even if the spirit and this Not Afraid guy got him, it didn't seem like his fate would be full of organ removal.

"Time and logic are not things Not Afraid cares for," Carlos said. He smiled briefly, his teeth flashing blue-white in the light.

"Bully for him," I muttered. "I think he's possessed by or working with a spirit. We have to get out of here."

"Would love to, but . . ." Carlos motioned at his collar and then jiggled his leg, making the chains rattle. "The little ones are only tied by an ankle each as well, and to the same chain. But the steel is new; I can't break it."

He was implying, of course, that if a lion shifter, and a Justice at that, couldn't break the metal, I had no hope. He was wrong. Probably.

Okay, I told myself. *All you have to do is destroy the metal. You like destroying things.*

The upside of sorcery is it is just raw power. It can be shaped to do or become just about anything if the will is there and if the raw power is there. The downside is that whole having to shape the power and have enough of it in the first place.

There was no way with my hands tied and no focus like my d20 that I would be able to keep up the light and somehow destroy my bindings. With the monumental headache I was nursing, the fact that my body had probably had to reconstruct part of my skull to heal me, and all the magic I'd already expended, I wasn't sure I could even do what I wanted to do.

But I was dead sure that I wasn't going to stay there and shit in a bucket while this Not Afraid dude and his evil spirit cohort slaughtered more people.

I let the light die. "Might want to back up," I whispered to Carlos, and waited until I heard him scoot away.

The easiest way to work magic you've never worked before is to have a path for it, a way for your brain to understand and enact the thing you want that won't fuck with your worldview and physics and stuff too much. It was that whole stones-and-hands problem again. Fortunately, the way I'd learned to control and channel my magic was through Dungeons &

Dragons, and D&D has a ton of spells in it. They wouldn't do shit for a normal human, but in the hands of someone with actual magic, they aided my will and imagination, gave me a focus.

Rust Ray was one I'd used as Dungeon Master, not for realsies, on a party and nearly been lynched by the players. They kind of hate it when you destroy their gear.

"Touch attack," I said softly to myself, focusing my power on the manacles around my wrists. I was touching them, so this could work. I pushed my magic at the metal, visualizing it corroding, weakening, rusting away under the onslaught of power. I twisted my arms, putting as much pressure on the metal as I could.

My magic stopped pouring through me, weakening to a trickle as I gasped, straining to hold the spell. My head throbbed and red danced across my eyelids as I squeezed my eyes shut in concentration.

The manacles broke with a discordant clang. I let my magic go and pulled my arms in front of myself, rubbing them to restore full feeling. A million tiny needles pricked at my skin, and I turned my lower lip into hamburger as I resisted indulging in more whimpering.

"You all right?" Carlos said.

"Yeah. Hands are free. Just got to get my feet. Hang on." I wasn't sure I could call up more magic, but I did it anyway. If I hadn't spent the last three months training and pulling on my reserves over and over, I don't think I could have managed. Score one for exhaustive practice. Emphasis on *exhaustive*.

It was easier to rust the manacle on my leg. My hands discovered it was only one leg that was actually chained. The other was tightly duct-taped to the metal, and I was able to rip the tape off without resorting to magic.

I crawled to Carlos, feeling for him in the darkness. "Hold very still," I said.

I was ready to drink a horse trough's worth of coffee and swear off ever doing magic again by the time I'd broken his collar, rusted out his leg binding, and freed all three children. I wasn't sure I could even walk, my head spun so badly. I managed a small ball of light in one hand and hoped that Not Afraid and his spirit buddy were far, far away. I was in no condition to do more than pass out on them.

Carlos had a rapport with the kids, keeping them quiet as he bundled Primrose, the youngest, who looked about six years old, into the blanket and motioned for the others to follow me.

We moved into the large chamber, Carlos sniffing the air and listening before he motioned me to keep going. I wanted to search the cavern for my necklace, but common sense won out. Escape was more important. I led us by memory back the way I'd come, every step seeming like it went nowhere, the walls tight and cold. One foot in front of another was the best I could manage, my head down, my whole being concentrating on walking and not losing the light.

Then there was light that wasn't mine, daylight dimly piercing the way ahead. The ground had turned upward at some point and I'd been too exhausted to notice. The steep main shaft loomed ahead of me as I turned a corner toward the faint light. Fresh air. Sunlight. Being deep underground will make you appreciate the small things. I had no idea why an adventuring party would ever, ever, ever go into a dungeon. Idiots, clearly.

Just a few more feet, I told myself. Then I collapsed. Warm fur caught me and I heard someone behind me curse in Spanish. Wolf. She was there, under my half-prone body, lifting me up. I clung to her and managed to stumble upward, my thighs burning and my vision blurred to uselessness.

Then daylight. Full, glorious sunlight and the heat of a summer afternoon. We were out of the mine. Now we just had to get the kids back to the camp.

Alek was there, coming toward me with concern in his eyes.

"I'm okay," I said, hopefully sounding more convincing than I looked.

I didn't want to think about how much dried blood was matted in my hair or how dirty I was. My kerchief hadn't survived the head wound. Without needing to hang on to my magic, I felt slightly better. I still leaned heavily on Wolf, but my breathing was coming back under control and my eyes no longer felt like they were squeezing out of my head.

"Alek!"

"Carlos!"

The two men looked as though they might embrace, except Carlos still had a wide-eyed little girl in his arms.

Then Alek looked at me and I guessed from the look on his face that the sight wasn't pretty.

"Are you all right?" he asked, gently touching the side of my face. Blood flaked off and I reached up, wondering where my kerchief had gone.

"You should see the other guy," I said.

"I hope I do," he said, his voice lowering into a growl. His eyes promised violence upon whoever had hurt me.

I wanted to throw my arms around him and tell him I loved him right there. My romantic timing sucked, but being hit in the head and chained up underground had apparently clarified some things for me.

"Alek," I started to say, but he shook his head slightly, softening the negation with one of his slight smiles.

"Back to camp," Alek said. "Then we will talk."

"I don't know if the kids can walk that far after being chained so long," Carlos said.

"I can walk," one of the boys said. Peter, I thought. He looked the least pale and weak of the two boys. Two weeks underground and chained wouldn't have been good for anyone, much less a little kid.

"I bet you can," Alek said. "But would you rather ride a tiger?"

Peter and Thomas looked at him, then at each other, then back at him, their dark brown eyes suspicious. "I don't see no tiger," Peter said.

Alek smiled and shifted. One moment he was a huge Viking of a man, the next a giant tiger. Dire tiger, Harper called him. It wasn't a bad description. Shifter animal forms are more like the Platonic ideal of the animal than any realistic version. They are bigger, prettier, stronger, faster. A giant white tiger is one of the most beautiful and most terrifying things ever. Alek was lovely and scary as fuck, is what I'm saying.

Carlos lifted the wide-eyed boys onto Alek's back. A tiger isn't made for riding, but I knew they would cling and Alek would take it carefully. It wasn't like their combined weight would give him back problems.

"I wanna ride tiger," Primrose said, clutching at the blanket.

"How about you ride a lion instead?" Carlos asked her. "You had better ride with her, Jade, keep her on."

It was a testament to how tenuous and dangerous the situation was that he would allow a virtual stranger onto his back. I was about to say I had my own ride but glanced around and realized Wolf was missing again. Great.

"Come on, Primrose," I said with what I hoped was a nice smile. "Let's ride a lion."

If Alek was a dire tiger, Carlos was definitely a dire lion. His ruddy mane reminded me of Narnia movies and I struggled not to make an Aslan joke. It didn't hurt that my brain was so fried and in pain that I couldn't come up with a good one anyway.

I put Primrose up onto lion-Carlos's back and then climbed on. He rose and I gripped his mane with one hand and held on to the little girl with my other arm. Alek and Carlos moved through the woods in big, ground-eating strides.

It seemed to take no time at all to get back to camp. I felt the hum of the wards on the boundary stones, and then we were through the ferns and out of the woods. The People were gathered around the big house, much as they had been when Alek and I arrived.

Sky Heart was there, standing over an indigo-wrapped body laid out on a stretcher. Wildflowers in little bunches were strewn around and the air was solemn, no one talking until we emerged into the big clearing. A woman cried out and ran toward me, reaching for Primrose, who squirmed and called out, "Mommy." I let her go, sliding to the ground as Carlos dropped low to let us off his back.

Staggering to keep my feet, I looked up and my eyes met Sky Heart's own. They were red, puffy, and full of fear.

CHAPTER SEVEN

For a long moment, we were swamped with people asking questions, relatives claiming the children. Carlos and Alek shifted back to human form, but none of us were able to answer much in the clamor and press of bodies. I swayed on my feet but forced myself to push gently through, heading toward Sky Heart. That man had things to answer for and I wasn't going to be shoved aside like yesterday. Whatever was going on, I had a strong feeling it began with the leader of the Crow.

I got through the crowd and stopped, facing Sky Heart over the corpse. "Who is Not Afraid?" I asked him.

"I do not answer to you, exile," he said, the fear in his face morphing into rage as he looked at me.

"Good thing I now have two Justices with me, then, isn't it?" I shot back. "You may pretend you are outside all laws, but I hear the Nine don't take well to shifters killing shifters. If you caused this somehow—"

He cut me off with an angry cry like the hunting shriek of a hawk and shifted. His huge crow form lumbered into the air with angry wingbeats, scattering the bunches of flowers and blowing dust into my face. Sky Heart fled into the tall trees surrounding the big house and disappeared among the shadowed high branches.

I stood over the corpse, too tired and shocked to react. A hand touched my arm and I jerked sideways.

"Come," Pearl said. Her dark eyes held only sorrow. "You may use our bath. Then we will talk."

"Damn right we will," I muttered.

She ignored my ungracious comment and led me through the crowd. I caught Alek's eye, and he gave one of his Gallic shrugs that I took to mean I should just learn what I could and we'd talk later. I hoped that now we had brought the children home safely, the People would be more inclined to let the Justices help, more inclined to share what they knew. Maybe I was still naïve, or maybe I'd been hit harder in the head than I thought.

I'd been hit pretty damn hard. The mirror in the single bathroom in my old home revealed a thick pink scar along the side of my face that was slowly fading out as my body did its quick-healing thing. Bruising would take longer to heal, unfortunately, but at least my vision wasn't impeded by swelling. The side of my head was caked with flaking dried blood, my hair was a nest of pine needles and dirt, and my clothes looked like someone had dragged me over a mud-covered cheese grater. I felt naked without my talisman and rubbed my chest where it usually rested.

Not Afraid had better start being afraid, I thought. I wasn't going to forgive that theft, not that I would forgive the murders, either. Or the being hit in the face with a two-by-four or bat or whatever the hell that had been. His list of transgressions was substantial.

I stripped and washed off the worst of the grime before running the hottest bath I could stand and sinking into it. My hair floated out around me like ink and I sighed. It would be a bitch to untangle and braid again, but relaxing completely in the hot water and letting the dirt and blood soak out of my skin was worth it.

Pearl knocked and then came in before I could respond. For a moment, I wanted to order her out, but she was still my mother in some ways.

She'd wiped my ass and breastfed me. I didn't have anything she hadn't seen before. Bonus was that it meant I could question her without having to move.

"Why do you stay here? Any of you?" I said. It wasn't the question I'd meant to lead with, but Sky Heart's fear and anger bordered on insane. It was worse than I remembered from when I was a kid. Maybe I just hadn't noticed back then.

"It is our home," Pearl said. "Without Shishishiel to protect us, who knows what might happen? The world is not a very nice place."

I almost started to argue that there was a lot of good out there, free-dom, people who didn't throw people out who weren't like them, but then I thought about how it might be for someone who had lived in a bubble for centuries. And I thought, fleetingly, about Samir. There was a lot of evil in the world.

Yet hiding from it hadn't helped me, and it didn't seem to have helped the People. Evil had still found them.

"Are you sure Shishishiel still protects you?" I said.

"Yes." Her tone allowed no further questions along those lines, and I decided to take a hint and drop it. She set down the folded stack of clothing and pulled over a small wooden stool from the vanity.

"Who is Not Afraid?" I asked.

"Where did you hear that name?"

"Carlos, the other Justice. He talked to the guy who has been killing your people. That was the name he gave." I watched her face carefully, but her expression was guarded; only a slight tension about the mouth and eyes gave away any emotion at all, and I wasn't sure what that emotion was yet.

"A little more than a hundred years ago, there was a murder like these. It only happened once then, because Sky Heart caught the man respon-sible and he was executed. That man was called William Not Afraid. He is dead. Whoever this man is, he cannot be Not Afraid." She shook her head emphatically, as though it would help make her words true.

"Who did Not Afraid kill back then?" That was what I envisioned a cop on *Law & Order* asking. Trace the original crime, see what started that, then you could find out why there was a copycat. Of course, cops didn't have to contend with near-immortal beings, magic, or spirits. Lucky them.

"Opal," Pearl said softly. "Sky Heart's second wife."

Figured he would be at the center of this. "Did he ever tell you why?" I didn't clarify if I meant Sky Heart or Not Afraid, because I didn't care how she took it. Either would do if she had an answer, so I left it deliberately ambiguous.

"No. It may have had something to do with Not Afraid's twin sister. That is what I have always suspected, but Sky Heart won't speak of it." She looked down at her hands and picked at imaginary lint on her jeans.

"What happened to his twin?" I asked after a moment when it seemed she wasn't going to continue on her own.

"She wasn't Crow. She was exiled." Pearl kept her eyes down, not meeting mine.

"Not Afraid was Crow?" I asked, thinking of Carlos telling me that he was sure the man who had captured them was not a shifter.

"Yes, but Buttercup was not Crow. She wasn't even shifter, but one of the rare normal human births. She was exiled, sent away to live with missionaries, as we usually did then with those who were not People. But Sky Heart wouldn't tell Not Afraid where he had sent his twin, and he wouldn't let Not Afraid leave to find her. They were very angry with each other. Not Afraid seemed insane with rage. They fought and it shook the forest. Sky Heart and Shishishiel had no choice but to kill him."

She looked up then, but her eyes stared past me, right into her memories. I realized I had no idea how old my mother was. Older than I'd thought. I wondered what I would remember in a century or three, what events would stick and what would fade into fog and be lost to me forever.

Buck up, kid, I told myself. *I doubt Samir will let you live that long.*

I closed my eyes and sank lower in the tub. At least I had some information. Carlos had said it was a man and not a shifter. Maybe it was a descendant of the twin. If she had harbored a grudge for her whole life and had children, it was possible she could have passed that grudge on to them and one grandchild or great grandchild had come to collect.

Which didn't explain the spirit, except that the grandchild or whatever was clearly possessed by it. Or working with it. Either way was scary enough, given what the spirit had been able to accomplish through the intermediary.

I must have drifted off. The bathwater grew tepid, and when I opened my eyes, my mother was gone. I had wanted to ask her more about my birth father, but the moment seemed to have slipped away.

I managed to pull on clothes, wrap a towel around my head, and get as far as the uncomfortable couch. This time, it was Em who appeared, holding out a knit blanket.

"Mom said you would want to sleep if the bath didn't drown you."

"I'm sure those were her exact words," I said, and was rewarded with a sheepish smile.

I sprawled onto the couch and crashed hard.

It was dark when I awoke to the smell of coffee and pancakes. Though it was after midnight, Jasper and Pearl invited me to stay and eat something, since they had leftovers, but I wanted to go check on Carlos and Alek. Okay, I'll admit, I wanted to get out of that house before any more memories stormed in and gave me unwanted feels. After the day I'd had, I wasn't up to sitting down and having family dinner.

"I don't suppose there is cell phone reception out here?" I asked them before I stepped out the door. I hadn't emailed or texted Harper like I said I would, and I knew she'd be annoyed and worried by now.

"No," Jasper said. "Sorry. No cell, no Internet. We live our own lives up here."

I managed to swallow about fifty snide comments I could think of in response to that and stepped out the door.

It was a warm night with a light breeze. The big house was all dark and I figured Sky Heart was probably still sulking in the trees. Or standing in a dark room, watching his little cult empire crumble from behind tinted glass.

The couch may have felt like it was covered in hide and stuffed with rocks, but sleep had done wonders for my body. I pulled up a thread of magic, just to test how it would feel. No headache. That was good. No talisman. That was bad. It was harder to focus without it, and I knew I'd be limited in the kinds of spells I could do without my d20. Maybe it was a crutch, but I missed it. Still, the power was there when I reached for it, so maybe I didn't need the crutch.

Which didn't mean I wasn't going to go get it back as soon as it was daylight.

A faint glow out in the trees to the west caught my eye as I walked across the gravel circle toward Alek's trailer. It was pale and flickering blue, not a light like would come from one of the cabins or trailers in the camp. I remembered the boundary stone from the morning and thought that might be about where it was placed.

Mentally berating myself as the stupid horror movie victim who goes off unarmed into the woods to investigate the weird thing instead of ignoring it and heading toward people and safety, I changed course and walked toward the flickering light. Horror movie victims aren't generally nearly immortal with the ability to cast Fireball. So, you know, I had that going for me.

The boundary stone wasn't the thing glowing. The light flickered just beyond it, hovering like a will-o'-the-wisp among the dark sword ferns and spiky broken branches. I stopped at the stone and peered into the dark.

151

"Not Afraid?" I called out softly. "Talk to me." Worth a shot and somewhat better than calling out the old cliché "Who's there?" right before I get eaten by something big and ugly.

"She is not Crow, but she is here," a young male voice responded, the words faint. I realized he was speaking in the Siouan language that the Apsáalooke, the Native American Crow tribe, used. It was the language some of the elders at Three Feathers had spoken when I was little and didn't want me to understand what they were saying. Their efforts had been useless, since even as a small child, I had understood languages I shouldn't have known. It was yet another thing that had set me apart.

"I am not a crow person," I called out in the Crow tongue. "Talk to me; tell me what you want, why you are doing this. Is it for Buttercup?" I added the last part as a guess, hoping to get a reaction.

Not Afraid seemed to materialize from the darkness, only feet away from me. He was very young, not much older than Emerald, and I wondered why Carlos hadn't mentioned that. Perhaps he hadn't seen him clearly. Not Afraid's face was gaunt, his hair ragged and shorn close to the scalp. He wore leather clothing that had seen better days and looked like something out of a cowboys-versus-Indians movie. His eyes glowed faintly in the dark with a blue-white sheen over their dark irises, and it sent a shiver down my spine. The spirit was definitely a part of him, either by possession or by him working some spell to control it.

I wondered if he even knew who was controlling whom anymore.

"Tell me," I said again. "Please." Knowing what he wanted might give me an idea of what kind of spirit it was, which would lead, I hoped, to a way to get rid of it. A young, angry boy, we could handle. It was the supernatural that was fucking everything up.

"You want the truth?" he asked, his head cocking to the side like a bird's. "Come with me."

Oh, sure. That was going to happen.

"You hit me in the head," I pointed out. "Why should I trust you?"

"You were sent away?" he asked. "When you did not become Crow?"

It was more a statement than a question. It worried me but I shoved away the nagging feeling that something was weird about that. Everything was weird—what was one more bit to chew over later going to hurt?

"Yes," I said. "I was sent away, told to never come back. Kicked out of my own home. They said I was dead to them." I let some of my own anger and resentment show. *Building rapport. Goren and Eames would be proud.*

"You were lucky," he said. "I will show you the truth. Follow."

"Give me back my necklace," I said.

Without hesitation, he pulled the chain out from under his tunic and tossed my talisman to me. It glittered in the odd, flickering blue light, and I managed to catch it. Damn, but it felt good to have the heavy silver d20 settle into place against my skin. I summoned my magic for a second, letting it flow through me and my talisman. Everything felt normal.

"Now you follow," he said.

I cast a glance back toward the cabins and Alek's trailer. I couldn't see it from here, the trees and darkness enfolding me, but I knew what Alek would say about taking this kind of risk. In my mind I saw Redtail's body, his chest ripped open, his ribs protruding. If taking this risk meant stopping that from happening again, it was worth it. No one else was going to die.

Except maybe Not Afraid.

I turned back to him, keeping hold of a thread of my magic so I had it easily available, and nodded for him to lead the way. Then I stepped beyond the boundary stone.

CHAPTER EIGHT

Moving through woods in daylight was enough of a pain in the ass. Walking through them at night was just plain crazy. I'd been working on some spells to augment myself during my training with Alek and my gaming buddies. One of those spells was Darkvision. It didn't work quite the way I had hoped, at least not yet, and it wasn't easy to maintain, but I didn't want to cast a light until we were farther away from the camp.

Ideally, the spell would have enabled me to see like it was daylight, only in black and white. The reality was more like an odd amber glow limning objects near me, making solid things shadowed and dark while their edges shimmered. It was good enough for me to follow Not Afraid without falling on my face or running into trees, but not much use beyond that. I couldn't move quickly, but Not Afraid patiently waited every time I stumbled or had to disentangle myself from a blackberry vine or dead branch.

He moved confidently through the woods, not making a sound. I couldn't tell if that was because he was just that good or if something seriously supernatural was going on. It had occurred to me that he might be a ghost, but then he would have been bound by the same general rules as a spirit and unable to affect the physical world this much without serious help from someone corporeal. I noticed that ferns and brush moved as he passed. So, he had some solidity. I mentally checked off the box labeled *preternaturally quiet* and left it at that.

I couldn't tell what direction we were going. Only faint patches of stars glinted through the thick tree branches, and I didn't spare much time for staring upward. With my darkvision running, light wasn't a pleasant thing to look at. Even the flickering blue in Not Afraid's eyes was disorienting any time I met his gaze as he waited for me to catch up.

After what felt like hours, I heard running water. A few minutes later, I could smell the stream and the air shifted to feeling more open. The forest fell away in an abrupt line and a wide, rocky ravine spread out below me. My vision wouldn't let me see too deeply into it, but amber light limned a field of boulders. To my right loomed a huge cliff, the top lost to the clash between the slowly brightening sky and my night vision.

The sky was turning from black to the dull grey of false dawn. It was enough that my normal vision could start to pick out details, I thought, so I dropped the night vision. I kept a hold on my magic, not trusting my companion or the spirit not to fuck with me.

The cliff rose a good hundred feet up from the floor of the ravine, the top outlined against the grey sky. The heavily sloping field was mostly rockfall but overgrown, as though the rocks had tumbled down a long time before and nature was filling in the cracks. Boulders dotted the terrain like the bodies of sleeping beasts half-covered in dew-speckled grass blankets. Down the hill to my left cut a creek, its cheery burble at odds with the mostly silent morning. Even the birds weren't speaking.

The rocky field had the same eerie stillness I associate with grave-yards, and it unnerved me. Places can have their own power, their own energy. Sometimes from ley lines and other earthly sources. Sometimes from events like earthquakes or eruptions. Sometimes from people, though it would be rare for a wilderness spot like this to take on power from humans. I had a sense that we were close to whatever Not Afraid wanted to show me.

Wolf materialized beside me and growled, her hackles up, her eyes fixed on the cliff. She didn't appear to like this place any better than I.

"What is it?" I whispered to her. She looked at me with her starry-night eyes and growled again. I took a step forward, moving out of the trees, but she stayed put, swinging her head from side to side, her growl fading into a whine.

"Fine," I muttered. "Stay here, then."

Not Afraid let me take in the surroundings, ignoring that I was apparently talking to myself, and then started picking his way across the rocks toward the cliff face. I followed, looking around me warily as the shadows deepened and the sky grew lighter.

Not Afraid reached the base of the cliff and waited for me there. I clambered up beside him to where it leveled out somewhat. The cliff face itself was pitted and gouged by the elements, too steep for vegetation to take hold. White streaks ran down the rocks like tears, and something about the place made me shiver as I stared upward.

The bottom of the cliff was missing. Time and water had hollowed out the base into a low cave deep enough I couldn't see to the back, though something deep within seemed to move. I refused to peer too closely. I had had enough of dark places for a long while after the mine. Stalactites hung from the roof at the mouth of the cave, giving it the appearance of a gaping mouth waiting to crunch down. The area in front of the mouth had been dug away into a rough pit. The pit was still in shadow, but there seemed to be bare branches stacked in it.

I gripped my d20 and called up light, sending it like a flare over the pit.

Not branches. Bones. Hundreds of bones in piles with more poking out from the earth beneath. The skulls were obviously human and I counted a dozen before I made myself stop.

"What is this place?" I whispered. It felt wrong to speak loudly in the face of so much death. Perhaps this was just a burial site? I doubted it. The graveyard where the People buried their dead was back behind the big house, and I knew there were graves there that were hundreds of years old, so this wasn't some ancient site for the Three Feathers tribe.

"This is where the fledglings who don't turn into crow go to die." Not Afraid came up beside me, his eyes fixed on the grim piles only a few feet below us. "Blood Mother and I are trying to find which bones are whose, but it is not easy. Most of the spirits here do not want to talk to us."

"Blood Mother?" I looked sideways at him. He was close enough I should have been able to feel heat coming off his skin, to smell his sweat. I might as well have been standing there alone.

"She is with me," he said. "She will be avenged."

He was talking about the spirit, I realized. A spirit of vengeance.

"Buttercup?" I guessed.

"She died here," he said, biting off the words like they hurt to say aloud. "I have only Blood Mother now."

"Did you kill these people?" I said, letting the identity of the spirit go for the moment.

He laughed, and the chill in my bones grew stronger.

"She does not see!" he cried, throwing his arms wide. His fingertips brushed my arm, cold but solid. "She will not believe, even here."

"Tell me," I said, turning to face him. "Tell me what this is."

I had a feeling already. I knew but didn't want to know.

"Sky Heart," he screamed at me, and I felt his breath sting my cheek, cold and smelling of dust and death. Another sign he wasn't a ghost, at least. "This is where he would bring them, the ones who did not change. The ones who changed but not into crow. He calls this 'the final flight.' But we call it the cliff of many tears."

"He throws them off the cliff," I said, taking a step back, unable to hold my ground in the face of so much rage and grief. "These are children."

I looked back at the pit; my light ball had died, forgotten by me in my horror, but the rising sun now cast light into it, enough light that I could make out the bones for what they were.

"If they did not change and fly, they died. If they did not die, because they were other than crow, he would come down and finish them. This is why I hunt the People. Eventually, the coward Sky Heart will have to face me. This time, he will die."

"But I was only exiled. I wasn't killed. Is this still going on?" I hadn't been thrown off a cliff. Not that it would have killed me, nor would any other means aside from having my heart eaten by another sorcerer. Perhaps Sky Heart knew that, knew somehow that he couldn't kill me.

"Do the others know?" I thought of my mother, of her confusion over what was happening, over why Not Afraid had killed Sky Heart's wife a century before, over her insistence, decades earlier, that Jasper be the one to drive me away from the ranch, that he make sure the new family picked me up.

"It does not matter," he said. "They let it happen. They must pay."

"It matters to me," I said, though even as I did, I questioned why I was trying to split hairs, to assign guilt. How does one process murder on this scale? Sky Heart, if what Not Afraid was telling me was true, was a serial killer. But Not Afraid had plenty of blood on his hands.

He'd let the fledglings live. Let Carlos live. Gone out of his way to make sure they were fed and unharmed.

Heartless killer with a drama streak out for vengeance. I had to keep that in mind. As well as the spirit, this Blood Mother. She had proven tricky, full of illusions in the forest.

I shook my head. "I cannot let you keep killing," I said. "Somehow, this has to end."

Cold blue light flared in Not Afraid's eyes, but he shrieked and violently shook his head.

"Let me show her," he said. The light flickered and he reached for me.

"What are you doing?" I took another step back and nearly fell over a rock. I gathered power in my hands, ready to unleash a blast of force at him.

"Do not fight it, please," he said. "Let us show you what happened."

Universe help me, I let go of my magic and he took my hands in his icy fingers. A wave of power rushed up through me.

For a moment, I was two people, myself standing at the base of the cliff, clinging to a man who should be dead, and also a girl in a blue gingham dress at the top of the cliff, my hair loose and whipping around my face.

Then the vision settled and I was just the girl. Buttercup.

"What are you doing?" she/I cried.

Sky Heart advanced on her/me. He was younger, stronger, his hair with its mane of feathers floating and flapping in the strong wind like wings. Shishishiel's power hugged him like a dark mantle and she/I cringed.

"You are not Crow," he said. "You have one last chance, fledgling. This is your final flight."

"Please, please, no," she/I begged him. Not Afraid had changed. He was Crow. She would too; she was his twin—she needed more time. Even as she/I thought these things, we knew that there was nothing inside her/me, no power, no connection to an Other, an animal self.

Her/my only connection was to Not Afraid. He wasn't there, but he was coming, her/my distress calling to him across the miles of forest.

Too late. Sky Heart lunged forward and grabbed her/my arms with bruising force. "Fly," he yelled, his breath hot on her/my tearstained cheeks.

Then she/I flew, thrown off the cliff. One moment there was dirt beneath her/my bare feet, the next just sky. The clouds were steel above, unbroken, the sun hiding its face.

"Brother," she/I screamed as the flying turned to falling.

I jerked away from Not Afraid just as I felt the horrible crushing pain of impact, pulling myself back to the present, back to life. I staggered, going to my knees, tears running down my face as his grief stayed with me, flooding my own senses. He had felt her die; her memories lived on in him. She might not have been shifter, but she was born a twin to one, born with inhuman blood in her veins no matter how human she appeared. Buttercup lived on in Not Afraid, lived on as Blood Mother. I was sure of it now.

"I found her in the cave," Not Afraid murmured. He knelt down in front of me, his hands splayed in supplication. "That is where Sky Heart left them. He stripped her body, leaving her for animals to find and scatter the bones."

The vision was over, but I still saw her broken shape, now naked and twisted, covered in blood and dirt, discarded like trash on the cave floor.

"How many?" I asked. "How long?"

"I have found sixty skulls," he answered. "I started before; this is when I built the grave here in front. I tried to bury them, to quiet their spirits. That is when Blood Mother found me. There is only one way to quiet the dead. Justice, vengeance."

"So, you confronted Sky Heart, but he killed you." I didn't wait for him to nod before continuing. The pieces were falling into place. "How did you come back?"

"Some things are too important for death to stop. Blood Mother needed to regain her strength. And now Shishishiel has abandoned the People. Now was the time." The blue light was back in his eyes, casting shadows on his gaunt face.

"If Sky Heart dies, justice will have been done. No one else will need to die." I forced myself to meet those cold eyes.

"If they knew—"

"If," I said. "That is a big if. I saw no one but Sky Heart in your sister's memory."

"I will kill them all if it means getting to Sky Heart."

I believed that. "You said Shishishiel has abandoned him. Why can't you get to him now?"

"There is still power in the stones, and Sky Heart carries a talisman.

Like yours, but it keeps Blood Mother away. Without her help, I cannot kill him."

Looking at his face, seeing the intensity there, the desperate need, I knew why he had risked bringing me here, why he had showed me the vision and the bones.

"You want me to let you in," I said.

"You have power." He reached toward my d20 talisman and I flinched. No way was he getting his hands on that again. "Our needs are not so different. You want to stop the killings; I want to kill only Sky Heart. He is the end." His expression grew slyer, and it was so adolescent and obvious that I almost laughed.

Laughing would have been pretty bad, so I held it in. Teen boys do not like being laughed at, and I doubted it would be any different with resurrected teen boys filled with the enraged spirit of their dead twin sister.

I leaned back on my heels, looking out over the ravine, looking away from the bones. He wanted to kill Sky Heart and he wanted my help. I wasn't sure how to feel about that. I did not like Sky Heart, and that dislike was quickly turning to hatred in the aftermath of the vision. It was hard to deny the evidence that my grandfather was a coldblooded killer as well as a narcissistic cult leader. I had suspected that he had killed Ruby, my grandmother, but it wasn't talked about and there had never been any evidence of it.

It would be simple to destroy the boundary, I thought. Magic like that worked as long as the anchors were sound. Destroy a boundary stone and the magic should snap. Sky Heart's talisman would be harder to get, but the danger of an object like that was that once it was removed, it no longer protected the person. If I could get it away from him, keep him from fleeing in his crow form. That was a lot of *if*s.

But Blood Mother, the spirit, had proven very tricky with her illusions in the forest the day before. She had tried to fuck with my emotions. I didn't trust the spirit and that meant I couldn't trust Not Afraid. The vision felt so real, the bones were real, and this place had the energy of sorrow and evil about it. All that I could accept. Perhaps.

"I will help you," I said, meeting his cold gaze again. "But there are conditions."

"What conditions?" he asked. His mouth pressed into a thin line, and I guessed from the flicker and dance of blue fire in his eyes that neither he nor Blood Mother liked the idea of strings attached.

Well, bully for them. They wanted my help, they could suck it up and do it my way.

"I will speak with Sky Heart first. He will tell me the truth, and when I have verified what you say about him is true, then and only then will I break the wards and let you in. And only if you give your oath, on the bones and memory of Buttercup, that no one else will be harmed, that Sky Heart's death will end this and you will rest in peace."

He considered that for longer than I liked, but perhaps his thinking it over was a good thing. Agreeing too quickly would have been suspect.

"How will you make him tell the truth?" he said finally.

"I have a spell for that," I lied. It wasn't really a permanent lie. I had a few hours of walking back to the camp to figure out how I was going to cast a truth spell. I had some ideas.

"We agree," he said. "We give our oath. Killing Sky Heart will end our vengeance and justice will be done."

I searched his face for signs of a lie but found none. He had given an oath. In my heart it felt right. I wanted to trust him, and an oath given from a spirit like this was serious. Breaking oaths for supernaturals like ourselves wasn't something done lightly. That would have to be enough.

Now I just had to figure out how to deal with Alek and Carlos. I doubted they were going to let me walk into camp, magically bind and interrogate Sky Heart, and then possibly let a murder happen.

As if reading my mind, Not Afraid spoke. "The lion and tiger have crossed the boundary. They hunt for you."

Their being out of camp would make things easier. If they didn't find me.

"Can you lead them away? Keep them busy until I can get back?" I asked. "Without hurting them," I added.

"Yes." Not Afraid flashed me a smile and, for a moment, looked as young as he had been when he died the first time. "I am good at being the deer."

"All right," I said. "You'll have to point me in the right direction to get back." I was going to do this. The killing had to end. As Not Afraid had said, justice needed doing, and it looked like it was up to me to see it done.

With grim thoughts and dangerous plans swirling through my head, I got to my feet and followed Not Afraid back into the woods.

CHAPTER NINE

I wasn't as far from the ranch as I'd thought. The darkness had made the going very slow, and it took me less time to return. The sun rose, cresting the trees, and I judged something like two or three hours had passed by the time I encountered the boundary stone I'd passed on my way out.

It was enough time for cold certainty to fight off my doubts. Enough time for me to come up with the basics of a plan. Three months before, a warlock had tried to turn some of my friends into living batteries. He'd been able to incapacitate shifters and trap them in their animal bodies. I had stopped him and eaten his heart, taking his power so I could free my friends.

I didn't like going into Bernie's memories, tapping into his knowledge. He hadn't been a very sane or very nice man. I felt like it should have bothered me more to kill him, but every time I touched his power or accessed his knowledge, I remembered why I wasn't bothered at all.

I stopped at the stone and placed a small rock I'd picked up in the woods an hour before on top of it. I had filled the pebble with my power until I felt it wouldn't hold more without blowing apart. Which it would, as soon as I told it to, in a blast designed to at least score if not break the boundary stone. The explosion would disrupt the ward.

If Sky Heart was guilty. I was sure he was, my mind going over and over the things Not Afraid had shown me and going over my own gut feelings about this place, about my grandfather.

But I would do what was right. I would cast my version of a Zone of Truth and I would hear his guilt from his own lips. I was sure this was the only way I could live with myself later. The murders had to stop, but justice needed to be done as well.

I looked around the gravel circle and saw a few people gathered in a group near one of the cabins, talking. The door of one of the pole barns was wide open and there were sounds of people using tools inside. Farther on I saw two women throwing pottery on wheels under the awning of another barn. The scene was more normal than it had been—domestic, even.

As I stepped into the camp and walked toward the big house, I wished for a fleeting moment that Alek wasn't off on a wild goose chase. I wanted to ask him what he thought, tell him about what I had discovered. I hesitated at the steps of the house. I was acting alone again, the way I was used to doing things. My whole life since Samir had killed my true family, the family of my heart, I'd been alone. I wasn't used to having friends who I could trust with difficult things, friends who could handle themselves in the magical world. The real world.

Alek wasn't there. I shook my head. This was my choice. My decision. I would learn the truth and I would stop these murders. Alek would understand that.

My thoughts felt like lies, and I shoved them away. If he saw the bones. If he knew.

The door opened and Sky Heart stepped out onto the porch, taking away my last moments to think.

"You will leave," he said, leveling the shotgun at me. "Now."

No more hesitation. I caught the gun with my magic and yanked, ripping it free from his hands to clatter uselessly onto the boards. Then I pushed my magic into a circle using the knowledge I'd gained from the late Bernie the warlock. The power formed a ward, locking Sky Heart inside. I layered on a second spell courtesy of Bernie, a spell to keep him from reaching out to that other plane, from calling on his crow half and shifting.

What would have taken Bernie multiple items carefully researched and gathered and the power of a full moon and hours of ritual took me a couple of seconds.

Now for the coup de grâce. Or, as Harper would call it, the cup-dee-gracie.

I layered one more spell, forming my magic into a glowing white circle, envisioning the purity of truth, a light that pushed away all lies, all shadows, a light that would let nothing hide within it.

My head started to pound and I knew I wouldn't be able to hold the spells for long. Time for a chat with Grandfather.

"Did you throw Not Afraid's sister off a cliff?" I asked, keeping the question as unambiguous as I could.

Sky Heart's mouth worked as he stood frozen inside my circles and his eyes blazed with rage.

"Yes," he said, the words hissing out of his throat.

Was that enough? No. I wanted to know more. I wanted to hear him admit to all of it.

"How many children have you thrown off that cliff?" I said, my voice rising. Behind me I heard people moving, coming closer. *Good*, I thought. *Let them come. Let them hear.*

"Jade?" Pearl called out to me, but I ignored her.

"Tell me," I said. "Tell them, Sky Heart. Tell them all how you killed their children."

"You don't understand. You are exile. You are not one of us. You should be dead. I should have killed you when you were a baby. I let your mother keep you. I was weak and now we are all punished for it." The hatred in his face shocked me and I almost lost the spells.

"How many?" I demanded. "Tell them."

"I do not know," he screamed. "All of them. All the ones who are not my people. They were abominations, insults to the pure blood of Shishishiel. Like you. Just like you."

I reached out with a thread of power and found my exploding stone. A slight nudge of more power and it went off. A crack reverberated through the camp.

"No! What have you done?" Sky Heart shrieked.

I sprang forward, clearing the steps in a leap, and broke my own circles by diving into them. I ripped the beaded bag from his neck, pulling him forward. I kicked his legs out from under him and jumped aside as he tumbled down the steps.

He sprang to his feet quicker than I expected and turned on me, snarling.

A huge crow dropped out of the clear sky like a comet of death, slamming into Sky Heart and carrying him back to the ground in a swirling cloud of feathers. He screamed as the crow's unnaturally curved and sharp talons dug into his chest. Blue-white fire ripped into Sky Heart, flowing from the crow's open beak.

He died screaming, his chest bursting open, as the crow ripped out his heart and turned it to ashes before my eyes.

I stood on the porch, the beaded bag in my hand, shaking as the adrenaline dump hit me in the aftermath of using so much power.

The crow, which I guessed was Not Afraid, looked up at me and cawed, his huge black wings spread.

"It is done," I said. "Justice is done."

"No." Jasper was the first to reach Sky Heart's body. He waved his arms at the giant crow as though he could shoo it away. "*No!*" he cried again.

The crow looked at me and something in its gaze warned me, but not soon enough.

Not Afraid beat his wings and flew up into Jasper's face, his talons hooking into my father's chest. Blue fire spilled around them and Jasper screamed in pain.

I gathered my magic but couldn't blast the crow without hitting Jasper. I jumped off the porch and attacked the crow with my hands, tearing at his feathers. Cold burned me, icy fire rippling up my arms. More on instinct than with clear thought, I thrust the beaded talisman around Not Afraid's neck.

The crow shrieked and shifted. Now I wrestled with Not Afraid himself. He looked fifteen, but his body had a strength I couldn't match. Jasper went down and Not Afraid shoved me off, then came after me, ripping the talisman bag from his neck. He was free of my father. Free and clear for me to blast the shit out of him.

I summoned my power and sent a bolt of pure force at him. It should have ripped him apart, but he merely staggered and then laughed. His hands and face were covered in blood. My father's blood or Sky Heart's, I wasn't sure. It didn't matter.

"You broke your oath," I said as I struggled to my feet.

"I had a prior oath." He grinned at me, his gaunt and bloody face a death mask. He reached into his shirt and pulled out a small, rectangular piece of paper, tossing it onto the ground.

I ignored it and lunged for him, sending another bolt of power at his face. His eyes flared blue and he shifted to a giant crow again even as he leapt to meet me.

Wolf sprang between us, her huge body slamming into the crow and knocking it aside. I twisted and managed to avoid colliding with her as well. She spun and snarled, spit dripping from razor-sharp teeth as long as my fingers.

Not Afraid beat his wings and lifted into the sky, circling once and then glowing with bright blue fire before disappearing into the sunlight like a ghost.

I let go of my magic, falling against Wolf's warm body as exhaustion hit me like a drunk driver with a lead foot. My foggy brain realized someone was crying, pleading over and over for someone not to leave them.

Jasper. I opened my eyes.

He lay in a spreading pool of blood, his chest ripped open, his heart a smoking ruin within a mess of pink lung tissue and too-bright red blood. I knew he was dead. Even a shifter can't heal a vital organ destroyed by fire.

Pearl knelt over him, his head in her lap, smoothing her hands over his hair again and again, her pleading a high keening, the words blending and melding until they meant nothing. Emerald stood behind Pearl, her face pale with shock, her green eyes wide and unseeing. As I watched, shudders and shakes took over her body, and she dropped to her knees and clung to her mother.

Movement to my side caught my eye as something fluttered on the ground. The paper that Not Afraid had removed from his shirt.

Slowly, as though I had aged a thousand years, I staggered over and picked it up.

It was a postcard.

CHAPTER TEN

I crumpled the postcard in my hand, igniting it with a thought as I let it flutter toward the ground again. It was ash even as it hit.

A scream that shifted to a high-pitched snarl was my only warning. Em rose to her feet and sprang at me, shifting in midair into a white wolf. I threw my hands up and pushed magic out into a shield in front of me.

She bounced off the shield and twisted, landing on her feet. She sprang again, and again I forced her away.

"Em," I yelled. "I don't want to hurt you."

Snarl. Leap. Bounce. Twist. Repeat.

Then people around us started shifting, turning into crows. They rose as a black swarm into the sky and descended at me, dive-bombing me like I was a bird of prey.

I pulled my power around me like a dome and hunkered down, throwing everything I had into keeping the shield up. Through the barrage of black wings, I caught Pearl watching, Jasper's head still in her lap, and I silently pleaded with her to stop this, to call them off.

She shook her head and looked away from me, her face quickly lost in the slam and flurry of winged bodies.

I couldn't hold the shield forever. They wouldn't be able to kill me, but I had no idea what happened to a sorceress who was torn apart. How long would it take to regenerate? Years? What would that pain feel like? Would I be conscious?

Em's wolf body slammed into my shield again, and this time, I felt the reverberation right down into my bones. I was going to lose it soon; there was too much physical force being thrown against me.

The deep, coughing roar of a lion echoed through the camp, and suddenly, the crows all came to earth, changing back into their human forms as they touched down. Em hit my shield one last time and rebounded, turning even as she twisted in the air back to a teenage girl.

A huge white tiger leapt between Em and me. Alek. I dropped my shield and called out his name.

He shifted to human and looked around, taking in the two mutilated corpses and the cluster of angry shifters. Carlos, still in his lion form, prowled through the People, cutting a line between them and where Alek and I stood.

"What happened here?" Alek said. His voice was deceptively soft but carried some of the tiger's growl still in it, a dangerous tone.

"She broke the wards," Pearl said, pointing at me. "She allowed the evil in."

"That's not the whole story," I protested. "Sky Heart has been killing the fledglings who don't turn into crows. He murdered dozens of them. I have seen their bones. He admitted as much to me, to all of us, before Not Afraid killed him."

Alek turned and looked at me, disbelief and a deep sadness in his eyes. "You let him in?"

"Yes," I said. I spread my hands, half-reaching for Alek as I stared up at him, begging him to believe my good intentions. "We made a deal. He could get his justice, then he would rest and the People would be left in peace. He gave me his oath."

"He broke an oath?" Alek looked like he wanted to understand, but he stayed where he was, and I dropped my hands.

"He had a prior oath." I couldn't share my suspicions about Samir's involvement, not here in front of everyone. "He betrayed me and killed Jasper."

"You stupid girl," Pearl said. She rose to her feet after gently setting Jasper's head on the ground. "Not Afraid is an evil spirit. That is no boy. I saw him die more than a century ago. Whatever that is, it cannot be him."

"You heard Sky Heart," I said. "You heard him. He killed those children. Why do you think Shishishiel has abandoned you? Why did the Great Crow not stop this?"

I knew it was unfair to invoke their missing guardian, but I had been trying to help them. They couldn't see that. They could only see the dead bodies. They hadn't seen the bones. Hadn't seen how many more deaths I was trying to prevent.

Gasps and questions from the crowd turned quickly to angry murmurs, and Carlos roared again, quieting them. I stood up, every muscle protesting and my head pounding like it was going to explode.

"Go," Pearl screeched at me. "Go from here, killer. We will take care of our own as we always have."

Alek reached for me then, his hand closing on my upper arm as he stepped in close. "Get in the truck," he murmured. "I will get you out of here in one piece if I can."

I looked past him, forcing myself to see Jasper's body. For fourteen years, he had been my father. For more than thirty after that, he had been as good as dead to me. Then I had learned he wasn't even my birth father.

But he had come to me for help. Not Alek, not the Council of Nine. Me. He'd been so desperate, but also trusting that somehow I could come there and make things better.

I had failed him. I had seen only what I wanted to see, believed what I wanted to believe. He had paid the price for it. He was the one walking along the road to hell my good intentions had paved.

"No," I said, blinking away tears. I had no right to grieve for this man. But I did have the duty to set things right, to fulfill the promise I'd made him by coming here. Samir was somehow at the root of this; I could feel it. My guess was he had raised Not Afraid from the dead, reuniting him with Blood Mother and setting them loose on my family.

"No," I repeated, pulling my arm out of Alek's grip. "I am going to kill Not Afraid and lay Buttercup's spirit to rest once and for all. No one else dies."

"You do not have that right," Pearl said.

"I have every right. Jasper begged me to come and I promised I would help. I am going to end this. I will not break my word." I started walking, glaring at the crowd, daring them to get in my way.

"Wait," Alek said, coming up beside me. "We will come with you."

"What if he comes back here?" I said. "Who will protect them?"

I didn't think Not Afraid would come there. I was pretty damn sure where he had flown off to. But Alek couldn't come with me. This was my fight and I didn't know if I could protect him, too. Or even if I could win. I didn't want to worry about him.

And there really was a small chance that Not Afraid would double back, counting on me to try to follow him and instead coming to finish killing the People.

"Carlos," Alek said. "He'll stay."

"Because he was so effective against this guy before?" I hated the mean whine in my voice, but I had to convince Alek to stay out of my way.

Carlos snarled at me.

"Fuck you," Alek said. I was pushing him away, as obviously as the physical distance opening between us. I wanted his anger. I needed him to stay there. Stay safe, away from me.

"Please," I whispered, turning to Alek. "Please protect them. Don't let anyone else die."

It was underhanded and totally manipulative and I felt terrible pulling the trick, but it worked. There was enough truth in my pleading, in my grief, that he fell for it. That or he gave up on me. I didn't want to know.

"Fine." The finality in his tone was like charging into a wall.

"Wolf," I called, and this time she appeared. She seemed to recognize what I wanted and bent low so I could drag myself up onto her back. There was no way in nine hells I was getting back to the cave without help. My body was exhausted, my magic a weak throb inside of me. I hoped I could find a second wind somewhere on the run there.

Wolf and I plunged through the crowd and no one made a move to stop us. Soon, the cool forest canopy closed over us. I clung to Wolf's fur and tried to think about how in the power of the Universe I was going to kill a man who was already dead.

CHAPTER ELEVEN ▶

The rocks in the ravine looked like poorly cut gravestones jabbing through the inconsistent moss and grass clinging perilously to their edges. The cliff loomed, the tears streaking its face glinting in the sunlight. It cast a shadow over its base, as though deliberately hiding the pit of bones there.

Wolf stopped at the tree line again and I slid off her back. My legs felt like rubber bands and my head still ached, but I was more rested than I would have been if I'd run there under my own power. I was grateful that Wolf was with me.

Back to normal, she and I against Samir. Or in this case, one of Samir's stupid plots.

Not that stupid, a treacherous voice inside me whined. *You fell for it. This is what you get for not running when you had the chance.*

"It ain't over yet," I said aloud.

Wolf and I picked our way across the ravine to the cave. I had hoped that Not Afraid would be outside, though fighting him in the open would give him the advantage of flight. Wolf had managed to rebuff him when he was in his crow form. Carlos had said that he didn't think the boy was a shifter. I figured that he had lost that power when he died and was brought back. The diabolical crow form was probably Blood Mother giving him her power, which meant that, in that form, Wolf could hurt him.

Rustling in the rear of the cave caught my attention. I crept around the pit and stopped at the entrance. I didn't want to go back into the dark, back beneath tons of earth and stone. I summoned my magic, debating just spamming bolts of pure power throughout the damn cave to see if I could flush Not Afraid out.

Great. My plan was apparently to Magic Missile the darkness. There had to be a better way.

"Not Afraid," I called out. "Come face me, you bastard."

Silence. Then rustling and hissing. With my luck, the cave was full of snakes or something. The hissing reminded me of the noise a crow makes when angry, however. Not a sibilant sound so much as air being forced out of a small throat.

I pooled power in my hands, willing it into a bright purple goo that phosphoresced. Then I flung the goo into the cave, throwing my hands wide so that it splattered across as wide an area as I could manage. The light goo painted the stalactites and the cave floor, revealing a wide cavern with a ceiling that would have forced Alek to duck along the outer edge but opened up toward the back. The glow illuminated enough that I could make out shapes. There was something at the back of the cave, a shape that clearly wasn't a stalactite or stalagmite.

With a deep breath and more power at the ready, I moved into the cave. I crept toward the rustling and movement from the shape at the back. As I neared, I formed another ball of light goo and spattered the stalactites above me with it.

The shape resolved itself into a cage of human bones. Inside the cage was a giant crow that looked like something out of a *Resident Evil* movie. Its feathers were caked with ichor and dried blood, with large patches sloughed off and others hanging by threads of flesh. Its mouth was open, making that horrid hissing noise I'd heard before. The crow looked at me as Wolf started growling again.

Its eyes were exactly like Wolf's eyes. Full black with pinpricks of light like a backcountry sky on a moonless night.

Undying. The ancient guardians of the beings who became the human's gods.

Shishishiel.

He hadn't abandoned the People. He was trapped. Tortured and somehow decaying.

Wolf's fur isn't perfectly black anymore. Down her belly is a thick line of white scar tissue. A parting gift from Samir. We had barely made it away from him alive. He was the only person I knew who could hurt an Undying.

"Beautiful, isn't it?" Not Afraid slunk out from behind a stalagmite at the back of the cave. "Samir was very helpful. Now you see why I had to honor my oath to him? He promised me vengeance. He stopped Shishishiel."

Shishishiel shrieked and tried to open his wings, but the bone cage prevented it.

I unleashed my magic, slamming pure force into the cage, not daring to speak first lest I warn Not Afraid of my intentions. Nothing happened. It was as though the cage ate my magic. I grabbed it with my hands and was rebuffed by a shield of power that hovered just above the bones. The force of it threw me back and I slammed into a stalagmite. Crystalline rocks crashed about me and stung my face and arms as they fell.

This cave was fragile. Good to remember. I didn't fancy getting impaled.

"That will not work," Not Afraid said.

"What will?" I asked. I didn't expect him to answer; it was more to buy time for Wolf to circle around behind me and come up on his flank.

Not Afraid just laughed, his face again a death mask in the purple light of my spell. Blue fire danced in his eyes and illuminated his body. I prayed that meant the spirit was in him, which would mean Wolf could help. He drew a large knife from a sheath at his waist. I wondered if it had always been there but hidden by illusions, or if he had come back here to weapon up. I thought of Gibbs's rule nine from *NCIS*: always carry a knife.

Another thing I was going to change if I made it out of this situation.

"Where is Samir?" I slowly got to my feet, careful to make no move that might provoke an attack.

Not Afraid shrugged. "Not here. He said if you could not handle us, you would not be worth his time. He was not even sure you would come. But I was. I know the Crow. Blood calls to blood. No one leaves Sky Heart's tribe alive."

Wolf sprang at Not Afraid and he twisted, slashing with the knife. The blade glowed with red fire, power I recognized.

"Wolf, no!" I yelled. Samir had enchanted that knife. It was too late. The blade cut into Wolf's shoulder and she howled, iridescent blood spurting from her wound. I threw a bolt of magic at Not Afraid. It was easily deflected by a burst of blue energy and fizzled before doing more than distracting him momentarily.

A moment was enough for Wolf to get away. She was the size of a pony and her ability to maneuver inside the cave was limited by the crystalline growths. She limped backward, snarling.

"You can't kill me," I said, taunting Not Afraid, trying to make him focus only on me. "Did Samir tell you that? He's setting you up. Fucking with you. This is all just one of his stupid games, a way to hurt me."

"There are worse fates than death," Not Afraid replied, turning to me. He wiped the blade on his leathers and grinned. "Just ask Shishishiel."

Shishishiel. Not Afraid was between me and the cage, but I could see the crow's pained eyes beyond us. As I watched, a droplet of milky water fell from an overhead stalactite and splashed onto the cage, running down the yellowed bones.

Shishishiel, my mind repeated. The crow spirit had stopped Not Afraid and Blood Mother a century before. He was dangerous enough that Samir had neutralized him before resurrecting Not Afraid. Free the crow, save the People.

It didn't have quite the same ring as "save the cheerleader, save the world," but I would work with the ideas I had.

The water got through. The crystals were fragile, but I was willing to bet a whole stalactite would be pretty heavy. Heavy enough to break bones?

"Is the cage made from your sister?" I asked, buying time as I gathered my magic again. I couldn't use gestures. Nothing could give away what I was planning, or Not Afraid would attack. I had to keep him talking. In the end, he was just a kid. A totally crazy kid with the insane rage spirit echo of his dead twin sister living inside him. Still, he had talked to Carlos. He seemed to want someone to listen.

"Yes," he said, his eyes narrowing. "Why?"

"After you cut me up or whatever, are you going to kill the rest of the People?" I formed my magic into a razor-thin disk over my head, not daring to look up and check my work. I hoped Blood Mother couldn't see my magic. Not Afraid wasn't reacting so far, and as they say, so far, so good.

"I will wipe out the bloodlines." His lips curled back from his teeth.

"Even my sister? She isn't Crow. She's just a kid, just like Buttercup."

"No," he said. "She isn't. She's of your blood, of Sky Heart's blood. They all must die. They all must suffer." He took a step toward me, brandishing the blade. "You will suffer first."

"You weren't going to keep your oath to me even if you hadn't cut a deal with Samir, were you?" I asked.

I didn't give him time to answer. I already knew what he would say. Envisioning the invisible weapon like Xena's chakram, I threw the magic disk at the stalactite above the cage.

The magic chakram sheared through the crystal. The stalactite crashed down, smashing into the bones.

Not Afraid screamed and attacked as the cage shattered. Bone and crystal fragments flew everywhere, pieces embedding themselves in my body with searing force. I threw myself sideways, my hands up to protect my face. Not Afraid came down on top of me and I grabbed at his arms, struggling to keep the knife away from my body. He straddled me, his superior strength winning out as the knife blade dug into my chest. Blue fire rippled around his arms and joined the red fire burning a hole into my breastbone.

The screaming was all me. I tried to fight the panic, fight the feeling that I was about to die. It is hard to remember you are immortal when your heart is slowly being burned out of your chest.

I wasn't even sure that Samir's knife couldn't kill me. I really didn't want to find out I'd been wrong all these years about how to kill a sorceress.

Wolf's jaws closed on Not Afraid's shoulder as she sprang at him and tried to drag him off me, her head whipping back and forth. I tried to gather power, to blast him off my chest, but the pain was too much. Red spots danced in my vision like blood spatter, and cold darkness closed in, fogging my mind.

Then a woman appeared over Not Afraid. She was Native, her skin perfectly red-brown and smooth, her face ageless, young and ancient somehow all at once. Her eyes met mine and all I saw were stars as she reached for his head with strong, graceful hands.

She broke his neck.

Blue energy swirled up from him, but the woman shook her head and opened her mouth. Blood Mother's power swirled in the air, seeming to resist for a moment like a child who doesn't want to go to bed yet. Then it flowed into her mouth and was gone.

She pulled Not Afraid off me and the knife clattered to the ground.

"Shishishiel," I whispered. I'd always thought of the Crow as a man. Sky Heart had always called the spirit "he." I guess we see what we want to see.

The woman turned away from me and touched Wolf's injured shoulder. The leak of iridescent blood stopped and the wound closed.

I realized then that Shishishiel wasn't Undying. She was one of the beings the Undying guarded.

She stared into Wolf's eyes for a long moment as though they were holding an intimate conversation. For all I knew, they were. Then she shifted to a crow shape and flew out of the cave, leaving only the faint murmur of wings behind her.

I used Wolf's leg to pull myself up and forced myself to look down at my chest. The bleeding had stopped, but there was a ragged wound with charred edges, and it smelled like bacon.

"You got some 'splaining to do," I muttered at Wolf. Which was pointless. Wolf wouldn't tell me anything even if she could. I had a lot of sudden suspicions about how she came to protect me, however, all of which led to a lot more questions.

Questions I could ponder when I wasn't two breaths away from passing the fuck out. I picked up the magic knife. Instinct told me to destroy it, but logic told me to bring it with me. I couldn't leave it. The blade was too dangerous. Not Afraid had a sheath belted to his waist with a leather cord. I pulled it free of his corpse and slung it over my shoulder after putting away the blade.

With Wolf as my crutch, I stumbled my way out of the cave, blinking in the bright sunlight. One foot in front of another, we made our way across the ravine and back toward camp. Despite Shishishiel closing Wolf's wound, my guardian was still limping, and I wasn't sure I had the strength to stay on her back. So, we walked. Or shambled. Shuffled. Stumbled. One foot in front of the other. Over and over.

I don't know how far I got. A mile? Less, probably. There were lots of trees still. And sword ferns, which rose up to catch me as I slumped into them.

The next thing I knew, Alek was bending over me.

"Is it over?" he asked. Not "Are you all right?" or another expression of concern. He didn't try to touch me, either. That worried me, but I shoved it aside.

"Yes," I croaked. "He's dead."

It wasn't over, however. I had a feeling this was just Samir's opening salvo. His shot across my bow.

"Good," Alek said. Then his voice softened, and he added, "Rest; I've got you." He picked me up gently in his warm arms.

"We have to stop meeting like this," I said. Then red-tinged darkness roared up and pulled me under.

CHAPTER TWELVE ▶

Either I had made it farther than I thought or I stayed passed out for a lot longer than it felt like, because it seemed like barely any time had gone by before we emerged from the forest and into the camp.

The People were gathered again, standing in loose rows, filling the open space in front of the big house. Pearl stood over the two bodies. Both had been wrapped now with indigo burial sheets. No one said a word. They watched us pass in eerie silence as Alek carried me toward where his truck was parked. It appeared we were going to get the hell out of Dodge.

"Wait," I said, my throat still feeling like I'd swallowed gravel, my chest still on fire with every breath. "Put me down."

"I don't think that is a good idea," Alek said.

I started to struggle and he had no choice. I stumbled, grabbing his arm to steady myself. Wolf was nowhere in sight.

"You must go," Pearl said. She seemed less angry now, but there was a hard finality in her words that allowed no argument.

"What will happen to Em?" I asked, gesturing at the angry girl standing near Pearl. My half-sister had shifted, but not into a crow. I wanted to believe that my mother wouldn't throw her off a cliff, at least, but this was the same woman who had sent me away to live with an abusive couple.

I thought about what Sky Heart had said about wanting to kill me young. I thought about the bones beneath the cliff. Perhaps my mother had known, had suspected. She had tried to save me. I pushed that thought aside.

"Em is staying with us," Pearl said. "We must change to survive. Sky Heart's ways brought evil to the People. We will not send our children away. Never again."

"Send them away? He was killing them." I couldn't believe she was still talking around his crimes.

"Enough. What is done is done. This is not for you to know, not for you to be a part of anymore. We cannot forgive you, but for your atonement in killing Not Afraid, we will allow you to leave." As she spoke, the shadow of wings unfurled at the corners of my vision, and I knew that Shishishiel was with her. My mother, the new Sky Heart. I hoped she would be a gentler dictator.

"What about my father?" I asked. I didn't need to clarify I wasn't talking about Jasper.

"His secrets are not mine to reveal. If he wants you to know him, he will find you." She came toward me, the mantle of Shishishiel's power fading back, leaving only my mother's familiar form behind.

"I'm sorry," I whispered.

"Go," she said, but this time the words were a plea more than a command. "We must take care of our own."

I had no strength left to argue. Emerald would get to stay in her home. That was something at least. I wanted to warn Pearl about Samir, but realized that Shishishiel had likely already done so. There was nothing here for me.

"Good-bye, Mother," I said.

I used Alek's sink to wipe the worst of the blood off my chest, and changed my shirt. The wound was closed already, but I knew I wouldn't be eating delicious pork products with quite the same gusto for a long while. Black-and-purple bruising was already spreading over my whole chest, creating a nebula pattern that would make Hubble fanatics jealous.

Then I climbed into the truck and Alek drove us away from Three Feathers. We were silent until we had made it well out of sight of the camp.

"Where is Carlos?" I asked to break the tension.

"They had hidden his car when he disappeared. He went to retrieve it after Pearl said that Not Afraid was dead. She said you were hurt. That was when I went to find you."

"Ah," I said. The long night, the longer day, and sheer exhaustion slammed into me. My father, the man I had thought was my father, was dead. Samir had tried to wipe out my entire bloodline.

I had almost played right into his hands. I had maybe almost died.

I had let a man be murdered. A terrible man, true, but his blood was as much on my hands as on Not Afraid's.

I started shaking and curled up in the seat, wrapping my arms around myself and taking quick, shallow breaths. Deep ones still hurt too much to manage. Fat tears leaked down my cheeks.

Alek looked over at me but said nothing.

"Aren't you going to ask if I'm okay?" I stuttered through my tears, trying to crack a smile. I feared it looked more like a grimace.

"No," he said with a look that made it clear he knew I wasn't okay. A look that said *we* weren't okay.

We left it at that. I turned my head and stared out the window, watching the land go by in a green blur through my tears.

I had stopped Not Afraid and Blood Mother. I had even mostly thwarted Samir's plan to wipe out the People.

I didn't know the cost yet, not fully. I had only learned how little I really knew about my past and my heritage, about how the world really worked. This was a Pyrrhic victory, at best.

But one truth I did know was that there was no going back. Eventually the tears dried up and I faced forward. Toward the future. Toward home.

PACK OF LIES

THE TWENTY-SIDED SORCERESS: BOOK III

THIS BOOK IS DEDICATED TO

DEMON FOX:
CURSE YOU FOR ALL THE TOTAL PARTY KILLS
AND ALL THE UNSKIPPABLE CUT SCENES.

CHAPTER ONE ▶

Four pairs of eyes watched the twenty-sided die bounce across the hex mat, life and death riding on its little blue plastic numbers. We had gathered in the back room of my game shop for our usual Thursday night game session. First one since I'd returned from Three Feathers. Steve hadn't been able to make it, but the twins were there, and Harper, of course. She'd stood by me while I moped and struggled to resume training to fight my psychotic ex-lover.

While I pined for my other probably ex-lover. Who hadn't called me in over a month. The leaves were going to start changing. Our summer together, the ending in total disaster, seemed like a weird dream now. I missed Alek like hell, but I was recovering. Sorta.

Okay, I'd admit it. I'd been a mess. It felt good to game again, to resume some semblance of normal life again.

"Nat TWENTY," Ezee yelled as the die finished its roll and sat in the middle of a knocked-over pile of orc miniatures. The coyote shifter flipped his thick black hair back from his forehead and pumped a fist in the air.

"All right," I said, hiding my grin. "You successfully perform the Heal check. Harper, err, I mean Liandress the Unlucky, stabilizes."

"Cheap bastard," Harper muttered. "You could have just given me a potion."

"Potions are reserved for people who don't cast Fireball in small rooms," Levi said, reaching over and ruffling Harper's hair. She flicked one of his many facial piercings, sending the dangling seashell shape hanging off his lower lip spinning.

"What are you doing next?" I asked before this could end in Harper or Levi flipping the table or tearing out piercings.

"I'll waste a Heal spell on this useless wizard here," Ezee said.

"I'll loot the bodies," Levi added. He winked at me, leaned away from Harper, and slid a note across the table.

"Not the notes again," his twin groaned.

Harper rolled her eyes.

I had to admit, as I watched my friends bicker, that it was good to be here, to be doing things with them again. I felt like I was coming out of a fog, finally. For a week after I had returned from Three Feathers, after my anger and arrogance had gotten my father killed, I'd been despondent. Samir's games had gotten to me. Had nearly killed my tribe, killed my whole family, such as they were.

I'd stopped the killings, true. I had been banished from my childhood home a second time. That part stung less than knowing that Samir had manipulated me, tricked me. I felt like his little puppet toy on a string, dancing until he got tired and smashed me.

It wasn't a good feeling. All the training in the world, training to become strong enough that I could fight him head-on, seemed pointless. He wasn't facing me head-on. Instead, he kept up his little postcards.

Alek had heard me out, heard the whole story of Shishishiel and Not Afraid, heard how I freed the spirit or whatever it was and saved everyone, though at a cost. He seemed to understand. He told me it wasn't my fault, that my only mistake had been acting so quickly and acting alone.

I was used to working alone, being alone. This whole having friends who knew who I was and the dangers that posed and who didn't care was a new thing. The whole idea of having a relationship with someone was a new thing.

A thing I apparently sucked at.

Alek and I had talked a little, but I hadn't been ready for more, not right after. I'd retreated, hiding from everyone, alone in my grief and my pain.

Then Alek left. Justice business, he said.

He didn't call. He didn't come back.

I didn't quite pull a Bella from *Twilight* and mope for weeks, but it was a close thing. Harper kicked my ass out of bed after a week of me pretending I didn't need to eat or bathe, and made me go run the store.

"Life gives you lemons, you poke it in the eye with a stick," she'd said.

"Fuck you," I'd said. "I am just making a mess of everything."

"So, he's gone. Either suck it up and call his ass or stop moping."

"It isn't just Alek," I had muttered. "I don't know how to stop Samir. I hate this waiting."

"So, get out of bed and train."

"It's that easy?"

"No. It's hard. But you gotta get up and do it anyway." She had settled down on the bed beside me and tugged on my admittedly greasy black braid. "I'm a professional gamer. And a woman. You know what that's like? I get told I'm gonna get raped, that I'm ruining the game, that I should go back to playing with Barbies, that my hair is too masculine or that my boobs are too big or small or whatever, and all kinds of stupid shit. All the time. It sucks. But I don't let it break me and I don't let it stop me from doing what I love, from being who I am."

I knew some of the things people said online to and about her. I'd seen the comments, read the tweets. She never seemed bothered by it. I realized I'd just assumed she wasn't and hadn't ever asked. Great; on top of everything, I was a shitty friend, too.

"How do you do that?" I'd asked, resolving in my head to ask my friends more about their lives. Be more involved. They were risking everything by wanting me to stay in Wylde, by helping me train. Maybe it was time I started risking my heart for them.

"I tell myself every morning that today, today I'm going to kick ass and take screenshots." And with another tug on my braid and a bright grin, she had leapt up and started raiding my closet.

Kick ass. Take screenshots.

I wanted to screenshot this moment, my three best friends gathered around a table in a comic-and-game store that I owned. Nobody trying to kill me. Just people who cared that I was there, people who I would die to protect. This was happiness.

"Okay," I said. "You walk down the long hallway and see a set of huge doors. They open as you draw near, as though inviting you inside. The room is circular, with an ornate ivory throne sitting on a dais at its center. A man in red robes rises and greets you each by name."

"I ready my crossbow," Levi said.

"I've got the Fireball wand online," Harper said.

I reached into the messenger bag at my feet and drew out a flashlight. I clicked it on and pointed it at the ceiling. The words UNSKIPPABLE CUT SCENE were illuminated instantly.

"Whoa. How long did that take you?" Ezee asked.

"Not that long," I lied. It had taken most of a season of *Highlander* while I wrestled with the stupid idea, trying to get the words to project properly.

Ezee, Levi, and Harper all swiveled their heads at the same time, just before a knock came on the back door.

"Pizza break! I'll get it." Harper jumped up.

So much for my big dramatic moment where I introduced them to the big bad who would hopefully become their nemesis throughout the rest of the campaign. Gamers. Universe save me.

Joel, the pizza delivery guy, came in and set the pizza-warming case down on the side table next to the half-size fridge I kept in there. He was a wolf shifter, one of the few who lived in town instead of out at the official pack home, a giant faux-castle estate that pretended it was a hunting lodge.

"You guys sounded slammed," I said as he pulled the two pizzas from the case, pepperoni and pineapple for Harper and me, everything under the sun plus mushrooms for the twins.

"It's the wake for Wulf. Every alpha in the States is here with their seconds." He sighed, rubbing a hand over his short brown hair.

Harper had explained that Wulf was the local pack alpha, a legend. I'd seen him once or twice in town, an old man with white hair and watery grey eyes. His last name was Leifson, supposedly the son of Leif Erikson, the famous Viking who discovered Vinland and the new world. Harper wasn't sure about that, but he was old even for a shifter, over a thousand if the legend was true.

He had died a week before. Wolf shifters from all over the States were trickling into our small town, causing a weird end-of-summer boom in the hotel and restaurant industry. The hunters weren't there yet, as only wolf season had started and hunting wolves was banned in this county, and the students up at Juniper College wouldn't be back for two weeks, so the business was nice. Not that it was much business for me. Apparently, not a lot of gamers in the alpha wolf gene pool.

"They're going to hold the wake on Sunday, right?" Harper said, handing Joel a can of Mountain Dew.

He cracked the lid and drank deeply. "Yeah. Not that nonwolves are supposed to know, you know. Geez, guys. Jade isn't even a shifter."

"Small town," Ezee said. "Can't keep anything secret here."

Except me being a sorceress. That was still mostly a secret. Everyone thought I was just a witch. Totally fine by me. Most people, my friends excepted, think sorcerers are evil.

Which might be true. I knew Samir was evil. Me? I wasn't so sure yet. Given how things had gone lately, I figured I could go either way.

I shoved that depressing thought aside. "Well, I wish they'd buy more comic books," I said, smiling.

"They still planning to fight it out for who gets to be the next alpha of alphas?" Ezee asked. Wolf shifters had a weird society, from what Harper and the twins had explained to me. They put a lot of importance and power into their alphas, with everything being run like a gang, more or less. Not a thing I was a fan of, after how I'd grown up in a cult and all. Alpha shifters were just shifters who were much stronger than other shifters, sometimes with extra powers. Like Alek, though some of his powers came from him being a Justice and were given to him by the Council of Nine, the shifters' equivalent of a ruling body or gods or whatever.

"Guess so. Glad I'm not an alpha. They are supposed to reaffirm the Peace, too, which I suppose is the real point. I'm keeping out of it. I just deliver pizza, man, and sometimes howl at the moon." Joel laughed, finished his drink, and left with a hefty tip in his back pocket. I'd delivered pizzas for a while, during one of my lives while on the run from Samir. I always tipped well after being in the trenches of pizza service.

We filled paper plates and shoved dice and minis aside to eat. I asked Harper about the Peace, but it was Ezee who answered me, taking on a professorial tone that I knew from his wink was totally an affectation.

"Back in like the eighteen forties, when everyone was coming west, a lot of wolves from Europe were coming here, making a name for themselves as hunters, trappers, guides, and such. They mixed with the local shifter wolves and formed pretty territorial packs. There was a ton of fighting between packs, enough that it got to the point where humans were starting to notice weird shit like people turning into wolves, and how many people were dying or disappearing."

"Wolves are always territorial. It's like they take the worst traits of wolf and human and combine them into something that resembles neither," Levi said in a tone that made it clear what he thought. His shifter animal was a wolverine, but he was one of the most laid-back guys I knew besides his brother.

"This was bad, though, way, way bad. The Council stepped in. Some say that's when they created the Justices as they are today. I don't know. But Wulf, who was still called Ulfr Leifson back then, brought together a huge Althing with an alpha from each of the major packs. To prevent the Justices and the Council from killing them all because they were risking exposure, he brokered a peace. Packs allow all wolves to pass through their territory, and allow nonaligned wolves like Vivian or Joel to live within their territory."

"Like Max," Harper added. Her brother was a wolf shifter as well. He lived with Harper's mom, Rosie, out on a bit of land beyond Wylde, at the edge of the River of No Return Wilderness.

"No fighting, no killing. It saved the wolves from the Council's wrath and kept them from exposing themselves to humans," Ezee said with a shrug. "So, now that Wulf is gone, I guess they are going to see who is top dog again and reaffirm the Peace."

"And you think sorcerers are weird? At least we just kill each other," I said with a forced smile. Shifters had seemed so simple. Like regular people, just ones who could turn into animals. I was learning, though, as I slowly paid more attention to the people around me, that they were like any people: far more complex than they first appeared. None of my friends were wolf shifters, so I'd never really asked about packs and politics. Learn something new every day, I guess.

I'd just bitten into my second greasy slice, pineapple juice and spicy pepperoni sliding over my tongue, when a knock came at the back door.

"Probably Joel," Harper said. "Bet he forgot something." She jumped up again and disappeared.

I was halfway through chewing my third bite when she came back, a weird expression on her face as she slid through the door. I swallowed a lump of cheese and started to ask her what was up.

Then I saw the man behind her. Over six and a half feet tall, white-blond hair, ice-blue eyes, and a grim expression on his annoyingly still-handsome face.

Alek. And here I was, my hair in a loose braid with pieces falling out, and pizza grease sliding down my chin and staining my tee shirt. Fuck me sideways with a chainsaw.

"Alek," I said, regretting swallowing that last bite so quickly, as it lodged in my throat. Or maybe that was my heart, which was trying to punch its way out of my chest in a fight-or-flight simulation.

"Jade," he said, his voice low and soft. He raised one hand, holding up a plastic bag with a wadded-up shirt inside. "I need your help."

CHAPTER TWO ▶

The air seemed to go out of the room and I found it hard to breathe for a moment. Anger. Yeah, that's what I was feeling. Hurt and angry.

"Sure," I said. "No problem. Let me drop everything and rush to assist you, Justice. I'll just get my coat." I didn't move.

A glance told me that my three friends were trying their best to turn invisible. Harper pressed herself against the wall to Alek's left, as though her *StarCraft* tee shirt would blend with the *Magic: The Gathering* poster behind her in a sort of nerd wallflower magic. Levi and Ezee, both flamboyant in their own ways, Levi with his Mohawk and tattoos and piercings, Ezee with his silk shirt and pressed trousers, were hunched in their seats, frozen like bunnies sighting the shadow of a hawk. Nobody made eye contact with me.

I guess they would have fled if they could, but Alek's bulk filled the only door.

"Do you know Doreen Reeves?" the bulk in question asked. He didn't seem surprised I wasn't rising to help him despite my words. I guess his lie-detection powers were still intact.

Levi sucked in a breath and then immediately looked like he regretted drawing attention to himself as Alek and I shifted our gazes to him.

"Dorrie. She drives an Explorer," he said with a tiny shrug. "Just fixed her CHECK ENGINE light last week."

"She's missing," Alek said, his cold blue eyes back on my face, turning my skin hot beneath his gaze.

A weird feeling twisted in my gut. "She's a wolf?" I asked, though it was half a question only. Town full of strange wolves. Woman missing. I watched a lot of *Law & Order*; I could do crime-victim math.

"Yeah," Levi said. His eyebrows pulled together as though the piercings in them were suddenly magnetized. "Shit."

"Can't your visions tell you where she is?" I said. I was half out of my chair though, holding myself down with an act of stubborn will. I already knew I'd help. I just didn't want Alek to think he could waltz in there after over a month and snap his fingers for his personal sorceress bitch to come magicking for him.

Okay. That was definitely the anger speaking. It left a bitter taste in my mouth that drowned out the pepperoni and pineapple.

"No," Alek said.

I waited, but he didn't say more. Everyone was looking at me. I felt their eyes like physical weights pushing me out of my chair.

"Game's postponed," I said with an exaggerated sigh. "Don't read my notes while I'm gone."

"You do not have to come," Alek said. "Just work spell like you did before; I can do rest." His usually faint Russian accent stood out stronger and hinted at his own emotions hidden somewhere under his totally stone-faced exterior. I couldn't decide if that made me feel better or worse.

"Nope," I said. "You get me or nothing."

He held out the bag without another word.

I climbed up into Alek's truck and breathed in the scent of hay in sunlight and his own vanilla musk. I'd missed that scent, missed the feel of him near me. It wasn't fair. But I had a job to do. I shoved away my resentment and the mixed emotions of anger and lust and pulled the tee shirt from the bag.

Reaching for my magic, I focused my will into a Locate spell, picturing a link between the shirt, which still smelled faintly of sweat and cigarettes, and the woman who owned it, who had, I assumed, worn it last. I'd been training these last few weeks, plus the ordeal in Three Feathers had pushed me to a new level, I guess; I didn't even have to touch my twenty-sided die talisman to work the Locate spell. Practice, practice, practice.

I felt a tenuous link stretching to the north.

"North," I said. "It's not a strong link."

Alek started up the engine with a nod and drove out of the parking lot, taking the single road out of town, heading north.

"What does *not strong* mean?" he asked softly after a moment.

"I don't know," I said. "I don't think it's good, though. Where did you get her shirt?"

"From her mate."

I risked a glance at him, at his perfect profile in the shifting light from the streetlamps. He didn't elaborate, so I turned my focus back to the spell, to that thin silvery thread only I could see stretching into the darkness.

"You didn't call," I heard myself say.

"We are going to talk now?" Alek said. In the corner of my vision I saw a muscle tic in his cheek. He had stubble, faint and only a shade darker than his white-blond hair. He looked tired, but that might have been a trick of the uneven light.

"No," I said. "Bad timing." I swallowed the *sorry* I wanted to put at the end of that.

After a long moment, he said, "Neither did you."

"Touché," I muttered. Point one to Alek. Great.

The thread of silver veered off to the left, growing thicker as we left Wylde behind. I sat up straighter, peering ahead.

"Left at that turnabout. There's a logging road there, leads to an old quarry. We'll have to park and walk, I think." The quarry was a popular hangout for college students to scratch their names and dirty slogans into the rocks and drink beer and make out. Despite the weak link to Dorrie, this made me hopeful. Maybe Dorrie had run out here with some hot out-of-town wolf to do a little extramarital mating. Maybe I was about to wreck a marriage instead of find something worse.

There are far more terrible things than a broken relationship.

Alek drove the truck as far down the logging road as we could go, until huge logs dragged there sometime in the past stopped our way. He killed the engine and we climbed out. The air was chillier there than in town, a breeze sighing in the tall trees and sticking my sweaty tee shirt to my back. Summer was definitely over.

I was about to call up a light, which would make holding on to the tracking spell fun, but as I said, practice is practice. Alek beat me to it, pulling a flashlight from under his seat. He shined it ahead of me as I moved carefully down the road and into the quarry.

The hillside there was cut away, a scar on the landscape. Alek's light caught bits and pieces of it as he moved, loose gravel crunching beneath our feet. Darkness pressed in on me. Somewhere, not as distant as I'd have liked—which would have been so far I couldn't hear at all—a wolf howled and was answered by a chorus.

"I've totally seen this movie," I muttered.

"This is the part where we get eaten by a chupacabra," Alek said. He came up close behind me, his muscular body a solid presence at my back. Comforting even as he annoyed me.

His joke made me smile and then get pissed that I was smiling. "Stop being charming," I said, refocusing on the tee shirt in my hands, on the silver thread of magic pulling me forward into the dark.

"We will talk, Jade," he murmured, his breath warm against my neck, stirring the small hairs there. It sounded like so much more than just a simple promise.

I pushed down the hurt that rose and just nodded curtly, not trusting myself to speak.

We moved slowly through the quarry, the thread growing thicker, pulling me toward where I knew there was a drop-off and a secondary rockfall where they'd mined bigger boulders. We had to be near now.

"Careful," I said. "There's a cliff here somewhere."

After Three Feathers and my out-of-body experience as a woman getting thrown off a cliff to her death by my grandfather, I wasn't overly fond of heights.

"Wait." Alek's hand touched my shoulder as he moved up beside me. He sniffed at the air and made a face. "Blood," he said.

So much for hoping we were going to wreck some tryst. Why couldn't my life be full of sex instead of violence?

That thought got shoved in the way-way-later file as well. Thinking about sex or violence while standing next to Alek was a supremely bad idea. I'd realized in the last month that I didn't really know this man at all. We'd had a thing, a good thing, I thought. But I knew next to nothing about him other than he was hot, good in bed, a Justice, and would happily watch *Babylon 5* and rub my feet at the same time.

"Old blood?" I asked, but he was already moving ahead, taking the light with him. I stumbled trying to keep up and plowed right into him as he stopped, his flashlight illuminating something blue and black and dead all over. I smelled the death, that horrid scent of drying blood, before my eyes took in the body.

My brain didn't want to make sense of it at first. The blue and black were what was left of the clothing. Blue jeans crusted with blood. Black tee shirt with a Decepticon emblem still emblazoned on it, torn almost beyond recognition. Also covered in blood and worse. Dried blood covered the stones all around the body. The tiny body. A child.

I lost my grip on the spell and the tee shirt. I sank down to my knees, shaking my head, trying to deny what I was seeing, smelling. Limbs going in directions limbs shouldn't go, attached by what looked like Silly String but was probably strips of flesh. Something had ripped into his belly, and grey intestine bulged out, sharp fecal stench mixing with the sick sweetness of pooled blood.

His face was intact. I knew that face. That face made faces at me, and every other patron of Lansing's Grocery, the only market in town. We all shopped there. Everyone in Wylde pretty much. You had to drive an hour to get to a Walmart, so Lansing's it was.

"Jamie," I said. "That's Jamie." What was he doing out there? No one had reported him missing. He was seven. A little brat of a kid who always hung around the store, cocky and funny. "He likes *Yu-Gi-Oh!* They could order them off the net, but they come to me instead. Every Christmas and his birthday." His birthday was in November. Not so far away.

"Jade," Alek said. He pulled me up and into his arms and I shook there for a moment, weakness winning out. I needed to be held. After a moment, I pulled away, not looking at Jamie's body.

"We have to call Sheriff Lee," I said. I patted my pockets, but I'd left my phone charging in the store. Shit. This really was like some stupid horror movie.

"Wait," Alek said. He had turned away from me, sniffing the air, his shoulders tense. He looked more beast than man as he moved off into the darkness.

I picked up the flashlight from where he'd set it on the ground and followed him until I saw what he had scented, not twenty feet farther into the quarry. More bodies, looking like just more rock until I was close.

I forced myself to walk toward them, carefully stepping around drying splashes of blood and bits of gore and bone. Two adults lay sprawled and torn to pieces. I hardly needed to see their faces to know who they were.

Emmaline and Jed Lansing.

"These are that boy's parents. We have to call Lee," I said, stumbling backward, turning away. Too much death. I was so sick of death. I pulled my braid forward and used it to wrap around my mouth and nose, trying to block the stink. It didn't work.

"We need to find Dorrie," Alek said.

Dorrie. I'd forgotten her. Whatever had done this to Jamie and his parents had probably gotten her, too. I didn't bank on finding her alive, not after seeing what lay near my feet.

I walked stiffly back to where Jamie lay and picked up Dorrie's tee shirt. The thread of silver reappeared as I reached for the comforting heat of my magic. I wished I could track whatever or whoever did that to Jamie, could tear into whatever it was and show it that this was my town, my people. I wanted to rip things apart, and my rage scared me even as it warmed me and shoved away my nausea.

We found Dorrie, in her wolf form, partially down the steep hillside less than a hundred feet from Jamie. There was no blood on her that I could see. I held the flashlight steady while Alek skidded his way down to her, loose stones bouncing away down into the dark below. He felt for a pulse, but we both knew there wouldn't be one. Then he lifted her easily and carried her back up the nearly vertical slope, acting as though she didn't weigh two hundred pounds. Shifter wolves, like most shifter's animal halves, are much larger than their wild animal counterparts. More like dire wolves.

I was stupidly glad there was no blood other than a bit of dried gore around her mouth. Then that sank in. The torn bits of Jamie, of his parents. Blood on the wolf's mouth.

"How did she die?" I looked at Alek as he set her down carefully outside of the patches of blood and gore staining the area around Jamie's body.

"Looks like a broken neck," he said with a shake of his shaggy blond head. His hair had definitely gotten longer and he didn't have it pulled back in his normal queue.

"That wouldn't kill her, would it?" Shifters healed quickly, almost as quickly as sorcerers from what I knew. Especially if they could just shift, trading their human or animal body for whichever one wasn't injured. Then, whichever they chose, the other went into in a kind of stasis, I guess, where they could heal the damage to that body while they ran around in their other one. They were tough to kill, what with all the metaphysical body-swapping.

"Not like this," Alek said. "If the connection between body and brain were severed, yes, but this is sloppy. Not even full spinal break. It is lie."

"And the blood around her mouth? Tell me that isn't what I think it is." I pressed my lips into a line and stared earnestly into his face.

"It is," he said. "I think those people were killed by wolves. I think we are meant to believe it was this one."

"But?" Please, Universe, let there be a huge-ass *but* attached to the words he was saying.

"It wasn't this wolf. I think she was dead already. There is something—I do not know how to say it—something wrong with her scent. Something tainting her." He raised an eyebrow at me in silent question.

I drew on my magic again, searching the dead wolf's body for signs of magic, signs a spell had been used on her that would either make her kill a child or kill her while making it look like she'd died falling down a hill.

"Nothing," I said as my magic slid over the dead body with the same reaction it would have had sliding over the boulders around me. "Now can we call Lee?" Sheriff Lee was a shifter, and she was a wolf, but she also had a duty to the human residents of Wylde. Humans like the Lansings had been. This was a crime scene.

Fuck. I swallowed the bile that rose in my throat.

"No," Alek said. "We cannot call police."

"Excuse me," I said, rising to my feet even as he did. "I swear for a moment you said you weren't going to call the police."

"Think, Jade," he said, biting off each word as though they would cut his tongue if he weren't careful. "Little boy and two adults killed by wolves? Here? Now? With the Peace being reaffirmed and every alpha around in town? Your town is crawling in wolves, in shifters. But they won't be able to stop the humans here from going on warpath, from hunting every wolf they find, wild animal or shifter, until they get enough bodies for retribution. And that is not saying what the alphas will do, how they might turn on each other as suspicion grows."

He shifted his weight and looked down at Dorrie's body, her red-and-brown fur lit up by the abandoned flashlight. "Someone killed her and tried to frame her, a Wylde pack wolf, for these murders. This is Justice work, not human police work."

"The Lansings are human, normals. Besides, Sheriff Lee isn't human; she'll understand the need for silence on aspects of this crime," I said, wrapping my arms across my breasts as the wind picked up. I pretended the shivers I felt were all the breeze and not the chill suddenly clutching at my heart.

"True. But more than local cops will get involved. A child is dead. A whole fucking family is ripped apart out here. This will bring in too much attention, too many complications."

"Alek," I said, but then stopped. I knew what he was proposing. He wasn't going to leave the bodies there, where someone could find them in the next day or so. This place wasn't exactly deserted, especially on weekends. He was going to hide them, cover up the crime. It might not have been Dorrie who killed Jamie or his parents, but we both knew no wild wolf had done this. "You can't."

"I have to," he said, his voice rough, coming out as more growl than human speech. "Wait in truck if you want."

"No," I shrieked. "No, fuck, no. I am not going to let you do this.

People are going to notice they are missing. They have friends, family. You going to deny their family closure? Fuck you. I won't let you do this." I shoved him, hard. He didn't even give me the dignity of stepping back.

"I have to," he said again, folding his arms around me. I struggled but the effort was half-assed. "They would have closure, perhaps, but there is too much more death down that path. Death of wolves. Death of innocents. The guilty is a shifter, maybe more than one. You and I know this. The humans aren't equipped to get justice for his family, to stop whoever did this from doing it again. I am." He pressed his lips to my forehead, burning hot against my chilled skin. "This is who I am, kitten. This is what I do."

It was the endearment that broke me. Or maybe his logic. He was right, but I hated him for it.

I refused to help with the bodies, stubbornly sitting in the truck after Alek loaded Dorrie's body into the back and covered her with a tarp. I pretended it was morals instead of cowardice and pain that kept me from helping Alek cover up the murders. A family murdered, three people I saw weekly, people I knew, if not well. A wolf shifter killed also, left nearby in a way where someone clearly intended whoever found Jamie and his parents to think the wolf had killed them.

I pulled my knees up and wrapped my arms around them, staring out the windshield toward where Alek was doing whatever he was doing. This was fucked up. I worried it was Samir reaching out to stir up shit in my life and see what I'd do again. Somehow, I didn't think it was, however. This felt too impersonal for Samir. Killing a child, a whole family, I'd totally lay that at his feet. But he couldn't have known that I would be the one to find the bodies. And he would have known I'd never fall for the whole "look over here at this dead wolf that must have broken its neck or been chased off by its pack after eating these people" trick. It was stupidly obvious. Too obvious. Meant for hysterical relatives, perhaps. Law enforcement faced with an angry and grieving community.

People who would be looking for the obvious, the easy answers, the easy way to retaliate.

This wasn't Samir. This was something else, someone else. Shifter business. Great.

Of course, I'd been wrong about that before. Recently.

When Alek finally returned to the truck, he was covered in dust and bits of gravel. Grime lined his face like bad makeup, highlighting his cheekbones and the wrinkles in his forehead. He pulled his sweat-soaked shirt off and used the inside of it to wipe his face. He grabbed another shirt from a bag I hadn't noticed stuffed behind the bench seat of his truck. I tried not to watch but couldn't help myself, grateful for the dim light from the nearly full moon as it crested the trees. Alek climbed in without saying a word to me, started the truck, and backed up down the logging road.

"There will be a huge search when the Lansing family is reported missing," I said after a tense moment.

"Yes," he said. That was it, just *yes*.

"They will look out in the woods. They will check the quarry."

"No one will find their bodies." He said the words as though they were a comment on the weather, but he said them in Russian. Alek sometimes reverted to his native tongue when truly upset. First his accent would get very strong, then English would fail him.

He sounded certain. I let it go for now. I didn't really want answers. Yet.

When tires hit asphalt, I spoke again.

"I want in. All the way in. No 'Justice business, you shouldn't get involved' bullshit from you. You made me a part of this and I'm going to see it through."

"All right."

I finally turned and looked at him. He glanced at me but his face gave nothing away.

"Good. So it's settled."

"It is," he said in an infuriatingly agreeable tone.

"So, where are we going with Dorrie's body?"

"The vet."

"I don't think Dr. Lake's practice is open this late," I said.

"It is now," he said. "I made a call."

CHAPTER THREE ▶

Vivian Lake, the town vet, let us in the back. Her office was the bottom part of an old Victorian-style house. The tiny wolf shifter merely pursed her lips and sighed as Alek preceded us into the house with Dorrie's body over his shoulder. I didn't know what he'd said to her on the phone, but unlike the last time I'd come there asking her for an autopsy, she definitely wasn't surprised.

It was weird déjà vu. Alek and I showing up with a dead shifter was basically how Alek and I had met. Only, that time, the shifter, Harper's mom, Rosie, hadn't been actually dead, just frozen by evil magic and being used as a battery by a warlock.

A trick that technically, since I'd eaten Bernie the bad warlock's heart, I could also do. Not a fun thought. I left Bernie's memories the hell alone most of the time, not wanting that power. The one time I'd touched them, I'd made a huge mistake and gotten my not-really-my-father killed. Fuck that.

Alek laid Dorrie on the exam table while Vivian pulled on gloves. She glanced at me.

"She's really dead?" she asked.

I didn't blame her for double-checking after what happened last time.

"Yeah," I said. I wanted to say something about the Lansing family, the horror of it all bubbling up inside me, but Alek touched my arm gently and gave me a tiny shake of his head.

Fine. I'd let Vivian do her thing, but I wasn't thrilled with his decisions, and I glared at him to let him know that. The sadness that flickered in his eyes before his stony mask came down made me feel slightly guilty. But only slightly.

"Oh, Dorrie," Vivian murmurèd as she began feeling over the body.

"Did you know her?" Alek asked.

"Yes. I do not run with the pack or live at the Den, but I still attend barbecues. Wulf was a very accepting and open alpha. Those of us who chose to live our lives without being officially in the pack were still always welcome." Her voice was steady, but her eyes blinked rapidly for a moment, as though she were fighting tears. When she looked up at Alek, her cheeks were damp.

"Her neck is broken, but that wouldn't have killed her, not like this. And what is this blood? Did she get a piece of her killer?" Vivian asked.

"What killed her, then?" Alek said, ignoring her questions.

Vivian shook her head and got out the scalpels. I excused myself and slipped out of the exam room. I'd seen enough internal organs for the day. Or maybe the year.

I read old *National Geographic*s in the semi-dark waiting room, turning on only a single small desk lamp at the receptionist's, Christie's, desk. Outside headlights came and went and I heard occasional murmurs through the exam room door. An hour passed, maybe a bit more.

Alek opened the door and caught my attention with a small wave. I rose and moved toward him. He stayed in the doorway for a moment, just staring down at me. Then he glanced over his shoulder and moved aside. Vivian had draped Dorrie's body with a blue hospital sheet, like they give you in exam rooms to pretend to cover yourself with. I realized Alek had been hiding whatever was under the sheet from my gaze until the body was covered. Annoyingly protective of my sensibilities, as though he understood I was reaching my limit for the night. Yet that little gesture gave me the serious warm-and-fuzzies.

Fuck. I still had it bad for this guy.

"Well," I said, not moving.

"She was poisoned," Vivian said. She stripped her gloves off and tossed them into the trash, then rubbed at the lines forming on her forehead. She looked like she wanted to go drink half a bottle of whiskey and cry for days. I didn't blame her.

"Poisoned? How is that possible?" Shifters healed too fast for poisons to work well on them; plus, they could just purge their systems by shifting and letting the whole magical place where the alternate body lived do the work. Maybe I'd missed something during my discussions on the subject with Harper.

"The poison isn't something I've ever seen," Vivian said.

"Nor I," Alek added, his own forehead creasing. Tension rolled off him like a scent, a tangible presence that tickled my nose and raised goose bumps on my arms. "The poison incapacitated her, put her out instantly so she couldn't shift to purge it. Then it traveled to her heart and ate its way through the organ, destroying it. It damaged her brain and a lot of other organs as well."

"That's fucking just great," I said. "How did they get it into her?"

"Broke her neck first—I found where it started to heal. Injected her in the chest, I think, while she was incapacitated, waited for the poison to kill her, broke her neck again." Vivian squeezed her eyes shut and leaned against the counter. She looked almost childlike huddled against the tall counters, but the pain in her face was old and very adult.

"So, someone managed to hold down a wolf, break her neck, then inject her with this new super poison that eats heart muscle, then waited . . ." I paused. "Wait. What do you mean, *waited*?"

"The poison would take time. Many hours, a day or more if the shifter was particularly strong. Even without being able to shift, her body would have been trying to heal the damage the poison was doing as it worked. It just does too much damage and eventually destroys the heart," Vivian said. "I just hope they injected it close to her heart, so it would work more quickly, so she would suffer less."

"This is not good," I said, mostly to myself. Someone was responsible for this, or more likely, some *ones*, because one person would have to be crazy powerful to subdue a wolf, poison her, then pull off abducting and killing a family. Especially in this small town. People would notice.

How the hell hadn't anyone noticed? The town was full of strangers at the moment; that was true. But still, the Lansings ran the damn store. They were fixtures. Jed was always in and out of the deli, recommending cuts of meat. Emmaline often worked the registers, chatting with people about their day. Jamie liked to sit on the mechanical horse outside and show people the gaps in his mouth from the teeth he'd lost. Why had no one reported them missing?

"Reported who missing?" Vivian said, and I realized I'd spoken the last part of my thoughts aloud.

"Jade," Alek said, his tone a warning.

Well, fuck him. Vivian was already elbow-deep in this. He could deal.

"The Lansing family," I said.

"They aren't missing," Vivian said, her eyes wide with alarm. "They are at Jed's sister's cabin by Bear Lake. Aren't they?"

I guess that made sense, then. They'd gone on vacation but not gotten very far. I just shook my head, looking up at Alek.

"Vivian," he said, his voice terribly soft. "This stays here. You must not speak of what you've heard or seen tonight. Not until I can investigate. Something awful is happening here, things that could threaten the pack and the Peace. Do you understand?"

She nodded. "I trust you, Justice," she said.

I turned away so my face wouldn't betray my disgust with her compliance. It wasn't fair for me to feel this way. Alek was a Justice. The Council of Nine was like gods to the shifters. She would trust him to handle these terrible crimes just like I guess I would trust the State Police or the FBI to solve a murder.

That thought was slim comfort. I didn't think I'd trust them, either.

Only yourself, my evil brain whispered. *Trust only yourself.*

Fuck that. Look where that had gotten me. Great.

I walked out the back door and breathed in the cool night air, trying to clear my senses of death, my head of its confusion. Alek joined me and stood silently beside me.

"I'm pissed at you," I said.

"I know," he said. "Please, Jade. Trust me on this?"

"For now," I said. "But we need to talk. Like really talk."

"So talk."

"No," I said. He laughed and it made me want to punch him. Or kiss him. I had missed that deep, full-bodied laugh of his.

"If I talk to you now, I'll just end up punching you or saying stupid shit I regret. I'm too mad. So, I'm going to walk home and you can come find me tomorrow. Call me if you figure out anything else." *Or if anyone else dies*, but I didn't add that last part aloud. It would have felt too much like a prediction.

I didn't wait to see his expression or his response; I just started walking, afraid if I waited, if he said something, somehow the right thing like he usually did, I wouldn't be able to hang onto the burning anger inside of me.

He didn't come after me or call out, just let me walk away. I guess some things don't change.

CHAPTER FOUR

*My store, Pwned Comics and Games, is sandwiched in a rectangular build-*ing between two other shops. On one side is my friend Ciaran's pawn shop, a place full of crazy art, antique everything, and a few small, actually magical items. Ciaran is a leprechaun and has a serious case of desire for shinies. He also makes a mean cup of tea.

On the other side of my shop is Brie's Bakery. Brie is some kind of magic-user, though I'd never asked her what exactly. It isn't the kind of thing that comes up in small talk, even in a town as full of supernaturals as Wylde is.

My guess was that she's some kind of hearth witch; her magic seemed centered on hearth and home and making people feel good through excellent cooking. I could sense a touch of magic in every bite of every baked good I'd ever eaten from her bakery, but it was the kind of magic you don't mind. Little things, touches of charms to make you feel good, to improve taste and flakiness. Her baking was literally magical.

I hadn't told my friends that, of course. I figured they knew Brie wasn't fully human, since shifters have a good nose for such things, but her secrets, like mine, were her own.

I left Harper in charge of the shop on Friday morning and ducked next door to the bakery to pick up honey scones and two tall teas to go. Ezee was due any minute to take me over to the college and sneak me into the indoor pool there so I could keep working on my training. With the students still gone, the college was almost deserted, and the time of year was too late for many people to be using the pool, indoor or not.

The bakery had a decent crowd for a Friday morning. I recognized a couple of locals, but the others were likely visiting wolves. Even predators appreciate a perfect croissant. Brie was behind the counter, handling orders herself this morning, a tall woman with fire-engine-red hair in thick curls piled on her head that would make for great Disney's *Brave* cosplay, and an apron that said SAVE THE UNICORNS on it. I greeted Brie with a wave and got into line.

A stocky woman about my height, with reddish-brown hair in a ponytail and a flannel shirt on, was ahead of me, speaking her order in an impatient, brusque tone that annoyed me. Brie was handling her fine, however, so I just glared at the back of the stranger's head and stuck my tongue out a little. I know Brie caught that, because she smiled extra wide as she handed the woman her order.

The stranger turned quickly and nearly collided with me.

"Excuse me," she said in a tone that said I was the one at fault. Her eyes were dark blue and there was something sharp and almost feral about her face.

I stepped back and started to murmur some meaningless apology when I caught the glint of silver around her neck. Her shirt was partially unbuttoned and a silver feather hung there on a chain. A necklace almost identical to Alek's.

Not that there aren't tons of feather necklaces in the world. But something about her reaction to me looking at it confirmed it. Her eyes widened and she sniffed at me.

"Who are you?" she asked. "You from the rez?"

Yeah, because all us Indians live on reservations. Right.

"Um, excuse me?" I said, dropping any pretense of being polite. "Do I know you?"

"Apparently, you do," she said, her already thin lips turning into a white line as she mashed them together.

"I'm just here for delicious baked goods, lady," I said.

She looked me up and down, as though measuring me for my coffin, and leaned in, sniffing at me in a prolonged, obvious way. I became aware of everyone in the bakery now watching us, the strangers and the locals all taking in this woman acting weird toward the comic book lady.

"We'll see," she said. Then she stepped around me and walked out of the bakery.

The tension slid out the door with her and the people parked around the tiny café tables went back to their conversations.

"Lot of strangers in town," Brie said with a smile as she readied my order.

"Yeah, guess so." I wondered if she knew about Justices and the Council. I had a feeling she did.

"Be safe," she said as I juggled my order and my change.

Yeah, she knew. I got that feeling.

So, two Justices in town. I wondered if Alek knew about her. The questions I had for him were piling up. There was a shitstorm building out there with this Peace, these wolves. I felt it in my bones. For a moment, I wanted to jam it all into the not-my-problem file, stick my head in the sand, and pretend the only thing I needed to worry about was Samir and training to be strong enough to kick his ass back to the Stone Age whenever he finally showed his face.

I couldn't solve everyone's problems. I couldn't even solve my own. So, I watched down the street for a moment in the direction the female Justice had gone, pushed away the thought of the Lansing family buried somewhere out there among rocks and silence, said *fuck it* in my head, and climbed into Ezee's car when he pulled up. Time to eat honey scones and then practice breathing underwater.

Everything else would just have to wait.

This was my third session in the pool. The first time had been a total fail, with some hilarious-in-retrospect almost-suffocation. Nothing like trying to figure out a water-breathing spell and accidentally making it so you can't breathe air normally anymore.

I was better now. Magic for sorcerers is something we are, not just something we do. Unlike a witch or warlock or other human spell-user, we own the raw power—we *are* the raw power. Which meant if I could conceive of it and channel enough power into it, whatever *it* was, I could make it happen.

The mental game was the issue. We're raised with laws. Laws of physics. Laws of nature. Laws about how we can move, what we can do, say, act. Some of these things are flimsy, like human laws about not killing or cheating on your wife or whatever. Some things, like the law of gravity, are pretty strong and, without some kind of other force acting on them, can't be broken by just anyone.

I can break the rules, but only if I can convince myself I can and summon enough power to do so. That's where my upbringing as a teen with the role-playing game Dungeons & Dragons had come in handy. As I came into my power, my adoptive family had used the only things available to make sense of what I could do, the only real manual we knew of that talked about magic. D&D is fake, of course. It's a game, like many I love and play. In the hands of most people, the spells contained in it are useless. You got to have magic to make magic.

I *am* magic. It's like an extra muscle only I and others like me are born with. The more I work with it, use it, the stronger I become.

Which is why I was spending my Friday morning sitting at the bottom of the Juniper College pool, my hair tucked uncomfortably into a swim cap, breathing chlorinated water like it was air, and practicing turning the top of the pool into ice lances and melting them again. Keeping the water-breathing spell and the ice spells going at the same time felt good—a challenge, but not as bad as it had been the last week. I was making progress. How this would help against Samir, I had no idea, but I figured the more power I used, the more control I developed, the better.

The trick hadn't been figuring out how to breathe in water. That proved pretty simple, just an act of channeling the power into my lungs, bringing my will in line with the magic. It's magic, after all. It's supposed to do crazy shit without scientific, detailed explanations. No, the real issue had been convincing my body that breathing in water wasn't the worst idea ever. Biological conditioning of tens of thousands of years of evolution said that human lungs breathing in water was a terrible idea. Once I convinced my body that it wasn't going to die horribly, once I forced myself to take that first awful, scary, wet breath, it got a lot easier.

Morpheus was totally right. *There is no spoon.*

I was feeling pleased with myself until a twelve-foot white tiger dropped into the pool. He splashed heavily into the water and swam down, staring at me with open eyes and his nostrils pinched shut like a seal's. I would have freaked out more, but I recognized Alek's tiger form.

With as much dignity as I could summon while sitting at the bottom of a pool in a swimsuit and cap, I let myself rise to the surface, clearing the water from my lungs before I transitioned out of the spell and back to breathing air. Reluctantly, I let go of my magic and climbed out onto the side of the pool.

Tiger-Alek leapt out of the water and shook himself before shifting in less than a blink back to his human form. He wasn't even damp, his blond hair loose and fluffy, his black sweater and cargo pants clean and dry.

"I could have accidentally speared you with ice," I said, glaring to make sure he knew I was still mad.

"I'd live," he said with a shrug.

"Ezee still out there? He just let you in, didn't he?" I grabbed my towel from off the bleachers and wrapped it around myself, aware of how nearly naked I was.

"Yes," Alek said. "He wisely did not argue."

He's a shifter, I wanted to say. *He wouldn't argue with a Justice, anyway.* Those words sounded petty to me, and I held them back. Looking around, I noticed a silvery shimmer on the walls. Alek was shielding the room, so at least Ezee wouldn't be able to eavesdrop on whatever we said to each other. Small blessings.

I pulled on a green thermal long-sleeved tee shirt over my damp suit and then struggled into my jeans. I didn't want to talk to Alek without a proper amount of clothing on. I couldn't trust my hormones around him, and we really needed to figure shit out before we just jumped back into bed.

If we jumped into bed again. My libido was making a lot of assumptions.

"Is Wolf here?" Alek asked, moving over to sit beside me on the bleachers.

He was talking about my spirit protector, one of the Undying, a guardian of the old gods. I had named her Wolf when I was four after she showed up and carried me to safety out of a mineshaft where my cousins had abandoned me.

"She's around," I said. She was usually around, though I couldn't see her at the moment. In the days following the disaster at Three Feathers, I'd worried that Wolf would abandon me, but she hadn't. As I'd lain in bed despondent and unhappy, she'd crashed on the floor, a huge black presence that occasionally sighed and looked at me with eyes full of stars. She'd disappeared about an hour before Harper showed up, gave me the pep talk, and dragged me out of bed. I hadn't asked Harper, but I had a feeling that Wolf might have fetched her.

Alek just nodded, not explaining why he had even asked. I pulled my swim cap off, shook out my hair, and moved into a cross-legged position facing him. I snagged a braid tie from my pocket and started finger-combing and braiding my waist-length hair into some semblance of order.

"So," I said. "You didn't call."

"So," he said. "You didn't call."

We both cracked weak smiles. I started to speak but he reached out with one hand, as though to touch my cheek, but he stopped short and withdrew it, curling his fingers into a fist in his lap.

"I do not like being away from you," he said. I raised an eyebrow at that but let him go on. "I have been with women before but never for long. Always, I had to leave. I am a Justice first. I cannot let attachments to people or place interfere." His tone implied old hurt, old pains. I wondered who else, or where else, he'd left that he regretted.

"Did I ask you to stay? Did I ever tell you not to do your job?" I asked, unable to stay silent.

"You did last night," he said.

"That's isn't fair, Alek. You covered up a crime. You basically said that the potential death of a shifter is more important than the actual pain and suffering of a human family."

"Because it is," he said, his voice so soft it was nearly lost in the *plink* and *shush* of water in the pool. "I am a Justice. This is what I do, who I am. I serve the Council. I protect shifters. I keep them safe, alive, hidden. Unless they cross the line. Then I kill them." His eyes were hard chips of blue ice, his mouth tight and drawn as he stared at me. "Last night, those bodies, the death. It shocked you. Upset you, no?"

I nodded, not trusting my voice.

"It doesn't upset me anymore," he said, looking away from me, eyes fixed on the water. "I saw that dead child, and all I can see are problems that require solutions. The need to find the killer is there, yes, but all I see is that I will have to kill again. Take another life for a life, and in the end, there will be only death. My job is not a matter of how many die, only a balance of how many I can save."

"That's . . ." I said, then hesitated. "Awful." It made a strange sense to me, and that feeling twisted me up inside. Part of me understood what he meant. Part of me was horrified by this.

He reached into his shirt and fingered the silver feather. "This is the feather of Maat—do you know the legend?"

I nodded. Maat was an Egyptian goddess of justice and truth. Lore had it that when you died, your heart was weighed against her ostrich feather. If your heart was lighter than the feather or the scales balanced, you were good and could go on to whatever reward awaited. I'd forgotten what that reward or place was supposed to be. If you were bad, another god would eat your heart and your soul would be stuck in limbo.

Thinking about it, there were some creepy parallels to sorcerers. I thought about Bernie's memories and power, which I'd gained by eating his heart. Had I consumed his soul? Trapped him in some weird limbo? Ick. Definitely wasn't going to dwell on that right then.

"I look at it," Alek said, still turning the silver talisman over and over in his long fingers. "And I wonder if my heart would balance the scale. Then I look at you, and I wonder if there could be more to life than killing, if I could be both man and Justice." Deep sorrow and confusion lined his face for a moment as he looked up from the feather and met my gaze.

There were things he wasn't telling me, words I could almost hear in between the ones he spoke, but what he had said resonated. I was afraid of the same things. I was used to being alone, to doing what I thought was best for me and me only. Doing whatever I thought would keep me safe from hurt, any kind of hurt. And I worried about killing, worried about how it didn't bother me like I felt it should.

"It isn't Sky Heart's death that bothers me," I said. "It's the collateral, the mistakes I made." I knew I wasn't explaining my leap in logic and topic well, or really at all, but Alek slid his hands over mine.

"There are many choices we must make," he said. "Things we have to try to balance. You saved them. Without you, many more would have died. Without you, your sister would have been thrown from that cliff by her grandfather, as so many others were before her."

"But better than worst isn't good enough," I said. "Fuck, I'm talking in tongue twisters. I really wanted to just yell at you, you know. I had a speech planned."

"Liar," he murmured, his mouth creeping into a smile as though against his will.

"We're a mess." I turned my hands beneath his, touching his, palm to palm. He felt so warm, so alive. Even through the chlorinated vapors coming off the pool, I smelled him—vanilla and that Alek-specific musk that was wild, comforting, and all him.

"I am not good at relationships," he said. "But I want to try. I want to stay, as long as I can."

"I suck at this too," I said. "I mean, the last guy I was with is currently treating me like his emotional chew toy in prep for smacking me down and nomming my heart."

"I will strive to set a better example," Alek said, his smile stronger, enough so that I could almost forget the deep sadness and confusion he had shown only moments before. Almost.

"Next time, call," I said, squeezing his hands. "Or email. I'm not picky."

"I promise," he said. He leaned forward and brushed his lips over mine. The kiss was a promise too, but it ended quickly, and I bit back a groan. It was good we didn't start making out, I suppose. My mouth still tasted like pool water.

There were so many things that I didn't know yet about him. But maybe this was a real beginning—maybe even someone as fucked-up as I was could make a relationship. I guess I shouldn't have expected it to be uncomplicated.

"So," I said after a far-too-comfortable moment just holding hands and staring at each other. "Where is your gun?" I had noticed he wasn't wearing it the night before, but hadn't had time to ask. It seemed odd to me he wouldn't have it.

"That is a long story," he said, his tone making it clear he had no desire to tell the story at the moment. "I have not replaced it yet."

Hint taken, I changed the topic somewhat. "Any news on the latest psycho killing people in my town?"

"No." The way he said the word made it clear how much that frustrated him. "There are many wolves to talk to, spread out all over. I will go and continue questioning them, but I have to be careful. No one knows yet what has happened, and the knowledge getting out in the wrong way could jeopardize the Peace."

"What about the other Justice in town?" I asked. "She know anything?"

Alek's hands tightened on mine and his eyes widened slightly. "Justice?" he said, tipping his head sideways.

"You didn't know." It wasn't a question. It was pretty clear he hadn't. I reached up and brushed a lock of hair from his forehead. "Doesn't your Council tell you guys when they send more than one of you?"

"The Council does not speak to us in so direct a way," Alek said. "What did this Justice look like?"

"Reddish-brown hair, dark blue eyes, about my height, sharp features, and wearing typical hiker gear. Feather around the neck, and a bad attitude. Know her?"

"Eva Phillips," he said, nodding. He didn't look happy about it. "She's a wolf, been around a long time. She was one of the Justices sent to witness the original Peace at Ulfr's Althing."

"I take it you two aren't close?"

"We all mostly work alone. Sometimes, when things are very bad, the Council will send more than one. I have worked with Eva once. It did not suit me. She has no mercy in her."

"It's kind of scary to hear *you* say that, honestly." I rolled my shoulders, thinking of how the woman had looked at me.

"Remember how I thought you were killing shifters? How I listened to you and let you prove you weren't involved?" He rose from the bleachers and paced a little ways down the side of the pool.

"That's sort of how it went, I guess," I said.

Alek turned back to me, his gaze fierce. "If the Council had given Eva that same vision, had sent her, she would have killed you first, asked questions never." The shadows were back in his eyes, worry putting fine lines in his pale skin and turning down the corners of his mouth. His expression sent a shiver down my spine as I sensed that somehow his worry was as much for me as about Eva Phillips. I didn't understand why. More secrets, I guessed. Awesomesauce.

"Fan-fucking-tastic," I said. I pulled my socks on and then strapped on the knife I'd taken from Not Afraid in its ankle sheath before tugging on my shoes. "I guess you should work quickly, then, if you can. Question the wolves in town. Want to drop me back at my store?" Part of me wanted to go with him, ask my own questions, see their faces for myself. But Alek was a Justice; they'd talk more readily to him than to him and some random woman who smelled nonhuman but not shifter. I'd be better later, if someone needed Fireballing or protecting or finding. Part of me hoped Fireball was the option.

"Great job, Cerberus," I told Ezee as we emerged from the pool.

He gave me a shrug that said it all as he tucked away his Kindle and stood up from where he'd been sitting beside the doors. "You need a ride back?" he said, looking between Alek and me.

"Nah, Alek will drop me off."

"Good," he said, putting emphasis into the word. With an exaggerated wink, he brushed off his trousers, picked up his bag, and scrammed like the coward he was. I glared after him, unable to really be mad. A little warning would have been nice, but eh. Friends. What can you do.

Alek held the door for me like a gentleman. I started to walk through, doing the automatic check for keys even though I hadn't driven, and realized that my phone was missing from my jeans pocket. Probably fell out near the pool. I swear that phone was possessed, never around when I needed it. Maybe it knew my rough history with phones. I stopped and turned back.

Which meant that the bullet that should have turned my head into fine pink mist instead cleaved off part of my braid before chunking into the wall and pinning my hair there in an explosion of concrete dust.

CHAPTER FIVE

Sniper. First thought that went through my head. Watched too many war movies, I suppose. But I wasn't wrong.

I dropped flat as Alek sprang over me. He turned into a tiger in mid-leap and charged the upper parking lot, where the shot likely came from. I blinked dust out of my eyes and squirmed backward into the doorway.

"Alek," I yelled. A car engine roared to life and I heard squeals as it peeled out. Risking a look, I raised my head and crawled forward again, just enough to see up into the lot. The sun was in my eyes but I made out a giant tiger charging after a small SUV. The SUV floored it out of the lot, which fed into the main artery of the school and out onto the highway running away from town. Even Alek couldn't keep up.

He stopped and shook himself, as though only now realizing that he was a twelve-foot-long white tiger standing in an Idaho college parking lot in broad daylight. Then he looked around and turned back to a man in a blink.

I pushed what was left of my hair, which was most of it, thank the universe, out of my face and gathered magic into a shield around me, hardening it to turn away bullets, just in case that car had been a distraction from the real shooter. Then I made myself get to my feet, fighting down the panic. A bullet in the head wouldn't kill me, but I had no idea how long I would take to regenerate from it, and I really, truly didn't want to ever find out. Getting shot hurts like a motherfucker.

I was making my way toward the upper lot when Ezee came running back down the hill.

"Was that a gunshot?" he called out.

"Yeah," I said, my ears still buzzing. "I think someone just tried to kill me."

He looked wildly around, sniffing the air.

"They took off in a car," I added. "I think we're okay now."

For now, but how much longer? Pushing that fun thought away, I walked to meet up with Alek, who was standing over something where the car had been parked.

"He left a note," Alek said, crouching down and breathing deeply, mouth half open as though he could taste the air.

A piece of parchment paper lay curled on the asphalt, a single bullet holding it down. There was something written on the paper, brush strokes that looked like kanji, but I couldn't see enough to make out the word. An odd tingle, a bitter taste of foreign magic like the afterburn of gunpowder on my tongue, warned me just before Alek touched the note.

"Wait," I yelled as I threw my shield bubble around the note, locking it down with as much power as I could pour into it in the fraction of a second before the paper ignited and then exploded.

The blast, even contained within my shield, rocked all three of us off our feet. I fell on my ass, concentrating only on holding all that horrible force inside my magic. Alek and Ezee twisted and rolled, each regaining his feet quickly and gracefully. Damn shifters.

The blast force had nowhere to go but down. The asphalt buckled and split, tar melting and concrete turning to powder. The bullet fired as the force and heat ignited it, shards fragmenting and smashing into my shield, pinpricks of additional force that stung as I wrestled with the blast, holding it down. Inside my body, my power waged war against the forces as my bones vibrated and an out-of-tune hum rang in my ears.

Then it was over and the air stilled as though the world held its breath. All I heard was my own coughing breath, my pulse racing. Sweat dripped between my breasts. The jangling feel of my magic stilled in my bones. Slowly, I let the shield down. A wave of heat, like standing too close to a bonfire, swept over me, then was gone.

"Fuck," Ezee said. "That was amazing."

"Yeah, that was a hell of an explosion spell," I muttered. I shoved away my bitter memories as they rose—unbidden and unwanted. My second family had died in an explosion. I was not a fan of them.

"No, you," he said, grinning at me with a wild look in his eye. "That would have killed us."

"Not me," I said before I realized how that sounded. I didn't want to think about the fact that my friends, that the man I might be in love with, were a lot less durable than I was. I preferred to think of them as indestructible. I knew in my heart that they weren't. Even I could be killed. But not by a bomb. Or a bullet.

"That shot was at you," Alek said. "Ezekiel left first; it would have been simple to shoot him. Instead, assassin waited until you emerged into light. If you hadn't reversed course like that, poof. No head." His blue eyes were dark with rage. Lucky for the assassin that Alek hadn't caught him. It was cute how protective he looked, how afraid for me he was. Scary, but cute.

"That wouldn't have killed me. Not forever. I'd have grown a new head or something." I waved my hands around to indicate big magic would have happened. I wasn't clear on exactly how much damage I could survive, only that supposedly the single way to kill a true sorcerer is to have another sorcerer eat their heart.

"Then why bother? Unless the killer doesn't know that, I guess," Ezee said.

I shook my head. As the adrenaline left my system, exhaustion set in. I'd slammed a lot of power into that shield and done it quickly. Six months before, we would have all been blown to bits. It was good I'd been training, and a little scary to me how quickly I'd gotten more powerful. Maybe more powerful than I had been when I was with Samir. Sadly, still not powerful enough.

Samir. This had him written all over it. I took a deep breath and struggled to my feet, shaking off Alek's extended hand as he tried to help me.

"I think the idea isn't to kill me, just incapacitate me while he harvests my heart and gives it to Samir." Unless, of course, Samir was here somewhere. Watching. Waiting. I looked around, trying to pierce the dim tree line, trying to pick out a watcher if there was one. Total paranoia. I wished that thought hadn't occurred to me.

"Could Samir be involved in the other murders?" Alek said softly in Russian, knowing that Ezee wouldn't understand him.

I shook my head, ignoring Ezee's questioning look. "Think we can dig out some of those bullet fragments? Maybe I can get a trace on the assassin."

"He another sorcerer?" Ezee asked as Alek pulled out a folding knife and bent down over the still warm asphalt.

"Maybe," I said. "This was definitely magic. Like something out of an anime, right? Exploding paper. Whatever was written on it looked like Japanese."

"Should we be standing in the open like this, then?" Ezee glanced around again, fidgeting with the strap on his messenger bag.

"Go to your office," I said. "I think Alek the giant tiger freaked the assassin out for now. Hopefully, no one saw that," I added.

Alek lifted a shoulder in a half-shrug. "I sensed no one else around. Just the person driving that car. He seemed alone."

"Eh, it's Wylde," Ezee added with a tentative smile. "Besides, almost nobody is on campus and the dorms are on the other side of the hill. I doubt anyone will even report a gunshot."

He took off up the hill after I assured him that yes, we would be fine. Alek carefully handed me pieces of the bullet, the metal warm in my palm.

"It was a .308," he said, as though that would mean anything to me.

I tugged on my magic, wincing at the headache starting to form. I pictured the metal, the hand that must have last touched it, the environment it would have been in, maybe touching all its little bullet buddies. I fed my magic into that, pressing my will into the spell, telling it to trace its friends, trace its owner.

And I got zip, zilch, nada back. It was as though the bullet had come into being seconds before it got melted in the explosion. Fire is a good cleansing agent, but I should have been able to pick up something, even if it were uselessly vague.

"It's clean," I said, dropping the fragments in disgust. "Like, magically it has no signature at all. Like it never touched anyone." A chill went through me. This assassin knew what he or she was doing. I would have been willing to stake my game store on the guess that this assassin had hunted and killed magic-users and supernaturals before.

The exploding note and the fact that they'd been willing to shoot at me in broad daylight, with friends around, was more disturbing. It meant that collateral damage wasn't really a concern for the killer.

Once again, just being me was putting everyone around me in danger. F-M-fucking-L.

"Jade," Alek said softly, stepping up to me. He wrapped his arms around me and I didn't resist. "We will find and destroy this assassin and send Samir his head."

"I love it when you go all Conan on me," I said, resisting the urge to rub my nose on his chest. "Then we will listen to the lamentations of his women, right?"

I pushed away from him and sighed. "At least, now I know someone is trying to kill me. I'll be more ready for it next time. I hope." All I wanted was a ten-year nap, but I had a store to run. I couldn't leave Harper there forever. She'd just come kick my ass again. "Take me home," I said.

I took a quick shower and changed. Alek hadn't wanted to leave me, but I pointed out he had work to do that was more important than babysitting someone who could take care of herself. I promised to be careful with windows and walking out doors, as ridiculous as that sounded. I knew he had a point.

I made it down to the shop just in time to stop a fistfight. Harper looked about ready to kill one of my regulars. Trevor came by and hung out on Friday and Saturday afternoons, painting minis that we sold on eBay in trade for me keeping him supplied with comics.

"You cannot be serious," she was shrieking at him. She had a stack of comics in her hands, where she'd been setting out the new releases on the wide display rack I kept for them, but she was now brandishing them like they were going to be weapon number one if fisticuffs happened.

"If your brain hadn't been fried by all the cartoons you watch, you'd understand," Trevor said. He was grinning slyly, clearly baiting Harper. Man had a death wish.

"Get out of my goddamn store—" Harper started to say, her pale skin turning an awesome blotchy shade of scarlet.

"Whoa," I said. "It's my store, furball, and no one has to go. What is going on?"

"He said," Harper started, then paused to take a dramatic breath. "He said that the Punisher would kick Batman's ass in a fight."

"You said that?" I turned to Trevor.

"I was just pointing out the advantages that the Punisher has." Sensing danger, he backed up and slid behind the card table he had set up to paint on, putting it between him and us.

I turned and walked to the tall bookshelf that held the graphic novels. I pulled out the hardbound slipcase of the *Absolute Dark Knight*. Slamming it down on the table in front of him, I leaned in close enough to tell he'd been eating Cheetos for lunch.

"You like painting minis here? You like the free comics?" I said, trying to keep the smile off my face.

"Sure do, boss," he said, his expression scared but his brown eyes dancing with humor.

"Then put your hand here and repeat after me," I said, indicating the slipcase. "I solemnly swear that Bruce Wayne is the bestest superhero ever and I will never profane his name or legacy by suggesting anyone could kick his ass. Because they can't. Because he is the fucking BATMAN."

He managed to repeat what I'd said with only a minimum of giggles. For a man who worked nights at a truck stop and still lived in his parents' basement, Trevor had a lot of pride. I then looked at Harper. "Good enough?"

"Fine," she said, rolling her eyes. She turned back to putting away the comics and I returned the hardcover to its spot.

"So, saw Alek dropped you off," Harper said, coming over to the counter as I booted up my laptop, hoping to lose myself in translation work.

"We talked," I said.

"And? You guys okay now?"

"Yeah. Maybe. We'll see." I shrugged. A chunk of hair fell into my face. I had tried to braid it all back like usual, but the part that had been obliterated by the bullet was too short to stay tucked in. I'd need to French-braid it or something. Another annoyance.

"What happened to your hair?" Harper reached over and tugged on the short chunk.

I glanced past her at the back of the store where Trevor had pulled his painting table and was setting up to get to work. He was human, so I doubted he could hear us. I still lowered my voice down to a near-whisper, knowing Harper's preternatural senses would pick it up just fine.

"Someone took a shot at me today, at the college," I whispered. I didn't really want to worry her, but Ezee had been there, so it wasn't like I'd be able to keep it a secret from Levi or Harper. I was somewhat surprised he hadn't texted both of them ASAP afterward.

Then I saw the total lack of surprise in Harper's face. Ezee had texted her. Bastard.

"Yeah, I wondered if you'd tell me yourself," she whispered back. "You are still coming to dinner tonight, though. No getting out of that."

"It isn't a good idea," I said. "Who knows when that assassin will try again? I would just put your mom and Max in danger. Plus, I think Levi is bringing Junebug. That's too many people I care about in one place for me to risk it."

"Bullshit. Who better to protect you?" She made a face at me. "You can't live your life looking over your shoulder, remember? We're here to watch your back. If you don't show up, I'll tell Mom why and she'll bring the whole damn thing to you, and you know it. Besides, you warded the shit out of the Henhouse. There's probably no safer place in town."

She had a point there. I had been practicing wards by layering them all around Harper's mother's bed-and-breakfast. It was remote enough I could work magic without fear of random discovery, and often had all my friends gathered there. And, until he'd taken off, Alek had been living there in his house trailer, which had been another reason to make sure the place was protected.

"Fine," I muttered. "Now will you please let me work?"

She looked like she had more questions but just sighed and grabbed her own laptop off the counter, retreating to the oversized chair she liked to game in.

I closed my eyes and tried to picture the word written on the paper, but it hung outside my memory, eclipsed by the explosion, the press of power on my body. Japanese, though, I was almost sure of that. Painted with ink; I remembered the shape of the symbol, the brush lines, the flow of it. I gave up eventually and opened my email.

The day wore on without anyone trying to kill me or accuse me of murder, or any other shenanigans. I was almost lulled into thinking things might stay normal. Almost. I pulled the shades on the front windows, though with the displays and the posters up, it was very difficult to see directly into the story, anyway. I had a hard time turning my back on the windows or doors, and for the first time in forever, I actually locked the rear door. It isn't paranoia when someone is actually trying to kill you.

Alek showed up just before I was ready to close for the night at seven. During slow seasons like this, I usually didn't bother keeping the place open later than that. Wylde during the nonschool year is usually a sleepy little town where everyone stays in after dark. Maybe because many of its residents are things that go bump in the night. Or run around howling at the moon.

It was getting dark as I hustled Harper out with a promise I'd be at dinner in an hour. Alek slipped in the door as I was preparing to lock up.

"Find anything?" I asked.

He shook his head. "I am keeping my inquiries soft at the moment. I do not want to draw attention to the missing humans if I can. Liam, Ulfr's oldest son and the interim alpha, knows the whole story. I questioned him closely and am convinced he is uninvolved and deeply invested in the Peace staying intact. Henry, Dorrie's mate, also knows some of it. He also appears uninvolved."

"So, what's our next step?" I said, emphasizing the "our" part of it.

"I am going to try to trace the Lansings' steps. I will start at their house and then follow the route Vivian said they would likely take to Bear Lake. Perhaps I can find where they were taken and track the killer or killers from there." Alek rubbed at his neck, rolling his shoulders. It was the only indication he gave of how tired he must be. I doubted he had gotten much more sleep than I had the last night.

"Great, let me lock up and I'll come with you." I latched on to the excuse not to put my friends in danger, and the excuse to be doing something, anything, that wasn't just waiting for someone to try to kill me again.

"No," Alek said. "I can do this on my own. I might be gone for hours. If something happens here, you may be needed. Liam has your number—and Harper's, since you have such terrible phone luck." He smiled at that last part, pulling my cell phone from his coat pocket. He must have retrieved it at the pool. I hadn't even remembered it after the whole being-shot-at thing happened.

"Thanks," I said. "You sure you don't want company?"

"It is likely another dead end," he said, folding his hand around mine.

"The Council's visions aren't giving you some help on this? What did they show you?" I asked.

The troubled look returned to his eyes, and he bent and kissed my knuckles. "Nothing useful," he murmured. "I'll see you tomorrow."

"Call me if you find anything," I said, uneasy with his answer, his almost-defeated posture.

"I promise," he said as he turned away and left.

I watched him go, then locked my door and flipped the sign to CLOSED.

CHAPTER SIX

"We got a last-minute guest, but he's out taking pictures," Max said as he walked me into the big house that served as home and business for Rosie, Max and Harper's mother.

Rosie wasn't Max's real mother. She'd taken the boy in when he was just a pup. Harper didn't know where Rosie had come by him; Max was just one of the strays that Rosie had adopted. She had a big heart, Harper's mom did.

I had a sneaking suspicion that I was another stray she'd taken in, but I was too flattered by inclusion in this odd little shifter family to ask outright.

"Oh, yeah?" I said to Max when I realized I was being too quiet. "Photographer. That's cool."

He continued talking at me, telling me about dinner and how he was going to take the photographer out on a ride tomorrow. Only thing Max loved more than his big sister was horses. Weird for a wolf, in my mind, but the horses seemed to love him right back and not mind at all that he was, at heart, a predator. They were strays too, rescued from auction blocks all over Idaho. Who knows? Maybe even the horses knew a good thing when they saw it.

The Henhouse Bed and Breakfast was a good thing. The house had that old country feel, lots of wood, handmade quilts on the beds, a big country kitchen with whitewashed cupboards, a giant gas stove, and an original river-stone fireplace with cooking hearth. The land and original ranch had been grandfathered into the River of No Return Wilderness area. The house and barn were relics of another time, slowly built on and updated by Rosie. I didn't know how old she really was, but I was guessing she'd settled this land a long, long time before.

Dinner smelled delicious, some kind of thick, spicy game stew bubbling in a huge pot, and the yeasty, comforting scent of fresh-baked bread. I helped Harper set the huge dining table while Junebug, Levi's owl-shifter wife, and Ezee bustled around the kitchen with Rosie directing with the efficiency of a drill sergeant.

I knew from the looks I was getting that Ezee had told Levi and Rosie at the very least about the assassination attempt. We should have been eating outside on the huge porch, enjoying the last dying warmth of summer. No one said a word about us eating inside and I swallowed my own protests. If being in here kept me safer, it would keep them safer, too.

As we bantered, bustled, and tried to stay out of each other's way, I felt at home, almost forgetting that a giant target was painted on my back.

Ezee snagged a roll from the basket as Junebug brought it out to the table. The tiny woman admonished him, her amber eyes flashing with laughter as he pretended to put the roll back and instead tossed it to Max at the last moment.

"We're about to eat, and I think I hear our guest coming in," Junebug said. She grinned and ruined her stern look, shoving her long blond hair away from her face as she tried to leap up and snag the roll. Levi caught her waist and lifted her in a smooth motion, and she snagged the roll from midair when Max tossed it back to Ezee. She smiled up at him as she returned it to the basket and, bending, he kissed the tip of her nose.

Nez Perce punk mechanic and tiny blonde hippy. Levi was all sarcastic humor and moody edges, Junebug smiles and earthy mothering that rivaled Rosie's. If the world had room for their love in it, maybe there was hope for me, too. I pushed away the weird longing that rose up inside. I was getting maudlin in my old age, apparently. Introspection had never been my strong suit.

I heard the front door open and turned, pulling on my magic for a moment as the back of my neck prickled.

A slender Japanese man entered, pausing in the doorway. He had a camera bag slung around his neck. The guest. I let go of my magic, sensing nothing off about him. He hadn't triggered any of my wards, so he was human as well. Just a guy.

I smiled at him and Rosie emerged from the kitchen.

"Please, Mr. Kami, come in," she said, bowing politely as she wiped her hands on her apron.

"I do not wish to intrude," he said in accented but very fluent English. "This is your family time."

"You aren't intruding. Please join us for dinner." Rosie smiled at him and the small man smiled back, unable to resist her charm.

We made introductions all around and everyone settled in. For a few minutes, peace reigned as food was passed around and dished out. I looked around the table and felt something, like a small chip of myself, settle in my heart. Family.

The warm feeling was only slightly dampened by remembering what always seemed to happen to my families.

I found myself studying Mr. Kami, who was seated across the table and one down from where I was. His face was lined enough to place him in his forties at least, with his hair pulled into a topknot that reminded me of old samurai movies. He wore loose black pants and a long-sleeved, dark green shirt. He'd hung his camera bag off the chair behind him.

There was nothing unusual about him. His face was bland, almost forgettable. His eyes were dark, though not as dark as mine. He was tanned, more so than heritage would dictate, which fit with a man who spent lots of time outdoors taking pictures. His fingernails were trimmed and he ate with a polite tidiness that drew no attention.

Maybe it was because someone had tried to kill me. Maybe it was the Lansings' deaths or Dorrie's poisoning. I felt on edge, paranoia damaging what should have been a happy evening. I shoved the feeling down and decided to make small talk.

"Kami is an unusual surname," I said. "Where in Japan did you grow up?"

His eyes flicked to me and he brought his napkin up, carefully wiping his mouth and finishing chewing before he spoke.

"A tiny village in the Oki-shoto islands," he said. "It is very remote."

"I'd love to go to Japan," Harper said. "I've been to South Korea for tournaments, but never any further."

"Tournaments?" Mr. Kami asked.

"Oh, God, don't get her started," Levi said with a mock groan.

"But I am curious. Please tell," Mr. Kami said.

Which led into an explanation about what Harper did for a living with video games that Mr. Kami listened to with very polite attention.

I'd heard of the Oki-shoto islands. Kami means *paper* or *spirit*. It's a weird last name. Japan has a huge diversity of surnames, it's true, but it was the only odd thing about a man who was otherwise completely normal-seeming. Human. Boring. Everything about him from his appearance to his mannerisms said, *Nothing to see here; move along.*

I was so fucked up that his sheer normalness bugged me. Or maybe it was that curling slip of paper earlier. What were the odds that in a tiny town like Wylde, someone would show up using Japanese on a spell scroll and it would not be remotely related to the one Japanese foreigner in town? I didn't believe in coincidence. Not today.

I closed my eyes for a moment, listening with my other senses to the conversation, to the people around me. I pulled on my magic, spooling up a thread of power from the huge well within. I touched my wards, letting my consciousness spiral to the outermost circles around the property. Nothing unusual. I pulled myself back in, listening with magically enhanced senses to my friends. I felt their own thrumming power, the soft rhythms of their hearts, the tickling feel of their sleeping animal selves. I could identify each just by his or her energy signature, that metaphysical something that helped define what they were. This awareness of life power in others, this second sense, was a gift, of sorts, from an asshole murdering warlock whose heart I'd eaten to save Rosie and Ezee's lives only a few months before.

Mr. Kami, however, didn't even register. It was like he wasn't there. He might have been part of the chair on which he sat, for all my metaphysical senses could tell.

He should have shown up. I could sense the horses in their stalls, sense the fat tabby cat out on the porch swing. Not Mr. Kami. He had less presence inside my wards, against my magic, than a cat. I opened my eyes and looked at him.

Then, deliberately, carefully, I prodded him with a touch of my power. To a human's senses, it should have felt like something brushed against him, a phantom touch. A truly oblivious human, like our friend and fellow gamer Steve, might have felt nothing at all.

Mr. Kami tensed and flicked his dark eyes to me. For a moment, it was like a mask slipped out of place, and his gaze went beetle-black and hard, intense and focused like a predator's. Then the bland look came back, but I felt an answering push of power. Just a touch, the smell and feel of it hot and alien.

Ink and earth, smoke and gunpowder.

I was sitting at dinner with the man who had tried to blow off my head only hours earlier.

I smiled at him, all teeth. "Have you seen the barn?" I asked him. I wanted to take his head off right there, but he had magic. I couldn't predict what he would do. His actions earlier had indicated a total disregard for collateral damage, and we were sitting around a table full of people I cared about.

Not exactly an advantage.

"Yes," he said, his mask back in place. "Max showed me earlier. It is very nice. This is a very nice place."

I gathered my power, letting it spread through me, ready to blast him or shield my friends. "We should go outside," I said to him in Japanese.

"I am fine where I am," he responded in the same as he leaned back, scooting his chair out a small ways. He draped one hand casually over the back of Junebug's chair next to him. "How did you recognize me?"

"You were too invisible," I said. I wanted to zort him right out of his chair, blast him away and end the threat, but I didn't know what magic he had, what it might do. There were too many people.

"Jade," Levi said.

I didn't dare look at him and risk the man in front of him making a move. "This man is the killer," I said instead, switching to Nez Perce.

I had engaged in long discussions on the dying-out of the Sahaptian language with Ezee, so I knew he at least would understand. And Junebug had been an academic, studying Northwestern Native cultures before she fell in love with a wolverine-shifter mechanic and took up pottery.

Levi, Ezee, and Junebug all tensed. Beside me, Max stood up.

"Anyone want more ice in their water?" he said, too brightly.

Mr. Kami's right hand slipped beneath the table. I took the risk and threw pure force straight at him, driving into him with my will, wanting to crush him like a bug. As he flew backward and flipped out of his chair, magic flared to life, burning sigils appearing in the air around him and turning aside the brunt of my blast.

On the periphery of my vision I saw my friends all leave their chairs, moving with the graceful speed only shifters can achieve. Ezee and Levi shifted, a huge coyote and wolverine materializing. They sprang at the assassin, snarling.

"No," I called out as I struggled to my feet, shoving my chair away.

Glittering kunai filled the air as the assassin leapt onto the table. I threw shields up around my friends. Fire started to swirl around the killer's body, sigils spinning faster and faster. Heat blasted over me, and I pushed more power into my shields. The table began to burn.

I had to get him out of the house or he would just burn it down around us. I slammed more force into him as my friends attacked. The assassin jumped away, moving out of the dining room and into the front entry.

I grabbed the pitcher of water off the table as I followed and threw it in his direction, turning the water into a thin spear of ice. Magic raged through me, my blood singing with it, but I felt the edge of fatigue as well. Keeping his fire contained, my friends shielded, and throwing magic at him was taking a quick toll on me.

I gritted my teeth as the front door flew open and he dashed through it, the ice spear melting away before it hit him. He threw more kunai at me, the small dark blades glancing off my shields.

Bits of paper tied to the loop at the ends fluttered as the knives bounced and fell. I threw magic tendrils at them, Mage-Handing them back out the door as quickly as I could. Explosions rocked the house and I stumbled, smoke and heat filling my nose. A furry body raced past me.

I made it through the smoking ruins of the front entry, rage rising inside me. The assassin was running for his car. He spun as I sprang down the steps, and he fired a pistol at me. The shots hit my shields like punches from giant fists, the force shoving me backward, off my feet.

A fox, her body a streak of red in my smoke-blurred vision, leapt straight through his wreath of flames and latched onto his arm.

Harper.

I rolled to my feet and ran at the assassin. He threw Harper aside as though she were a puppy, not a hundred-pound fox. His lips moved and he thrust his arms out. His shirt curled and burned, the pieces lifting and turning into their own slips of dark paper, sigils flaming to life on the ruins of his clothing. I poured everything I had into my shields as a wave of flame rushed at me.

Belatedly, I remembered the house behind me, the people who might be there. Harper somewhere to the side of me, a crumpled form in the dry summer grass.

My shields took the heat and I threw my will into directing it upward, toward the sky, toward nothing that it could burn and hurt and kill. My eyes squeezed shut against the heat. I held my breath, ignoring the stench of burning hair as I spread my shields as thin as I could, trying to funnel the flame wave away from everything. Away from the people I kept failing to protect.

Pain radiated through my forearms and I felt my own clothing catching fire. It wasn't going to be enough. I needed more power, another answer. No time. I hung on, gripping my twenty-sided talisman with hands gone numb from pain, pouring all my strength into blocking the flames as the unfamiliar magic roared over me, resisting, almost alive, hungry for death.

And then, as it had before with the explosion in the parking lot, it suddenly ceased. Blood roared in my ears instead of fire.

I raised my head, catching sight of the retreating taillights of the assassin's car. Again. He turned a corner, speeding off. I had no energy to go after him. I wanted to breathe. To curl up in a bath of ice and forget what fire tasted like. My body vibrated with spent power. With terror. With pain. My arms were raw, skin bubbling into blisters even as I stared at it, trying to gather my mind back into itself.

Rosie ran past me, toward a charred shape in the smoldering grass to the side of the driveway. Then she started screaming.

CHAPTER SEVEN

Harper was alive, barely. Her scorched chest rose and fell in uneven breaths. Clumps of charred hair fell off her as Levi and I carefully got her moved onto a blanket and brought into the house.

"Why isn't she shifting?" I asked, ignoring the pain in my hands and arms as the blanket rubbed on raw, burnt patches of skin.

"She's not conscious," Levi said. "She's breathing, though. Her body will start to heal."

"Can you do anything?" Max asked me. "Heal her?"

I shook my head. Healing was complicated. I didn't know anatomy or what her healthy skin was supposed to be like, exactly. I was scared to try using my magic that way. I'd attempted to heal Wolf once and had failed miserably, my magic sliding uselessly off her bloody chest.

Wolf appeared as though thinking of her had called her. I wanted to curse at her, ask her where she had been, but she couldn't have stopped this. The assassin was human—using some kind of magic, sure, but not a magical being himself, not enough that she would have been able to help.

Still, part of me thought she could have at least warned me. She should have smelled the magic on him. Instead, she'd been absent. I felt betrayed but shoved it away. Irrational anger wouldn't save Harper.

"Max," Rosie said. "Go help Ezekiel put out the fires."

He glared at her but left, throwing a last worried look over his shoulder at Harper.

We put her on a bed in the first-floor guest room. Her fox body was small for a shifter, her normally red and glossy fur charred away in ugly weals, burned to brown and black and patches of raw red flesh.

Guilt swamped me as I stood there, helpless.

"I shouldn't have come tonight," I said.

"You don't know what he would have done if you hadn't," Rosie said. "Don't start blaming yourself, dearie. If we start that game, then Harper shouldn't have run out the door like an idiot. That man was bad news. He is the one to blame. He set my baby on fire."

"But only because I was here," I said, turning to her. My vision blurred as tears leaked out my eyes, tears of rage, tears of guilt. "And I didn't stop him. How can you look at her and not hate me?"

"You saved me from the slowest, most terrible death I could ever envision. You risked your life, your freedom to protect my family. As far as I am concerned, that makes you family." Rosie's mouth set into a line and her hazel eyes were uncomfortably kind, full of a deep understanding that wrapped around me like a physical presence.

"Family," she continued. "Family doesn't give up on family just because things get dangerous. Azalea risked her life for you, same as you'd risk your life for her. Don't belittle that choice by pretending you could make it for her. You don't have that right."

She squared her shoulders as I shut my mouth on any protest I would make. I stared down at my burnt arms, my flaking and crisped shirt. Something was hard and uncomfortably hot in my pocket. A fried plastic smell leached from my jeans.

I pulled out my cell phone, wincing. It was dead, totally slagged by heat.

"Jade," Rosie said.

I looked up. Levi had slipped out of the room. It was only Rosie and

I now, with Harper's heavily breathing body on the bed between us. At least she was still breathing.

"Go get a clean shirt, clean those burns off. She isn't going to die."

"I'm already healing," I muttered, the guilt not quite gone. I did as she asked, however, slipping up the stairs to Harper's room. Peeling off the remains of my clothes sucked more than I want to say, but the burns on my arms were turning pink now, the blisters fading down into the skin almost as quickly as they'd appeared.

As my head cleared, rage replaced the guilt. I didn't know where Mr. Kami had gone, but I was going to find him. I was going to end him.

I washed my face off, biting down a scream as the water hit freshly healing skin. My hair wasn't as damaged as I'd feared, but it would take a true shower and a lot of conditioner to return it to some semblance of pretty. I left it as it was and went back downstairs.

Harper wasn't a fox anymore. Her human skin was clean of burns, but she lay on the bed whimpering under her breath as Rosie covered her with a clean quilt. Her green eyes were open and clear. Relief dumped the rest of the adrenaline from my veins and weighed me down.

"Hey, furball," I said, sitting on the edge of the bed. "You okay?"

"I will be," she said. She winced, as though it hurt to talk, and her voice was rough.

"I thought you told me that shifting healed you," I said with narrowed eyes.

Her lips formed a faint smile. "It does, eventually. I still feel pain through the link, though, am still weak. I didn't want you worrying about us anymore than you already do, though. So, I kinda fudged the truth a bit, sorry."

"I'm sorry I didn't protect you," I said.

"I ain't dead yet," Harper said. "'Sides, I totally got a chunk of that guy. Won't be throwing ninja stars with that arm anytime soon."

She was right about that, unless he knew spells that healed, which I supposed wasn't unlikely. I'd seen similar things, though not in real life outside of shops where they weren't truly imbued with magic. Ofuda, like you'd find at a Shinto shrine. Or omamori, protective Japanese talismans. Nothing I'd seen outside of animated movies looked like what the assassin had managed. Spells inscribed on paper. Fire and ink. I suspected the sheets of paper stuck to his body were for physical enhancements. It sucked he was trying to kill me, because his kind of magical practice was fascinating. Maybe I'd ask him questions before I kicked his ass.

Chuckling at that, I imagined myself like a monologuing villain, giving the enemy the chance to recover and surprise me. Maybe I wouldn't be holding another conversation with Mr. Kami. I wondered for a moment why I cast myself as the villain in my head, but shoved the rising tide of dark thoughts away for later examination.

"You promise you'll be okay? And never do that again?" I asked.

"Yeah, yeah," she said, her eyes slipping shut. "I learned my lesson. Fire bad. Tree pretty." She closed her eyes and her breathing slowed, deepened.

If she was cognizant enough to make a *Buffy the Vampire Slayer* reference, I figured she just might live after all. I watched Harper sleep for a few minutes until I heard voices. Reluctantly, I rose and left the room. Levi, Ezee, Max, and Junebug all trooped back into the dining room, spent fire extinguishers in hand.

"Fire is out; don't think we're at risk of a wildfire," Levi said.

I nodded, looking around the charred dining room. The table was a mess of burn scars and smashed dishes. The chairs were overturned. Next to one was a familiar bag. Mr. Kami's camera bag.

I picked it up, reaching for my magic. The bag seemed normal at first, then that normalcy fell away and the alien touch of foreign magic brushed against my power as I tried to link this object to its own.

It wasn't the smoke-and-ink power of the assassin that touched me but another power, one I had once been very familiar with.

Cool sweetness flowed through the bag, a seductive song against my senses, like watching the ocean waves roll in and out. Deep, vast, a power that knew no limits and would take you into its embrace with hardly a ripple.

Samir.

I dropped the bag, my heart punching against my ribs. Without thinking, I ripped into the magic there, the physical bag itself as well, smashing in, rending it piece by piece and turning the pieces to ash.

"Jade, Jade!" Ezee's voice finally penetrated my fear, my hatred.

I looked up at him, amazed to find myself on my knees, a smoking pile of ashes at my feet.

"It was evil," I said, aware I looked totally crazed.

"It's dead now," he said.

It was. And with it any chance I had of linking it to the assassin. I took tiny consolation in the fact that it was unlikely I could have anyway, not with Samir's power all over it.

"What was it?" Max asked, poking at the ashes with his sneaker.

"A container," I guessed. "For my heart."

"Gross," he said.

A search of the room that Rosie had rented to the assassin revealed nothing, not a stitch of clothing or a metaphysical trace. I had already half-expected that.

Weary to the bone, I made my way back to the room where Harper still slept, and collapsed into a chair. Her steady breathing reassured me, but I still wanted to stay, to keep watch. I didn't trust that the assassin wouldn't come back.

Rosie sat on the other side of Harper for a while, knitting. I heard the others moving around out in the front rooms, cleaning up. I almost went to help them, but my body had decided that sitting was all I was going to be good for at the moment. Exhaustion crawled over me, and I found myself drifting off. At some point, Rosie put a blanket over me, and Harper's soft breathing carried me into uneasy sleep.

▲ ▲ ▲

Alek woke me with a kiss. The sun streamed through the window and I had a hell of a crick in my neck. The clock on the nightstand said it was after ten in the morning. I opened my eyes, half-convinced I was dreaming.

He looked far too tired for this to be a dream, however. His ice-blue eyes were bloodshot, and shadows had taken up residence below them. I looked from him over to where Harper still slept.

"Max told me what happened," Alek said.

"Rosie promises she'll be okay," I said.

"She will. Come have breakfast."

I sat in the kitchen and picked at my pancakes for a few minutes under Alek and Rosie's watchful gazes, then pushed the plate away. I was too keyed up to eat much. I wanted to lay some hurt on someone, preferably a damned ninja assassin someone, but I'd settle for whoever killed the Lansings.

"You get anywhere?" I asked Alek, though I was guessing he hadn't, from his exhausted and frustrated expression.

"No," he said, then switched to Russian as he glanced at Rosie. "I could find no trace of them. Their car is missing. But no unusual scents at their house, no sign of struggle. Nothing on the road between here and Bear Lake, or at their cabin."

Rosie slipped out of the room with a murmur about looking in on Harper. I felt bad about talking in front of her in a language she didn't speak, but Alek clearly wanted to keep the murders as quiet as possible.

"Bear Lake? You drive all night?" I asked. It was obvious he had. I sighed.

"Most of it," he said. "I have Liam and a few of his pack he trusts, and who I vetted, out looking for the car. If they were taken anywhere near Wylde, the wolves should be able to pick up a trail." He didn't look as hopeful as his words sounded. He just looked tired.

"You need sleep," I said. "Where is your trailer?"

"On the side, in the RV parking." He drained the last of his cup of tea and started to rise.

"Rosie won't begrudge you a room, you know."

Alek shook his head. "Too much to do."

"Too many ways to fuck up if you don't sleep," I said. "What about that other Justice? Shouldn't she be helping?"

His expression soured, and he sighed. "Vivian told her about the murders, said Eva came and asked about Dorrie. She came to the Lansings' house before I did—I smelled her presence there. She does not wish to work directly with me, I do not think. We do not get along."

"What about the Council? They not giving you useful guidance? You'd think they'd want you two to work together since this Peace is so important."

"Yes," he said, his jaw clenching. "Perhaps." He shook his head at my questioning look.

"Will a shower with me cheer you up?" I asked. It was a shameless move, but he needed rest, needed to relax. We both did.

We borrowed one of the empty guest rooms on the second floor. The shower cheered up both of us and we lost ourselves in skin and comfort and heat for a little while. He pulled on his underwear, then crawled into the bed when I pointed. I tugged on my borrowed tee shirt and jeans, then pulled a quilt over him and lay down on top of it.

Alek's arms came around me and he tucked my head under his chin.

"I fucked up," I said softly. "I almost got everyone killed again."

"Don't blame the victim," he said. "That assassin doesn't care about collateral damage. He was here, in this place, for a reason. Perhaps Samir wishes for your friends to be killed, to be hurt, as well. This is very like him, yes?"

"Are you trying to be comforting?" I muttered. I shook my head, rubbing it against his chin, and took a deep breath, inhaling Alek's vanilla-and-musk scent.

"I meant it in a more general way," I added, trying to order my thoughts. "I have been so defensive. Yesterday, when he shot at me, I ducked. Then I threw up a shield. I didn't blast his car off the road. I didn't try to go after him. I just went for cover, went for minimizing damage. And last night, I did the same. I hesitated when I should have just struck for a kill. And then I used so much power shielding and none attacking."

Somehow, I knew that Alek might understand what I was thinking, what I was trying to say, that he, more than anyone in my life, would get my desire to stop reacting. To start acting.

"You think if you had acted more quickly, gone on the offensive, Harper would not be hurt?" he said softly.

"Yes."

"You might be right."

Okay, that stung a little. I mean, it was what I was thinking, but hearing someone else say it hurt.

"Ouch," I said, pulling away and sitting up.

He tucked his arms behind his head and looked up at me.

"You are afraid of your power," he said. It wasn't phrased as a question.

"A little, yes," I admitted. "There is so much of it, and it's growing all the time. When I was younger, I just stuck to little stuff until Samir came along, trying out spells I found in the D&D manual, but I didn't do too much. I was afraid even then, afraid I would hurt people. I don't feel like I have control. I don't know what my limits are until I hit them. I don't even know if those are real limits or if my brain is just imposing them to save some shred of my psyche. I'm terrified of hurting people around me." The words flowed out of me in a rush, leaving behind a strange relief that I had finally said them aloud.

"With great power comes great responsibility," he said, nodding sagely.

"Did you just quote *Spider-Man* at me?" I raised an eyebrow, impressed.

"*Spider-Man*? No. Voltaire. Or, technically, Jesus, if you believe the gospel of Luke. I believe he said, 'To whom much is given, much is expected.'"

ANNIE BELLETT

Oh. Right. That made more sense. Alek was still cute when he was smug and all full of the brains.

"Well, Uncle Ben said it too," I said, making a face at him.

He smiled but it didn't last, his serious expression returning.

"You did what you felt was right, for you, for that moment," he said. "There is no shame in that. Learn from it, from these doubts and feelings and fears. Next time, make a different decision. Just remember to always decide. Inaction is death."

"I don't know if I can be a killer," I blurted, saying the words that had hovered in my mind since I watched, helpless, as my father died in front of me, torn apart because of my decisions. If I had killed Not Afraid. If I had killed Sky Heart. If I had never gone back. If, if, if. I was terrified that all the solutions I saw looked like death for someone.

I was terrified that part of me wanted that death. Killing Bernie hadn't sucked. I didn't like his slimy, psychotic memories living in my head, but I didn't regret eating his heart and ending him for even a second.

And that scared me too.

"Liar," Alek murmured, his voice incredibly soft, almost a purr. Looking into his eyes felt like falling into the sky.

I sank back down, laying my head on his chest. His arms came back around me.

"I don't know," I said. "I'm tired of death, but I'm tired of worrying so much about it, about causing it when it seems like my enemies stack up and don't give a shit. I'm tired of every problem looking like a nail. Does it get easier?"

"Does what get easier?" he asked.

"Killing," I said.

"Yes," he said, his voice deep and sad. "It does."

After a while, we both slept.

CHAPTER EIGHT ▶

"Lean on Me" by Bill Withers was playing as I sleepily lifted my head.

"Fuck is that?" I mumbled, lost for a moment as to where I was. I knew the warm body trying to move out from under me was Alek. Then the rest of it flowed into my half-conscious brain.

"My phone," Alek said. He lifted me off him and grabbed his pants from the floor, fishing his phone out of them. "Yes?"

I smiled at his choice of ringtone. I'd missed his sense of humor. The room was dim, and I looked out the window toward the barn. Long shadows from the trees clung like tentacles along its red roof. The sun was setting.

"We're coming now," Alek said, all sleepiness gone from his voice and his posture.

"What is it?" I asked as he shoved his phone into his pants pocket and started dressing with preternatural speed. He didn't bother with his sweater, pulling on his undershirt as he checked for his car keys.

"Liam has been murdered," he said.

We raced down the stairs, pausing to throw on our shoes in the entry. I glanced toward the room where Harper was, realizing I was leaving her without my protection. I hesitated and Alek looked back at me, the front door already open.

Rosie appeared in the door to Harper's room. "Trouble?" she said.

"Yeah," I said, glancing at Alek. "But I can stay."

"Harper ate three sandwiches and went back to sleep an hour ago," Rosie said, making a shooing motion. "She'll be fine. We'll all be fine. Go watch the Justice's back."

"Jade?" Alek said.

"All right," I said. I turned and followed him out.

In the shadows of the porch, I spied Levi and Junebug sitting in Adirondack chairs. Junebug had a carving knife and a length of rosewood in her hands, whittling away. Levi had a hunting rifle across his knees. They both nodded to us as we went by, heading for Alek's truck.

I expected Alek to drive us back to town and through to the other side, to head toward the Den where the Wylde pack lived. Instead, he headed out farther along the road after leaving the offshoot that led to the Henhouse, taking us right along the edge of the wilderness. We pulled into the large turnaround and day-use lot at the Three Firs trailhead. Sheriff Lee's official SUV was pulled up there, along with at least four other vehicles.

There was enough daylight left to see the crowd gathered in the grassy area beyond the lot. I recognized a few of them, faces I knew from around town, but there were at least half a dozen men and women who I couldn't place as belonging in Wylde. Alek and I climbed out of the truck and I felt the suspicious looks and tension like a physical weight pressing on me.

I walked toward the crowd beside Alek, refusing to look down or away from any of the eyes that met mine. I was not prey. I was there because a Justice wanted me here. I was there because I wanted, no, *needed* to help. Someone had to remember the human side of things, to remember the Lansings in their unmarked graves. To use Alek's metaphor, I was there to help balance the scales.

Eva, the other Justice, stood near a tarp on the ground spread over

I didn't want to know what, talking to Sheriff Lee. The sheriff was an American-born Chinese; her family was original to the non-Native settlement of the area. They had come to work the gold mines in the Dakotas and kept moving westward as time wore on. I didn't know how old she was, but I'd chatted with her a time or two in Brie's Bakery and got the impression that she hadn't been one of the original family members to come to Idaho but was born there, sometime inside this century.

Of course, with shifters, you never know.

I liked her. She was solid, steady, and good at making drunk tourists and college students back down from a fight. She kept a town full of supernaturals and shifters nearly crime-free. Well, with a few exceptions in the last year. Mainly *my* exceptions. I felt a pang of guilt and shoved it away.

Eva I did not like. I'd formed a snap impression of her, true, but her expression as Alek and I walked through the crowd of wolves toward her was sour and mean. Her dark blue eyes were hard and judgy. Yeah, I didn't think she'd become my favorite person anytime soon.

"What is she doing here?" she said, ignoring me and looking at Alek.

"She's with me," he said. "What happened?" He motioned at the tarp.

I breathed through my mouth, ignoring the buzz of flies and reek of death. More death. I was pretty sure I didn't want to see what was under that tarp.

"Someone murdered my brother," a woman said, stepping forward. "Someone is trying to kill their competition." She was tall and lean, with freckles and wheat-colored hair. Her face seemed familiar, but I was pretty sure we'd never officially met.

"Freyda," Alek said, and I got the feeling he was using her name both to calm her and for my benefit. "Perhaps this is less related to becoming the new alpha of alphas and more about the Peace," he suggested softly.

Murmurs went through the small crowd. I assumed some of them were visiting alphas. They looked diverse enough. Two tanned brothers with green eyes and thick beards, wearing jeans. A white man with silver in his light brown hair, dressed incongruously with the forest setting in business casual attire. A woman in a blue sundress with skin so dark, it made mine look pale in comparison. All of them radiated power and control, their bearing reminding me a little of Alek. Definitely alphas.

Only one stood out, and he lurked a handful of paces back from the others, a dark-haired man who looked as though he hadn't slept in days and had spent much of those crying. His hair was crinkled and stuck up in places, as though sweaty hands had run through it over and over. I guessed that this was Henry, Dorrie's mate. It must have been he who called Alek.

Freyda stared him in the eye, then slowly let her gaze drop. "There is no trail. We found sign of a pack, of at least three or four wolves, but they must have left in a vehicle. The trail ends." She pointed at the parking area.

"Sheriff." Alek turned to Lee. "May I see the body?"

She nodded even as Eva shook her head. "This is pointless. We should be questioning the sorceress." She glared at me.

Every set of eyes turned to me and the tension ramped up to epic levels. I was desperately thinking, *Don't be prey,* but at that moment, I felt a lot like the rabbit in the shadow of an eagle. A flock of eagles. Hungry, angry eagles.

Yeah. Uh. Shit. So, that was a cat out of the bag that wasn't ever going back in. I wanted to take the proverbial bag and smother that righteous bitch with it.

Alek stepped in front of me, all six and a half feet of him towering over everyone else, tension radiating from him, careful, controlled, but no less dangerous. Maybe more dangerous. Even Eva seemed to deflate a little under his sweeping icy gaze.

"Jade is here to help," he said, his words a growl.

I didn't need him fighting my battles for me, but on the other hand, this was his realm. I was no shifter; I had no idea about pack politics. Hell, apparently some of what Harper had been telling me about shifters wasn't even the full truth. I'd make her fix that later. If we weren't all dead.

"Her number is the last one dialed in his phone," Lee said, bravely cutting in. "It is a valid question why he called her, what he said."

"I didn't talk to him," I said, moving back beside Alek so I could actually see the people I was talking to. "When did he call me?"

More important, *why* did he call me? I didn't say that aloud, though. I remembered Alek saying something about giving Liam my number, telling him to call me if anything came up or he found the Lansings' car.

"Early this morning," Lee said.

"My phone kind of fell in a fire last night—it's been dead since nine PM or so."

"His heart is missing," Eva cut in. "I hear sorcerers like hearts."

"His heart is missing?" Alek asked, looking at Lee, not Eva.

I cast a glance around, wondering if others noticed the snub. From the speculative look the black woman and Freyda were giving Justice Eva, I thought at least some had.

"Yes. And his intestines. And a large chunk of his throat." Lee glanced at Freyda as she spoke, her light brown eyes soft and sad.

"Would you like to see?" Eva offered, her smile all teeth.

I swallowed bile and shook my head. I'd had way more than enough of death and dismemberment this week. Instead, I took another step forward, meeting her eyes.

"I can prove I had nothing to do with this," I said. "You are a Justice, so you can tell when someone lies, right?"

The smile slid off her face as she nodded, her eyes narrowing with displeasure. She saw where I was going with this.

I looked around at the gathered wolves, making sure everyone was paying attention. Then I looked back at Eva and said, "I did not kill Liam, son of Wulf. I did not talk to Liam at any time in the week before he died. I had no prior knowledge of his death, nor anything to do with it. Satisfied?"

She looked like she wanted to choke me, but she took a deep breath and glanced at Alek.

"Yes," she said grudgingly. "The sorceress is telling the truth."

"We should not be looking at outsiders," the man in the suit said. "This is clearly pack trouble."

"We will question the pack," Alek said. "We will question every alpha. If this is wolf-caused, those responsible will be brought to justice. It is what we do."

"And if the alpha responsible is not here?" asked one of the green-eyed brothers.

"Softpaw," Freyda said, eyes widening. "He has not come yet."

"Softpaw?" I asked Alek quietly.

"The Bitterroot pack alpha." It was Henry who answered me.

"The wild wolves live apart, and Softpaw was the only wolf to deny the Peace, to never acknowledge Wulf as the alpha of alphas," Freyda added.

"What is the point of reaffirming the Peace if not all sign? If all won't keep the Peace, why should any of us? The Council will not be happy," business-suit guy said.

"Do you know the will of the Council?" Alek said, moving toward the man, seeming to grow taller and wider with each step. "The Peace was good enough to last well over a century, even without the Bitterroot alpha. Do you think this Peace so weak, this situation so unimportant, that the Council would not care? If they did not care, would there be not one but two Justices here?"

He paused and looked around, again meeting the eyes of everyone present. Except for Eva's.

"Whoever has done this, whether their goal is to disrupt the Peace or sabotage the true and fair competition for alpha, he or she or they will be found. They will face the Council of Nine's Justice. Do you trust the Council's will?"

His words were clearly a trap, and everyone there flinched as he finished, his question hanging in the twilight. Everyone was looking at Alek except Eva, I noticed. She stared straight at me, her face twisted with a hatred I didn't understand. Then she met my eyes and a mask fell into place, her features smoothing out, her expression stern but bland.

"I trust the will of the Council," Freyda said. The others slowly followed with their own murmurs of agreement.

"Go," Alek said. "Calm your seconds. Talk to the other alphas. The wake will happen tomorrow as planned. We will not let a killer ruin Wulf's legacy."

They dispersed, except for Lee, Henry, and Eva.

"The body?" Alek said to Lee as the cars drove away. "Before we lose all the light?"

I sighed and steeled my nerves. Apparently, I wasn't done seeing mutilated corpses this week. Awesomesauce.

Eva hovered but didn't interfere as Lee donned gloves and pulled back the tarp.

Liam had looked like his sister in life, but with more pronounced cheekbones and something familiar about the shape of his eyes that made me think he had Native American blood in him. His eyes were closed, his face spattered with blood but otherwise untouched.

His throat was missing, only a mess of torn flesh left holding his head on. I saw vertebrae in it and had to look away for a moment. It was a good thing I rarely dreamed. I could add this body to the list of horrible things I could never unsee.

His heart and a lot of his internal organs had been ripped out through a huge hole in his stomach. I was grateful for the dying sunlight, which softened the colors, painting everything in a muted palette and making it look waxy, a touch unreal.

"Tooth marks," Alek said. "Did he get a piece of his killer?"

"We think so," Lee said. She pulled an evidence bag out of her coat pocket. Inside was a tuft of black fur. "It is wolf but not a scent any here recognized."

"Can you use this to track?" Alek said, taking it from her and turning to me.

"You would use her tainted magic?" Eva said.

"What is your problem with me?" I asked. "I don't even know you, and you really don't know me. I don't even know how you knew what I am."

"I met a sorceress once," Eva said. "I have never forgotten the way she smelled."

Sorceress. Female. So, not Samir. I wondered who it was, if there was a chance the woman was still alive. I wished I could ask and expect a real answer.

"Well, she wasn't me. So, get the fuck over yourself and let me help," I said.

Sheriff Lee and Henry both took a couple of steps back, their shock radiating like heat off their tense bodies.

"Eva," Alek said softly. "We must find the killer. Let her work."

Her eyes literally flashed, sheening with golden-brown light for a moment. I had the impression she wanted to shift, to let her wolf take me down. Or take Alek down. I pulled on my magic, letting it fill my veins, sing in my blood, and pool in my hands. *Let the bitch come at me,* I thought. I was ready to lay down a beating on the next person or thing to piss me off. I was too fucking tired of death and posturing and people trying to hurt me and the people I loved.

She turned abruptly and walked to the parking lot, climbing into one of the last three vehicles left. She snapped her fingers at Henry, and he looked at Alek with an apology in his puffy, reddened eyes, and left with Eva.

When the crunch of their tires on the gravel had faded, Alek looked at me. "Track?" he said.

Sheriff Lee watched with interest as I shook the fur out of the bag and into my palm. I pictured the wolf it must belong to, pushing my magic into the spell. Silver thread spiraled out from the fur, then hung in the air, pointing one way, then another, like a compass in the Bermuda Triangle.

I pushed more power into the spell, wondering if the owner of this fur was out of range. I had no idea what my range even was. I had never tracked someone more than maybe twenty miles. The spell fizzled, the connection too weak to form a link. Which was weird, since I'd formed stronger links off things people had only been in contact with. This was a piece of someone or something. It should have created a nice strong link. Unless . . .

"It's not working," I said. "I think this fur is very old. So old it has lost any real connection to its original body."

"Hmm," Lee said. Her lips pressed together and she looked skeptical. I didn't blame her. To her eyes, it probably looked like I'd stared really hard at a bit of fur in my hand.

"Dead end," Alek said.

I slid the fur back into the bag. "Maybe science and the crime lab can tell you more," I said, handing it back to Lee.

Her laugh sounded tinny and bitter. "What do you think we are? CSI Idaho? Besides, this crime will never see a report."

Alek took his keys from his pocket and handed them to me. "Go back to your friends. I will help Lee, go talk to the other alphas, and then meet you later."

They were going to cover up another murder. I sighed. Somehow, the sheriff being involved made it slightly less awful. Slightly. I knew that they couldn't bring this body to the county medical examiner, just as I had known, before Alek made his case the other night, that in the end, the Lansings' bodies couldn't be found by normals either. There was a whole world of magic and danger that humans couldn't see. I had a hard enough time wrapping my mind around this stuff. Universe knows what the rest of the world would do if faced with so many things that didn't follow what we all thought of as "the rules."

"Be careful." I squeezed Alek's arm. "I'll try not to crash your truck."

CHAPTER NINE

I realized that Alek's truck was almost out of gas, so I detoured past the B&B turnoff and headed into town. I grabbed a change of clothes from my house and checked on the store, taping up a note saying we were closed for the weekend. I hoped my few regulars would forgive me. The wards on both apartment and shop were intact and undisturbed. Then I filled Alek's tank, amazed at how much fuel fit in it as opposed to my little econo vehicle, and headed back.

I hadn't realized how worried I'd still been until I heard her laughing and teasing Max as I entered the Henhouse. Harper was awake and sitting up.

I took a moment to check my wards, though they'd done a fat lot of good against the ninja assassin. Still, it made me feel slightly better, though that could have been the feel of my magic rushing through me. All the sleep I'd gotten had done a decent job of fighting back the exhaustion, my nap with Alek refreshing me more than I realized.

If the assassin returned there tonight, I would be ready. I had an idea or three about how to deal with him. No more hesitation.

Harper and Max were playing Electronic Talking Battleship with an original board, a relic from the late eighties. The electronics still worked, little pings and crash noises coming through the speaker.

"Hey," Harper said as I came in and settled into the chair I'd slept in the night before. "Where's your handsome half?"

"Out," I said. I didn't know what to tell her.

"Still riding the secrets train, I see," she said, making a face.

"Glad you are feeling better," I said.

"She's fine. She's just lapping up the attention." Max entered a number and a letter. A crashing noise rang out from the Battleship board.

"Fuck, you sank my battleship." Harper stuck her tongue out.

Max laughed and then straightened as his phone buzzed loudly in his pocket. He pulled it out, flicked the screen, and then handed it to me. There was a text from Alek, telling me he was going to meet with Justice Eva to interview alphas and work on the case.

"There's a second Justice in town?" Max asked.

"Wait, what? Who?" Harper set the game board aside with a wince.

"Some woman, a wolf, named Eva Phillips. She's kind of a bitch. Oh, and she told Sheriff Lee and some of the Wylde pack what I am. So, I give it a day or two at most before every supernatural in town knows. Kickass, eh?" I pulled my knees up, tucking my feet under me, staring at the text message on the phone.

Phone. Oh, right. "Max, can I check my messages on this thing?" I asked.

"Sure, if you know how to work it, and you know your box number and password."

"I don't know. I'm so ancient, I might have forgotten." I smiled at him. "I touch this screen thing here, right?"

"Okay, okay," he said, putting up his hands in surrender. "I could have worded that better. You are as bad as Lea."

"That's not my name," Harper said. "Don't make me kick your ass."

"Like you could catch me right now, gimpy."

"Guys," I said. "I'm trying to check a message here?"

They continued making silly faces at each other as they cleared the Battleship board and began a new game.

I had one message, sent this morning at seven fifty AM.

"Jade Crow? This is Liam Wulfson. Alek gave me your number. He said if we found the car to call you, since he wasn't expecting to be in town. He said you could help and would want to see it. I'm out at the . . ." He paused. After a breath, he called out, "Justice!" and I heard a woman's voice answer, followed by a shuffling noise and a crack that sounded like a gunshot. Then the message ended.

Fuck.

I played it again. And again. Each time hearing the same thing. Him telling me they found the car. Him calling out "Justice" and then the sound of a gun. Adrenaline hit me as I realized that Alek was going to meet with Eva. I dropped the phone as I jumped up and had to scrabble for it under the bed.

I called Alek back but his phone went straight to voicemail. I checked the text message and it was time-stamped over twenty minutes before I'd seen it.

"Jade?" Max and Harper looked at me, alarm in their faces.

"Why didn't you see this before?" I yelled at Max, shoving the phone in his face. "Why is it here twenty minutes after it was sent?" Why did I stop for gas? For clothes? How much time had I wasted? Would she hurt Alek?

"Jade!" Rosie came into the room, flour from the bread she had been kneading floating off her hands and arms. "Stop yelling."

I stopped and looked at her, shaking. The twins and Junebug appeared in the doorway behind her, all my friends watching me for an explanation.

"The Justice," I said. "The woman. I think she killed Liam."

"Liam? Like, Wulf's son, Liam?" Rosie said, her hands twisting in her apron.

"Yes. I have to find him. Alek is going to meet her." I threw the phone at Max and pulled Alek's keys from my pocket. I could trace these—they were his; he kept them on him all the time.

Except I needed them to drive. No, wait. Someone else could drive me. I looked desperately at Levi over Rosie's shoulder.

"Can you drive? I have to track Alek. We have to save him."

"Go," Junebug said. She and Ezee stepped aside as I rushed out the door, Levi at my heels.

Levi's Honda Civic didn't look like a speedy car, but he had clearly made some aftermarket modifications to it. We gunned down the drive and out onto the road. I poured magic into the keys, visualizing Alek, his smell, the feel of him. The link was strong, an undeniable pull and a thick silvery thread stretching out into the dark.

I wasn't that surprised when it took us back to the quarry.

"She has a gun," I told Levi as he cut the lights and stopped the car just off the highway. We were going in on foot, just in case.

He nodded and shifted to his animal form. Wolverines look somewhat like bears but cuter. Until they open their mouths or reveal their claws. Then they are kind of fucking scary. Wolverines the size of a Doberman? Scarier. Levi slipped silently into the shadows, leaving me alone on the track.

I ran. Eva would be able to hear me coming no matter what I did, so I gave up stealth in favor of shields and speed.

Mental note: definitely taking up running if I lived through the night. My lungs and legs burned. My pool exertions were clearly not enough to counter my sedentary, geeky lifestyle.

Alek was ahead, his keys yanking me toward him with the power of a rare-earth magnet. I dropped the tracking spell and stuffed his keys in my pocket, stopping only long enough to pull Samir's knife from its sheath at my ankle. If this thing could hurt an Undying, I figured it could really fuck up a shifter.

I threw light out ahead of me, not trusting just the moonlight, though the rising moon was nearly full. Soft purple light spread across the quarry like bioluminescent graffiti. Just beyond where we'd parked the night before, I saw Alek.

He was on the ground, not moving, looking like an apparition in the ghostly mix of silver moonlight and violet spell light. A furry body streaked toward him and I almost blasted it off the stones. Then I recognized Levi's shape as he shifted from wolverine to man and bent over Alek's body.

I skidded to a stop and fell to my knees on the rocks, my hands reaching for Alek, feeling for a pulse. He was warm to my touch, his chest still rising and falling. I looked up, looked around.

"No one around that I can smell or hear," Levi said. "There is something on him, though, something wrong with his smell. And I smell blood." He touched Alek's collar where a smear of greenish fluid had stained his grey undershirt.

I saw a stain along Alek's side and lifted his arm. Blood soaked his side and the back of his shirt. Cursing, we turned him carefully and found the bullet wound. Bitch had shot him in the back.

"Alek," I said, shaking him. "Alek, you have to wake up." I knew what the smear was before I found the puncture mark in the side of his neck, near where it joined the shoulder.

"We have to get him to Vivian," I said. "He's been poisoned."

"Poisoned?" Levi shook his head. "But—"

"Don't fucking argue. This is how Dorrie died. We don't have time."

"Dorrie is dead?"

"Levi! Please." I tried to lift Alek but couldn't even get his torso off the ground.

"I've got him," Levi said. He lifted Alek as though the man weighed only a hundred pounds, but Alek's body was long and awkward. I grabbed his feet and we managed to carry him to the boulders. Levi sprinted down the road and brought his car as close as he could get it, while I hovered over Alek, nervously watching the shadows of the quarry for movement. Getting him stuffed into the small vehicle was another exercise in frustration. Everything was taking too long.

Vivian lived above her practice, and my shouts and banging on her back door brought her downstairs quickly.

The three of us managed to get Alek inside, but his body wasn't going to fit on an exam table, so Vivian had us take him into her office. There was a narrow couch there along one wall, but it was far too short and cramped for him to fit, so we laid him on the floor. She listened to his heart, checked the puncture wound, and pressed a bandage to the bullet wound in his back. Then she checked his reflexes and poked and prodded him while I tried not to chew off all my fingernails or blow the place up with the rage and magic boiling inside me.

"We can try adrenaline straight to his heart," she said finally, looking up at me. "If we can rouse him, enough that he can shift, he might stand a chance."

"Do it," I said. I remembered her description of the poison. How it was eating away at his organs, his heart. I grasped my talisman and prayed to the Universe not to take him. I had just gotten him back. He couldn't die like this. It wasn't fair. It wasn't right.

She left and came back with a long-needled syringe that looked like something out of *Pulp Fiction*, partially filled with greenish liquid. She knelt over Alek and deftly sliced his shirt open. With a murmured prayer of her own, she jammed the needle into his heart, depressing the plunger.

We all held our breaths. The silence was complete, only the sound of Alek's ragged breathing, like the ticking of an old, erratic clock, breaking our vigil.

Nothing. His eyelids didn't even flutter.

"More," I said.

Vivian shook her head. "That's all I had. That stuff is highly regulated."

"No," I said. "I won't accept this. Get out." I needed them out, needed time and space to think, to figure this out. I had power. Lots and lots of fucking power. What was poison against a motherfucking sorceress?

"Jade," Levi said, touching my shaking shoulders with gentle hands.

"Out," I said. Whatever he saw in my face convinced him it was in his best interest to go.

They left me alone with Alek. I placed my hands on his chest, trying to send my magic into him, visualizing the poison as a foreign agent, as a thing that could be burned out and destroyed.

For a moment, it felt like his body responded; his breathing changed, grew steadier beneath my palms. I sank into him with my consciousness and my heartbeat changed, turning erratic and painful. My lungs burned and a headache to end all headaches speared me between the eyes. I was dying.

I lashed out with magic, recoiling from the acid eating away at me. Recoiling back into my own body. Bile rose in my throat and I vomited blood, barely turning my head to the side in time to avoid splashing Alek's chest. The headache continued but my heart steadied and the feeling of my insides burning away faded.

That was not the way to heal someone with magic, apparently.

"Alek," I said. "Tell me how to do this."

No answer.

So much power, and here I was, helpless again. I got up, took a folded throw blanket from the narrow couch, and spread it over him. I found tissues and cleaned up my vomit as best I could before lying down next to Alek, pressing myself against him. His heart was still beating. He was still fighting.

I touched the puncture wound on his neck, imagined Eva luring Alek out to the quarry. What would she have told him? How did he not see her lies? I guessed that she would be very good at not quite lying. Did she have others helping her? No way to tell. Alek would have been vulnerable, anyway. He didn't like her, perhaps didn't even trust her, but she was a Justice. They had both been sent by the Council. He would trust in that. Let her get close enough to shoot him in the back. To drive the poison needle into his flesh.

Tears choked my throat, burned my eyes. That bitch was going to die. I wanted to go find her, but I couldn't bring myself to leave him. The least I could do was stay, keep trying with my magic to heal him. I pressed more power into him, not sinking into him with my mind but just letting magic flow into him. But I might as well have been channeling at a rock. A rock would have absorbed the magic better, probably.

Sorcerers can't eat shifter hearts. They have a level of immunity to most kinds of magic and their power can't transfer. The same thing that protected shifters from sorcery was preventing me now from helping him. The best I could do was kill him more quickly. I smashed that thought to pieces as I rubbed the tears from my eyes.

The door creaked open and Levi poked his head in, one hand on the door as though ready to flee and close it behind him if I snapped at him again.

"Jade," he said softly. "Can we help?"

"No," I said. "No one can." Then I froze, a memory rising in me. Alek and Carlos roaring and crows falling from the sky, changing back to their human forms.

"Wait," I said. "If he shifts, could he heal? Ask Vivian."

"Yes," she said, looking in at me from under Levi's arm. "I think he is strong enough. But he can't shift if he doesn't wake up. I think there is too much damage."

"But what if someone made him shift?" I asked.

"No one can force a shift on another," Levi said.

"I've seen it. I watched Alek make crow shifters come back to human."

Levi looked down at Vivian and they both shook their heads. "Perhaps that is a power the Council grants. I've never heard of such a thing, but Justices are special."

"So, we'd need a Justice?" I asked, defeat stabbing the hope in my heart to death. "I thought it might be an alpha thing."

"No," Vivian said.

The only Justice I had access to wouldn't do it; I was sure of that. For a moment, I indulged in a very violent fantasy of hunting her down and forcing her to make Alek shift, but I knew from the tiny bit of logic left in me that she would never cave. Eva had too much at stake if she was willing to kill another Justice.

"The Council; what about them?" I was grasping at very tiny straws but any glimmer of a chance . . .

"They do not directly interfere. We may as well ask Jesus Christ to intercede," Levi said, a bitter note in his voice. I wondered at it but shoved the questions aside.

"Jade," Vivian said. She licked her lips and glanced up at Levi again. "The Justice is strong. He's suffering. He will take a long time to die. That isn't right."

"No," I whispered. "It isn't. Just . . . give me a few minutes. Let me say good-bye."

My real words were unspoken. *Give me time to think. Give me time to figure out how to cheat my own personal hell, my own Kobayashi Maru.*

She nodded, and they left me alone with him again.

My magic was no good, not the way I wanted to use it. Bernard Barnes had been able to affect shifters with his magic. I didn't want to think about the evil warlock who had nearly killed my friends, who had used dark rituals to bind shifters into their animal forms and turned them into living magic batteries for his use.

I hated touching his memories. The last time I had, I had done so quickly, using Bernie's knowledge to lock Sky Heart into his human form, preventing him from fleeing Not Afraid's wrath. I had been so full of rage, my heart full of images of death, that delving into Bernie's power inside me hadn't fazed me then. It had barely registered. Yet in so doing, in using Bernie's knowledge, I had brought about the death of my father. Or at least, the man I'd thought was my father.

Bernie had been a serial killer. His psyche and therefore his memories were sick, full of things I didn't want to see or experience, twisted experiments, a full spectrum of human suffering and death. A PowerPoint presentation in full sensory detail on how awful one being can treat another.

But somewhere in that knowledge could be my answer. If Bernie could lock a shifter into animal shape, he could force a shift. He had laid a magical trap that had nearly forced my friends to turn on each other, had pushed them to shift. Somewhere in the hellish miasma of his memories, there might be a way to save Alek.

I had to look.

I slipped my hands around Alek's limp fingers, closed my eyes, and sank down into my own mind.

But the first memory that came wasn't Bernie's. It was my own.

"Come on in, Jess; I won't bite," Ji-hoon says. He sits at his drafting table, pen in hand. There is ink on his lip where he chews the pen nub while inking.

I slip into the room. I'm in trouble, I think. I lit a boy's hair on fire with my mind. Pretty sure that was going to be the final straw. I don't want to go back onto the street, but at least I am a couple years older now. Stronger.

"I'm sorry," I whisper. "I lost control."

"That boy called you some pretty awful names." Ji-hoon has his own kind of magic, like how he always knows things. I know that the school called him, so it isn't really magic, but something in his face calms me. He's not mad.

It's weird.

"I know that is no excuse," I say, trying to show how mature I am. How I can take responsibility for my actions.

"The school can't prove you did it, since all witnesses say you were standing ten feet away," he says. "Relax."

"*But I hurt someone.*"

"*And you feel terrible about it, even though he was totally being an asshole. That's good. The fire only burned his hair, from what the principal told me. So, you stopped yourself, put it out, right?*" He smiles at me and goes back to inking, putting clean black lines over his sketches, bringing the comic to life.

"*I did, but . . . I don't feel good. I feel like a freak, like a bigger asshole than he was.*" Now I'm a little mad. I want him to tell me I'm a bad person. This power inside me, it isn't normal. I couldn't be like my real family, and now I'm not like my new one, either. I'm a freak.

"*You don't feel good because you* are *good,*" Ji-hoon says. "*Your magic is just magic, Jess. It is like lightning or the ocean. A part of the world. It can be harnessed and used for good or ill. But it just is. You choose. Today, you chose to hurt. Now you know what that feels like. Tomorrow, you can choose differently.*"

"*My magic hurt him,*" I say.

"*No,*" he says. "*You hurt him. Your magic is no more to blame for that than my pen is for creating this line.*"

The memory faded and I sank deeper, cursing at my subconscious. It hurt to see Ji-hoon, even in my memories. I had buried that family, hiding them so I wouldn't dream, wouldn't hurt. Parts of me felt like they were waking up now. Parts I wasn't sure I wanted to see again, things I didn't want to feel.

I shoved that away, too.

Bernard Barnes. Ah. There he was. Brown, thinning hair. Watery blue eyes. Pudgy, pale body. His memories started to flood me but I scoured through them, burning away the images, the impressions. Setting fire to every crime, every murder, every pain perpetrated by his choices, his use of the power he gained. I faced the deaths in my memories and rejected them. Not my actions, not my choices. They had no power over me, no more than death on a TV screen would.

I did not want those things, but I faced them unflinching. For Alek. For myself. What I was and who I was, as Ji-hoon had pointed out when I was way too young to listen, were up to me. My choices. Not Bernie's, nor that boy's who so long ago had looked at my brown skin and called me names.

I faced the pain and suffering Bernie had wrought and set it alight in my mind. I sought only his knowledge, the bright core of what he had learned. I wanted the tool, not its wielder. Ji-hoon was right. Power was power.

There, amid the coals in my psyche, I found the knowledge I wanted. A ritual inscribed in an ancient book, a trap to set for men who could change their shape, forcing them from man to beast.

I am a sorceress. I have no need of ritual to raise power. I had Bernie's power, now scrubbed clean and joined with my own. Just power. Just magic. A tool, a means to whatever end I wanted.

Balancing the scales, perhaps, a little more in favor of good. Not undoing what Bernie had done to gain such knowledge, not justifying it, but perhaps adding my own feather to the opposite side. Bernie had chosen to use the knowledge to bring death. I chose life.

I swam up to consciousness with the bit of knowledge clutched in my mental fist like a pearl. Alek still breathed beside me, his heartbeat fainter now. I pressed my magic into my newfound knowledge, following the unfamiliar patterns and shapes of the ritual with my mind, painting a circle around us in golden light. Magic oozed from me, filling each line as I drew it.

"Alek," I whispered, pouring my will into the circle. "Be a tiger."

Then the circle snapped into place and the hand I held became a paw, too big for my hands to encompass. The man struggling to live beside me became a huge white tiger, his body shoving aside the desk with his weight.

His heart steadied. His breathing evened out. He slept.

Levi and Vivian must have heard me shout with joy as I let the circle fade away. I didn't know what words were coming from my mouth, which languages I spoke to them in. I clung to his paw and rubbed my cheek on his rough fur.

Vivian checked his vitals, drawing blood. She left, but after a few minutes, she returned, her face full of awe. When she looked at me, there was a shadow of fear in her eyes. "His body is untainted by poison. He will sleep for a while, I think, while his other self fights the poison, but I think he is strong enough to purge it. The twilight is a powerful place."

"Twilight?" I said.

"Nothing to do with the book," Levi said as he knelt beside me, touching Alek's fur as though to reassure himself that the tiger was real. "It's what some of us call the place where our nonphysical self lives. Ezee calls it the Cave, after Plato's work."

His dark eyes met mine, and I was relieved to see no fear in them. Of course, he had known for months what I was. Vivian, not so much. I had a feeling my days of living anonymously as just another low-power witch in a town full of supernaturals were about to be a distant memory after the events of this weekend.

That would be a bridge I'd Fireball when I came to it.

"Can we move him?" I asked.

"It's safe to move him," Vivian said with a wan smile. "But I am not sure we are physically capable of getting him out of here."

"I'd like to try," I said. "I'd rather have him at the Henhouse than here. You, too, Vivian. If Eva figures out he didn't die in the quarry, she might come here."

"Eva? The other Justice?" Vivian looked like she might faint. Her face got splotchy and she took a couple of deep breaths.

In my rage and pain, I'd forgotten to mention who had shot and poisoned him, and apparently Levi hadn't mentioned it either. Oops.

"Yeah," I said. "I'm pretty sure she's the one killing people and framing wolves. I think she wants the Peace to fall apart. Just wish I knew why."

None of us had answers for that, alas. Yet.

Levi called Ezee and Max. Turned out that three gamers who all played *Tetris* could figure how to move a tiger out of a small room and into a truck. The whole four-people-with-preternatural-strength thing helped, of course. We only had to remove two doors to do it.

I rode in the back with Alek, my cheek pressed to his chest, listening to his heart. In my own heart, the joy of knowing he would survive was fading. In its place, rage simmered. White heat flowed through my veins, my magic responding to my mood.

As soon as I was sure Alek would live, as soon as he was okay, I was going to balance the scales another way. I was going to find Eva, and this time, I was going to choose murder.

CHAPTER TEN

Using a lot of shifter strength and a heavy-duty canvas tarp, we managed to get Alek into the Henhouse and onto a makeshift pallet of quilts in the formal living room. I hovered as they moved him, not wanting him out of my sight. He breathed easily, his heart steady when I pressed my face against his chest.

"He'll live, I promise," Vivian said to me. The awe was still in her eyes.

"I know," I said, still pressed against his fur.

Everyone crowded into the living room, asking questions in low voices. Rosie shushed them and handed me a warm washcloth. She was wise enough to realize I wasn't going to leave Alek's side until he woke up, until I heard from his own lips that he was going to survive. I must have looked a mess. My shirt was stained with Alek's blood and covered in long white tiger hairs. My hands had blood under the nails and streaks of dust and dirt going up my arms. I couldn't imagine what my face looked like. Or my hair.

"Eva did this," I said as I handed back a much grimier washcloth to Rosie with a nod of thanks.

"The Justice?" Rosie asked. The others echoed her, their faces full of disbelief.

"I believe her," Max said. He looked at me with unhappy eyes.

"I, too, believe her," Harper said. She came into the room, a quilt wrapped around her. Her normally pale face was even whiter, but she moved easily and without evidence of pain. "I heard Liam's message. Max and I listened to it after you left."

"She is a Justice," Junebug said. "How could she kill like that? Attack another Justice?"

"It's worse than that," I said, and I told them everything. About the Lansings, about the poison, the setup with Dorrie's body.

Stunned silence followed my story.

"But, the Council—" Ezee started to say.

"Fuck the Council," Levi said. "They pick and choose. You know that, Ezekiel. Where were they, where were their Justices when we needed them? When Mama needed them?"

"Levi," Junebug and Ezee both cried out, looking at him.

Levi's eyes were shiny with pain and unshed tears. "I'm sorry," he said as he took a deep breath. "I . . . This situation, it's too hard. But I believe Jade. The Justices are not infallible, the Council is not infallible, and I think it will only get more of us hurt to continue believing such things."

"All right," Rosie said softly. "If this Eva woman is corrupt, why is she doing this? Why now?"

"I have a guess," Vivian said. She was curled on the overstuffed couch, her legs tucked up against her chest, her arms wrapped around them. "You are all too young to remember how it was before the Peace. You are not wolves. You do not understand. I was a child then, but it was still dangerous to be without pack. My mother moved us around, unwelcome because she was an alpha, but she had no desire to run a pack. An unmarried woman, traveling with a small child, was crazy in those days. There was little work, and I won't speak of the work she *could* get. We were always in danger. From other wolves. From humans."

She paused and looked down at Alek's huge, slumbering form. "There was too much fighting among wolves; too many alphas and not enough pack. Stories started being told around human campfires, in human brothels and taverns, of wolves the size of ponies, of men who changed shape and howled at the moon. Men were dying. Men disappearing. Then the Council of Nine sent their Justices to America and the shifters of the new world learned the power of the Council. They learned to fear. Back then, a Justice only showed up when someone was slated to die— they were executioners as much as judges, killers as much as protectors."

I brushed my hand over Alek's fur. He couldn't hear this story, lost as he was in healing sleep, but I knew he would agree with Vivian. He would be thinking that the Justices were killers still. I recalled his face, his eyes piercing and earnest as he told me that this was who he was, what he was.

"Eva was one of those Justices," I said. Alek had told me as much.

"Yes. She put down the bloodiest of the packs, killed their alphas as examples of what the Council would do. She formed her own pack, a group of bloody hunters she called her Hands of Justice. If it hadn't been for Wulf, who knows how long the killings would have gone on? My mother and I lived on the edge of Wulf's territory by that time. He gathered alpha wolves from all over the new territories and the original States, and they pledged in blood on the sword of his father to keep the Peace, to allow wolves to live within their territory, to allow alphas to be pack brothers and sisters. Because all territory would be his territory. All alphas subservient to the alpha of alphas. He fought and defeated all challengers for weeks, until they had submitted, until they had signed."

"What about the Bitterroot pack?" I asked, thinking of what the wolves had said as we'd stood by Liam's body.

Vivian shook her head. "Aurelio, who is called Softpaw now, refused to sign. He refused to challenge Wulf as well. Instead, he left, taking his pack. They live as wolves. Perhaps they thought the Peace a concern for those of us who walk on two legs."

"And Eva?" Harper asked.

"She was one of three Justices who witnessed the Peace. My mother told me a Justice tried to challenge Wulf, but that she was sent away by the other two. I had never met Eva before yesterday, but the story fits together now."

Furniture creaked as everyone settled back, and a chorus of held breaths released sighed around the living room.

"So, she wants to be the alpha of alphas?" I speculated.

"Or she wants more chaos, for the wolf packs to fight again, so that she can bring her own version of justice down," Levi said.

"I guess that fits with what Alek said about her," I said. "He said she liked to execute first and ask questions never." It fit somewhat too with the whole "trying to set up wolves to look like killers of the humans in Wylde." A massive wolf hunt and lots of human attention would cause huge risk to the shifter population and to their secrecy. The Council would send a Justice. Eva clearly believed it would be her.

I just wanted to know how the Council hadn't seen this coming. If they were really some kind of gods, why wasn't there an army of Justices here to stop Eva? Why only Alek, and why hadn't they warned him?

"What are we going to do?" Ezee asked.

"We? Nothing," I said firmly. "I'm going to wait until Alek wakes up, then I'm going to go kill me a wolf bitch."

"But she's a Justice," Junebug said.

"She's evil," I said. Didn't get much more evil in my book than murdering a family, killing and framing an innocent woman, and then killing anyone who got in your way. Oh, and the fact that she shot and poisoned my lover was like the deserves-to-die-horribly cherry topping on a giant I-will-smite-you sundae.

"But the Council—what if they come after you? She is still a Justice," Harper said.

"Fuck the Council," I said, smiling grimly at Levi as he nodded. "What's one more thing trying to fuck up my life, right?"

"We have to warn the alphas. At least call Sheriff Lee and whoever is in charge at the Den now." Max had his phone out.

"Freyda," I said, remembering Liam's sister. She had seemed smart and steady. I just hoped she would believe us. "Will they believe us?"

"I don't know, but warning can't hurt," Ezee said. He pulled out his phone as well.

"Straight to voicemail at the Den," Max said. "Says they are closed this week and to leave a message."

Vivian got up and retrieved her coat, getting her own phone out. She tried calling Henry, then Freyda directly. Every call went to voicemail.

"Sheriff Lee is busy," Ezee said. "So dispatch tells me. They said, if it is an emergency, to call nine-one-one."

"No," I said. "That would get humans responding; too many problems with that."

"They are holding vigil tonight," Vivian said. "They will inter Wulf's body at dawn in the Great Hall. Then the challenges will start and go until there is only one alpha. It was likely to have been Liam. I am not sure who is likely now. At moonrise, they will pledge their blood to the sword and reaffirm the Peace."

"So, we've got until dawn or maybe later even before things get really hairy," I said. "Will Alek wake up by then?" *Please, Universe, let him wake up by then.*

"He might," Vivian said. She stared at her phone and then sighed, shutting it off.

I realized everyone was looking at me, waiting. I felt like the game master of my own life suddenly, caught without the notes or my dice, woefully unprepared. I didn't even know what system we were playing.

"You all have seen the evidence for yourselves and yet find it hard to believe Eva could do these things. If we try to go warn them tonight, we'll be outsiders, interrupting and accusing a Justice with no way to prove what we're saying," I said, thinking aloud. "We need Alek. I don't see a way to salvage the Peace and stop Eva without him." I wanted to go after her myself, as soon as possible, but I knew that just killing her would make things worse for my friends, for Alek. For a lot of shifters, probably.

It wasn't what Alek would want. Balancing the scales. Killing, but only to save as many lives as possible.

"We stay here, we stay alert, and we wait for Alek to wake," I said. It was something like a plan, at least. "At dawn, we will go and try to warn the wolves and stop Eva."

"And if he doesn't wake by dawn?" Harper said, worried green eyes focused on the huge sleeping tiger at my side.

"I'll storm the castle and do shit the hard way." My magic responded to my anger, rising in me until my normally light brown skin glowed pearl and violet for a moment. It felt like there was a switch inside of me now, waiting to be flipped. I was ready to stop reacting, ready to stop defending.

Ready to kill.

None of us slept much that night. Levi and Ezee and Rosie traded off watching out a crack in the front blinds and sitting with the rifle. People came and went from the living room, but mostly my friends left me alone with Alek. Rosie brought me a hot cup of sweet orange tea at some point. I stayed seated on the floor beside my tiger, watching him breathe.

I must have dozed off at some point. A damp nose against my neck woke me. Wolf. She walked to the window as though she could see through the curtains, her lips peeling back from teeth as long as my fingers in a silent snarl.

An odd hum buzzed in my ears and my skin tingled. My wards. Something or someone was moving out there. I sent my awareness spiraling out into the circles I had placed around the Henhouse. One, two, then others. At least six bodies out there, not human.

So, not the assassin. I was willing to bet they were shifters, wolves. But friend or foe? Looking at Wolf's snarling face, I assumed *foe*.

"Where have you been?" I whispered to her. "You could have warned me about Eva a little sooner." It was useless to complain. Wolf had her own priorities and ideas about things. Eva was of the physical world mostly, not a threat that Wolf could protect me against. I guess, technically, not one she needed to, since Eva couldn't kill me. Still, I couldn't help feel a little warning would have been nice. She was warning me now, after all.

Next to me, Alek moved. His huge head lifted and his eyes opened. He twisted, scrabbling in the quilts, pulling his legs beneath him, his lips coming back in a snarl. Then recognition bloomed in his pale eyes and he shifted to human.

"Jade," he said with a wince. His shirt was torn and bloody, with the bandage still on his back.

"Should you shift yet?" I said as he pulled the ruin of his shirt off and contorted to rip the bandage free.

"The poison is gone," he said. "I'll live."

I crawled onto the quilts and ran my fingers over the bullet wound in his back. Only a pink scar remained. He pulled me into his lap and we clung to each other for a long moment.

"I heard you," he said. "In my mind, I heard you calling to me, telling me to shift. I felt you send me into the twilight."

"You're welcome," I said, smiling against his chest.

He pulled away from me, looking down into my eyes. "It was Eva," he said.

"We know. Liam left me a message and I heard her kill him."

"How did you find me?" he asked, and then smiled ruefully. "Ah, let me guess. Magic."

"Alek! Alek's awake!" Max stopped at the edge of the carpet and started yelling, a huge grin on his face.

Everyone came running to the living room. Alek held on to me as he quickly answered their questions, confirming for all of them that Eva had really gone rogue. I was okay with that, not wanting to break contact with him, not trusting yet that he was okay. The image of him dying, burning up on the inside, was too fresh.

Wolf snarled again, still staring out the window, and I remembered the bodies, my wards. Shit.

"There's people outside," I said. "Six or so, I think. Shifters is my guess."

"Fuck," Harper said.

"It is nearly dawn," Vivian said.

"Is Eva out there?" Alek asked me. "Can you tell?"

I shook my head. "I don't think so, but I can't tell. All I know is six nonhumans are just inside the edge of the wards. They rang the alarm, basically."

"So, they are staying in the tree line, out of sight. Show me where," Rosie said.

I reluctantly got up and went into the dining room, grabbing a piece of notepaper off the sideboard. Harper handed me a pen, and Alek followed, standing over me as I sat at the table and drew a rough diagram of the property, marking out where I felt the bodies.

"So, two at the back door, four covering the front and angles there. I think they are here to keep us inside. Pinned down." Alek's eyes narrowed.

"She's afraid of us showing up and ruining her party," Harper said.

"She knows I'm a sorceress," I said. "She should be afraid. I'm going to kill her."

"No," Alek said. "You are not."

I twisted in the chair and glared up at him. "Did you just say what I think you said?"

"She will die," Alek said. His tone softened but held a dangerous, deadly edge. It made me think of forest shadows and screaming prey. "I will bring her to justice."

I almost argued. Alek wasn't at full strength; he had nearly died only hours before. His face convinced me to shut up. Eva had betrayed more than Alek and the shifters she had killed. She had abused and betrayed her position as Justice. Betrayed her gods. This was Justice business, and I understood Alek's need to balance the scales. I understood, too, that a Justice killing the rogue Justice might be necessary to salvage their reputations.

And hey, if it kept his Council from wanting to kill me in retribution, I was okay with that as well.

"I'm coming with you," I said. He might be able to take on Eva, but I was going to make sure he got to her in one piece, and be there to lend my power if needed.

That was when the wolves watching the house got bored and started shooting at the cars.

CHAPTER ELEVEN

"They shot my car," Levi snarled as he peeked out the front blinds. He looked ready to shift and go lay some serious wolverine rage down on them.

"They shot all the cars," Ezee said. "Sounds like automatic fire, too."

"Where did they get automatics?" Vivian asked. "Used to be, we solved our problems with tooth and claw." Her disapproval was almost funny in its schoolmarm way.

"It's 'Murica, fuck yeah," Max said with an eye roll.

I looked through the blinds. The sun was rising. False dawn tinged the horizon the color of fresh meat and cast a hazy shroud over the tree line.

"I could go out there," I said. "Bullets won't kill me. I think I can shield against them."

"Hold up there, Rambo," Harper said. "They might not kill you, but they won't do you any favors, either. How are you going to stop Eva if you burn yourself out trying to stop bullets?"

Furball had a point. I sighed, frustrated.

"Can you shield enough to distract the two in back?" Junebug asked me.

Two people shooting at me was better than four. I nodded. "True, there are fewer out there. Maybe we can break out and circle around, take the others by surprise."

"You want to sneak up on shifters? Who have machine guns?" Rosie pursed her lips, clearly not on board with anyone going outside and getting shot at.

"They can't use the guns if they aren't human," Alek said. The killing look was back on his face, his eyes glacially cold and scary.

I remembered him forcing the crows in my former tribe to shift. "How close do you have to be?"

"They only need to hear me," he said.

"You can make them shift?" Ezee asked.

I saw Vivian and Levi both glance at me before looking back at Alek. I'd told those two as much.

Alek inclined his head slightly, a grim smile touching his lips. "I am a Justice of the Council of Nine," he said softly. "They will rue this day."

"Good," Junebug said. She brushed her hands over her skirt and took a deep breath, glancing at Levi. "Distract them, and I will fly out of here. You will need a car to get to the Den. I can fly to the shop and bring one. Just make sure they are gone before I return."

"What? No," Levi said. "It isn't safe."

"Don't you lecture me about *safe*," she hissed at him. I could almost envision her feathers ruffling as her eyes widened and her shoulders hunched up. "You run around with your brother and your friends, getting yourself nearly killed by a warlock. You are ready even now to run out there and fight a pack of wolves. I am your wife, Levi, not a sweet little princess sitting helpless, waiting for her knight to come home. Let me help."

"Dude," Ezee murmured with a smile, "I think your princess is in another castle."

"Shut up," Levi said to his twin. He moved away from the window and wrapped his arms around Junebug. "All right," he murmured into her hair. "Bring the Mustang. We'll have them cleared out."

▲ ▲ ▲

I pulled my magic around me like a cloak, hardening it until I felt encased in stone. I hoped it was enough.

Opening the back door just enough to slip through, I dashed out and across the porch, diving down the steps. Gunfire crackled from the trees at the back of the house. Pieces of the porch splintered as bullets *chunk*ed into the wood. I was definitely going to dig into my savings and buy Rosie some serious home repairs after this weekend.

I dodged behind a low brick flowerbed. Poking my head over it, I threw bolts of white light at the trees fifty yards or so out. That was where gunfire had originated. The light was meant to blind them in the dim light, distract. Give Alek a chance to get out the door if we determined the wolves were close enough for his magic to take effect. And to give Junebug a chance to fly from an upper window.

Behind me, a coughing roar rang out, vibrating with power. Alek.

Tiger-Alek stood on the porch, half through the rear door. I climbed to my feet, holding my shield in place. No one shot at me.

Still roaring, tiger-Alek sprang down from the porch and stalked toward the woods. Ezee, Levi, and, surprisingly, Vivian had agreed to handle the four wolves in front. They were not immune to Alek's power, so everyone except me was currently furry. Rosie had forbidden Max and Harper from fighting, pointing out that Max was only fifteen and Harper was still hurt. She'd threatened to lock them in a closet if they didn't agree, and I didn't think she was bluffing.

Two large wolves hurtled from the trees and sprang at Alek. He snapped one wolf's neck with a bat of a huge paw and spun, catching the other in the shoulder and flinging it back.

The wolf twisted in midair and scrabbled to its feet, snarling. I gathered power, ready to blast it, but Alek sprang before I could do anything. His mouth closed on the hapless wolf's throat and blood spurted, staining tiger-Alek's white fur. He threw the body down and resumed roaring as he ran for the front of the property.

I gulped in a deep breath, staring at the dead wolves. It was one thing to say you were ready to accept killing, to know that your lover killed people as part of who he was, as part of his job. It was another thing to face it, to see the sheer power and violence right in front of me.

They did this to themselves, I told myself. *They shot at us. They chose Eva's side. They chose wrong.*

I gave myself a mental shake and ran after Alek.

The fighting had spilled out of the woods. Wolverine-Levi tangled with a huge white wolf, fur and blood flying as they engaged and came apart. A smaller, red-furred wolf who I guessed was Vivian circled a bigger grey wolf, driving it back toward where coyote-Ezee crouched in the long grass, snarling and watching for an opening.

A third wolf leapt at Vivian, blood streaking its grey and black fur. Tiger-Alek reached the wolf before it landed, bounding across the distance in giant strides and slamming the wolf down into the grass with a sickening crunch I heard even from forty feet away.

Coyote-Ezee took advantage of the distraction of Alek's arrival and darted in, teeth ripping into the grey wolf's hamstring. Vivian leapt as the wolf twisted and yelped in pain. Her jaws closed on the bigger wolf's throat and together they went down in the grass, struggling.

A snarl and movement in my peripheral vision warned me as the fourth wolf streaked toward me from the side. I guessed that it thought that the lone human would be an easier target for its rage. I spun and lashed out with my magic, focusing it into bolts of force.

The bolts hit the wolf, sizzling in its fur and knocking it down. Shaking its body, the brown wolf leapt at me again, refusing to stay down.

Another wolf, its fur red and white, streaked in, moving with impossible speed. This one was young, lanky, and much smaller than the brown wolf. They collided and rolled away from each other, snarling and circling as they regained their feet.

Max. Damnit. Rosie hadn't locked him in a closet after all. Probably hard to do as a fox without thumbs.

The two wolves circled around me, moving with such speed that I didn't trust myself to aim true if I threw more magic at the brown one. I dropped my shield, fatigue starting to send little heralds of headache pain into my brain. Crouching, I went for Samir's knife in its ankle sheath.

It wasn't there. Cursing, I recalled it had been in my hand when we found Alek. I'd dropped it in the quarry. Fucktoast on a stick.

Something to worry about later.

Max darted toward the wolf, leaping past my legs close enough that I felt the brush of his fur. The brown wolf was quicker, more experienced. Its mouth snapped shut on Max's leg with a crunch, and Max yowled in pain.

I jumped on the brown wolf, digging my fingers into its eyes, biting an ear and ripping with my teeth.

The wolf let go of Max and whipped its body around, trying to dislodge me. I let myself fly free, spitting a piece of its ear out as I hit the grass and rolled. The wolf was impossibly fast, on top of me again before I could regain my feet.

A huge white shadow ripped the wolf away from me, leaving only a warm spray of blood behind. Alek shook the wolf as though it were a rat and sprang onto the body as he dropped it, raking it with his back claws, rending it to shreds.

"Alek," I cried out. "It's dead. Stop."

He looked at me, mouth scarlet in the light of the rising sun, his lips peeling back in a snarl.

"Or, you know, shred away," I said, crawling to my feet without taking my eyes off his. "Knock yourself out."

An odd look came into his deadly gaze, and he coughed. I realized he was doing the tiger equivalent of laughing. I relaxed. Slightly.

Then he shifted, turning from giant, bloody tiger to tired-looking Viking in less than a blink.

"Are you okay?" he asked.

"Yeah," I said. "Max?" I turned and looked for him.

Max shifted from wolf to human, his face scrunched with pain. "Broke my leg," he said, rubbing the human limb, which appeared straight and unhurt. "I'll be okay if Mom doesn't kill me."

"I'll tell her you saved my life," I promised. "Idiot."

Ezee called out to us and we all moved back toward the house, leaving the bodies where they had fallen. Ezee and Vivian were unhurt, but Levi walked with a limp even in his human body and cradled an arm against his side.

"I'll live," he grunted at his brother. "Stop looking at me like that. You're worse than my wife."

Alek disappeared into the trees and returned a few minutes later with an armload of automatic weapons. "Shouldn't leave those out there," he said.

Rosie nodded and brought a sheet to wrap them in. Junebug arrived with the Mustang, gunning down the driveway with a reckless speed that rivaled Levi's driving.

"That's my princess," he said with a pained smile.

I convinced the others they had to stay at the Henhouse. Levi, Harper, and Max were in no condition to fight more, and Alek and I had no idea what we would face at the Den.

"We still don't know where the assassin is, either," I pointed out. "Alek and I can handle Eva." After seeing Alek fight, I was pretty sure Eva was worm food. Especially if I was there to make sure it stayed one on one. Turned out, dire tigers were really scary in action.

There were protests, but Alek and I were out of time. He took the keys to the Mustang and I followed him out the front door and past the bullet-riddled cars. Even his truck had eaten a magazine or two. Broken glass crunched beneath my feet.

"Have fun storming the castle," Harper called out from the porch.

I turned and waved, yelling back, "Think it'll work?"

She grinned at me, obscuring the fear in her expression if not in her posture. "It would take a miracle," she said, finishing the *Princess Bride* quote.

I was fresh out of miracles, but I still had magic. And I had a Justice with me. It would have to be enough.

"We need to make a detour," I told Alek as we drove away from the Henhouse. "I left Samir's knife in the quarry." The knife was magical, a blade able to hurt things that shouldn't have been able to be hurt by physical weapons. I couldn't leave it lying around. Besides, having a weapon like that going into whatever we were driving toward at the Den wouldn't hurt.

"All right," he said. His expression was grim. His eyes met mine for a moment before returning to the road. "Are we all right?" he said softly.

I thought about the dead wolves. The blood, still drying, sticky on my shirt. I'd wiped the worst of it off, but I could still smell it, feel it on my skin. They had made their choices. We had made ours. All we could do was keep fighting, keep making choices, and hope the scales balanced in the end.

"Yes," I said grimly. "We're just fine."

CHAPTER TWELVE

The sun was high enough by the time we reached the quarry to fling shadows across the stones and highlight the scars and ridges in the naked rock. Alek drove the Mustang right up to the boulders.

"Keep it running," I said. "I'll be quick."

I jumped out of the car and jogged toward where Levi and I had found Alek's body the night before. There was still a dark stain on the ground from his blood and I shivered remembering his crumpled, dying body.

Samir's knife was still there. The air felt oddly still, though the scene looked undisturbed. Another shiver ran up my spine and goose bumps broke out.

A hint of smoke touched my nose as I reached the blade. Smoke and ink. Magic. Enough of a warning that I dropped flat and the first shot missed.

One of the boulders moved, resolving itself into the assassin as he raised a gun and fired again. He'd made a mistake, coming this close, choosing terrain that wouldn't burn, choosing a place where I didn't have to worry about witnesses or collateral damage.

I lashed out with magic, ripping the gun from his hands. My power raged through me. I was ready for this shit now.

I sent my magic out in a circle, throwing up a dome of force around us, boxing him in with me. He was faster than I was, in better physical shape. Clearly, he knew how to fight. All advantages I didn't have.

The assassin tried to back away, drawing two more kunai as he sprang backward and slammed into my magical Thunderdome.

His breath hissed out through his teeth as he steadied himself, and his face lost its perpetually bland expression.

"Who are you?" I asked. I tied off the spell, anchoring it to the rocks. It wouldn't last forever, minutes perhaps, but I couldn't keep channeling it and shield myself as well. Or go on the attack.

"Who are you?" he asked back, his beetle-hard eyes narrowing.

I pushed my magic into a shield just over my skin, much like I had at the Henhouse before trying to attract the attention of men with machine guns. One of his kunai spun toward me and I slapped it out of the air with a glittering, shielded fist.

"Jade Crow casts Harden," I muttered. "It's super effective." I tightened my grip on Samir's knife and crouched. "Only way to get out of here is to kill me," I told him. I figured saying "Come at me, bro" would have been too much. Adrenaline pumped through my brain, carrying me into a high that fueled my power, made me feel like I could do anything, take on anyone. I felt giddy with magic and bloodlust.

The assassin came at me, darting in so quickly, I barely got my knife up before he was slashing at me with his own blades. I felt every cut and impact on my shields, felt my power being used up, draining, each blow pushing me around, off-balance. I tried to slash back, but he was far too quick, my dome giving him just enough room to maneuver on the uneven ground and circle me.

I threw bolts of force at him, recklessly spending magic. Beyond the slight shimmer of the dome, I saw Alek rush up. Saw him pause, his mouth moving. I couldn't hear his words.

Looking at Alek distracted me, and the assassin came at my back, his knife slicing into my leg, cutting through my weakening shield. White-hot pain lanced up my hip. The assassin slapped something to my back and retreated. Reaching back, I snatched the paper and flung it away from myself, dropping low as fire raged around me.

The air grew thin, breathing more difficult. My shield had cut off everything, apparently. Things to think about and refine later. Smoke filled my nose, made my eyes water. My leg gave out under me and I slashed at the dark shape as the assassin hit me again, this time taking me to the ground. I couldn't breathe. The fire had eaten all the oxygen.

He rolled me under him, trapping my legs. I looked up into his face as he sat up and pressed a kunai to my chest. His skin was blotchy, his lips turning blue. He was out of air as well.

I don't need to breathe, I told myself. *Air is optional. Remember the lessons of the pool.* I stopped breathing and focused on the magic inside myself, pouring my power out to encase the assassin in icy cold, envisioning everywhere he touched me as frozen, dead.

He tried to scream as frost rimed over him, speeding up the blade to his arm, wrapping itself around his throat, locking his limbs. Ice didn't need air. Ice was good against fire.

I pulled my arms free and smashed the dome, breaking the circle.

Air rushed in and I gasped for breath. I put Samir's knife against the assassin's throat, exhaustion making my hand shake. He was still frozen, though I felt his skin warming where he knelt on my stomach, his body starting to twitch.

I jerked the kunai out of his hand, pushing his frozen arm away from my chest, keeping my own knife against the pulse in his neck. The assassin's eyes watched me, unafraid. He was ready for death.

I wondered if he was ready for worse than death. I set my hand against his chest, felt the beating of his heart. Samir had sent him to kill me. This man had tried to kill my friends, had hurt people I loved. Plus, he had really pissed me off.

Old Jade Crow might have let him go. Months before, I might have. He was human. A week ago, I would have merely killed him.

Today, I flipped the switch inside. No more defensive. No more playing by rules that only got people I loved hurt.

New rules.

"I'm sorry," I said softly. Then I focused my magic into my hand and ripped out the assassin's heart.

Power and knowledge surged through me as I swallowed a bite of the assassin's heart. His name was Haruki and he was forty-one years old. He hadn't lied about growing up in the Oki-shoto islands. His life flitted through my mind and I pushed it away for later examination.

I felt Alek pulling Haruki's body off me and opened my eyes, still vibrating with the new power as it mingled with my own magic, joining. Like dumping a pond into an ocean, the ripples went on for a while before fading away.

Alek helped me to my feet. I carefully sheathed Samir's knife and then tossed the remainder of Haruki's heart onto his body.

"You are injured," Alek said.

I tested my leg. The cut was already closing. "I'll live," I said. "Go to the car; I'll be there in a moment."

He studied my face for a breath and then nodded. There was no judgment in his eyes, only concern. I watched him walk away before turning back to Haruki's body.

I wiped my bloody mouth on my equally bloody tee shirt, annoyed that the blood tasted almost sweet, almost good to me. Then I crouched and closed Haruki's clouded eyes. Using his own blood and his own memories, I drew a sigil on his forehead, imbuing it with power.

"Good-bye, Katayama Haruki," I said softly in Japanese, using his surname first and then his given name. Then I turned and limped to the car as his body ignited behind me, a last wave of inky heat following me. I did not look back.

CHAPTER THIRTEEN

Stonebrook Hunting Lodge, the official name of the Den, was about six miles out of town down a partially paved road that wound up a hill through pristine old-growth forest. It was a faux castle, a hulking stone-and-wood building with two main wings joined by a three-story-tall great hall and flanked by squat, mostly decorative stone towers. There was only one approach to the Den, a long driveway that climbed the hill and terminated in a circular drive in front of the huge stone steps leading to the giant red doors of the great hall.

Cars filled the parking lot carved into the hill beside the Den, shining like Skittles in the morning sunlight as Alek and I stopped the Mustang at the bottom of the hill, pulling as far off to the side and into the shadow of the trees as we could.

"How many alphas are here?" I asked.

"Counting their seconds?" Alek thought for a moment as we stared up at the big stone building. Only the upper part was visible from where we were. We'd have to go farther up the drive to see the doors. "Two hundred and thirty wolves, I believe."

I wondered who the wolves we'd killed at the Henhouse had been, what pack they were with. I hoped it wasn't Wylde's pack helping betray everything their former alpha had lived for, had worked to build.

"I believe your line is 'time's up; let's do this,'" Alek said with a slight smile.

"We live through this, I'm going to make you watch that YouTube video," I said, smiling back at him. Nerves fluttered in my belly and then calmed. We would live through this, I promised myself. This was a beginning, this new start between us, and I wasn't going to give it up so easily this time.

We climbed out of the car and slipped into the woods, sticking to the trees as far up the hill as we could. The forest thinned and then terminated a couple hundred yards away from the doors. From here I could see the wide stone porch. Four figures lay prone in its surface, sunlight glinting on metal in their hands. I squinted. Guns. Big guns. If anyone was dying inside that hall, we were too far away to hear the commotion.

"Wolves?" I asked Alek.

He took deep breaths of the air, mouth partially open as though tasting as much as smelling for their scents. He shook his head. "Human. I can't force them to shift," he added, clearly following my line of thought.

"Damn," I muttered. I reached for my magic. We were a long ways out, but I had to try to reach them. We needed inside that hall. Universe only knew what Eva was doing, what was happening in there. She had hired these men to keep anyone else from coming in. Humans with guns. Another breach of the Council's rules, I guessed, a shifter dealing with humans, using human muscle. Mercenaries. Fucked-up world.

"Wait," Alek muttered. His head swiveled and he tasted the air again.

I sensed movement in the trees behind us. Wolves.

But it was a man who emerged from the denser forest and made his way to the stand of fir we lurked within. He was about six feet tall with long, shaggy black hair that had a dramatic shock of white running through it, a thick beard, and skin a shade darker brown than my own. He smiled, his hands spread in a nonthreatening gesture. Something about how he moved was almost awkward, as though he had not walked in a long time and was trying to remember how with each step. He wore only a pair of green sweatpants, no shirt or shoes.

"Justice," he said, his voice rough and gravelly. "I am Aurelio, called Softpaw, alpha of the Bitterroot pack."

Alek moved so that he was halfway between Aurelio and I. "That your pack in trees?" he said.

"Yes," Aurelio answered. "I have come to swear the Peace. My daughter is dead; the Justices have no hold over me any longer."

Alek and I exchanged a confused look, which Aurelio saw.

"You do not know?" he asked, the determination in his face turning to confusion. "No, I guess it has been many, many years. You are too young. One of your own, a wolf called Evaline, made me leave. My daughter killed a human trapper, and the Justice said the price for her life was for me to fight Ulfr, stop the Peace. I could not fight my friend, but I did not sign. I took my pack and we fled deep into the wilderness. But my daughter is gone. I wish to redeem my cowardice."

He said the words as though he had been rehearsing them, which I guessed he might have. It had likely been a very long time since he'd spoken with a human throat, since he'd shared words with other people.

"Good," Alek said simply. "Eva has broken the trust; she is not acting with the will of the Council."

Aurelio searched Alek's face and whatever he saw there satisfied him. "My pack is yours, Justice," he said.

"Don't suppose you know another way into the Den?" I asked.

He looked past Alek at me and shook his shaggy head. "Your mate is human? She will be in danger here," he said.

"Whoa, I am not his mate," I said. "Or totally human. Check your nose."

His nostrils flared and he cocked his head. "No," he said in his rough voice. "Not human. The blood on you is, but it is not your blood."

All right. I had literally asked for that. I sighed.

"That still doesn't get us past men with machine guns." Turning, I leaned around the tree behind me and peeked at the top of the hill. "They look spaced within five feet of each other to you?"

"Yes, why? Can you make a shield again?" Alek asked.

"Maybe," I said, though I had something else in mind. I pulled on my magic, ignoring the dance of red spots at the corner of my vision and the sharp pain that did a jig between my eyes. I was tired, but I hadn't hit my limit. Not yet.

But I was tired of shields. Tired of bullets. There had to be another way. I looked around and fixated on Alek's shirt. He'd pulled on a white tee shirt from his house trailer and a black sweater over it. The tee shirt showed a little above the collar line of the sweater. I was sure Ezee would have been horrified.

"Give me your undershirt," I said to Alek, the stupidly crazy idea forming in my head growing more and more real by the second.

He pursed his lips, but to his credit, he pulled off his sweater, then his tee shirt, and handed it over, tugging his sweater back on. I picked up a dry stick from the ground and tied the shirt to it. Pulling my braid over my shoulder, I yanked out the tie and shook my hair down my back. I wanted to look unmistakably female and human before I walked out into the open.

"Wait for my signal," I said. "I'm going to try to get closer."

"They are going to shoot you," Alek said.

"Maybe," I said. "But those are human men up there. I know a thing or three about men."

"You are covered in blood."

I looked down. He had a point, but fuck it. "That might help sell the whole 'helpless and in need of saving by dicks.'"

"What's the signal?" Alek asked with a resigned look on his face.

"Them dying or me getting shot. Whichever happens first." I picked up my makeshift truce flag and grinned. I didn't give him a chance to respond, stumbling out of the tree line and into the grass, walking straight up the hill toward the men holding machine guns.

Behind me I heard Aurelio mutter something that sounded like "mates."

The men didn't shoot. I saw movement among them, and the murmur of voices filtered down to me as I walked, waving my flag.

"Don't shoot," I called up to them, pitching my voice higher than it normally was. "I need help!" I fake-stumbled and moved closer, letting my magic fill my veins, readying a spell in my mind. I knew what I wanted to do; it was just a matter of getting close enough, of connecting.

"Lady," one of the men yelled, sitting partially up. "This is a restricted area. Back down." He sounded distressed. I didn't know what Eva's instructions had been, but shooting unarmed women who looked already hurt and were asking for help clearly hadn't been covered.

Just a few feet closer. Closer. I labored up the hill, covering another ten feet. Then another. I could make out their eyes through their balaclavas. One of the men on the side dropped low over his gun, sighting down on me. The others still looked confused and unfocused, but I was running out of time.

Forty feet out, I threw the spell. Purple lightning arced from my outstretched hand, zapping into the man who had spoken. It hit him hard and threw him back before spreading between him and his companions, forking out to either side in a spectacular light show. I dropped flat to the hill, wincing as my injured leg twinged, and pressed my face to the still damp grass.

Silence. Then I heard Alek and Aurelio running up the hill behind me. I sat up and looked at the porch.

The mercenaries lay where the lightning had thrown them away from their guns. None of them were moving. I shoved away the pang of guilt about it. Alek was right—it did get easier. It helped, of course, that I was pretty sure they had been about to gun down an unarmed woman. Hard to feel guilty in the face of that little fact.

We climbed the remainder of the hill together.

"What did you do to them?" Aurelio asked me as Alek checked the bodies methodically for signs of life, stripping them of their weapons as he went.

"Chain Lightning," I said. "When you absolutely, positively got to kill every last motherfucker in the room, accept no substitutes."

"You are very odd," the Bitterroot alpha said. He turned away from me with a frown and, putting his fingers into his mouth, whistled back at the woods.

"Guess you don't watch a lot of movies," I muttered. My badass references were wasted on this guy.

Wolves streamed up the hill behind Aurelio. He met the eyes of a leggy white wolf and nodded as though it were speaking to him.

"These are the only men with guns out here. Everyone else is inside," he said.

I looked up at the huge doors. "I think I can blast through these," I said. High on magic, I was pretty sure I could blast through anything at the moment. I was going to pay for this later.

"Or we could go in the side door," Alek said, pointing to a smaller door set near the corner of the hall, at the edge of the stone porch. "With the key Liam gave me before he died."

So much for a super-grand, dramatic entrance. Some guys just don't know how to have fun.

Aurelio agreed that he and his second, the white wolf, would come in with us, but that the rest of his pack would stay outside and guard our flanks. He actually said "guard our flanks." It was kind of adorable. I wished that Ezee had been here to hear it.

Alek unlocked the door, and we entered the great hall with him leading the way. I readied shields just in case there were more men with guns.

The side door led into a small foyer where a second door opened into the great hall proper. That door was also locked, but Alek's key opened it. The door opened inward and Alek poked his head around before nodding and walking through.

As soon as we passed through the door, I heard people talking, the sounds of a crowd washing over me like a tangible wave. The air inside was heavy and warm—the ceiling was far above and there was plenty of space even with hundreds of bodies inside, but the hall was still crowded enough to heat the air, to change it. The stone walls shimmered slightly and I recognized the kind of soundproof shielding that Alek sometimes used. Eva's doing.

The hallway we'd emerged into opened wide almost immediately to reveal a cavernous room. Benches lined the walls and there was a gallery level above, an iron spiral staircase on my left leading up to it. Men and women covered the benches, many sitting, and some standing above in the gallery. A large stone slab engraved with knotwork sat in the middle of the floor, raised a few inches from the stones around it. Wulf's final resting place, I guessed. A small group of shifters stood at the head of the slab, Eva among them.

The crowd's murmuring conversations turned to exclamations as we entered. Bodies moved aside, eyes questioning, as the four of us walked into the open center of the hall.

"The hall is sealed," Eva said, fear and anger clouding her face and making her look meaner and uglier than ever. "This is a place for wolves. You are not welcome here."

"Am I not?" Aurelio asked before Alek or I could respond. He looked around at the assembled alphas. "I am wolf. I am alpha. This woman once prevented me from pledging to Ulfr's Peace. I will not be turned away again." His eyes dropped to the elaborately carved stone. "He was my friend."

A shorter speech than he'd given Alek and me, but it worked. Murmurs of "Softpaw" and "Bitterroot alpha" rippled around the hall.

"The Peace? It does nothing for us. It has neutered us. We are wolves. We are alphas. Do not be stupid." Eva strode forward, spitting onto the stone.

Freyda stepped out of the group as well, following Eva, outrage in every line of her body.

"Eva Phillips," Alek called out before Freyda could speak. He raised a hand, his gesture and words commanding immediate silence. "You are a murderer and a liar. I am here to bring you to justice."

"Justice? You know nothing of what we were, cat. Once, we were feared, respected. The Council gave us real power, ultimate authority. There was a time when they spoke to us directly instead of feeding us vague visions and unhappy dreams. I will be the alpha of alphas and there will be no Peace. Let the Council come and stop me."

"I am still Justice," Alek responded, moving forward with the stalking grace of a hunting cat.

Aurelio and I backed off. Freyda looked at Alek and she, too, moved backward, until just the two of them stood on opposite ends of the stone slab.

"So, the Council sent you?" Eva mocked.

"No," Alek said.

From the soft exclamations all around me, I wasn't the only one surprised by this revelation.

"But," he continued, pulling his feather talisman out of his sweater and holding it so that the silver caught the dim light filtering in through the upper windows and glinted, "I am still a Justice. The scales will balance."

Eva's eyes widened, and she snarled at him, flicking her hand in a "now" gesture.

Movement and a soft cry from the upper gallery dragged my gaze away from Eva. I recognized the two green-eyed brothers from the parking lot by Liam's body the day before as they stood up in the gallery, machine guns in their hands. Every man and woman near them also pulled out a machine gun.

The hall had just become a barrel, and we were the fish.

CHAPTER FOURTEEN

Alek roared; the same deep coughing sound as earlier at the Henhouse reverberating throughout the hall. It was an impressive sound coming from a human throat, human lungs. Around me, bodies turned from human to wolf, dropping from two legs to four, until I was standing at the edge of a sea of wolves. Beside me, a huge black wolf with a wide white streak down his back crouched and growled, golden eyes focused above. Aurelio. I stepped in closer to him and looked up.

In the gallery, the men and women holding machine guns had stayed human as well. I squinted, making out earbuds and the lines of cords running from their ears. No wonder Eva had gestured to signal them. One of the brothers held a gun that looked more like one of the paintball rifles we used. It made me nervous, though I didn't know why.

Eva was still human as well. She laughed. "Thank you. Saved me the trouble of forcing them to shift later."

Alek glared at her and snarled. "I challenge you, Eva. You want the old ways? Then let us fight, tooth and claw. We shall see who is right."

"You are a tiger," she said. "Hardly a fair fight."

"I am still weak from your poison," he said.

"Good point," she said. "That reminds me." She gestured again, pointing at Alek and making eye contact with the brother holding the air rifle.

"No," I yelled in warning as I threw my power at Alek, trying to shove him aside. I recognized the gun now. It was like the ones some of the scientists used when tagging wolves out in the River of No Return Wilderness. A tranq dart gun.

Only I knew it wouldn't hold a tranquilizer.

The dart stuck him in the shoulder instead of the neck as my magic shoved him sideways. With a snarl, he ripped it out and threw it down, then shifted immediately and sprang at Eva.

She pulled a small cylinder from her pocket, gripping it in her hand before she shifted as well. She wasn't that big a human, but her wolf form was massive, thick with muscle and covered in sleek red fur.

Tiger-Alek dwarfed her, but his leap missed as she sprang sideways. Around the edges of the hall, the wolves pressed backward against the walls, giving the two Justices room. One wolf tried to climb the stairs, snarling up at the shifters with guns. A gun cracked, impossibly loud in the hall, and the wolf fell back, screaming in pain.

Alek and Eva circled each other. He kept lunging and trying to grab her, but she was too quick, leaping out of reach and circling around, snapping at his legs and forcing him to twist and turn. She was waiting, I saw—waiting for him to weaken. My hands tightened into fists and I wanted to fry her where she stood. Alek's pale eyes caught mine, and I held back. He had made me promise that Eva was his. This wasn't my fight, unfair though it was.

I had to trust him. He had shifted before the poison had gotten deep into him. He could take her. I hoped.

Beside me, Aurelio moved away, stalking along the edge of the wolves, heading for the stairs. I hesitated for a moment, worried about Alek, but gave myself a mental shake and followed Aurelio, turning my attention to the gunmen above.

The brother with the dart gun noticed us moving and nudged his brother. I hoped I was close enough and sent a bolt of lightning streaking into him. The lightning arced between them and blasted both brothers off their feet, smashing them back into their companions. My spell was weaker than the one I'd thrown at the men outside, the lightning dying out before traveling to more than the two of them. Fatigue turned my legs to lead and my head felt about ready to explode, but I threw another bolt into the gallery, then another, striking as many as I could.

The remainder started trying to shoot me, but automatic weapons aren't exactly accurate. I threw up a shield, trying to angle it so bullets would skip off at an upward angle, away from the wolves trying to back away from me.

"Get out," I yelled at them. "The side door, go." But no one was listening, their attention either on the gallery where Aurelio had gained the stairs or on the tiger and wolf fighting in the center of the hall.

The alphas meant to see the fight through. Idiots.

Aurelio and his white wolf companion ripped into the gunmen above me, and I dared not throw more lightning around. The gunfire stopped as the few remaining found they had more pressing—and toothy—problems. It looked like Aurelio had things in hand as three more brave alphas flowed up the stairs and joined in subduing the last of the gunmen.

I staggered against a bench and sat heavily, trying to breathe through my exhaustion, my gaze returning to the fight. Wolves around me were turning back to men and women, taking up seats again. They all gave me wide berth, leaving me with a perfect front-row seat.

Blood ran down Alek's flank, staining his pristine white coat. There was blood on his mouth as well, and a wound gaped in Eva's right shoulder where his teeth had found purchase. She glanced up at the gallery and snarled. Alek took advantage of her distraction to spring, his tail whipping back and forth as he landed on her, pinning her partially beneath him. His jaw snapped closed just above where her head should have been as she shifted to human and then back to wolf in a blink, avoiding the killing blow. Her jaws sank into his foreleg, and he twisted, ripping into her injured shoulder again with his teeth. She rolled out from under him, fur and blood dripping from her mouth.

Alek didn't let her go far; his teeth were still locked in her shoulder. He tore free a huge chunk of fur and flesh, revealing the white of her bone before a curtain of blood covered it. So much blood, spurting from severed arteries. She was too hurt to continue. She had to be. I leaned forward, holding my breath, waiting for Alek to deliver the killing blow.

Eva screamed, scrabbling away from him. She couldn't stand, however, instead crouching low on the stone slab, her blood gushing down and slowly painting the knotwork engravings crimson. She became human again, her hand still clutching whatever she had pulled from her pocket before the fight.

Alek shifted back to human as well. His face was gaunt, his eyes filled with rage and pain.

"It is over," he said. "I find you guilty of murder, Eva Phillips. I find you unworthy to wear the mark of the Justice."

She laughed, her eyes darting around crazily. "It's a stupid charm I bought from a stand on the road," she said. "My feather melted away like ice in sunlight the night I killed that stupid wolf bitch. The Council has already turned on me. But the Peace will never succeed, even if I die. The Council is sick. This way of life is over. We will find a new way."

"I am here. The Council is here through me," Alek said. "It does not matter. You will die by my hand." He walked toward her cautiously, not trusting her. I applauded that.

"No," she said, spitting blood. "You'll all die by mine." And she raised her hand, revealing the silvery object. It looked like a pen but with a button on top.

I'd watched enough action movies to recognize that. A switch.

"I had Wulf buried with a little something extra," she said, still cackling as blood frothed from her mouth.

CHAPTER FIFTEEN

I didn't stop to think, to breathe. I hardly knew I was moving, only that I wouldn't make it to her in time. Grabbing my d20 talisman with both hands, I threw my magic out and anchored it like a tether to the bloody stone beneath Eva's body. Then I pulled. The tether yanked me forward and I went flying across the floor and slammed into Eva as she pushed down on the button.

"Get out get them out go go please go," I was screaming as I threw my arms around her, wrapping my magic all around us and the stone, pouring every ounce of myself into the shield.

I couldn't see if Alek obeyed before the world exploded.

There was pain, but it was the kind of pain that became abstract very quickly. Like being cut deep with a very sharp blade. The ache is there and intense, but it doesn't feel real. The cut looks like it has happened to someone else and your body tries to tell you that this isn't your limb, that isn't your wound.

This won't kill me. But it felt like dying. My eardrums exploded, my head ringing like a million bells. Darkness threatened, but I fought it back with my power, pushing against unconsciousness, embracing the blinding pain. I couldn't feel Eva in my arms anymore. I wasn't convinced I still had arms. My world became a thought, narrowed down to a single desire.

So much pressure. White hot, molten, bubbling up against me like lava. My shields strained, the power in me waning, drained too far.

Keep the shield up. No more family, no more friends are going to die because of a bomb. Ever. Not if I still live to stop them. Never. Again.

Something inside me broke loose. Like a joint popping back into alignment that I hadn't known was out until it set itself again.

The lava turned to warmth. The pain disappeared. I floated in a sea of power, breathing in it, channeling it into the shield as though I had the universe itself at my fingertips. I breathed in flame, inhaled the pressure of the explosion, and breathed out magic, pure, unfamiliar power that was both mine and not mine.

If this is death, I thought, *I don't mind it so much.*

Not death, said a gentle, masculine voice in my head. *But you aren't ready yet. Go back to sleep.*

And then the power slipped away and the warmth faded back into heat.

There was something hard and smooth as glass beneath my body. My head pounded like a motherfucker. For a long second, I just breathed, amazed that I could, afraid to move in case the blinding pain returned. I tested by wiggling my big toe.

It was there and intact. I felt it scrape against the smooth surface beneath me. My hands were underneath me, my talisman pressing against my palm. I opened my eyes and blinked a few times, trying to figure out where I was. Glassy red stone curved upward in front of my face, as though I lay in a steep bowl. I rolled onto my back and my foot hit something that clattered on the glass as it moved.

Above me, the roof of the great hall looked intact. I moved my eyes as Alek appeared at the lip of the giant bowl I lay in.

"Jade?" he said, his voice and face filled with disbelief and then joy. He slid down beside me as I sat up.

"I'm okay," I said. My voice sounded like I had smoked a few too many packs of cigarettes, and I coughed, trying to clear my dry throat. A memory of breathing in fire, of bathing in flames and having more power than a god flickered through my mind, slippery and unreal. I pushed it away and looked around.

There was no sign of Eva. At my feet was Samir's dagger. It had survived the blast, which didn't surprise me. My clothes, not so much. I sat in a depression in the stone floor about eight feet across and three or so feet deep. The stone was bloodred and melted smooth like glass. Alek crouched down beside me but didn't touch me.

I climbed slowly to my feet, taking the hand he offered. Other than being totally naked, I felt fine. My body looked fine—not a burn mark or wound on me. My hair fell over my shoulders, waist-length and glossy, as though I'd washed and combed it recently. I reached up and felt for the shorter bit where Haruki had shot off part of my hair, but that was gone. Twisting my leg, I looked at the back of my thigh. No sign of that wound, either.

"Huh," I said, bending and picking up Samir's knife.

The hall was empty, the great doors thrown wide open. Beyond, I saw shifters milling around. Aurelio and Freyda stood side by side on the porch, just outside the doorway, talking with their heads together.

I took a deep breath. "So, that's over, I guess." I tried on a smile and looked at Alek.

"No," he said. "But our part is, I think."

I tried to climb up out of the bowl and slipped. Alek's arms came around me and he lifted me up. Fucking hell. Not again.

"Put me down," I demanded as he jumped easily out of the bowl.

"You can barely stand," he said.

"But I *can* stand," I said. "This happens, like, every fucking time. I pull off big magic, knock myself on my ass, and then you show up and carry me home. Fuck that. This time, I am walking out of here on my own two feet."

His lips twitched and the concern in his eyes turned to humor. He set me down, keeping a steadying hand on my elbow.

"Would you like a shirt, Lady Godiva?" he asked, his smile turning into a smirk.

I looked out at the gathered crowd and then down at my naked body. My hair was doing a Godiva thing, covering my breasts if not much else. It was definitely a sign of my exhaustion that I had forgotten in the last twenty seconds that I was sporting the emperor's latest wardrobe malfunction.

"Yes," I muttered. "Shirt might be good."

He gave me his sweater. I pulled it on and it covered me nearly to my knees, the sleeves falling over my hands. I rolled them up and picked up Samir's knife again. Good enough. I turned to Alek and gently touched the purple and black bruises on his arm and shoulder.

"You okay?" I said, looking up at him.

"I will live," he promised me, bending to kiss my nose.

"All right," I said. Squaring my shoulders and trying not to lean on his offered arm too heavily, I walked out of the hall on my own two damn feet.

I passed out cold about thirty seconds later, but that's beside the point.

CHAPTER SIXTEEN

Freyda became the new alpha of alphas, Alek told us later. Aurelio and many others pledged their blood to Wulf's sword, but some of the alphas left without pledging and there was still a great deal of suspicion around who had sided with Eva or not.

It seemed the future of the Peace was still up in the air.

Eva was dead, assumed vaporized in the explosion. Wulf's body was now sealed beneath the depression I'd created with my power, though I guessed it had been vaporized as well.

I told my friends my version of events, leaving out the weird experience in the middle of the explosion. I didn't know what to think of it. My power felt normal after a day of sleeping and eating vast quantities of Rosie's French toast. No strange warmth, no sudden desire to inhale flames.

Haruki's memories lurked in my mind, his knowledge waiting for examination, but I had had enough of fire for a while and left them there. I left my shop closed for a few days, too, choosing to stay at the Henhouse.

I pretended it was because I needed to recover and make sure all my friends were healed, but the truth was, I was afraid to resume my life, afraid of what might happen now that people knew what I really was. I didn't believe for a moment that what had happened at the

Den would stay quiet among the supernatural residents of Wylde.

It was Harper, as usual, who made me go home and return to work. Harper who nagged me into resuming my normal life.

My shop felt musty, but it aired out after we propped the door open for a while. It was Thursday morning and nobody came in, which wasn't unusual. The college would open for classes in just over a week, so I figured business would pick up then. I didn't mind the quiet.

Harper was camped out in her chair, playing *Hearthstone* and swearing at the RNG gods. I sat up on my stool, a full box of unopened *Magic: The Gathering* booster packs in front of me, debating if I should just open them and sell the individual cards or keep the packs intact. I kind of wanted the mindless work of sorting them, and the little bits of happy discovery that came from each opened pack as I looked to see what the mythic or rare card was.

"Shouldn't you have the blinds down, just in case that assassin comes back?" Harper asked, glancing at the front windows and open door.

"He's not coming back," I said. I'd neglected to tell my friends about Haruki and how it had ended. There had been too many other things to say, and the moment had passed. No one had asked about the assassin all week, either.

"Wait, you sound really sure."

"You could say I'm dead sure," I said, giving her a grim smile.

"Okay, back up; when did that happen?" Harper slapped her laptop closed and sat up straighter.

I sighed and told her the full story. Or almost, anyway. I tried to leave out the part at the end.

"You stopped off on Sunday morning and had a ninja battle? And you seriously didn't think it was worth telling me about?" She shook her head at me. "Crazy lady."

"I killed a man," I said softly. "I didn't really want to talk about it."

"He's not the first man you've killed," Harper said with a shrug.

I flinched. "I more than killed him," I told her.

Understanding dawned on her face, and she took a deep breath. "Good. You need more power to stop Samir, right? Why not use the tools you are given?"

"This doesn't remotely bother you, does it?" I searched her face but she only looked back at me with open, honest eyes.

"Some people need killing," she said.

"Easy for someone who has never killed to say."

Harper went very still and then shrugged far too casually.

"What?" I said. "Azalea! Who did you kill? When?"

"Someone who needed killing," she said. "You want the story, I want cake." She pointed at the door.

"Cupcakes okay?" I said, taking pity on her. She looked profoundly uncomfortable, and I understood the feeling. Talking about murder wasn't a comfortable thing.

"Lemon, please," she said, relaxing a little.

I grabbed my wallet and walked next door to Brie's Bakery. The nice weather was holding and the morning sun sparkled off the display cases. The bakery smelled amazing as always. It was too late in the morning for the coffee-and-paper crowd and too early for the lunch crowd, so I almost had the place to myself, and there was no line. Two regulars sat at a table in the corner far from the door by the window, playing checkers and eating fruit tarts.

I walked up to the front and contemplated the cupcake selection while Brie finished loading a fresh tray of Danishes onto a shelf. There was lemon today, but I wanted chocolate. Or vanilla. One of each? Oh, the difficult choices in front of me.

"Hey, Brie," I said when she turned around. "Two lemon and two vanilla with chocolate frosting." I pointed at the cupcakes.

"No," she said.

I straightened up and looked at her. Her normally cheerful face was cold and hard, all warmth missing from her eyes. Shit.

"No?" I asked, confused.

"You are not welcome here," she said. Her eyes flickered to the two customers at the table and she lowered her voice, adding, "Sorceress."

My confusion melted away into unhappy anger.

"I'm the same person I was yesterday, or last week. Or these last five years," I said.

"I will not clasp a snake to my breast," she responded. "Now leave. You are banned from this place."

A snake? What? I backed away. "Brie," I said, trying to think of words that would help, that would stop the hatred pouring off her. The air crackled with magic, her usual warm, healing power turning bitter and sharp to my senses.

"Do not make me call the sheriff and have you arrested for trespassing," she said.

The two regulars stopped their game and looked up at us with wide eyes. We were starting to make a scene. I realized there was nothing I could say or do that wouldn't just make things worse, so I turned and left.

I walked the dozen steps back to my shop in a daze. The door chimed as I entered and Harper looked up.

"No cupcakes?" she asked, seeing my empty hands.

"The cupcakes were a lie," I said, trying to joke through the tears that threatened.

"Jade," she said, not fooled for a moment. "What happened?"

"Word is out," I said. "As I knew it would be. Small town. Brie banned me for being a sorceress. She's afraid of me now."

"But you've lived right next to her for, like, half a decade."

"She called me a snake," I said. "Like I was just waiting to bite."

"She's an idiot. I am never eating her pastries again. Ever. And neither will the twins or my mom or anyone else I know, once I tell them about this."

"Harper, that isn't necessary. Sorcerers don't have the best reps; you know that. She can't be sure I'm not a danger to her." Her fierce protectiveness made me smile and pushed down the sadness inside.

"Fuck that. I bet that is all Samir's fault, anyway. You don't deserve this shit." She got up and wrapped me into a bony hug.

"Thanks, furball," I said, hugging her back. It was good to have friends.

I sent Harper to get sandwiches an hour later, not quite ready to go back outside. I was pretty sure the sandwich guys at Pete's Deli were human, but better safe than hungry.

I was in the back part of the store, dusting off the painted display miniatures, when my door chimed and my wards hummed, warning me of magic. The scent of cloves preceded the woman into my shop. I walked to the counter where she waited, recognizing the head librarian. I couldn't recall her name, however. It started with a P, I thought. She was middle-aged, with brown hair laced with grey pulled up into a tidy bun. She had on jeans and a tee shirt that read Books are Grrrreat over the picture of a goofy-looking tiger.

"Afternoon," I said, though I had the feeling from the sharp scent of her magic that this wasn't a social call or her wanting games or comics for the library.

"I'll make this brief," she said, wrinkling her pale nose as though my shop smelled like dirty laundry. "You are not welcome in this town, sorceress. I require you to leave as soon as possible."

"Um, no?" I said, standing up very straight. I resisted the urge to summon my magic and push back on the power she had clearly readied and brought with her. A protective spell, I was guessing. I was willing to bet it was no match for what I could throw at her. But petty escalation wasn't going to help my new PR issue. "I've lived here in peace for five years. I'm a business owner."

I didn't mention I actually owned the whole building, including the bakery next door and Ciaran's Curios. Both Ciaran and Brie leased from me, though neither knew it. I'd bought the building through one of my fake names and figured I'd let that part stay a secret.

"We allowed you to stay because we thought you were just a young witch. You did not bother to introduce yourself to the coven, but we considered that ignorance on your part, not secrecy."

"Coven?" I said. "I had no idea there was a coven." That meant there were at least twelve others. Great.

"We are more powerful than you might believe," she said, folding her arms across her chest. "Do not think you can come after us. Our power will never be yours."

"I don't want your power; I have my own, thanks." I dropped all pretense of politeness and glared at her. "I'm staying right here. Live with it."

"You have thirty days to leave. After that, we will make life very, very unpleasant for you," she said, her mouth pressing into a tight pink line.

"Oh, for fuck's sake," I said. "Are you seriously threatening me?"

"Thirty days," she repeated. "Or else . . ."

I started to ask her "Or else what?" but was interrupted by Ciaran.

The leprechaun who had been my friend and neighbor for half a decade filled the doorway of my shop and clapped his hands together sharply, drawing both my and the witch's attention.

"Peggy Victoria Olsen," he said in a booming voice that was completely at odds with his short, stout stature. "You will not threaten my friend. Leave. Now."

"Ciaran, do you know what this woman is?"

"She is my friend," he said. "You have no power here, Peggy. No authority. Go. I am not so much a gentleman that I won't make you leave by force if I must."

Peggy the witch librarian sniffed loudly and turned on her heels. She stomped past Ciaran, who moved aside just enough to let her pass.

I wanted to hug him but settled for thanking him profusely in Irish.

"Think nothing of it," he said, accepting the offer of a seat in Harper's chair. "I do not care what you are. Only who."

I narrowed my eyes. "You've known this whole time, haven't you?"

He winked at me and tugged on a springy red curl near one of his oversized ears.

"It's a poor leprechaun I'd be if I couldn't keep a secret or three," he said. "Ah, there is Miss Azalea with your lunch, I think." He stood up. "You are welcome for tea anytime, Jade Crow."

"As are you, Ciaran Hayes," I said formally, offering my hands.

He took them and squeezed briefly. Then, exchanging a greeting with Harper, he breezed back out my door with the same energy he'd entered with. I felt a deep relief that he was still on my side.

"What'd Ciaran want? Don't tell me he's banning you, too?" Harper said as she put the bag of sandwiches down on the counter.

"No, he's still my friend. The librarian, on the other hand . . ." I sighed.

"Mrs. Olsen? What did she want?"

"She's a witch," I said. "And she's given me thirty days to leave town. *Or else.*" And with that, I collapsed into giggles, because it was better than crying or screaming.

CHAPTER SEVENTEEN

After staying at the Henhouse for a few nights, it felt strange to be alone in my apartment again. I took a long bath and then put on a season of *Clone Wars*. I needed something fun to distract me from the events of the day. At least no one else had come in and threatened me or banned me from their business.

I picked up the folded copy of the *Wylde Gazette* I'd grabbed from the counter in the store where Harper had abandoned it. The front-page article was about the Lansings. They had been reported missing on Tuesday by Jed's sister. Last night, they had been found, following a huge search effort. Their car had apparently gone off the road and caught fire in one of the twistier parts between there and Bear Lake. The bodies had been so burned that the cops refused to confirm it was the Lansings, but the VIN on the car matched, so the paper was comfortable reporting it.

I didn't know how Alek had managed that one, but I guessed it gave the family closure while still protecting the shifters. Balance again. I sighed and tossed the paper into the recycling.

I heard the creak of someone coming up my back stairs and paused by the kitchen door. A light tap followed, and I opened the door.

Alek stood there with a bag of Chinese in his hand and a gentle smile on his face.

"You are getting sloppy," I said. "I heard you coming up the stairs."

He shrugged. "I made noise on purpose."

"Sure you did. That lo mein?"

We settled down on my couch with chopsticks and passed the boxes back and forth, just eating and sharing company for a while. After my belly was full of noodles and spicy chicken, I told him about my day.

"It will be more difficult for you here now," he said with a sigh. "But you will stay?"

"Of course," I said. "I'm sort of in for the penny and the pound at this point. I am done running away from my problems. From now on, I run at my problems, preferably armed to the teeth."

"Good," he said.

"What about you?"

"Me?"

"Yes," I said. I set down my chopsticks and curled up on the couch beside him, tucking my feet under his thigh. "The Council didn't send you back here. You told Eva that."

"No. I came back because I missed you. Missed this." He waved a hand around, gesturing at the apartment, at the food, at me. "I ran into Henry at a gas station outside town. He was searching for his mate and recognized me. He thought I was here to help him, and I let him believe that."

"You totally lied," I said, smiling to take some of the bite out of my words.

Alek ducked his head and took a deep breath. "Yes. I maintain that you are a bad influence." That thought seemed to sober him further and he looked at me, searching my face. "Before, when I left? It was because the Council sent me away."

"To help somewhere else, to work a case, right?" I reached out and tucked a stray lock of hair behind his ear.

He pressed his cheek into my palm. "Yes and no. They warned me to stay away from you. They do not want me here."

I looked into his ice-blue eyes and saw shadows lurking there. "What else?" I asked, because I knew there was more he wasn't saying.

"They showed me my death," he said, his voice dropping almost to a whisper, a growl. "They showed me that if I stayed here, I would die."

"I don't fucking accept that," I said, curling my fingers into a fist and pulling my hand back. "They didn't warn you about Eva. They didn't send anyone to stop what happened here. I'm sorry, Alek, but I am beginning to seriously doubt this Council of yours."

I had watched him dying beside me, had felt the poison burning away his heart. No way was I ever going to let anything happen to him. Never. Fuck the Council and their stupid visions. I was a sorceress. I would change the future, make it mine.

"I am as well," he said so quietly I thought I'd imagined the words. He wrapped his hands around mine, warming me. "I still sense them. I still have my gifts, my talisman. I do not know what their plan is. But I will stay here. That is not negotiable anymore."

"Good," I said. "Because we have some serious talking to do."

"We do?" He raised an eyebrow at me. "Should I be nervous?"

"No, but I want to know you, Alek. I mean, I don't even know if you have a family, siblings. Where you grew up. Anything. You've at least met my family."

"You never asked," he said. "And I only met your family because someone tried to kill them and they came asking for help. You didn't exactly share their existence or that you'd been born to shifters before that."

Touché. Another point for Alek.

"All right, so both of us need to be better about this whole actually-sharing thing." I made a face at him.

He dragged me into his lap and tucked my head under his chin. I curled against his impossible warmth, relaxing into him.

"I was born in Siberia," he said, his voice rumbling and making his chest vibrate against my cheek. "In the Irkutsk Oblast."

"Gesundheit," I said.

"Hush, kitten. If you want others to talk, you first must be silent."

I leaned up and nipped his chin. "Go on. Siblings?"

"I have two siblings. A brother and a sister."

"Let me guess: you are the oldest?" He seemed like an oldest, with his overdeveloped sense of responsibility.

"Technically, I suppose. By a minute or so."

"Wait," I said, sitting up and twisting in his lap so I could look at him. "You are a triplet? That's like crazy rare, right?"

"Yes, well, Mother was an overachiever." His eyes were unfocused, looking at memories far away and long ago. I remembered then that he was over sixty years old.

"Was? She's dead?"

"She died giving birth to us. Hemorrhaged, but she refused to shift with us inside her—she was convinced it would kill us. By the time they cut us out, it was too late."

Oh. I laid my head back down on his chest. "Are you close to your siblings? Did your father raise you?"

"We are tigers. I do not even know who my father was." I felt him shrug. "We were raised by my grandmother. She lives still, in Russia. It has been a long time since I spoke with her or my siblings."

"When did you become a Justice?"

"I was sixteen when I was called, chosen. Carlos, who you met at Three Feathers, came to me not long after and took me away to the States for training."

"And you've never been back?"

"I have. But it was not the same."

I understood that, too. "Thank you for telling me," I said.

"Anything," he murmured into my hair.

Anything? I decided to test that. I sat back up.

"When Eva triggered the bomb, did you see anything?" I recalled his face as he looked down at me, the awe there. I had caught hints of that awe in him, speculative glances in the days after.

He looked away from me, staring into the middle distance again. Then shook his head. "I do not know. There was much chaos, people trying to leave, getting the doors open. Your magic shoved me away from you. Then there was a bubble of light, and inside . . ." He shook his head again. "I think I know what I thought I saw. But it is impossible. And the memory is unclear; it won't stay for me to look at it."

"As though it's something you knew but have forgotten and now can only remember that you have forgotten, but not what you forgot," I said.

"That almost made sense," he said, smiling. "But yes, it is slippery like that."

"What do you think you saw?" I asked.

"A dragon," he said softly.

"Oh." I searched my own memory. The heat, the light, that lingering sense of wonder and power. No dragons.

Alek pulled me tight against him and kissed my forehead. "I told you it was crazy."

"Crazy is my new middle name." I nuzzled his neck, glad to be held. Glad he was whole and safe.

"While we are on the subject of crazy things," he said.

"Go on." I licked his throat. He even tasted like vanilla. I probably tasted like soy sauce.

"I love you, Jade Crow," he said.

I froze, my mind going blank for a moment. I struggled to form the perfect response, to find the words to tell him how much hearing that meant to me, how my life was better with him in it, how I wanted to give us a real chance, to make this relationship work and let our past be

ANNIE BELLETT

damned. I hesitated too long, unable to find the right words to begin, and the moment stretched out and became awkward.

So, I settled for a *Star Wars* reference instead.

"I know," I said, burying my head in his shoulder.

And somehow, with those two words, he heard all the things I had meant to say.

CHAPTER EIGHTEEN

Tess watched Samir from the corner of her eye as he spoke quietly into his cell phone. Tension built in his broad shoulders, and his golden eyes flared with power as he snapped the phone shut and turned away from the huge picture window that overlooked the valley below his mansion.

"The assassin has failed," he said.

"I told Tess it wouldn't work," Clyde said in his nasal, whining voice.

Tess vowed, again, to rip out his vocal cords before she killed the little bastard. But Clyde was still Samir's apprentice, sharing her station in life like a sibling. Samir expected them to get along. So, she could go on pretending.

She was faking the rest of her life—why not this little thing, too?

"It was diverting," Samir said. "But now it is Clyde's choice."

Tess knew what Clyde would choose. She looked over to where he sat, resting like a pampered lapdog on the white leather sofa. His blond hair was artfully messy, his silk shirt unbuttoned just enough to show off the smooth muscles of his chest. He was slight but kept himself in excellent shape. Samir preferred his lovers to be in shape. He required beauty in all things around him.

"I want to go," Clyde said. "Enough fooling around. Let me bring you her heart myself."

Jade Crow. Samir's obsession. It grated on Clyde. He hated that Samir cared more for a woman who had left him years before than for the man who lived with him now, fawning after his every whim.

Clyde did not understand Samir. He was young, and he did not yet see the danger in a life lived too long. Boredom was a terrible burden, and Samir was easily bored.

Soon, Tess knew, Samir would grow tired of Clyde. Then the young sorcerer would become another heart for the reaping.

Tess did her best to never be boring. A delayed execution was better than nothing.

She looked at Samir, drinking in his aquiline, dark features and his masculine beauty. She focused on her attraction to him, pushing down her revulsion, her fear, shoving it aside.

"I wish to go as well," she said. She lifted a thin shoulder as though to say "Why not?" To convey to him that she merely wanted in on the fun, that this wasn't an important request either way. If she showed it was important, he might refuse her out of spite. Or start asking her questions that wouldn't be safe to answer.

"I don't need her," Clyde said, staring daggers at Tess.

She smiled blandly at him. "Of course not, dear."

"Enough, both of you." Samir chuckled and shook his head, his expression benevolent and amused but his golden eyes sharp. "You will both go. Bring me Jade's heart. I will make a new container tonight. I will be watching closely. Do not fail me."

"What about her friends?" Clyde asked. "That big blond guy?"

"Do with them whatever you like," Samir said.

Clyde's smile made Tess's skin try to crawl off her bones. She bit the inside of her lip and kept her feelings off her face. Clyde's expertise was in raising demons, in perverting spirits of nature. He reveled in cruelty in ways that surprised even Samir on occasion.

Which was probably why Samir let him live. For now.

Tess's talents were subtler. She would find a way to make Clyde's rapid bull-in-a-china-shop methods mesh with her own. She smiled at Samir and inclined her head. "We will not fail you," she said.

Turning away before her face could betray her thoughts, she left the study. Only when she was safely behind her own wards, in her own room, did she relax.

Jade Crow had escaped Samir not once but twice. She had thwarted his attempts to find her for many years. And now she was visible again, surrounded by magic and inhuman friends. She had killed the assassin Tess had suggested they send after her. Tess had known that Samir wouldn't mind fattening Jade up a little more. Just as she knew he half-expected his errant former protégé to kill both his apprentices.

Their lives meant nothing to Samir.

But Jade's life. Her life might mean something to Tess. Win or die, Tess was certain that the beautiful Native American sorceress held the key to Samir's death.

And that was something Tess was very interested in indeed.

HUNTING SEASON

THE TWENTY-SIDED SORCERESS: BOOK FOUR

CHAPTER ONE ▶

I carefully glued another piece of rice paper beside the front door of Pwned Comics and Games, mirroring it with the one on the inside. The sigil on it was something I'd learned from an assassin named Haruki, and his memories assured me that this bit of magic would work like, well, a charm for keeping out vermin.

If only I could figure out how to modify it for keeping out witches entirely. The first plague Peggy Olsen and her coven had sent me was to set off the sprinkler system in my shop. Fortunately, I've got wards up to protect my goods from water and fire damage, so mostly it was just the pain in the ass of cleaning up a thousand gallons of stagnant, brownish water. I'm not great at wards, but protecting something from the elements isn't too tricky.

I couldn't prove it was witches' work that had caused the inexplicable malfunction in the sprinklers. But when you've got a coven of witches trying to run your ass out of town, every issue starts to look like a hex.

This week, it was roaches. I hadn't even thought to ward against insects. I own the damn building and keep it in shape and inspected. I mean, there's a bakery next door, whose owner was possibly one of the witches. My roach problem was localized, my shop and apartment only.

Thousands of the little filthy critters skittering around. The exterminator said he'd never seen anything like it outside of a big city. Around there, he mostly dealt with wasps and ants.

"Back door is secure," Alek said as I walked back into Pwned Comics and Games.

"Everything lined up?" I asked. When he nodded, I knelt down on the floor and pressed my hand onto the sigil I'd carefully scratched right into the boards. Gripping my twenty-sided die talisman, I pushed magic into the sigil, imagining lines shooting out and conjoining all around my shop and the apartment upstairs. I'd mixed drops of my own blood into the ink I'd used to create the magic papers, a link between Haruki's magical knowledge and my own actual sorcery. His ability to use the sigils and this kind of spell had relied on decades of careful study and many special ingredients in the creation of both paper and ink.

I didn't need the bells and whistles to make magic work. Only my innate ability and the will to make it happen.

Power hummed in my head and a spiderweb of magic spun out between the various bits of paper, igniting them in purple flares. High-pitched squeals and pops resonated around the store as cockroaches of all shapes and sizes poured forth from the dark nooks and crannies of my shop only to burst into purple flame and vanish, leaving no trace but a pungent haze of smoke in the air.

"Lovely," Alek muttered.

Wrinkling my nose at the acrid burned-toast smell, I looked at the front door, still seeing the tracery of magic. Nothing remained of the paper we'd secured around the shop.

"That was cool," Harper said as she poked her head up from behind the counter. "No more bugs?"

"Universe willing, no," I said, letting go of my magic. "We can reopen for business tomorrow."

"The roaches going all vaporizy kind of proves it was the witches, right?" Harper asked.

"Who knows?" I said. "Can't do anything about it, anyway. The moment I retaliate, I'm an asshole proving everything they think about me is right."

Alek slid his warm fingers under my hair and caressed my neck as he gave me a sympathetic look. We'd been arguing about this for weeks now as the one-month "get out of town or else" deadline the coven had given me approached. I wasn't leaving, but I didn't know how to deal with the witches without being a worse bully. I could fry them all where they stood, though I only knew who a couple of them even were. That was the point and the problem, however.

Alek wanted to go put the fear of giant Justice tiger into them. I had convinced him it wouldn't do much good.

I was the bigger person here, both magically and morally. I had to be. I didn't want to be Samir when I grew up, after all.

"Sucks," Harper said. She looked at the clock and clucked her tongue. "I should be getting home, and it looks like you two need to get a room."

I grinned and leaned into Alek's solid heat. "Levi and Junebug still staying with your mom?"

"Yeah, she keeps trying to send them home, but not very hard. You know Mom; she loves having people around. She's going to have to open the B&B again soon, though." Harper shrugged, the motion too casual.

She'd almost been killed by an assassin, the same one whose knowledge I'd just used to de-bug my shop. Her mother's bed-and-breakfast had been damaged as well. None of us were quite sure how to handle the aftermath of the wolf council and Haruki's assassination attempts. Alek's mentor Carlos had told him that he couldn't do their Sunday talks anymore, that things with the Council of Nine, the shifters' gods, were on shaky ground right now as word spread that a Justice had tried to kill an entire building full of alphas. No one knew much, but speculation was pretty wide about how that had even been allowed to happen. Faith could consider itself totally shaken, from what I could see. Even Alek's, though he hadn't said much about it since Carlos had stopped talking to him.

Other than the stupid shit the witches were pulling, the last month had been almost too quiet, a calm that seemed more like a held breath than actual peace. Even Samir's stupid postcards had stopped coming.

I didn't know if it was the calm before the storm, or if this was the eye of the storm.

Only thing we were all sure of was that a storm was coming. Nobody felt comfortable. Nobody felt safe. All I could do was keep training, learn the things Haruki's memories had to teach me, keep gaining power and strength and pray it would be enough to protect my friends.

I gave Harper a hug and a promise to come out for dinner another night, then locked up the store. Wylde, Idaho, dies out on weeknights after about seven in the evening. The October air carried the first hints of winter in it as Alek and I climbed the back steps up to my apartment. We'd get snow soon.

My apartment was roach-free as well; the same lingering scent of charred toast greeted me as I opened the door. The wards had been for the whole building, and I was already sure if they'd worked down in the shop, they would have gone off upstairs too, but it was still comforting to smell the evidence and see the faint trace of power hanging in a protective web around my little place. I was tired of bugs.

Alek started pulling steaks from the freezer as I grabbed a couple of candles, put them on the kitchen table, and lit them with half a thought and a touch of power.

"Show-off," he said, nuzzling my hair as he wrapped his arms around me.

"Practice," I said. "You know, you don't have to cook. We could go celebrate, grab burgers at the bar or something."

"I promised. You rid place of roaches, I cook dinner. Go shower, and dinner will be ready soon."

"You saying I smell?" I turned in his arms and poked him in the stomach.

"Like burned roach," he said.

"That's not me; that's the apartment!"

"Perhaps, but that shampoo you use will drown it out."

I poked him in the stomach again, harder. I knew he liked my shampoo and was just giving me shit. It was nice he felt like joking, at least. "If I have to shower, so do you."

"Then steaks won't be cooked," he said. He smiled at me with half-lidded ice-blue eyes, and a low, purring growl started in his chest as I slid my hand down lower and poked another part of his anatomy.

"They will later," I said, then shrieked as he picked me up and tossed me over his shoulder.

"I accept," he said as he carried me into the bathroom. The doorway was narrow enough that the two of us wouldn't fit and he had to set me down. I had his shirt off and he had mine half over my head when he froze, letting go of me.

"What?" I asked as he turned his head toward the door. Then I heard it too. Footsteps coming up the back stairs.

I yanked my shirt back on as a knock came a moment later. "If that's Peggy the bitch librarian," I muttered, "I'm turning her into a toad."

Gathering my magic just in case, though I had a shield more in mind than a transformation spell, I threw open my door, shivering as the chill autumn air blasted over me.

Not a witch or a librarian. Just Vivian, the local veterinarian and a wolf shifter. Her thick down jacket was streaked with drying blood and her eyes were dark, tired hollows.

"Please," she said. "I don't know who else to go to. We need your help, Jade Crow."

CHAPTER TWO

Vivian explained very little, ushering us out the door as we grabbed coats. She told us only that she needed my magic to help her with a hurt animal and that it was better if I just saw things for myself.

"I can't heal for shit," I said.

She shook her head, halfway down my stairs already as I zipped on my hoodie and followed.

"It isn't like that, not exactly," she said over her shoulder.

"You said 'we'—who is 'we'?" Alek asked as he followed me out and settled his gun into a hastily buckled-on holster. He didn't bother with a coat, having told me more than once that our Idaho autumn weather was like a Siberian heat wave to him.

"Yosemite," Vivian said. "He'll meet us at the Henhouse."

"Mountain man?" I asked, but Vivian was already getting into her car, which she'd left running in the middle of the small lot behind my building. Only, it wasn't her car, because she drove a truck. I recognized one of Levi's loaners and wondered. More questions for later.

I climbed into Alek's truck and we followed the frantic vet out of the parking lot, heading toward Rosie's bed and breakfast.

"Who is this Mountain Man?" Alek asked me as we pulled onto the main road.

"He's sort of a local legend," I said. "Brie is his sister or something, I think. He comes into town sometimes to get supplies, but mostly he lives out in the River of No Return Wilderness. Huge guy, bushy red beard. That's why everyone calls him Yosemite, after Yosemite Sam."

Alek's eyes flicked to me and then back to the road. He clearly had no clue what I was talking about. I opened my mouth to try to explain and then closed it. I could always show him cartoons later.

Vivian broke all the speed limits, and since we were following her, we broke them too. On a night like this, it was unlikely that Sheriff Lee or one of her deputies would be out trolling for speeders. They were likely all at the diner or catching up on paperwork. The whole town was subdued by the apparently accidental deaths of the family who had owned the main supermarket, and the events that had followed among the wolf shifters.

Approaching the Henhouse, we saw all the lights were on out at the barn and saw Vivian's truck and trailer parked there. She pulled up her loaner car beside it and waved us over.

Harper, Max, Levi, and Ezee were all there, crowded around the biggest stall.

"Move," Vivian said, her voice half growl.

Everyone moved. Their faces when they turned toward me were grim and horror-struck. The air fairly crackled with shifter anger. I noticed as I passed that the other stalls were empty, and I wondered where the horses had gone.

Vivian pulled open the stall door, and I looked over the short woman's head as I came up behind her. The barn usually smelled of horse and hay and sawdust, but tonight, all I could smell was blood and something rotten, like a compost heap in high summer.

Yosemite, who had a few inches and at least eighty pounds on Alek, knelt inside the stall, a white horse prone beside him with bloody gashes oozing blackish fluid all along its pale sides and flanks. He leaned back as he turned his head to me, revealing the head of the horse, which he cradled in his lap. A long, pearlescent horn stretched out over a foot from the forehead of the animal.

"Unicorn," I said, frozen in the door of the stall.

"He's dying," Yosemite said. "Fix him."

I crept into the stall. The unicorn's eye rolled toward me, his gaze dark and pained. There was intelligence there, more than I'd ever seen in all my years of working with horses. I'd been a working student at a barn once, during my twenty years of living on the run, and helped Max with their horses from time to time out of nostalgia. I'd ridden show jumpers worth six figures and trail ponies saved from auction. All beautiful. None as beautiful as I imagined the unicorn would have been.

His abdomen was torn open, guts glistening where they weren't caked with blood and woodchips. His breathing was labored, rasping. I didn't know how he was still alive. Unicorn magic, I guess. I understood my friend's anger now, why everyone in the barn looked ready to go to war and tear something apart. Whatever had done this to such a magnificent creature was evil, pure fucking evil.

"I don't know how to heal," I said. I tried to fix Alek once, to drive poison from his body, and almost gotten us both killed instead.

"He could heal, but there's something wrong. I feel magic at work, but it is nothing I've ever seen, something foul and tainted." Yosemite's eyes were multicolored, one green, one blue, like a white cat Sophie had once rescued when I was still in high school.

I knelt down, pushing my sleeves back and summoning my magic. I laid my hand gently on the unicorn's shoulder. His coat was soft and thick; it felt like I was touching rabbit fur instead of horsehair. Closing my eyes, partially for focus and partially because I couldn't stand to see any more exposed guts, I pushed my magic into the unicorn and tried to *see* the taint.

Yosemite was right. Clinging dark magic twisted and writhed within the unicorn, covering the bright pure light of his own innate power. The taint reminded me of those pictures they show you after oil spills, where the animals are coated in inky black sludge, barely visible as a creature beneath the filth.

The magic was alien to me, however. I didn't know how to fight it or how to kill it. I pictured my own power as dish soap and attempted to scrub away the filth. The filth reacted by spreading and writhing, not retreating. Nausea ate a hole in my stomach as I swallowed bile and struggled to retain focus, to keep the magical bond with the unicorn. He was trying to fight, but his light was so dim, his own power nearly extinguished by the filth.

Fireball? No problem. Shields? Lightning? Destruction? Finding lost socks? I was good at these things. When it came to this kind of thing, I was lost. Helpless. I hated it.

A long gasp rattled from the unicorn's throat and he stilled beneath my hand.

"No, you fucking don't," I muttered. I was not letting the unicorn go gentle into that evil damn night.

Turning my magic into a lance, I speared through the filth, reaching for the dimming sparkle of his power. "Rage, rage," I whispered, barely aware of the sound of my own voice.

The iridescent power touched mine and joy filled me, pure and wild. The joy of a flower blooming through the last frost of winter, sunlight breaking warm and golden through a clouded sky. The burble of a brook, clear water cold and sweet on the tongue. The joy of storm winds whipping down a valley and the quiet of a forest buried in fresh snow.

I clung to that joy though it hurt like staring into the sun. I fed it strength, trying to remember every time in my life I'd ever felt like this, giving over everything good and happy that I had for this creature until one memory stood clear.

It's dark and everyone was saying there would be below-freezing temper-atures tonight. I had nowhere to go, so when the little Asian guy offered me a warm meal and somewhere to sleep tonight, I figured even if he wanted a fuck or something, I could talk him down to a handjob. He's pretty short and thin. I'm in a weird old house and he's arguing with two women in the other room. I try not to listen. I guess they don't like the idea of this guy bringing home a street kid, but now I'm not so certain why he did. Seems weird to pick up a kid when you already have two women, right? Maybe they are only into each other.

I'm debating what the wooden clock on the wall might be worth if I can get out of here and pawn it, when the women come in to the kitchen. One starts making me another sandwich. The other sits down across from me at the little table.

"Ji-hoon says you have nowhere to go?" she asks.

"No," I say. I wonder if they will call the cops. I wonder if I care anymore.

"Why?" she asks.

Screw this, I think, but I decide to answer her. "My family kicked me out because I'm not like them." I give her my best hard stare. She can have the truth, but no one will ever get my tears. Not ever, not over this.

She glances at the other woman and they seem to telepathically decide something as she nods. "I'm Kayla," she says. "That's Sophie. We're not like anyone else either."

Then she smiles, and weirdly I know that life has changed, and for the first time in a year, the sun comes out in my heart.

The unicorn's power fed on mine, drinking in my memory, my moments of true relief and joy. Magic—mine, his, I wasn't sure—cascaded through both of us like a tidal wave of glitter. I was barely in control, hanging onto my magic through will alone, unaware of anything outside myself and the unicorn.

The filth burned away as though we'd thrown a match onto gasoline.

I felt bones knitting together, wounds closing. Then the wave ebbed and the unicorn let me go. Reality came back to me in stages. First it was touch, my hand still clutching soft fur. Laughter, voices exclaiming, a sense of deep relief replacing the anger and tension. Cautiously, I opened my eyes.

The unicorn breathed again, his dark eye closed, but his nostrils flaring gently with each easy breath. Blood still stained his coat, red now instead of inky black, but the gashes were closed and only deep pink scars remained where the gaping wounds had been.

"You saved him," Yosemite said as he ran a sweaty hand through his dark red curls. "Thank you." His tone made it pretty clear he hadn't thought I could. I remembered that Brie was his sister or something and wondered what she'd said about me.

"I think he mostly saved himself," I said, stroking the unicorn's fur gently. I didn't want to stop touching him, to release myself from the joy, but I made myself let go. My chest hurt and my legs barely wanted to hold me up as I got slowly to my feet. "What did this to him?"

Yosemite gently laid the unicorn's head on the stall bedding and unfolded himself. He was definitely taller than Alek. "We should talk inside," he said, motioning with his head toward the house.

Rosie and Junebug had joined the crowd outside the stall, but everyone took the cue and made their way to the house, except for Max, who said he wanted to stay and keep an eye on the unicorn after he brought the horses back in. It was a sign how subdued everyone was that both Levi and Harper missed an obvious joke about virgins as we left the barn.

"They went crazy when Yosemite showed up with the unicorn like that," Harper explained about the horses as we walked up to the Henhouse.

"Unicorns are guardians of the wild things," Yosemite said in a deep, smooth voice behind me. "The whole forest will be going mad over what has happened. It was good we were able to save one."

I waited until coats and boots were off and we were settled in the living room before I asked him what he meant by "save one."

Vivian passed me her phone as she and the mountain man exchanged dark looks filled with grief. On it were pictures, flashes of horror taken with a cell phone camera in the dark. Unicorns, at least three, ripped to pieces, their bodies black with filth and gore.

"The Bitterroot pack is guarding their bodies," Yosemite said. "I will have to try to lay them to rest, though I do not know if the forest will allow it."

"Aurelio? I mean, Softpaw?" I said, surprised. "I figured he and his would be long gone from here."

"They were, but dark things have been stirring in the wilds, beasts slain for cruel sport instead of food, spoor from creatures that we've never seen before. He found me and we were tracking a pack of whatever did this when the forest went mad, and I followed the treesong to the unicorns. The stallion was the only one still alive. I tried to use my knowledge to help, but this was far beyond my power." Yosemite's hands clenched into fists in his lap.

I looked closely at him, really looked, now that he wasn't bundled into a thick jacket, and I had a moment. His skin was tanned and freckled, his arms covered in red-gold hair, but his tattoos were visible and looked very old, faded and blue. I made out shapes of animals, a fish, something like a cat, a stylized wolf's head, and spirals mixed in. It reminded me of the tattoos on a Celtic woman they'd found in a bog, her body preserved for a couple thousand years. I reached out magically, touching him with the lightest brush of my power, and felt the answering thrum of his own, smelling to my metaphysical senses like pine needles and the air before a snowstorm.

He looked into my eyes with a suddenly ancient gaze and I let my magic go, lifting a shoulder in a half-shrug of apology. "You are a druid," I said. Hey, if there were unicorns, why not druids? I'd always thought that Brie might be one. "Brie is your sister?"

He laughed, a quick bark that died as soon as it was out. "No, she's not my sister. But I am a druid. Taking care of the Frank is my charge." He looked away, staring into a middle distance, seeing none of us. "And I am failing."

I looked at the phone in my hands, glad the screen had gone dark, and could find nothing to say.

"Hey," Ezee said. He'd taken a seat on the couch next to the druid and now scooted over the scant distance between them, putting a hand on Yosemite's arm. "The unicorn will live, right? And now you have not only the Bitterroot pack to help, but all of us."

"It's true," Harper said. "We've vanquished a little evil in our time, for sure."

Rosie made a noise in the back of her throat, threw up her hands in dramatic fashion, and mumbled something about making tea as she left the room. If I had to guess, I'd say that the idea of all of us, her real and adopted family, running out into the woods to fight evil didn't sit well with her. But she wouldn't stop us, either. After seeing Vivian's pictures, after feeling that filth clotting and killing the unicorn's wild purity, I was ready to go lay down some serious pain on whatever had done it.

A whining voice in the back of my mind told me it might be my fault. This couldn't be coincidence. I didn't believe in it, couldn't afford to, after everything. Somehow, this would be tied to Samir. I felt it in my exhausted bones. I still mentally shut that voice into the closet, however. Nothing I could do but fight whatever came and try to protect the people I loved.

I leaned into Alek's warmth as he wrapped an arm around my shoulders.

"Do you want help burying them?" he asked Yosemite. "I can dig."

"There will be no digging," Yosemite said. "I will ask the earth to take her children inside of her. If they are too tainted, we will have to burn them instead."

Ezee squeezed Yosemite's arm and the druid slid his hand over Ezee's own. I realized that they must know each other, though neither Ezee nor Levi had ever said anything to me about the mountain man. He'd never really come up, since his visits to town were pretty rare, from what I knew. There was a familiarity between them, the kind people only get after years of knowing someone. Or the kind you get between lovers. I raised an eyebrow at Ezee and he raised one back, his expression clearly telling me we could talk later.

Rosie brought out tea and we mostly drank it in silence. The mood was grim despite the miracle I'd pulled off with the unicorn, and I had trouble keeping my eyes open after a few minutes as the aftermath of using power like that hit me. I knew I'd be fine come morning with a little sleep and food in me; my recovery times were getting shorter and shorter as I got stronger. Didn't help the exhaustion now.

Alek and I said our good-byes with a promise to come check on the unicorn tomorrow. Yosemite promised to keep us advised of the situation in the wilderness and call upon me again for help if he needed. We drove home in near-silence and I found myself drifting off in the warmth of the truck cab. Alek touched my knee gently as he parked.

"There's someone sitting at the top of your steps," he said softly.

I could barely make out the shape of a person as I squinted through the windshield at the figure under the porch light. The figure was seated but stood as Alek shut the truck down. It was a woman, in a thin coat that looked like leather, with a thick ponytail of hair spilling off the back of her head. Her face was in shadow as the porch light backlit her, but she didn't seem familiar.

"Want to go get a motel room?" I asked Alek, only half-joking. I didn't want to deal with anything else today.

"Want me to eat her?" he said, smiling.

"She's probably a witch," I muttered, wondering what stupid thing they were going to try now.

"If she's a witch, you can turn her into a toad." He squeezed my knee and climbed out of the truck, letting all the nice warm air out.

Sighing, I climbed out and summoned my magic, wondering if I could turn someone into a toad. The wards around my building weren't going crazy, so she wasn't actively working magic or anything, but they hummed slightly as I checked them.

I stayed at the bottom of the steps and let her come down to me, though the light here was worse. "Who are you?" I asked.

Her eyes were dark and big in her thin, heart-shaped face. She was strikingly beautiful despite her tired look, her face made up as though she'd walked off a magazine photo shoot and found herself on my stairs by accident. She wore a thin leather jacket that hung in a flattering way down to midthigh, jeans, and four-inch red heels, which would have identified her as an out-of-towner if nothing else had. Around her neck was a silver chain with a delicate heart-shaped lock hanging from it that seemed to catch the light and glint on its own.

I stopped breathing as I looked at the lock and power poured out around me in visible, purple sparks as I dragged my gaze up to her face.

"Where is he?" I asked.

I'd had a lock and chain like that once. I'd melted it off of myself over twenty-five years before. Looking at hers, I could feel the blinding pain, the heat on my skin as I forced the magic lock to melt and come loose. As I broke the bond between Samir and myself for good.

"My name is Tess," the woman said. "Please, you have to protect me."

CHAPTER THREE

Wolf, my spirit guardian, appeared beside me, her dark hackles raised but otherwise calm as she stared at the woman. I let the moment stretch out and then sighed as Wolf looked toward me and cocked her head in a silent question.

I let the woman into my apartment. It was late, cold, and I was tired. I wanted to be inside my wards, on familiar ground where at least I wouldn't have to worry about a sniper or some bullshit like that. Wouldn't be the first time Samir had done something underhanded like that.

I pointed at a kitchen chair and said, "Sit."

She sat, her arms wrapping around her body as though inside were colder than out. Looking at her terrified, unhappy face, I almost felt pity for her, but I shoved it aside.

"Why are you still wearing his necklace if you want to get away from him?" I asked.

"I don't know how to take it off," she said, fingering the charm with a shaking hand.

Alek growled. We had taken up positions forming a triangle around her, Wolf's large form to my right and Alek to my left, both where I could see them without having to take my eyes off the woman.

"That's strike one," I said. "Lie to me again and I'll let him serve me your heart for dinner."

"All right," she whispered. "He'll know when I take it off."

That was true. I didn't even need Alek's nod to confirm it. The charm tied her to Samir; it was a promise inside a delicate spell. He and I had worn matching ones, our love made into filigree metal and sealed with power and blood. I felt a twinge that I worried might be jealousy, and angrily shoved the feeling away.

"Where is Samir?" I asked.

"I don't know," she said.

Alek gave a slight nod. Truth.

"Does he know you are here?"

"I am sure he has guessed," she said. "He likes to keep an eye on you."

"How?" I asked. It was something I'd been wondering for months. He seemed to know so much about me that it made me wonder if I'd hidden as well as I'd hoped all these years, or if he'd been busy elsewhere and decided to finally turn his attention to me.

"I don't know that, either," she said. She glanced at Alek as he narrowed his eyes and nodded. "He doesn't like to tell me things. Knowledge is power, and he prefers all the power be his."

I took a deep breath and forced my hand to unclench from my talisman. I had a d20 imprint on my palm that faded as I stared at it. I knew what she meant all too well. Every instinct in my body was screaming at me to fry her where she stood, that this was another trick. It probably was, but I could have been looking at myself twenty-five years before. If I had known of a former lover of his, of someone who got away, would I have gone to me for help? I thought perhaps I would have.

"Why come to me?" I asked, pacing the short distance across my kitchen. I let my fingers trail through Wolf's fur, her strength reassuring.

Tess gave me an odd look. She couldn't see the giant black wolflike creature I was petting, so my gesture must have appeared odd. Most of the time I avoid interacting with Wolf in front of people for that reason, but tonight I really didn't give a fuck.

"You got away from him," she said. "He's going to kill me, eat my heart, and take my power. It's what he does."

"Yet you swore devotion to him," I said, indicating the heart-shaped lock.

"As did you, once," she said, her full lips pressing together and her chin coming up in a new show of will. In the better lighting inside my apartment, her irises appeared to have deep reddish-brown whorls in them, her eyes taking on the color of firelit brandy. She looked like a perfect damsel in distress, damp ringlets escaping her ponytail, her body not so thin that she didn't have an obviously heaving bosom to complete the picture. She could have given Queen Amidala a lesson in distressed bosom-heaving.

I gathered my scattering thoughts.

"Are you here to kill me?" I asked.

"I want free of Samir," she said without hesitation. "I think you have the best chance of anyone of protecting me and killing him."

Alek pressed his lips together and nodded with a grimace. I didn't need him to tell me she spoke the truth, though the confirmation was nice. I could hear her desire in her voice, read it on her terrified but determined face.

I sank my fingers back into Wolf's fur and closed my eyes. I was so damned tired of everything. The wild joy the unicorn's magic had spawned inside me had shined a light into my exhausted heart. I didn't want to run anymore, but the waiting was killing me, bit by bit.

Waiting for Samir to make a move. Waiting for someone else to try to hurt me or the people I loved. Waiting for the right moment, for some day in whatever future I had where I'd somehow trained enough, gotten strong enough, become someone who could stand up to him and say, "No more."

I felt like the characters in the second act of my favorite musical, *Into the Woods*. I wanted to belt out the lyrics to "No More" and crawl under the covers. There was no convenient orchestra for me there, however, and I was pretty sure my audience would ruin the drama of it. No more hiding for me. No more running. No more waiting.

Perhaps Tess was a gift, a tool placed in my hands by fate.

"Fine," I said, opening my eyes to find Tess and Alek watching me, both of their expressions grim and guarded. "You know where Samir lives? Let's go. Tomorrow, you and me. If he's not there, we'll wait for him."

"But—" She stuttered, stopped, then started again, "I don't know where he lives. I mean, I know he has a mansion in a valley, but I couldn't tell you where it is."

"Why not?" I asked. Samir and I had lived in a beautiful house in Detroit after he had seduced me away from New York. He'd let me come and go as I pleased, though my freedom had been an illusion, and I hadn't wanted to leave him, anyway. Not until the end.

"He always flies me there in a private plane, then a helicopter. Everything is warded and I'm always blindfolded. If I want to leave, I have to go the same way. I don't know if it is even in the States. The landscape is carefully groomed; too many differing plants for it all to be native." She spread her hands. "You hurt him, and now he doesn't trust anyone or anything."

"*I* hurt *him*?" I choked down a bubble of irrational laughter, swallowing it like an unpleasant burp. "He nearly killed me. He . . ." I stopped, my eyes burning as I blinked back tears. This woman was a stranger; she didn't need to know about my losses. She was dangerous, sincere or not. Having her there was a mistake, for both of us. Especially if she couldn't help me.

"So, you can't tell me where he is or where he will be?" I reiterated.

"No," she said. "Though I imagine he'll come for you eventually. He's reluctant to face you. That's why I'm here. You are the only person he seems wary of."

That was mildly comforting. Very mild. Like tepid-bathwater mild.

"Take off your charm," I said, forcing away any pity I felt for her. I'd melted mine off, not knowing the trick of opening it. I was curious how she would do it, and I didn't care if Samir knew she had. Let her prove herself if she wanted my help. I wanted to feel her magic, to see it.

She lifted her hand to the necklace and her sleeve slipped back, revealing a silver charm bracelet. Only one charm dangled from it, a cross with a tiny crucified body on it. Her power, when she called it, was cool and crisp to my senses, tasting somewhat like sucking on an ice cube. She closed her eyes and hummed a soft, clear note. The air around us grew thick and still, as though time itself hung for a moment on that note. With a quick tug, the necklace broke free, sliding through her neck as though the chain or her throat were merely illusion.

It was amazing . . . and terrifying. Not because she used a lot of magic, because she hadn't. I felt only the merest breath of power, barely more than I had exercised earlier that night when lighting the candles now burned to nubs on my kitchen table. It was her control, her finesse, what she managed to do with so little magic.

I knew in that moment that whoever Tess was, I would be stupid to underestimate her. And more stupid to keep her around. Either she had been sent by Samir to kill or weaken me, or he'd severely misjudged his new apprentice and lover. Maybe both.

And yet I was tempted. She seemed so afraid, so certain he would kill her. Which he would, sooner or later. It was what Samir did, after all. She had knowledge of magic—I felt it, saw it in her economy.

"How old are you?" I asked, unable to keep the awe out of my voice completely.

She looked up at me, surprise flickering in her brandy-colored eyes. She started to turn her head slightly and look at Alek, but seemed to think better of it. "Older than you," she said. "I was born a decade or so before the American Civil War."

"You avoided Samir for more than a century, no?" Alek asked her.

"Yes, but I could not do so forever. He has eyes and ears everywhere. The moment anyone gains enough power to be noticed, to be identified as a sorcerer, he pounces. The pretty ones, the young ones, he keeps as lovers until he grows bored. And it seems he grows bored more quickly with each passing decade." Her body was tensed, poised for flight.

I got the feeling she hadn't planned on telling me these things, had hoped I would take her at face value. I hadn't been around a hundred and fifty years, but I wasn't exactly born yesterday, either. She was good at deception, and I wondered what I would have done if I hadn't had Alek here to keep her on the truthful path.

"Look," I said. "I can't trust you. You fear me, too. This is a disaster in the making and we both need to just admit it. I believe that you are genuine in your fear of Samir. You don't strike me as a stupid woman, and I'm guessing you figured you could pretend you were a naïve young thing for a while until you found a way to bring him down or get away. How am I doing?"

"Better than I expected," she said, the ghost of a smile touching her ruby-red lips.

"I can't help you. I am not sure I would if I could, honestly. I mean, I'll do my damnedest to bring that bastard down if he ever deigns to show himself, but having you here is just one more fucking worry I don't need on my plate." I paused as I realized her showing up here and the unicorn getting mauled were probably related. Coincidences? Don't exist on my planet.

"You can help—" she started to say.

I cut her off with a raised hand. "You know anything about evil creatures in the woods killing unicorns?"

"What? Unicorns?" Her confusion seemed genuine, and Alek raised an eyebrow at me. "Unicorns aren't real."

"I just patched one up tonight," I said. I still didn't believe in coincidences,

355

but it was clear that if the unicorn murders were related to Tess, it wasn't in a way she was actively in on.

"Unicorns are real?" she said.

"Yep," I said. I took a deep breath, marshalling my thoughts. She couldn't tell me where Samir was. She was dangerous in many ways, most of which I probably hadn't even thought through yet, because damnit, I was tired as hell and hadn't had time.

"You can't stay, Tess," I said, trying to be kind. "You need to destroy that charm and then run, far and fast. Don't use your magic. Hopefully, Samir will think you came to me and that I'm hiding you. His attention, at the least, will be divided, right? So, you've got a chance. Take it. You need money?" I doubted from her designer clothes that she did, but who knew how controlling Samir had gotten.

"No," she said. "I have money. But I have nowhere to go."

"Neither did I, twenty-five years ago," I said. "I made do. You're a survivor, I bet. You'll be fine. Run, and don't look back."

"I can help you," she said. "You are powerful, right? But I know magic. I've been using it a long time. We can be stronger together than apart. Two against one. Don't send me away, Jade Crow. Please."

I think she would have sunk to her knees if she'd thought it would help, but instead, she rose, staring me down eye to eye. She was white, her skin milky pale, and her hair was a deep reddish-brown with a gentle curl to it, but in other ways, she and I were mirrors of each other. Nearly the same height, though her heels were giving that illusion, same thin body type. I lacked her generous chest, but we shared high cheekbones, dark eyes, long hair.

I wondered if her desperation and terror had ever been reflected in my eyes. I guessed it probably had, the day I'd shown back up on my adopted family's doorstep. The first time I ran from Samir.

It broke my heart a little to turn and walk away. I opened the kitchen door, letting the cold October night sweep inside.

"I can't help you," I said. "You are a risk I can't afford. Go. Run."

She left without a word, leaving behind a silent room and the faint scent of blackberries.

I closed the door and leaned into it, listening to her footsteps retreat down the stairs. Only after I heard a car engine start and the crunch of tires on gravel did I turn and look at Alek.

"Did I just make a horrible mistake?" I asked.

"Perhaps," he said. "That was cruel."

"Geez, tell me how you really feel and totally don't hold back."

I unzipped my hoodie and hung it beside the door, then walked past Alek and into the bedroom. My limbs and heart felt like lead, and I debated crashing without bothering with clothing or shoe removal. Alek had been sleeping over most nights, so we'd made a nest of quilts on the floor. It looked safe and inviting, if empty without a twelve-foot white tiger keeping watch over me.

Said tiger in human form came up behind me and pulled me into his arms. He tucked my head beneath his chin.

"It was cruel," he repeated. "But I understand. She is a dangerous unknown. There is too much at stake here, and we cannot trust her."

"The good of the many over the good of the one," I muttered. I felt shitty anyway. I had told her she was alone, on her own. She wasn't one of us, part of me and mine.

The safe decision, perhaps even the smart one. Definitely not the kind one. It was not what Sophie or Todd or Ji-hoon or Kayla would have done.

And look where it got them, the cold part of my heart whispered. *They are dead.*

I turned my face into Alek's chest and let my tears soak unnoticed into his shirt.

CHAPTER FOUR

The next day was completely and almost suspiciously uneventful. I hung around my shop, half-expecting every person who walked through the door to be Tess, but none were. My friends were all busy with unicorn fever, taking turns watching over the recovering stallion. There was a minor argument over the name to give him, but common sense had prevailed and we all agreed on Lir, after the prince who had loved the last unicorn.

Depressing thought, really, in some ways. As far as Yosemite knew, Lir wasn't the last, but he might be the last in this wilderness. Unicorns were very rare, the druid said, and thrived only where the wilderness wasn't overly damaged. That was precious few places in the world anymore.

Harper called me two days after and said she was running late, so I opened the store by myself. Alek had gone with Yosemite into the woods that morning, leaving our makeshift bed in the wee hours with a soft kiss and assurance he wouldn't do anything stupid like get himself hurt or killed. I tried to pretend I believed him.

I was tidying up things that didn't really need tidying and avoiding doing translation work, which is what I do to actually pay the bills that comics and games don't cover, when Brie walked in. The tall baker was without her usual apron, but she had a box in her hands that smelled like sugar, spice, and everything buttery, fattening, and delicious.

It had been exactly a month since she'd told me in no uncertain terms that I wasn't allowed in her shop, that she wanted nothing to do with me, and that she considered me and my kind the epitome of all that was wrong with everything, ever. Well, those weren't her exact words, but she'd been pretty clear she meant it. I had been shocked and hadn't had the heart to tell her that she paid rent to me every month, though for a second I'd been tempted.

"Don't give me a look like that," she said, setting the box down on the glass display counter that ran down one side of my store. "Iollan told me what you did. I admit I might have judged too harshly and too quick."

For a moment, I couldn't figure out who Iollan was. "Yosemite?" I said.

She nodded, bright red curls bouncing with the motion, and looked down at the box. "I brought those little cupcakes you and Harper like."

"This mean I'm allowed to talk to you again?" I asked, raising my eyebrows. I really was trying to be civil, but her outright rejection of me had stung. But I really did miss those damn cupcakes.

"I knew a sorcerer once," she said, her eyes meeting mine. "He talked a woman I loved out of her home, away from family, hearth, and all who loved her. When he tired of her, he took her heart." Her eyes were shadowed with pain and she swallowed visibly.

"Sounds like we might know the same guy," I muttered.

"I guess we might," Brie said. "I do not like losing the ones I love. Ciaran assures me that you are different, but it is hard to trust."

I flinched inwardly at that. It *was* difficult to trust, and I was feeling the full consequences of that these last two days. I wanted to cast my eyes skyward and tell the universe that it was okay, I got the freaking message already.

"I'm glad I could help the unicorn," I said instead.

"I am also," she said. "He would not have let you help if you were of an evil disposition, I don't think."

Remembering that wild rush of power, the pure joy, I knew she was right. I tried to take some comfort in it.

"I am not sure I am very good," I said. I brought my hand to my mouth, surprised. Damn out-loud voice, sneaking up on me.

"None of us are only one thing or another," Brie said with a gentle smile that made her look strangely ancient and almost painfully beautiful from one breath to the next.

I wondered what she was, revising my idea she was just a hedge witch. I made a mental note to ask Ciaran when he got back from his latest antique-buying trip. Not that I expected a real answer from the leprechaun. He had a way of keeping secrets.

Brie had to get back to her bakery, and I resigned myself to waiting for Harper before I opened the cupcakes. Harper would never forgive me if I ate them without her, and it wouldn't be worth the whining and reproach. Besides, she'd be shocked that Brie and I had made up. I couldn't wait to see her face when I told her. So, I turned to my computer and opened the latest work file, making my brain move away from the world of unicorns and mysterious red-haired people with ancient Irish names, and to Japanese car documentation contracts that needed to be put into English.

Harper's face was priceless when she showed up that afternoon and saw the box from Brie's bakery sitting on the counter.

"Did you check for traps?" she asked after I told her the story of my morning.

"Nope, I figured I would wait until the rogue got here."

"Maybe there's an invisible ooze or something," Harper said, poking at the box.

"Maybe it is poisoned. Should we call a cleric?" I sniffed the box, though I didn't really need to, since the smell of sugar and lemon had been taunting me for hours now.

"Tell Max he can have my Game Boy," Harper said, pulling open the box and lifting a mini-cupcake out. She popped it into her mouth.

"It's a good day to die," I said, snagging a cupcake and following suit.

Harper replied but I couldn't make out a word of it around the mouthful of cake. Guess I'd finally found a language I didn't understand, har har.

"How's Lir?" I asked when we'd finished off all half-dozen cupcakes.

"He's standing but still pretty weak. Max won't leave his side. It's kind of cute. But I get it, you know? I could almost like horses as much as he does if they all looked like a unicorn." Harper flopped into her usual chair and pulled her laptop from her backpack.

I almost told her about Tess, but she started humming and wasn't paying any attention to me at all, so I turned and went back to translation. The weather outside had turned blustery, and rain spat from the sky. It was a weekday, so there wasn't much traffic through the store. We worked in near silence, Harper playing *Hearthstone* and swearing about the RNG gods.

Possible conversational openers ran through my head. I wanted to share what had happened with her. She was my best friend. I trusted her more than anyone, maybe even more than Alek. I was afraid I'd made a horrible mistake with Tess, that I'd turned away someone in real need over stupid fears. I wasn't sure what I wanted Harper to say, how talking to her about it would assuage the guilt and doubt eating me alive, but it was getting messy to keep it inside. Part of not hiding anymore meant trusting the people around me with the ugly things as well as the good.

Besides, for all I knew, Harper would say good riddance, tell me in her best Mr. Torgue impression that Tess was going to betray the fuck out of me, and I'd find some kind of closure there.

"So," I said, "I had a visitor the other night."

Harper looked up from her game and tipped her head to one side. My face must have given away that this was serious, because she slapped her laptop shut and set it on the counter beside where my phone was charging.

My phone buzzed, choosing the worst time, of course. I checked the text and saw it was from Alek.

"What's the word?" Harper asked.

"Nothing. He and Yosemite are doubling back; he says the trail keeps going in circles." I closed my phone after checking the battery level. I'd bought a cheap one this time, having lost the last two in pretty quick succession.

"So, someone came to see you?" Harper said.

The bell chimed as a figure pushed through the front door. This business would be so great if it weren't for the customers and their immaculate sense of timing, right?

Only, it wasn't a customer. It was a bloody witch. Well, not literally bloody. Not yet.

"Hello, Peggy," I said to the head of the Wylde coven, putting a bit of frosty power into my tone so that my breath literally puffed with chill. I wasn't above theatrics, even if I couldn't turn her into a toad. Not yet, anyway, not before I heard her out. It would be impolite.

"Today is the thirtieth day," she said, no preamble, no pleasantries. Her hair was in its perfect bun, though damp from the rain, and she held a dripping umbrella in one hand, which she pointed dramatically at me. "You are to be gone from this town by dawn or else."

"Oh, for fuck's sake," Harper said. "Ms. Olsen, you are a total asshole, you know that?"

"Out of respect for your mother, young woman, I will ignore that you run with such a crowd and spare you."

"Spare me what?" Harper said, coming around the counter. "Plagues of bugs? Snootily looking down your nose at me? You are a fraud, all of you stupid witches. Jade could fry you like hotcakes into dust with a wiggle of her little finger, you dumb bitch. But you know she won't, which is why you feel okay threatening her, right? 'Cause you wouldn't be so goddamn stupid if she were actually dangerous."

Wow. I sat back, forgetting to be mad for a moment. I'd never seen Harper go after anyone like that, not even in the infamous flame wars on the net that she often found herself immersed in. I had to admit I was impressed and more than a little warmed by her profanity-laden defense and display of friendship. I prepared a shield, holding my magic tightly, my hands loose on my thighs, just in case Peggy the librarian got frisky when challenged.

Harper's jeans pocket began playing "The Imperial March" at the same time as my phone rang with "Bad to the Bone." It sounded like Max was calling his sister at the same time Levi was calling me. That couldn't be good. I froze, unable to decide between going for the phone and dealing with the witch.

"I will not be spoken to like this. You will rue this day, both of you." Peggy stuck her nose in the air in a bad high-school drama way and shook her umbrella. "Hexen!" she shouted. The lights, my phone, both computers, and, judging from Harper's sudden leap sideways and subsequent outpouring of swearing, Harper's phone all flickered, crackled in spectacular sparks, and died.

Peggy fled as soon as it happened, making a very undignified exit out my door as quickly as she could.

I had no time to get a shield up, distracted by the ringing phones and more expecting an attack directly on Harper or me, not our poor innocent electronics. Summoning light into my d20 talisman, I held it aloft and surveyed the damage. The bulbs in my strategically placed lamps had all turned smoky black. Greenish, acidic smoke trailed off both computers. My phone was a useless brick of plastic. Light still shone from the streetlamps and the bakery, so I had hopes the hex hadn't damaged anything outside this room.

"She fried Cecilia!" Harper cradled her laptop in her arm, blowing at the smoke.

"I really hate witches," I said.

"We could go after her," Harper offered.

"Nope," I said. "We can't. One, she's probably in a car halfway across town by now, and two, you were right. I can't do shit about this without looking like a total asshole."

"I'm revising my opinion on that. This is, like, totally the gauntlet thrown, dude. So not cool." She opened her laptop and tried to turn it on, but we both knew it was a doomed act. "You would think she'd obey that threefold law thing. Bitch."

"*Threefold law thing?*" I asked.

"Yeah, I read it in one of the Wiccan books at the library. Supposedly, if you do magic, it comes back to you threefold, especially the bad stuff. So, like, you are supposed to avoid cursing people and crap, 'cause it'll just go like mega worse for you. Haven't you ever seen *The Craft?*"

"Guess I missed that one," I said. Wheels in my brain started turning as an idea began to form, as ephemeral as the dissipating smoke from my dead computer. "We should figure out why the guys were calling us, and then you can tell me more."

We never got the chance to do either. Brie rushed through the door into the mostly dark shop, cell phone in hand.

"They are under attack," she said. "We have to get to the Henhouse."

CHAPTER FIVE ▶

Clinging to the oh-shit handle in Harper's car as we barreled down the road toward the Henhouse, I finally understood the phrase "hell for leather." Brie was crammed into the back seat behind me, hanging on as well. All she knew was that Rosie had called her, saying there were demons trying to get to the unicorn, and telling her to go find me.

Harper pulled a turn worthy of an action movie as we hit the driveway for the B&B and bounced down the slick gravel driveway. The floodlights were ablaze around the paddocks and barn as we pulled up. The barn doors were closed, but the hayloft door was wide open, figures backlit against it. As I sprang out of the car before the engine had even died, I heard the panicked scream of horses followed by the crack of a rifle.

Rosie and Junebug stood side by side in the open doorway of the loft, rifles in hand, shooting into the seething mass of bodies around the paddocks. Max, in his wolf shape, and Levi, in wolverine shape, guarded the barn doors from the demons. I couldn't see Ezee.

"Demon dogs" was a more accurate description. The creatures were about the size of Great Danes but heavier, with muscles that bulged beneath mottled grey skin. They had single eyes in the middle of their thick heads and single horns curving out between ratty, floppy ears. The horn was nothing like the unicorn's, more like an elongated rhino horn, pitch black in color and shiny as though wet, glinting in the light from the barn. Long, spike-like teeth gleamed in their widely gaping mouths, and their claws would've made a velociraptor feel inadequate.

In other words, the demons were ugly and scary as hell.

I charged right toward them, trying to count as I went, magic singing in my veins as I threw a bolt of force into one demon, drawing the attention of three others, who peeled away from trying to approach the barn door and charged at me. The bolt sizzled with purple fire as it threw the dog off its feet, but the creature rolled with the blow and joined its buddies in charging me.

Time for more firepower.

A large red fox streaked past me, snapping at a dog as she went, distracting the creatures from their charge as she flew by them.

"Harper," I yelled. "Reflex save."

She understood and dodged at a ninety-degree angle, using her superior speed and smaller size to advantage.

I threw the Fireball, pushing every frustrated, pent-up bit of anger I had into it. Which was a lot, apparently. I couldn't fry the annoying witches, I couldn't take back sending Tess away and being a terrible person, but damnit, I could throw down some serious burning pain on these reeking, evil monsters. It was nice to have something I could fight. Finally.

The ball of fire blew into the middle of the charging pack, changing growls and snarls to screams of pain as the dogs split in different directions. Two in the middle collapsed, burning and writhing. I cleared a path to my friends in front of the bar with a second Fireball, trying to keep the range and size tight. Brie sprinted up beside me, a freaking longsword in her hands that blazed with white fire. I gawked as she twisted and spun, stabbing one of the dogs through its eye.

"Go for the eye," she gasped as we ran.

I did just that as another ugly monster sprang at me. I was too close to the barn now to risk another Fireball. I aimed at it with a bolt of purple force. My bolt slammed into that red, evil eye, and the monster fell, not even twitching as it died.

"Go for the eyes, Boo!" I yelled, euphoric with the power running through me as I reached my friends.

Putting the barn door to my back, I surveyed the battlefield. The stalls were closed off from the paddocks by heavy metal doors, unlike the more decorative wooden door behind me. Junebug and Rosie were doing a good job of shooting the eyes out of anything that came over the fence into the small space of the paddocks. The demon dogs seemed intent on getting into the barn, but the women with rifles and the steel doors helped create a funnel toward Levi, Max, and now Brie, Harper, and myself. The pack decided the bodies looked easier to go through than the metal, but they hung back now, gathering in a dark half-circle at the edge of the light. More bodies were visible in the tree line.

"How many of them are there?" I asked, throwing another bolt at another glowing red eye. My bolts weren't quite quick enough at this distance, and the monster dodged it with preternatural speed.

Beside me, Levi shifted to human, his breathing ragged and his lips still peeled back from his teeth in a snarl.

"At least two dozen," he said. "They got one of the horses, and Ezee is injured. He's inside. And he'll be okay," he added as I glanced at him, concerned.

"The fuck are these things?" I said.

"Fomoire hounds," Brie answered. "Creatures of filth and evil. They are here to finish the unicorn, I think." Her hair had come loose and spilled in deep red waves down her back and over her shoulders, and her green eyes glowed as though lit from within. I'd never seen anyone look so badass in a flour-dusted apron before.

"Great, so we kill them." I rolled my shoulders, gathering more magic. I knew it was partially the adrenaline, but I felt ready to take on a couple dozen uglies. The air was filled with the scent of churned earth, gun smoke, and burning flesh. An undercurrent of rot teased at my nose and I snorted, pushing it all away.

The uglies charged, this time with their heads down, horns in front. This made it hard to pick out eyes but easier to Fireball. I was glad for the recent rains as I threw a small orb of flame that expanded and grew with my will and power as it zipped over the ground to smash into the monsters.

At least three went down in flames, but more filled in to take their place. They moved across the open ground between the woods and the barn in a roiling black wave. My euphoria died down as I realized how many there were, but I pulled on more magic, willing another ball of fire into my outstretched hands, determined to take as many down as I could before they reached us. No way were these things going to finish Lir. I hadn't saved the unicorn just to let him die.

My next Fireball was the last I could manage as the first line of hounds reached us. Wolverine-Levi barreled into one, his powerful jaws snapping its leg. Brie waded into the fray, her blade a white-hot streak as it sliced through grey flesh and slashed across red eyes. I refocused my magic, visualizing it as a beam of searing light, one hand now clutching my talisman as I drew on more and more power, ignoring the sweat pouring into my eyes.

Purple fire streamed from my hand in a thin line, cutting into the eye of a hound as it tried to snap at and then gore the quick red fox leaping past. Harper didn't try to inflict much damage, just kept dodging and distracting, her sharp teeth snapping at tendons. Wolverine-Levi screamed in pain as one hound got its claws into him and I smashed my light beam into the monster, clearing it off my friend.

Levi scrambled back beside me, snarling. His shoulder was scored with bleeding claw marks.

"Keep back," I hissed at him as I passed my beam across two more hounds, forcing them to retreat.

He shook his bearlike head and his muscles bunched as he prepared to leap once more into the fray. Harper and Max took down another hound between them, tearing into its hamstrings and flank, and Brie was a killing machine with her sword, but it seemed for every hound we felled, two came to take its place. We were hemmed in on three sides and I was running low on juice.

My head throbbed and I lost concentration, barely managing to avoid a black horn as it swept toward me. I sprang back, my shoulders slamming into the barn door, and threw my hands out, shoving magic at the creature with very little thought beyond *Get it away from me.*

The hound went flying backward like a boulder hurled by a giant, tumbling through the ranks of its companions. The effort left me weak, and red dots swam in my vision. I had spent too much power too quickly.

The hounds retreated for a moment, the ones I'd knocked down climbing to their feet. They closed ranks, still at least a dozen or more of them left, and stalked toward us, walking over the smoldering and whimpering bodies of their fallen kin. Beside me, wolverine-Levi crouched, shoulder still welling with blood. Harper and Max faced toward our open left side while Brie, her apron covered more in gore than flour now, faced slightly right, her sword still blazing, but her breathing audible and strained.

Even the horses in the barn were quiet now, and the rifles had stopped firing. I hoped that Junebug and Rosie were all right, but couldn't risk trying to look up and see.

One of the hounds in the front of the regrouping pack died to a rifle shot and I sagged in relief. They were still up there and still had ammo. It was something.

We straightened up, ready for the next assault. The last assault. I wasn't so sure, if we didn't take them out now, that we'd be able to survive another wave. I shoved that sobering and awful thought away and dragged on the last reserves of my magic, feeling like I was scouring a soup bowl with my fingers for leftovers. Feeling like I *was* the soup bowl.

Beyond the hounds, the trees started to shake. Eerie howls picked up and the hounds seemed strengthened by it. A fresh wave of bodies burst forth from the trees, howling in greeting to their companions. Once again, we were outnumbered by way too many to one.

"Fuck my life," I muttered. I had to manage at least two more Fireballs for us to even stand a chance. It would probably knock me unconscious, but I had to try.

As I gathered power into my hands, bright green light poured out of the forest, and I realized the new hounds hadn't been howling in greeting, but in warning.

You haven't lived until you've seen a red-haired giant wielding a cudgel burst forth from a huge old oak tree on the back of a twelve-foot white tiger. Trust me.

Yosemite sprang from tiger-Alek's back in a cinematic leap worthy of Legolas and smashed apart the skull of a hound, his cudgel crushing through horn and bone as though they were rotten wood. Tiger-Alek's massive jaws ripped a monster's head clear from its body. One of his huge paws, claws extended like a fistful of katanas, swept aside another monster.

Brie cried out something in Old Irish and charged the pack. I threw my last Fireball, the energy crackling out from my hands and fizzling pathetically into the front rank of creatures, doing not much more than singeing skin and angering them. Bending, I yanked Samir's dagger free from its ankle sheath and pushed what little power I could still summon into a half-shield in front of me. I knew the dagger was powerful, but it had come from Samir, and I was loath to use it. Desperate times, desperate measures, and all that jazz.

Yosemite smashed another hound and started yelling, his voice booming across the field as he chanted. Vines and roots exploded from the grass, snatching at the hounds and dragging them down. The ones that ran for the trees found branches that lashed out, the forest around the barn beating any monster that came in reach to death with whomping blows as saplings bent and snapped in their fury.

Wolverine-Levi and I found ourselves fighting side by side again, keeping the barn as much to our backs as we could as three of the hounds decided we looked like less trouble than the bellowing giant, the woman with the flaming sword, or the dire tiger. I slashed with the dagger, painfully aware I had little idea how to fight without magic. My shield held, sparking purple as a hound slammed into it. Pain lanced up my leg as I barely dodged a clawed swipe. I prayed it was only a flesh wound and stumbled back.

My stumble left Levi's side open and a hound sprang in past me, horn aimed right at the wolverine's unprotected side. He twisted, trying to avoid the blow, and a second hound's jaws closed on his leg with a sickening crunch. Levi went down and the first hound sprang onto him, its jaws wide and aimed at my friend's unprotected head. I screamed and threw my shield as though it were a physical thing, trying to turn the killing jaws aside.

Time seemed to slow, then scramble, then speed up again, as my vision stuttered and a blast of air took me almost off my feet. It was as though reality had become a faulty VHS tape recording.

Instead of closing on Levi's head, the hound's jaws snapped shut on Tess's abdomen as she materialized between the wolverine and the hound. She buried a large hunting knife in its burning red eye with a scream.

Adrenaline and power flowed into me, and I threw the dead hound off Tess and Levi. Levi struggled to rise, but Tess collapsed, blood spurting from the gaping wound in her stomach. The second hound sprang for Tess, and I threw every last shred of magic inside me at it.

"NO!" My voice was raw, the word clawing its way from my throat with the roar of blood in my ears.

The hound exploded. Chunks of fetid, warm flesh rained down on me as I stumbled to Tess's side and crouched there, holding the dagger, waiting for the next attack.

It didn't come. The hounds broke and ran, tiger-Alek and Max giving chase as far as the glowing woods. It sounded from the shrieks that the trees did the rest of the killing work. I dropped Samir's dagger and yanked off my filthy tee shirt, pressing it to Tess's stomach.

"I'll live," she whispered.

"I know," I said. "Because you are a motherfucking sorceress, and so am I."

I held her gaze, willing her to stay with me as people came up around us, talking. My head swam in a lake of pain, and darkness pressed in on the sides of my vision. I was vaguely aware of Alek and Yosemite moving up beside me. I let them transfer Tess to a horse blanket and convey her to the house, reluctantly letting go of the blood-soaked tee shirt.

Harper slid herself under one of my arms, and I was surprised that Vivian, the vet, appeared and inserted herself under the other. She had a hunting rifle slung over one shoulder and a grim look on her face. I thought she said something to me, but my brain wasn't up for processing language anymore. Barely conscious, I managed to stumble with their help up to the house. I looked around as we went, making sure I saw each friend. Ezee, in human form, was limping with his twin, who was also back in human form. It wasn't clear who was holding up whom, but they were breathing, conscious, and alive. I didn't see Max until I looked back and caught sight of movement up in the hayloft. Max waved tiredly to me from his perch. Behind him, I could just barely make out Brie's figure, now holding a rifle instead of a sword.

Rosie and Junebug were on the porch, blankets in hand as we climbed the steps. Rosie said something to Harper and then darkness ate my brain.

CHAPTER SIX ▶

I woke up on the couch in the main living room of the Henhouse to the soft murmur of voices and the smell of vanilla and musk. I was wrapped in a quilt with my head resting on a warm, muscled thigh. I knew that thigh, that warm energy, that scent. Alek.

"Hey," I said, struggling to unwrap myself as I turned my head and looked up at him, squinting into the light from the lamp beyond his shoulder.

"You all right?" he asked. He helped me sit up.

"Yeah." If I hadn't been, the concern and love emanating from his ice-blue eyes would have fixed any ill, I was sure. I poked at the yellow-green bruise and thin pink line on my leg that were all that remained of where the Fomoire hound had slashed at me.

"Good to see you again, Jade," said a rough, almost gravelly male voice, and I looked over to see Aurelio, the alpha of the Bitterroot pack, sitting cross-legged on the floor. His shaggy black hair with its shock of bright white was loose over his bare shoulders, and I swear he was wearing the same green sweats I'd last seen him in, a month earlier.

"Wish we could meet when things aren't trying to kill us, eh?" I said. "I thought you were leaving the area."

"I tried," Aurelio said with a grim smile. "Seems my pack is still needed. The forest is unquiet."

I looked around the living room. Judging from how healed my wound was, I'd been out an hour or so. Max was wrapped in a quilt similar to the one around my almost-naked torso and fast asleep in one of the over-size chairs. Harper and Rosie sat at the dining room table, their heads together as they spoke in voices too low for me to understand.

"Ezee is with Levi and Junebug upstairs," Alek said. "They are hurt, but nothing a few days of rest and Rosie's cooking can't cure."

Memories flooded back and I stared down at the dried blood rimming my fingernails. "Tess?" She was a sorceress, like me. She'd live through a wound like that, but it wouldn't be fun.

Alek jerked his chin toward the hall and the room where Harper had convalesced the previous month after nearly being turned into furry BBQ by Haruki the assassin. "Vivian is with her, seeing what she can do to get the bleeding to stop and close the wound."

"She'll heal, like I always do," I said. I stood up, wrapping the quilt around my body like a towel and tucking in the corner, since I had nothing but my bra covering my chest. Alek caught my hand and raised a pale eyebrow at me.

"I'm getting some water," I said. "And maybe finding a shirt."

I walked to the kitchen, not wanting to go see Tess yet. She'd come back. Part of me was relieved, in no small part because she'd probably saved Levi's life by appearing when she had. Part of me was afraid.

It was no coincidence that all this was happening now. I couldn't afford to be that naïve or optimistic. She'd shown up at precisely the right time, hadn't she? I hated myself a bit for being so suspicious. I clenched my hands into fists and went to wash her damn blood off them.

Harper and Rosie both looked at me, but I shook my head in a "later" gesture and they let me pass without conversation. The kitchen was occupied, however. Brie and Yosemite stood there, arguing in Old Irish, keeping their voices low, but clearly not so concerned that anyone would hear them. I paused in the doorway, but they did little more than glance my way before resuming their conversation. Ciaran must not have told them I spoke Irish, or if he had, they assumed he'd meant only the modern language, not all its iterations.

"You cannot come with us," Yosemite said. "Ciaran comes home tomorrow, but he will not be in time. I cannot wait. You know that. If you were to lose yourself without him there . . ." He trailed off.

"You need my help. The two of you alone are not powerful enough if it is what we fear," Brie said. "I cannot let you go into the woods alone, not again."

"Who will stay and protect the unicorn?" Yosemite countered.

"The pack is here, and the sorceress can handle herself."

I finished rinsing my hands and poured a glass of water, taking a sip, swishing, and spitting it out. I drained the cup and turned to face them both. Yosemite's dual-colored eyes were shadowed by dark circles and his thick shoulders were hunched. He looked more exhausted than I still felt, a tree ready to topple in the next stiff breeze.

Brie appeared different. There was no trace of exhaustion around her. Her green eyes were bright, her curls somehow bouncier, and her lips and skin practically dewy with health and youth. She looked ten years younger. Her apron was gone, replaced by a tee shirt that read "Frag the Weak," which I recognized as one of Harper's.

"I'll go with you," I said to Yosemite as they stopped talking and regarded me in turn. I'd already figured the second person Brie had meant was Alek, and I wasn't letting him run off into the wilderness without me again.

"You?" Brie snorted. "You can barely stand up."

"I'll be fine by morning," I said, mostly sure I wasn't lying. I was tired, but the worst of the exhaustion had passed and my magic was there and strong when I reached for it.

"Please, Brigit," Yosemite said in Old Irish. "Stay and wait for Ciaran."

Brigit? The way he said the name rang a bell in my head, but whatever thought it was ran off before I could grasp it. Whatever Brie was, she was no hearth witch.

"Fine," she said after a moment. "You better let nothing happen to him."

"I believe Iollan can look after himself," I said in Old Irish, enunciating the words. "Or perhaps you missed the fight I just witnessed."

"I miss very little. Something it would seem we have in common, Jade Crow," she said, her mood changing from pissy to grinning in the blink of an eye. "I will wait and keep watch while you sleep," she said to Yosemite. She walked out of the kitchen and toward the back door.

"Who is she?" I asked the druid. We both knew I really meant "What is she?"

"That is a long story, and not mine to tell," he said. "I must rest. We will leave at dawn, before the trail goes too cold." He moved to follow Brie, stripping his clothing as he went, his steps lumbering and pained.

I set down my glass. Hadn't expected a strip show. Who were these people?

"He's going to recharge," Ezee said behind me. "He'll sleep out under the sky tonight, his body in contact with the earth. Tomorrow morning when the sun rises, he will be ready to go off and be a big damn hero again."

I looked over at my friend. Ezee wore another borrowed shirt, this one just plain black with a power button symbol on it. His hair was pulled back from his tired face and still damp from a shower. His brown eyes closed for a moment as Yosemite, now stark naked, left through the back door and vanished into the night.

"So," I said. "You and the druid, eh? When did that happen?"

"It didn't," Ezee said. "I mean, it does, sometimes. It isn't serious; we just see each other when he's in town sometimes. Rarely."

"Methinks you doth protest too much."

"Funny," he said, waving a hand at me in a vague STFU gesture.

"Seriously," I said. "You two seem pretty close."

"A bird may love a fish, but where would they build a home together?" he quoted.

"You know, they get together and live happily ever after at the end of that movie," I said.

"What? What movie? I'm quoting *Fiddler on the Roof*."

Ha, whoops. "I thought you were quoting *Ever After*. I'll take NERDS MIXING UP REFERENCES for six hundred, Alex."

We smiled at each other. Our smiles didn't last. Too much had happened.

"You know about folklore and stuff, right?" I said. "Why is *Fomoire* familiar to me?"

"So, you'll actually take WHITE PEOPLE'S LEGENDS for six hundred," Ezee said. "The Fomorians were the original people in Ireland, I think. Irish myth isn't exactly my area of expertise. They were bad folk, but of course, the people who fought against them and destroyed them would say that."

We shared another, sadder smile. Try growing up Native American if you ever want a stark lesson in how the conquerors rewrite history and even myth to suit themselves.

"Yosemite said those demon things were Fomoire hounds. They seemed pretty damn evil to me," I said.

"I'll ask him tomorrow," Ezee said. "Who is the woman that Vivian is trying to patch up? Seemed like you knew her."

Shit. I knew I couldn't dodge this question forever. But maybe a little longer.

"How is Levi?" I asked, aware of how obvious my ploy was.

"He'll be fine, thanks in part to that woman showing up and saving his ass, apparently. So?"

"I'd better tell everyone at once," I said.

"Levi is asleep and Junebug won't leave his side, so the rest of us will have to do," Ezee said, following me into the living room.

Harper and Rosie had moved from the table to the second couch, probably trying to give those of us in the kitchen some privacy. Max was awake, sipping tea.

"Can I borrow a shirt?" I asked Harper.

She jumped up and ran upstairs, returning with a grey long-sleeved tee shirt that had Pikachu on it. Mistake on her part, because I wasn't sure I'd give this one back. It was one of my favorites of hers. I pulled it on and took up a spot on the couch next to Alek.

"The woman who showed up tonight," I said, motioning with one hand toward the room where Vivian and Tess were. "She's a sorceress, like me. Kind of exactly like me." I took a deep breath, searching for the words. "She ran away from Samir this week and came to me. Or so she says."

"Samir?" Aurelio asked.

"Psycho sorcerer ex-boyfriend," Harper supplied. "He's been fucking with Jade, trying to kill her for, like, years now."

"Why didn't you tell us she was in town?"

I glanced at Alek, but he only raised his eyebrows at me. This was my mess, and while his arm came around my shoulders in silent support, he wasn't going to clean it up for me.

"Because I sent her away, or at least I tried to. I don't trust her. You think all this stuff happening right when she shows up is a coincidence? This is more of Samir's stupid games."

"So, she's here to kill you?" Ezee asked.

"I don't know," I said. "She said she wasn't, and Alek says she's telling the truth, but I just don't know. I can't take the chance. Things are dangerous enough."

"If she wanted to hurt you, she has one heck of a way of showing it," Rosie said. "I saw her appear like that, put herself right between that demon and Levi."

"She saved my brother's life," Ezee said. "He told me. And now she's half-dead in that room, her guts everywhere, half her blood on the driveway. Pretty shit plan if she wanted to harm us, no?"

I hated their logic. I hated that I still felt so much suspicion. I hated that I had sent her away and she had come anyway, shown up in my moment of need and done something I had failed to do. Saved my friend.

Letting out my breath slowly, I pushed all the hate away. Maybe that was the problem. Too much hatred for Samir, too much pain, so much it was blinding me when it came to him, to anything he'd touched. Maybe it was time to try accepting Tess at her word, give her a chance.

"I know," I said. "I might be wrong. I'm going to talk to her, see what she knows. This isn't a coincidence."

"Maybe he's pissed that she ran," Harper said. "Could he be here? Summoning those things? They weren't natural."

A small thrill went through me, followed by a spike of dread. If he was here, I wasn't ready. But I didn't know if I would ever be ready.

"I don't know. I'm going to talk to her when she's awake."

Vivian emerged from the room, stepping into the hallway and turning toward us as our worried gazes all fixed on her. She wiped a bloody hand over her forehead, leaving a pink smear.

"She wants to talk to Jade," she said. "Don't overtax her. She's healing, but it'll be a while and she needs rest."

Be a while? I raised my eyebrows at that. Vivian didn't know how fast sorceresses healed. Tess's wound would already be closing after an hour. She'd have a hell of a bruise by morning and probably be tired and slow for a day or two, but by week's end, she would be right as rain with just an ugly, fading mark to show for being nearly bitten in half.

I got up, and Alek followed me. Behind me I heard Rosie offering Vivian a room and a change of clothes.

Tess was in the bed, quilts pulled up to her chin. Her face was pale, her cheeks sunken hollows. She opened her eyes as we entered.

"So," I said. "We meet again."

CHAPTER SEVEN

I sent Alek out of the room after asking him, in Russian, to ward it off for sound. I didn't want the details of the conversation I was hoping to have to reach my friends' ears before I could digest whatever information Tess could give me. Alek looked as though he would protest, but in the end all he did was sigh, set the silvery ward that would soundproof the room, and leave.

Tess watched me with tired eyes as I sat on the edge of the bed.

"How do you feel?" I asked.

"Like something ugly tried to bite me in half," she said, a ghost of a smile playing at her mouth. She was beautiful even with smeared makeup and exhausted circles under her eyes. The effect made her look delicate and ethereal.

"You followed me," I said, then winced. I should have said something like *thank you for saving my friend*, but the words came out way wrong.

"I told you; I have nowhere to go. I thought maybe if I stayed, I could help somehow, convince you I'm not going to kill you." Talking looked like it hurt her, and she closed her eyes.

"Thank you," I managed to say. "You saved Levi. How did you move so quickly?"

"I wish I'd moved faster," she said. "It looked like you would be okay, so I hung back. I'm sorry."

"But how did you do it?"

"Time," she said. She opened her eyes, seemed to have trouble focusing on my face, and closed them again. "My powers mostly revolve around manipulating time. I can slow time down or speed it up, sort of. It is very localized, but I can make myself quick or someone else slow. It's my specialty, like elemental magic is yours."

Elemental magic was my specialty? That was news to me. I was good at throwing around power, good with fire and ice, or just pure magical force. I could do a lot of other things, however, like shields, basic wards, finding things and people. Even breathing underwater now. I'd been trying lately to teach myself to fly, but it was difficult to wrap my head around the whole defying-gravity-for-long-periods thing, so I hadn't managed more than a few feet of gliding so far. Samir had always encouraged me to use as much power as possible, to do the flashy, showy stuff like using fire or turning water to ice. Elemental magic, now that I thought about it.

I had never brought up the D&D spells I'd practiced and learned to control my magic with. The book was from a game for children and I had wanted Samir's approval, had wanted so badly for him to love me and respect me and see that I wasn't just any girl, that I was mature and worldly. I shook my head over how ignorant he had kept me. Hansel in the cage, being fed sweets until slaughter time.

Tess's breathing evened out as she seemed to lose consciousness. Feeling like a creep but doing it anyway, I gently pulled back the quilt and peeled up a corner of the huge gauze pad across her abdomen. The wound was ragged still but not bleeding. The edges were pressed closed as best Vivian could manage without sutures. From the clear beads around edges of the wound, it looks like she might have used glue. I looked around the room and spied a half-used tube of Super Glue on the dresser.

"Making sure I'm really wounded," Tess said.

"Sorry," I muttered. I pressed the bandage back down as gently as I could. "Why aren't you healing faster?"

"I am too tired to speed up time around myself," she answered. "I'll start tomorrow. Even with that, it'll be a couple weeks before I'm whole again, at least. So, I guess I'm not much threat now, huh?" Her chuckle ended quickly in a grimace of pain.

Alek wasn't in the room to tell me if she spoke the truth or not, but I had a feeling she did. A week until she was whole. I would have healed that wound in a day or three at most. My ignorance settled on me like a cloak I hadn't realized the weight of until just now.

"So, you can't use magic other than the time stuff? What about what you did to the necklace?" I asked, trying to get more information without seeming as stupid as I felt.

"I removed it by making myself be elsewhere in time for a moment and letting the necklace remain," she said, as though it were perfectly clear what she meant.

Okay. Yeah. Not helpful. I filed away what she'd said for later examination.

"I can do small things. Power is power, after all, but it does not want to flow in ways we are not naturally inclined," Tess continued. "Have you never tried to do something very different from what you are good at, and failed?" Her eyes were open again and she stared steadily at me, her gaze intense, serious.

I thought about the time I had tried to heal Alek. Healing is apparently super hard. "Sure," I said, trying to nod in what I hoped was a sage manner. "I can't heal for shit."

"Who healed your leg?" She looked at my thigh, where my jeans still sported a bloodstained hole.

Well, fucktoast. I couldn't dodge that question gracefully. "I did," I said. "I mean, it healed on its own."

"You left a scar on him, on his arm," Tess said. "It never healed. He hides it with illusion and sometimes even makeup. He doesn't know I have seen it."

I knew she meant Samir. "It never healed?" I asked, pushing back the tide of memory that came with her words. My last meeting with Samir. My doomed charge to try and kill him after my family had blown themselves up rather than be used to torment and trap me. I'd thrown so much power at him, but it was all a blur in my memory. Wolf had come, had bitten him, the only time I'd seen her affect the physical world like that.

Turning my head, I looked toward where Wolf lounged on the floor. I hadn't even realized she was there, but somehow in that moment, I knew she was and that if I turned my head, she would be there. Life was getting weirder. My guardian perked up her ears and lifted her head. The slash of white down her chest where Samir had wounded her showed starkly against her pitch-black fur.

"That is why I came to you," Tess said. "You got away. You hurt him, hurt him so badly that even after decades, it has not healed but remains puckered and red, as though freshly closed."

"I can't remember what I did," I said, which was partially true. He'd nearly killed me, and Wolf had dragged me away. I took a deep breath and got to the topic I was dreading. It had to be talked about, or I could never even start to trust her. "Do you have anything to do with what is going on? You show up in town, terrible things start happening in the woods. I don't believe in coincidence, Tess. I can't afford to."

"Not directly," she said. "I think I know who might, though. I think it is partly my fault. I'm so sorry." She shivered and I realized I'd left her half uncovered.

"Samir followed you here?" I asked, helping her pull the quilt back up to her chin.

"No, not him, I don't think. Clyde, his other apprentice."

"There's two of you?" Samir apparently had been busy.

She nodded. "Clyde has been with him for a while. He's awful. All of Samir's cruelty, none of his reserve or finesse. I would have killed him years ago if I could, but the idea of eating his heart makes me sick."

"You ever eaten someone's heart?" I asked. She seemed to know what it entailed, at least, which made me think she had.

"Only once," she said, her eyes leaving mine and staring off into the middle distance that was memory.

She did not elaborate, and I found myself unwilling to ask more. I knew firsthand what a weirdly intimate experience it was, having done it twice now. And I understood what she meant about not wanting to repeat it with someone she loathed. The first heart I had taken had been of a serial-killing warlock, and his evil, sickening memories still gave me nightmares sometimes.

I asked her questions about Clyde, and the picture she painted was a bad one. His specialty was in raising spirits, warping them and infusing them with his own cruel and twisted desires. It made me think of Not Afraid, and Tess confirmed that as far as she knew, Clyde had been involved in that, though mostly she thought it was Samir's doing. She claimed she hadn't been, that Samir didn't seem to include or trust her as much as he did Clyde. Apparently, she was pretending to be very young and inexperienced in the hopes that Samir would continue to believe her not worth harvesting yet. She was tiring quickly, I saw, and I decided the rest of my million questions could wait.

"One last thing, just in case," I said. "What does Clyde look like? What does his magic smell like?"

"Smell like?" she asked, her face a picture next to the word *confusion* in the dictionary.

"Magic has a smell, a feel, a taste. I don't know how to describe it," I said, waving my hands in the air. "Yours is cool, crisp, like a frosty morning."

She blinked up at me and her tongue flicked over her lips. "I cannot smell or taste someone else's magic," she said. "I can see the effects, see the obvious things like you throwing fire. I have never heard of anyone who can sense another without taking their power first."

I racked my brain. Surely this was something Samir and I had discussed. I couldn't remember it ever coming up and I wasn't willing to take a super in-depth trip down memory lane to find out if it was something he knew about me or not. "Huh," I said.

"Clyde is blond, looks midtwenties, and is very pretty," she said, her eyes keen but her voice fading almost to a whisper with exhaustion. "He's a little taller than you, but almost as thin, and his voice is nasal, whining. He's also completely devoted to Samir and a total idiot about what Samir will do to him when he finally tires of Clyde."

"Thank you," I said. "Rest. I have to go away in the morning to help hunt down those hound things, but you'll be safe here, I think."

"I can stay?" she said, and the hope in her face broke my heart all over again.

"Yes," I said, because I no longer had it in me to say no.

Max, Ezee, and Harper were arguing in the living room when I emerged.

"What? I'm totally Oona!" Harper said.

"I called dibs on Jack already. I mean, I totally helped save Lir both times," said Max.

"I think that makes us Screwball and Brown Tom," Ezee said with a tired grin.

"So, wait," I said, figuring out after a moment what the hell they were talking about. "I'm Lili, right? I look good in black."

"That would make me Jack," Alek said, rising from beside the door where he'd stationed himself and coming up behind me to wrap his arms around my waist. "But I'm far too tall and blond to play Tom Cruise."

"Wait, you showed him *Legend*?" Harper asked.

I looked up at Alek, impressed. "Nope," I said. "He got this reference all on his own."

"In Soviet Russia," Alek said, smiling down at me and playing up his accent, "references get you!"

When everyone had stopped dying of laughter and shock, we regrouped in the living room. Aurelio had left to check on his pack and Rosie had gone to bed.

"Is she staying?" Harper asked me.

"Tess? Yeah. I think so. I am going into the woods with Alek and Yosemite tomorrow. We might not be back for a couple days. If she tries anything, just cut her head off and stick it in the freezer, and I'll deal with her when I get back."

"I'd laugh, but one, my sides hurt already, and two, I think you are like totally serious."

"Mostly," I said, smiling at my friend. "She's pretty damaged. Just . . . Be careful."

"We'll keep an eye on her for you," Ezee said. "But seems like she could use friends, too."

CHAPTER EIGHT ▶

We gathered just after daybreak. Alek and I had made a run to my apart-
ment to collect things like clean clothes, sleeping bags, and my hiking
boots. Yosemite said he had a feeling where the hounds had come from,
now that he'd seen them, but it was going to be at least overnight to hike
out, maybe longer, since we'd have to track the survivors if we could and
make sure they weren't doubling back for more.

I described Clyde as best I could from what Tess had told me, and
Aurelio said he would pass it on to his wolves. Everyone was going to
stay at the Henhouse. I'd put the CLOSED sign up on my shop, as had
Brie. There'd be some questions from regulars about it, but we'd deal
with those later, I figured.

Tess woke up long enough to promise me that Clyde would get to
my friends only over her dead body. I still wasn't sure what to make of
her yet, but from the grim approval in Alek's eye after she said this, I had
to believe she meant it enough to pass his lie-detector senses. That was
some comfort.

I walked out to check on Lir, the unicorn. One of Max's ponies had
been mauled, a little grey named Merc, but Ezee had told us all about
how the unicorn had touched his horn to the wounds and brought the

pony back from the brink of death. The little gelding would have scars to show, I saw, running my fingers over the long pink lines, but he was alert and munching hay.

Lir greeted me with a huff of air and a gentle bump on my shoulder with his nose. I stroked his uber-soft fur.

"Lend us some luck, okay?" I murmured.

His intelligent dark eyes watched me in silence as I left the stall. He was magnificent, and my heart hurt looking at him, a tightness in my chest full of wonder and fear for his life. I wanted to kick even more Fomoire ass and this Clyde guy, too.

Alek had been right. Killing did get easier, especially when the stakes were so high.

Yosemite explained what he thought might be happening, and to my surprise, he said that he'd spoken with Tess and she agreed it was in the realm of possibility for Clyde to do.

Apparently, back in the time of legend in Ireland, there'd been a really bad dude named Balor Birugderc, also called Balor of the Evil Eye. He'd led the Fomoire against the Tuatha Dé Danann and been slain by a guy named Lugh.

The part of the legend that hadn't made the books and retellings was that the head of Balor had been given to the first druid for safekeeping, and passed on through the ages until it fell to one of the last druids, a youth named Iollan who, after a few centuries, emigrated from Ireland to what became the United States, and buried the head in a wilderness full of powerful nodes and unbroken ley lines.

Working theory was that Samir, and thus Clyde, had somehow learned this and figured out a way to peel back the lid of Balor's evil eye.

"Seven lids," Yosemite said as we hiked. "Balor's power is much reduced by his death, but it could still kill this whole area."

The forest we hiked through was in full autumn foliage, the deep greens of the evergreens mixing with red and gold from birch, maple, and oak. The ponderosa pine needles had turned to flame red, and fallen leaves created a thick carpet under our feet. Deer flashed tails at us as they took offense at our intrusion. We climbed elevation, the forest growing sparser. Many of the bushes and ferns had turned to red and gold as well, and the grasses between boulders and sheets of grey rock were yellowed. For hours, we hiked mostly in silence, moving more slowly than the two of them might have without me. Yosemite would pause and point out a wildflower or a tiny squirrel. His love of the land radiated from him, showed in how he moved through the woods and over the open, rocky areas with ease and comfort.

Occasionally, he would stop and confer with Alek about the trail we were following. I tried to pick out tracks, look for signs, but broken twigs looked like broken twigs to me, and the hounds hadn't left much. Yosemite and Alek agreed about which direction we should keep moving in, so I put my trust in them and tried to keep up.

I'm a nerd, I hang out in my store, I play video games. My idea of a workout was playing paintball for a couple of hours. I'd been getting in better shape over the last few months out of sheer self-defense, swimming, even lifting weights with Levi's coaching. Alek and I had started going for runs now that he was back. I still found myself breathing hard as the sun climbed, hit its zenith, and began to descend.

There was that whole we-could-be-attacked-at-any-time tension, too, which didn't help. I couldn't just relax and enjoy the nature walk. I kept looking around us, waiting for the proverbial killing shoe to drop.

Day moved to night and we set up camp on a wide stretch of open ground on a hill above a large creek. Two huge boulders had crashed together at some point in the last million years and created a wedge-shaped shelter. With rock on three sides, we felt safe enough camping, though we didn't risk a fire. Dinner was protein bars and water.

Alek slept in tiger form, eschewing a sleeping bag. I dragged myself into mine and curled up against his huge, furry side. I was used to sleeping next to a giant tiger by that point. There's something comforting about it, like knowing you have the biggest, baddest mofo in the room on your side, keeping watch over you. Even so, it took me a long time to get to sleep. I stared up at the stars, wondering where Samir was, worried about my friends back at the Henhouse. Eventually, the physical exertion of the day won out and I faded into sleep.

The second day, we crested a ridge and then began a slow, painstaking descent down shale-covered slopes toward a thick patch of forest below. The sky was overcast, but so far, the day was mild for October and it hadn't rained on us. Even to my untrained eye, it was clear something was wrong with the land there. The leaves were off the trees and the trees themselves looked charred, as though from recent fire. The air smelled of smoke and wet charcoal. The grass was all dead—not the aged yellow it had been the day before but a wet, unhealthy, slimy brown color.

"Was there a forest fire here?" I asked. "I don't remember that being on the news." Fires this late in the autumn would have been reported, especially one close to Wylde. We'd hiked all day, but I doubted we were more than twenty or thirty miles inside the wilderness area.

"No," Yosemite said. "This is worse than it was even days ago when I last came this way. I fear I am right about Balor's Eye."

We had hit the bottom of the valley, almost to the tree line, when movement caught my eye. I froze, turning toward the wide expanse of dying grass to my left.

The dead forest covered much of the valley floor and the far side, but there was nothing but open ground to our north. Shale and grass and brush spread out from the edge of the dying forest in a wide plateau. In the very edge of the distance I could see, a huge grey boulder stood up and shook itself with a roar that crackled in the dead trees and echoed down the valley and back with eerie reverberations.

Then the giant rock charged, shaking the ground as it moved. Moved straight at us.

CHAPTER NINE

Alek went from man to tiger in a blink beside me. Yosemite shouted at me to run for the trees, but he had his feet set like he was preparing for a fight, so I said fuck that and summoned magic, bracing myself as well.

The rock monster bounded closer. It looked like something dreamed up by the artists of *Shadow of the Colossus*, only without the pretty green mossy bits or the shiny scrolly bits. Instead, it had cracks between plates of grey stone that gleamed with dull red light. It was shaped like a rhino crossed with a turtle and a bit of insect thrown in, its six legs stumpy but apparently effective in moving its bulk. Its head was huge, with thick horns protruding from the sides like a bull's and a round nose like the head of a hammer. If it had eyes, I couldn't make them out at that distance.

Distance that was quickly going away. Yosemite shouted in Old Irish and vines burst up from the ground, wrapping around the rock beast's legs. They might have been made of dental floss, for all the notice it took of them. The vines fell away, snapping like Silly String, with no effect.

"The earth here is too sick," Yosemite gasped out, sweating beading on his forehead. "It cannot fight properly."

"Maybe we should move," I said. I didn't think a Fireball was going to do much to that thing. It definitely looked like it was made of rock.

"Trees," the druid said.

The three of us turned and bolted for the forest, but it was clear from the shaking of the ground that we weren't going to make it. I veered at a ninety-degree angle and dove painfully over a chunk of rock as the beast reached us, its huge head sweeping side to side as it reared back and tried to stomp on Alek. Tiger-Alek leapt for its face, knifelike claws extended. He didn't even scratch the surface, and the beast threw its head around until he was forced to leap free. He landed with a rolling skid and regained his feet, a deep roar coughing from him as he retreated and circled toward me.

I aimed bolts of force at the dull red cracks in the stone, hoping that would be a weak point. No dice. My bolts sizzled, fizzled, and did little more than attract the creature's attention. It bellowed again and backed off, pawing at the ground.

We ran for the trees again, putting distance between the beast and ourselves. The dead forest would provide little coverage, but little was better than none.

I stumbled into the tree line next to Yosemite and looked at the druid. "How do we stop that thing?"

"I have no idea," he said. "Drop trees on it?"

"Can you do that?"

"In another part of the forest, perhaps. Here, there is not enough life to answer my call," he said, shaking his head. "This was one of the guards set long ago. But something is wrong with it. She will not heed my call; she is no longer tied to the land."

The beast shook itself and oriented toward us, pawing the earth, sending grass, topsoil, and chunks of shale flying. It was going to charge again.

"Like something out of a freaking anime," I muttered, trying to figure out how to stop it. Transmute rock to mud? It was an oldie but goodie from the Dungeons & Dragons spell book, but I wasn't sure I could pull it off, not without that thing holding still so I could concentrate. "Wish

393

we could summon Goku." Never a Super Saiyan when you needed one.

Or was there? I stood up straighter as the beast pawed the earth again. Tess had said we had specialties, right? She thought mine was elemental magic, but I knew that wasn't really the case. I was best when it came to throwing around lots of raw power. I had been training all summer to gain more finesse, more control, to do more with less. Shoring up the areas I was weak more than trying to strengthen the things I was good at. Maybe I'd been going about it all wrong.

"Get behind me," I shouted as the ground shook and the beast charged.

I pulled power into myself, grabbing at every shred I could summon and hold without losing concentration. I slid my left foot forward and thrust my arms out behind me, focusing all that energy into a ball between my hands.

Yosemite and Alek moved, retreating farther into the trees. Smart men.

The beast wasn't so smart. It crashed toward me like a wrecking ball. What happens when an irresistible force meets an immovable object? I had no idea why that popped into my head, but I went with the thought, pouring every ounce of strength and belief in my own irresistible power. I waited until the stone beast was almost to me and then . . .

"KAMEHAMEHA," I screamed. I threw my hands in front of me, unleashing the beam of pure force right in the beast's ugly face.

The beam exploded into the beast, lifting it completely off its feet and rolling it up like a potato bug before flinging it back along the ground like an out-of-control, off-balance bowling ball. I had to turn my head away from the sudden gritty wind that erupted as debris flew into the air in its path.

Rubbing my eyes with my shirtsleeve, I peered out of the trees and down the deep furrow the rolling beast had left. It lay, unmoving, about two hundred yards away, half buried in the side of the valley. I reached for more power and stumbled toward it.

Up close, it smelled like ash and rot. The beast wasn't dead, its side rising and falling very slowly, but its chest was caved in and rust-colored ichor leaked out, too thick to look like proper blood. I really didn't want to touch it, but I couldn't have pulled off another giant spell if my life had depended on it.

Gripping my d20 for focus, I pictured what I wanted to do and laid my hand on its bulbous nose. The beast snorted, dull red nostrils opening and closing as fetid smoke gushed forth. I choked and hacked as my eyes watered, but kept my hand where it was.

Rock to Mud. I couldn't remember all the details of the spell, though I knew there was something in there about not working on magical stone. Fuck that, because the manual wasn't a spell book, not in reality. In reality, I just needed to have the power and the belief I could do it.

At that moment, I believed I could do anything. I'd just cast Kamehameha, or Turtle Devastation Wave, as translated from the Japanese. It had seemed appropriate, given the way this beast looked. Super effective, if utterly exhausting.

I pressed power down into its rocky skin through my hand. The magic animating it was inky and black, just like the corruption I'd burned out of the unicorn. Clyde, if I had to guess. My power sank in and the stone bent to my will, softening, cracking, turning to black, sludgy mud and finally splitting and sliding away in huge chunks. Rust-colored smoke gushed from the melting head and I held my breath, keeping my magic sinking into the sludge beneath my palm until the creature stopped breathing.

Stumbling back, I spat to try to clear the filth from my mouth and then gasped in mostly fresh air. Alek, back in human form, was there to catch me as I collapsed. This time, I didn't even resist as he lifted me into his arms. I buried my head in his chest and let exhaustion take me away.

▲ ▲ ▲

I came awake tucked against Alek's side. It was nearly dark, the moon rising above the rim of the valley. He'd brought me back up to the top and we were tucked against a large rock.

"Didn't want to camp down in the valley of death?" I asked.

"Not safe," Alek said. "How are you feeling?"

"Like I just stopped a freight train with my face," I said. My mouth tasted of smoke and sour beer, and my eyes were gritty when I rubbed them. I took the water Alek offered and tried to drink slowly.

"Where's the druid?" I asked, looking around.

"Valley," Alek said. "He went to check on the head."

"Hope there aren't any more of those stone turtle things."

"He says there are two others."

"Great," I muttered. "Can we fight them tomorrow? Because I don't think I can do that twice."

Alek's smile flashed white in the gloom. "Whatever that was, it was impressive."

This was what I got for falling for a non-nerd. Harper or Levi or Ezee would have been gushing with glee over what I had done. They'd be talking about it for months. I just hoped they'd believe me, but there was no way it would be as cool when I told it as it would have been if they had witnessed it, damnit.

"Gee, thanks," I said, knowing he'd see my eye-roll with his much better low-light vision. "We got any more of those power bars left?"

Yosemite returned sometime in the night, long after I'd drifted back to sleep. I awoke with the sun and he was there, wide awake, watching the sun rise over the ridge. The air was cool and the wilderness quiet as a grave. No morning birds sang.

"What's the story?" I asked the druid.

"I cannot get to Balor's head. There are two more guardians in the way, camping directly over the burial mound, plus I sense a pack of Fomoire hounds nearby and coming closer. I am not sure it would matter, in any case. I cannot close the lids." He rubbed his hand over his face, looking older and utterly tired.

"So, we gather up the gang, bring as much firepower as we can muster, and come lay down the hurt," I said. I was not looking forward to fighting two more of those rock monsters or another pack of hounds, but what choice did we have? I hoped that with Tess's help, maybe I could track Clyde and put a stop to his shit as well.

Of course, I might not have to. If I ruined his little Balor party, he would probably come to me. I was his end goal, after all.

"Did you not hear me?" Yosemite said. "I cannot close the lids. I cannot purge the land. It is too late—even if we stop this sorcerer polluting and twisting the spirits of the forest, I do not have the knowledge to close the eye."

"Who does?" I asked. "I mean, the druids gave you this head but didn't teach you how to stop it if something happened?"

"Jade," Alek said softly in that tone he used when I was being a bitch.

Yosemite waved his hand in an *it's okay* gesture, quieting Alek.

"There is a ritual. There were once many rituals, most lost to time now. But some, the most important, were written down by the druid who trained me. He had three copies of the book made. So far as I know, only one has survived the centuries."

"Great," I said. "So, we can do the ritual and stop this. Where is the book? Ireland? Buried inside a glass mountain and guarded by a fox with nine tails? I'm up for a quest." I smiled at him, trying to bring some lightness to his grim, unhappy face.

I failed.

"Seattle," he said. "But it doesn't matter. I cannot read it."

"Seattle?" That was only an eight-hour drive away. "Why can't you read it?"

"My teacher wrote it in an ancient script known only to a few. He meant to teach me the letters, but he was killed before he had a chance. His knowledge died with him, for he was the last who knew the secret tongue."

"Okay, let me get this right. There is a ritual in a book in Seattle that can close Balor's Eye and stop this?"

"Yes, and also, I think, a ritual that will wake the soul of the wilderness here and cleanse the land. But as I said, it doesn't matter." He got to his feet and turned away from us, his face lifting to catch the first rays of the morning sun. His cheeks above his thick red beard were suspiciously damp.

I looked at Alek and watched as comprehension dawned on his handsome face. He smiled, and I returned it, brushing my fingers over his. He squeezed my hand and then let go.

"So, if you could read the ritual—or rituals—we could fix all this?" I got to my feet and waved my hand at the valley below.

Yosemite rounded on me and snorted in frustration. "Yes," he said. He closed his mouth on whatever he was about to follow that with, looking down into my smiling face.

"Cool," I said. "Because I can read any language. It's kind of my superpower."

"Any language?" He blinked at me.

"Yep, so far as I know." I could tell he was skeptical, so I took a deep breath. I wasn't fond of talking about Samir, but it was getting slowly easier to share. "It's how I found out my psycho ex was going to kill me. He keeps journals written in a mix of dead languages and some words he's made up all on his own, I think. He believed that no one could ever decipher them. He was wrong. So, I'm pretty sure I could read your book."

Yosemite pursed his lips and folded his arms. After a long moment, he nodded. "What have we to lose?" he said.

Howling broke the morning silence. It sounded distant, but not distant enough for my taste. I started stuffing my sleeping bag into its sack as quick as I could. Alek rose to his feet, sniffing at the air.

"Let's get out of here," he said. "They are closer than they are letting on."

"We shall find healthy trees," Yosemite said. "Then I can open the leafway to get us back to the Henhouse."

"Not that again," Alek said with a grimace.

"We can't waste another day, not when we must travel to Seattle and lose time already. The forest sickens; the land will die permanently if we delay too long. We must move with haste now."

"Tree travel it is," Alek said with a resigned sigh.

"How bad can it be?" I asked as we took off over the ridge. Famous last words, right?

CHAPTER TEN

The uneven ground had entered into a conspiracy to slow me down, trip me up, and make me dog food. Swear to the universe. I was never going hiking again. We raced over the ridge and down the other side, Yosemite and Alek leaping and gliding over rocks and brambles toward the line of healthier forest far below and beyond us. All those hours climbing up this ridge to get to the valley, all that effort, and now I had to stumble my way down at breakneck speed. I would have sighed, but I had no breath to spare.

Breakneck speed was an accurate phrase for it. I gave up after the second fall ripped my jeans open at the knees and embedded thistle needles in my palms. I reached for my magic, letting it run through my muscles, strengthening me, lifting me up as I sprang a few feet off the ground and forward, leaping like a long jumper. Using my magic, I pressed down, willing myself not to land but to keep going. I'd learned in my AP physics class in high school that gravity is considered a weak force, and I intended to ignore the shit out of it for as long as I could if it meant not face-planting again before reaching those trees.

Even with magic, I could barely keep up with Alek and Yosemite, their long legs eating up the distance, their huge bodies apparently good enough at defying pesky things like air resistance and gravity all on their own.

Behind me, the baying of the Fomoire hounds grew louder, closer. I couldn't risk a look, but it felt as though they were closing the distance, definitely over the ridge by now. I wanted to turn and tear into them, but memory of our barely won fight at the barn kept me gliding forward, kicking off the ground for another long glide. All I needed was a Hidden Leaf headband or an Anbu mask and I'd be right at home in a *Naruto* manga.

The healthy forest spread out ahead of me, the leaves looking like they were on fire in the morning sunlight, lit from the side by the rising sun. We were nearly in its shade when the first of the hounds caught up.

Fetid and heavy breathing warned me, and I threw myself sideways, using my magic like a ski pole to shove my gliding body aside as a hound sprang at me from behind. I shouted a warning as I hit the ground, the impact jarring me from ankle to teeth. I managed to keep my feet and spin, lashing out with a beam of purple fire. The hound dodged and went for Alek instead.

Alek shifted and sprang, his huge jaws ripping into flesh with satisfying crunches, paws bigger than my head with claws longer than my fingers tearing the hound to whimpering shreds.

Yosemite had reached the trees, and he turned as well, a thick branch, its length still covered in twigs and leaves, dropping from the trees to his hand. He spun it with mastery, cracking into one monster's skull and spinning back to trip another and send it flying into the trees. Vines ripped up from the ground, glowing green in the dim light beneath the trees. Any hound that shot past us was caught, yowling in pain, and dragged into the earth.

The pack backed off as a high whistle sounded and the ground shook. There were less of them than before, I noticed as I edged toward Alek and the druid, gasping for air. Still too many; twenty or so at least. I raised my eyes as Yosemite cursed in three different tongues and looked back up the hill.

One of the stone turtle insect guardians, its craggy body oozing rusty smoke, lumbered down the hill. It wasn't moving very quickly, but it was picking up steam as it went. The one the day before had moved better, and after a moment, I could make out why this one was more cautious.

It had a rider. A man stood on its back, his golden hair bright, a motherfucking crimson cloak streaming out behind him.

"Fucking theatrics," I muttered.

"That the sorcerer?" Yosemite asked. He had half-turned away and was looking at the trees around us as though searching for something.

"A sorcerer," I said. "Not Samir. I think that's Clyde."

I set my feet, one back, one front, and started to pool magic into my hands, balling force as I had before. Bowling that stupid turtle down would be even more satisfying with that clown on its back. He was an idiot to come out in the open. I smiled.

Just a little closer, fuckwad, I thought, watching Clyde come down the hill. I could make out his features now. Delicately pretty, like Tess had said. He was grinning fit to split his face. Well, that made two of us.

"Jade," Yosemite hissed, his voice filled with fear and urgency. "The other guardian, it's behind us."

I risked a glance behind, clinging to my focus, holding the gathering ball of magic in my hands. Something grey and black slithered between the trees, brush crackling as it came closer. I made out a snakelike head and rust-colored eyes or maybe nostrils, smoking beneath the trees.

"I don't think I can take out two and the hounds," I hissed back.

"I can open the way, but only in that tree," Yosemite said, pointing toward an oak about twenty yards to our left. It was bigger than the trees around it, growing at the edge of the wood, where it had gotten plenty of light and water.

Alek crouched by my side, growling low in his throat, his whole body vibrating with tension.

The stone turtle insect stopped its advance, and Clyde called out to me, "Good morning, Jade Crow."

Cocky cocksucker. My whole body shook from holding the spell. It wouldn't be as strong as yesterday's; my reserves were still low.

"Good morning, Clyde," I called. Then, in a whisper, I said in Old Irish, "Start going to the tree; I'll distract him," and added the words in Russian for Alek's benefit.

"I see our little traitor has been talking," Clyde yelled. "You think she won't betray you, like she did Samir?"

Something about his words bothered me, but I shoved them aside. I couldn't hold the spell much longer.

"Fuck off," I yelled. Out of the corner of my eye, I saw that Alek and Yosemite had halved the distance to the tree. It would have to be good enough.

"You are trapped," Clyde called out. He started to say something else stupid and gloaty, but I threw my hands forward, unleashing the Kamehameha.

The energy ball ripped along the ground, tossing hounds out of its path like sticks. It slammed into the polluted guardian, rocking the creature backward and bowling it off its feet in a cloud of dirt and shale.

I bolted toward the tree, not watching to see what further effect my spell had. The stone snake guardian rushed us, crushing ferns and saplings in its path as it abandoned stealth for speed.

Yosemite was chanting, green light streaming from his hands and into the oak. A glowing portal opened in the trunk and he half-shoved tiger-Alek through it and reached for me as I made one last magic-assisted leap. The snake's jaws snapped just where I had been, its breath an ill wind at my back. I dove into the leaf-way.

There was no ground, no up or down. I flew through empty space, feeling like I was moving or that perhaps the filtered green light that danced all around me was moving, and that I was just falling. Falling forever, my heart in my throat. If that was what skydiving was like, I made a solemn vow right then and there to never, ever try it.

I clutched at my d20 talisman with both hands, needing something solid to remind me I was there and real. I was a sorceress. Hitting the ground after a fall like that wouldn't kill me. If there was ground. Hadn't Alek and Yosemite come out through the ancient oak at the Henhouse, safe and sound, only days before? I tried to cling to that memory, to the knowledge that whatever was happening would pass and I would survive it.

I slammed back into daylight, ground beneath my feet for a moment until my toes tripped me up as my forward momentum carried me into a full-on face-plant in the dewy grass outside the Henhouse. I almost kissed that ground as I realized I was there and it was solid, but I was afraid if I opened my mouth, I'd barf.

Alek, back in human form, leaned down beside me, helping me to my feet.

"How bad can it be?" he said, eyebrows raised.

"Okay, you win," I said, swallowing hard. "Let's never do that again."

Yosemite leapt from the tree behind us as though he'd been on a stroll and turned, banishing the green light and closing the leaf-way. I really wished he'd said something cool like "The way is closed," but you can't have everything, I guess. Besides, hadn't I just been disgusted with Clyde the evil sorcerer for being overly theatrical? That was partially sour grapes on my part, I knew. His little distraction plan had almost worked, though I wanted to believe I could have taken him and his little dogs too. All two dozen of them. And two giant monster things made of nearly impregnable stone.

Yeah, those grapes would have tasted like shit. The fox was so right.

▲ ▲ ▲

We walked into the Henhouse after checking on Max and the unicorn. A few lights were on and I heard voices as I entered. The whole lower floor smelled of buttered popcorn. The first person I saw was Harper walking between the kitchen and the open door to Tess's room, a huge bowl of popcorn in her hands—which explained the scent, at least. She looked tired but had a smile on her face that grew grim when she saw us.

"You guys are a mess," she said. "You okay?"

"Yeah," I said. "Everyone in Tess's room?"

It sounded that way, at least, their voices spilling out into the hall.

"I must make a phone call," Yosemite said. He went up the stairs without another word.

I followed Harper into Tess's room, Alek behind me. Levi, Ezee, and Junebug had all set up camp there, as far as I could tell. They'd brought one of the flat-screen TVs into the room, and I recognized the closing credits from *Firefly* paused on the screen. Tess had more color in her cheeks but still looked delicate and weak in the bed, propped up on half a dozen pillows.

"You guys been up all night?" I said.

"We were worried about you guys," Levi said.

"So, we started watching *Firefly*," Ezee said with a shrug.

"Next thing we knew, it was morning," Levi finished.

"You are just in time, though," Tess said. "We finished the first season, but we haven't started season two yet."

"Season two?" I said, raising an eyebrow at the twins. "You didn't warn her?"

"We didn't have the heart," Harper muttered as she set the popcorn down on the nightstand.

"Warn me about what?" Tess asked, looking between their faces.

"There is no season two," I said, glaring at my friends. I felt like I was in some alternate universe. I went away for a few days and everyone was hanging out like old friends, turning our new friend into a gorram Browncoat while they were at it.

"What do you mean there is no season two?" She looked crushed. I knew the feeling.

"Fuck this," I said, throwing up my hands. "I'm going to go take a shower. You guys can explain things. Then we'd better tell you all what we found."

I left to the sounds of another fangirl heart breaking in twain.

CHAPTER ELEVEN

It appeared that the Henhouse and surroundings had been quiet while we were gone, which was a relief. No one had tried to get to the unicorn again. If I had to guess, I would have put my money on Clyde being distracted hunting us through the woods, trying to catch up to us once he'd realized we were tracking the hounds and heading for Balor's burial site.

We wasted little time, despite being exhausted with almost no sleep. Clyde had no reason not to come after us, perhaps bringing the stone guardians with him this time. Yosemite thought we had a day, maybe a day and a half on them because of the tree travel. Ciaran, surprising me, showed up as I wolfed down an omelet. He and Brie would go into the woods, he said, and see what they could do to slow the pack's progress.

I tried to protest, of course, but he just looked at me with his ancient eyes and I shut up. All three of them—Brie, Yosemite, Ciaran—were a lot more than they seemed and I had to accept that I wasn't the only badass in the room. In some ways, it was a relief. I wasn't alone against Clyde and his filth.

I'd spent a lot of the last month feeling alone, despite my reconciliation with Alek. My tiger was still conflicted about killing a fellow Justice and his Council's apparent withdrawal of their support from him. His feather still hung from his neck, and I often caught him fingering it with a sad look on his face in unguarded moments. He'd been busy with the local wolves, dealing with the fallout, sometimes gone for days at a time.

The loneliness came because I knew that time was growing short. Samir would tire of these games, and then we'd find out if everything I could do, everything I had, was enough to keep the people I loved safe. My helplessness against Wylde's stupid witch coven didn't help my confidence. How was I to fight monsters without being the bad guy? How to fight people who weren't monsters but were just bigots? I didn't think I could kill someone for just being an asshole, much as I sort of wanted to in the deep dark parts of my soul.

But, sitting at the dining table in the Henhouse, listening to my friends scheme and make plans to help me take out the latest big bad to throw himself at us, my loneliness faded into the background. I had some pretty awesome friends and they weren't running away, weren't cowering or coming up with excuses. They were tackling every problem like proper gamers, as though our enemies were a puzzle that just needed the right solution.

We had to wait until late morning before Yosemite was ready to leave. Alek wanted to come with us, but I made him stay. He'd barely slept in two days and his ribs were poking out. He needed rest and a ton of food. Yosemite didn't have a driver's license, or any ID at all, so I asked Ezee if he'd come to split the driving with me. No ulterior motive there, I swore, ignoring Alek's disapproving face at my lie.

Ezee had an SUV, which would make the trip more comfortable for all of us. I let him take the first leg to Seattle and curled up across the back seat, pillowing my head on my arms. As I drifted off, I heard Ezee chuckle at something Yosemite said, and I smiled.

"Haruki," soft voices whisper around me. I can't tell where they are coming from. Bamboo towers over my head as I run, the thin, sharp leaves slicing

my bare arms. My heart pounds and my leg muscles are tired. I've come all the way from the village by the sea. Sweat stings my eyes, but I resist wiping it away.

"Haruki, Haru, Haruki-ki-ki," the voices sing out, movement in the bamboo around me giving them away.

Children, *I scoff to myself. I am not like them. They can torment me all they like. I am sure Mother put them up to it, another layer of distraction. I shove my anger down, letting it burn inside me, an ember keeping warm for later. Today, I do not need it.*

The bamboo ends at the edge of a clear stream and I leap over, falling into a silent roll on the other side and coming to my feet beside the walled garden. I lick my palms to ignite the words carved upon them, the fine cuts stinging, and climb the smooth stone wall like a spider. At the top, I pause. Below me is the garden, spread in a spiral of careful paths and shaped trees leading to the inner courtyard.

There, standing on the bridge over an empty stream, is my target. The woman stands with her back to me, her long black hair loose over her blue robe. Too easy.

I leap down from the wall, rolling again, and slip the kunai from my vest. I have only one spellblade. I must choose the right target, or I will fail.

Failure has no appeal, no honor. I am a poor loser, Mother tells me. I would always rather win. Wouldn't everyone?

A songbird sings out in a cage on a pole high above as I run by, startling me. The wind picks up, making fallen petals dance along the path.

Another woman waits in the center of the spiral, sitting calmly in seiza, her hands open on her knees, palms facing the overcast sky as though waiting to collect the rain that will surely fall tonight. Her hair is unbound as well, falling over her shoulders like ink spilled from a broken bottle.

I let the kunai fly, my aim true, and it buries itself in her chest with a dull thud.

The woman vanishes, a block of wood with a smoking piece of rice paper stuck to it all that remains of Mother's illusion.

The woman at the bridge turns and bows respectfully as she approaches. I have not failed.

"Haruki," she says. "What have you learned?"

"That illusion is immune to wind," I say, unable to hide my smile. "Her hair did not move."

Mother shakes her head, her hair swaying gently with the motion. "I suppose that must be close enough to the lesson, then. You must observe, always, Haruki-kun. Very little in this world is as it appears."

I woke from my half-dream, half-memory to find that it was dark out, with large buildings looming around us. I swept the dream from my head, shoving it away to examine later. Living with the echoes of the people I'd eaten inside my brain could get pretty creepy, and I wasn't up for dealing with whatever my subconscious was up to right now.

"I thought you were going to wake me to help drive," I said to Ezee, sitting up. "Looks like we are here." I'd slept for nearly nine straight hours, cramped in the car, and I couldn't decide if I felt better or worse. My mouth tasted thick with sleep and slightly sour.

"You looked so peaceful, we didn't want to wake you," Ezee said.

He seemed relaxed, more so than when we'd gotten in the car. I wondered how much of the intervening time he'd spent talking to Yosemite. The druid looked calm as well, and I had a feeling something had been worked out between them, whatever it was. More birds and fishes, maybe. Maybe not. I didn't want to ruin the comfortable vibe by asking personal questions. I could try grilling Ezee about how his love life was shaking out later, in that magical future where someone wasn't trying to kill us.

"Are we there yet?" I quipped, smiling at Ezee as he flicked his gaze to me in the rearview mirror and made a face. I rolled my shoulders. Two nights of sleeping on cold, rocky ground, and now cramped in a car seat, made my muscles do their best Rice Krispies impression. *Snap, crackle, pop.* I felt old.

"Nearly," Yosemite said.

There turned out to be a huge old warehouse in West Seattle. We pulled into the dark parking lot. Ezee turned off the car and pulled out his phone, plugging in headphones.

"You aren't coming up?" I said as Yosemite got out of the car. Salty, cold air from the Sound washed in over us.

"No, just you two. Apparently, this guy doesn't like a crowd." Ezee said it in a casual way, but I could see it bothered him a little.

"I'd say call me if there is trouble out here, but I'm phoneless."

"I'll hit the horn, no worries," he said. "Go on."

Yosemite hadn't said much about the mysterious owner of the book, only that he was a man known as the Archivist. It sounded ominous.

The warehouse was at least two stories, with dark windows high above and a heavy steel door. The door buzzed as we approached, and Yosemite pushed through it. He led me directly up a metal stair, running lights along the steps our only illumination. I could make out a hall beyond the stairs, with what might have been more doors. The place was cool without being cold, but the air had a slightly dusty quality to it that reminded me of a museum. Or a mausoleum.

At the top of the steps, an ornate wooden door carved with huge Fu dogs stood partially open. As we stepped through, lamps came on around the room. Shelves lined the space, stretching up into the shadows, with tall library ladders adorning them at regular intervals. The gentle lamplight gleamed on leather spines embossed with gold leaf and engraved titles. The room was empty other than the books, two padded benches, and a small writing desk. Also, it was much smaller than the outside dimensions of the warehouse said it should be. Like a reverse TARDIS.

I looked around for doors but saw none. There must have been more rooms on this level; I was sure of it.

Movement caught my eye and I realized a man stood just outside a pool of lamplight, watching us. He'd moved deliberately, I felt, just enough to catch our attention.

"Archivist," Yosemite said, inclining his head in greeting.

The man stepped into the light. He was slender with an angular, not-quite-pretty face. His eyes were eerie, a flat, inhuman silver, with pupils that looked more catlike than round. He motioned to the benches, watching me intently. I felt like the mouse and it didn't feel good.

Going on instinct and probably no little amount of nerves built up from the last few days of fighting and running for my life, I sent a light brush of magic at him, trying to discern what he was. His flat silver eyes watched me and his mouth curled in the hint of a smile as nothing happened. I might as well have brushed my power against the desk at his side or the books on the shelves.

Or a corpse. I listened, using my magic to enhance my senses. The Archivist stood still, too still, frozen like a mannequin, no hint of breath or normal movement to him. No heartbeat.

"Curiosity is known to kill cats, Ms. Crow," he said, raising an eyebrow in a gesture that looked utterly practiced and precise.

"Satisfaction brings them back," I said, letting go of my magic. I didn't want to accept what my brain and senses were telling me. "Do you sparkle in sunlight?" I asked.

"No," he said. "I burn."

I looked at Yosemite, who had seated himself on a bench and was watching us with a guarded, bemused expression. "Great. First unicorns, now vampires. What's the next not-so-mythical thing we can encounter this week? Bigfoot? Ooh, I know! How about a dragon?" I looked back at our silent host.

He had a very strange expression on his face and I had no idea what it meant. "Please," he said after a moment. "Sit."

I sat, realizing I was ranting a little, and tried to get control of my nerves. I was dating a perfect predator, for Universe's sake. This guy was scarier.

Shifters I knew; I'd grown up with them. A vampire? I had no idea what was myth and what was reality. It was becoming quite clear to me that there was a lot about the world, the magical world especially, I didn't know. I felt very small all of a sudden, and it made me want to lash out.

"Do you have a name?" I asked, trying to curb my tone to something polite.

"Noah Grey," he said, and this time his smile reached his eyes briefly. I wasn't sure if that was scarier.

Yosemite gave a start of surprise next to me when the Archivist answered, but recovered quickly. "We would like to read the book I discussed."

"All information can be had, for a price," the vampire said. "I doubt you can afford this one."

"I do not want to take the book, only to let Jade read it." The druid was prepared for this. He had a small bag of various rare and special plants and seeds. "I am willing to trade so we may read and copy what we need."

"A week," Noah said, looking at me. "I will take a week of your time, working for me here. Then you may copy the pages you want."

"What?" I said. I leaned back on the bench and folded my arms over my chest, aware it was a defensive position and not caring. "We don't have a week. And what the hell do you want me for?"

"I have books that even I cannot read, information hidden from me. A week of your time to translate certain texts; is that so much?" His smile was back, this time revealing a hint of sharp white teeth.

"Yes," I said. "For one, we're sort of on a clock here. For another thing, how do you even know I can read the things you want me to translate?"

"But of course you can," he said, tipping his head to the side.

I wished he would blink. His unwavering stare was fucking unnerving. I couldn't help but bend forward, searching his face for a clue as to his thoughts. What did he know about me? How did he know about my gift with languages? Yosemite had promised he would only tell the

Archivist that I could read the book and I trusted the druid's word.

"How do you know that?" I asked.

Samir's dagger chose that moment to fall right out of its ankle sheath and clatter to the smooth wooden floor.

I didn't see Noah move. One breath the vampire was standing by the writing desk, the next he knelt in front of me, the dagger in his hands. He turned it over and over and then looked up at me. I tried not to flinch.

"Sorry," I said, reaching for the blade. "It does that."

"As well it should," he said, standing up at a more human speed. He kept ahold of the knife. "This blade is not complete without its twin, so it will always seek to leave its bearer unless he or she holds both."

"What is it, besides mine?" I asked, emphasizing the *mine* a little and holding out my hand. I hoped that Samir didn't have the twin. That would be awkward. The dagger was scary enough on its own.

Reluctantly, Noah handed me back the blade. "What will you pay for that knowledge?" he asked.

I almost said *What do you want?* but realized the answer would probably be something like *Another week of your time.* I thought about pointing out I had paid translation services easily available on the web, but if this supposed knowledge broker couldn't figure out that much, I wasn't about to share. Maybe later, if I felt like ever dealing with him again, which I really kind of didn't.

"Look," I said, standing up. Noah and I were almost of a height. "We aren't going to loan you my time for a week. We can't. And I'm not going to play these stupid bargaining games. Lives are at stake here, which I realize dead guys probably don't give a flying fuck about, but we need to read the druid's book."

"Trade me the dagger," he said.

"Give us the book outright," I countered. "Not just to read but for Yosemite to keep. It should be his, after all."

"Done," he said.

I couldn't repress a small jerk of surprise. I hadn't expected him to cave like that.

"Won't the dagger just try to leave you, too?" I asked as he turned and walked to the desk, pulling a receipt book from one of the little drawers.

"No," he said. "I possess the twin." This time, his smile was all teeth.

I bit back all my other questions and glanced at Yosemite. He hadn't said a word in minutes. He stood slowly and shook his head at me, but I sensed a part of him was pleased at the bargain. Why should he not be, right? I'd given something up, not he.

I hated that dagger. I carried it on my person despite its many attempts to get left behind, dropped, or lost, because I wanted to keep it close, keep it out of the wrong hands. I wasn't sure a vampire constituted the right hands, but he wasn't actively trying to kill me, so I was pretty sure that made him a better candidate for holding on to the thing than most of the other people who knew about it.

Noah signed a receipt, listing one druidic tome for one dagger, magic, and handed it over. He disappeared through a sliding-bookcase door at the back of the room, leaving us alone.

"That was probably a mistake," I said quietly to Yosemite.

"Perhaps," he said. "The Archivist is not good, but he is not so bad, either. He lives for the preservation of knowledge, all kinds. Objects, rumors, myth, prophecy, art, literature. It all flows through here and he squirrels it away, a lot of it. Often the most dangerous things. That knife will likely never see the light of day."

"Well, sure," I said, trying on a smile. "Daylight burns that guy, don't you know."

I paced the room as we waited, thinking that Ciaran would have been doing a jig in here if these titles were authentic. I feared touching some of the books, not knowing if the bindings were just decorative or if they were as old as they looked. I found one, a slim volume with a red leather binding and an inlaid figure of an oriental dragon. I reached for the book, forgetting my caution, but Noah returned before I could pull it from the shelf.

"Curiosity and cats, Ms. Crow," he said, clucking his tongue as he walked by me, hauling a thick tome in his arms.

The book was a good foot across and nearly as deep. The cover was carved wood inlaid with semiprecious stones, and I could almost smell the age of the vellum inside. Knotwork illuminated the first few pages as I pulled my sleeve down over my hand to protect the pages from the oils on my skin.

"It's magically protected," Yosemite said, peering over my shoulder. "Your hands won't hurt it."

"How did the other two get destroyed?" I asked, flipping a page. There were many drawings, diagrams with notes on plants, animals, even a star chart. Something about it was familiar. The book reminded me a little of pictures of the Book of Kells I'd seen online, but not quite so ornate.

"Witch hunters," the druid said, pain straining his voice.

"The Inquisition was not a good time for magic," Noah added. He almost seemed to sigh. "Do you wish to read it here?"

"No," I said. I'd paid pretty dearly, probably more than I knew, for this book. I could read in the car on the way back. I couldn't get motion sickness. "We don't have time."

The vampire walked us to the ornate doors.

"Nice to meet you," I said, trying to sound at least halfway sincere.

He took my hand, his fingers strong and cool against my skin, and bent over it before I could react, brushing his lips against my knuckles. "Until we meet again," he murmured so low I thought I imagined the words—until I saw the predatory look in his strange silver eyes.

I won't say I ran down the steps, but hey, we were in a hurry, so taking them two by two was perfectly natural and not all because the vampire gave me the heebies.

Ezee was relieved to see us and swore that as long as we grabbed some of Seattle's finest coffee, he was good to drive back as well, so I could read the book and find the rituals we needed to stop Clyde and save the trees. I gulped down scalding coffee after we hit a late drive-through, and dragged the huge book onto my lap, summoning light into my talisman to read by.

The text wasn't easy to read. The handwriting was precise, but like many things from its time, the script was difficult to decipher and it was written in about four different languages, only three of which I'd ever seen before. If my gift hadn't been wholly magical, I would have been screwed. Fortunately, magic saved my ass as soon as I stopped squinting so hard and trusted my ability to let me read and make sense of what I was reading. Slowly, I grew used to the druid's handwriting and odd diction, and the words and phrases began to make more sense. I shoved away the nagging feeling of familiarity and searched each entry, looking for references to Balor, hearts of the forest, and other keywords. I wished the damn thing was digitized so I could have just used a search function, and lost about ten minutes musing if I could create a spell that would hunt the text for me.

Unfortunately, I didn't want to risk messing with the magic preserving the book or risk the book itself if my spell went sideways somehow, which new spells of mine often did if they were detailed. Settling back against the seat, my thighs growing numb under the weight of the tome, I turned page after page. I found the ritual I thought we needed after over four hours of carefully searching the book, and a lot of pieces fell into place.

"Drive faster," I told Ezee. "We better hope the unicorn is still safe."

"No one has called me," Ezee said. "I'm sure they are fine."

So, of course, no sooner were the cursed words out of his mouth than his damn phone began to sing "Lean on Me," which was his ringtone for his brother.

417

CHAPTER TWELVE

Levi hadn't meant to call Ezee. Exhausted from keeping watch with the wolves, he'd tried to shut off his phone before he crashed for the night and hit redial instead. Gave us all heart palpitations.

After pulling over and managing to call back and figure all this out, I made Ezee switch seats with me and drove. I explained to Yosemite what I'd read, promising him a full translation of the ritual later. He listened with the patience of an oak tree, asking me minimal questions, seeming to understand what I was saying better than I did. Which was good, because while I could read the words, that didn't always mean I knew what they were talking about without greater context.

It was early morning when we reached the Henhouse. We needed more sleep and to prepare. Yosemite had certain plants to gather as well. I wished I understood what needed to happen enough to just magic it into being so, but the book was by druids, dealing with druidic magic. I wasn't sure I could eat a druid's heart and gain his power. Probably. Even the thought was unnerving and I shoved it away, climbing into bed next to Alek.

"Briefing at high noon," I murmured to him, curling up against his warm chest.

"Read the book?" he asked.

"Brought it back with us," I said. "I had to trade Samir's dagger to a vampire for it."

"Vampire? They don't exist." He shook his head and ran a hand down my spine, tugging at my braid where it ended at my waist.

"Yeah, turns out they do."

"You are telling the truth," he said.

"Hey, it happens on occasion."

"I like the druid," Alek said. "I am glad you and Brie are no longer fighting."

"Where is Brie?" I hadn't seen her or Ciaran when we got back.

"Patrolling. She is different somehow. I can't place it. Even her scent has changed. It is like she is a different person."

"Yeah," I said. "I guess a lot of us aren't exactly what we first seem." I was thinking about myself but also about Tess. Even Alek had given me a very different impression when I'd first met him.

I rubbed my nose in his chest hair and breathed in his vanilla-and-musk scent. This was home. This was safe. We had the book, we had the ritual, and we had the unicorn. Later today, we could end this whole mess. I could take out Clyde, which would be some kind of blow to Samir, at least. And there was enough time for me to cuddle with a handsome man who loved me. It was a win all around so far.

I lay there for a while, feeling like something was terribly wrong. Maybe I was just not cut out for winning.

Unable to sleep, I went down to see Tess after Alek got up to get breakfast. She was still propped up in bed, watching *Farscape* on the TV. The sun was out, streaming in through the light blue curtains, bathing the room in gentle light. Tess looked thinner, but her smile was strong as she paused the DVD and motioned for me to come sit in one of the chairs pulled up by her bed.

"I see my friends got you hooked on science fiction," I said, closing the door behind me.

"I never watched a lot of shows before. Mostly news shows and occasionally that reality TV junk so I could keep up with fashion, slang, and that stuff." She lifted a thin shoulder in a half-shrug. "Harper promised that this show has more than one season."

"Oh, it does." I sank into a chair, my back to the window so I wouldn't have to squint at her.

"So far, it is funny," she said.

"You must be watching the first season." Harper was evil. I had almost been jealous that my friends were bonding with Tess so well, but they were doing their own version of nerd hazing, from what I could see. Trial by fire. Heartbreaking science fictional fire.

She looked at the TV and then back at me. "You didn't come here to talk about television."

"I met Clyde," I said. My brain had been turning the experience over and over, searching it for meaning. The wrongness started there, I was sure of it. I just couldn't find it. Clyde had been exactly as Tess had described. Flashy. Arrogant. Utterly evil. "He knows you are here."

Her gaze sharpened and she pressed her lips together, nostrils flaring. "I guess I'm not surprised. Samir will know by now I'm gone, and I told you he has eyes everywhere."

"He told me you would betray me," I said.

"He doesn't understand why I ran," she said with a snort. "All he sees when he looks at Samir is a handsome man who lets him get away with murder."

"How did you know who Samir really is? What he intends for you both?" I knew how I had discovered it, but I knew too how seductive and sweet Samir could be. Tempting with his offer of knowledge, binding you to him with promises, playing to your strengths and flattering your ego until you felt like you were the most special person in the world. It was a hard thing to break away from, to see the rotten core of him, covered in so many layers of deception. Samir was the best manipulator of desire and fear I'd ever met.

"I've always known," Tess said, closing her eyes. Her voice took on a tight edge, as though her throat hurt. "I watched him kill my grandmother when I was a little girl."

I waited, saying nothing, watching her face as she visibly struggled to control her emotions.

"She was so beautiful. Said that God had given her a gift and she was going to use it. She could heal, you know. She hid it with herb lore and such, but she had a magic touch. No one dared call her a witch—she was too sweet, too kind. Too devout. I think she scared the priests, even. They called her Sister Mary, even though she wasn't a nun. Everyone thought she was my mother, but she'd come and taken me away from Papa after Mama died giving birth. She could do more magic, though. I remember how good she was at hiding things, hiding people. She helped slaves escape along the Eastern Shore, sometimes hiding whole boats in Chesapeake Bay."

Tess stopped and took a deep breath. I waited again to see if she'd continue, but she opened her eyes, now bright with unshed tears, and shook her head.

"Why didn't he kill you?" I asked.

"I don't know," Tess said. "I've thought about it over and over. He looked right at me after he ripped her heart out, though Grandmother hid me under the bed. She had a spell on me, I know that, but he bent right down and looked me in the eye. I remember the blood on his lips, and how my chest was too tight, how I couldn't even scream. Then he smiled and got up and left. Just like that." Her hands fisted in the quilt and the tears spilled from her eyes.

I got up and found her a tissue. She was a crazy-strong woman. I'd been with Samir because I hadn't known better. The moment I figured out what he was, what he intended, I was so damn pissed, I confronted him, and when it became clear he was too powerful to face, I ran. Tess had waited over a century, and when faced with him again, she'd pretended to be naïve, new, just a young sorceress waiting for him to fatten and slaughter. I had to admire her survival skills, her patience.

"You really want him dead, don't you?" I said softly.

"Yes," she said, her brandy-colored irises catching the sunlight, the highlights in them like sparks. "It was almost a relief when I realized he was close to finding me. I was teaching pottery at an art school and had to use magic to save myself when the kiln exploded. I knew it was enough that I was likely exposed."

"Why come to me now?" I asked. I'd asked her before, but I wanted to hear it again.

"You hurt him," she said. "And he is getting moodier, more paranoid. Clyde, too. I felt as though his games with you are coming to a close. So, I took my chance." She rubbed her fingers over the crucifix charm on her wrist in a gesture that reminded me of how I touched my talisman for comfort sometimes.

"You are Catholic?" I said. "After all you've seen, you believe in God?"

"You believe because you have seen. Blessed are those who have not seen, and yet believe," she answered, the words sounding old-fashioned.

"Scripture?" I guessed.

"Jesus Christ spoke those words to Thomas the Doubter. I guess your people have their own god, right? A Great Spirit?" She closed her hand over her bracelet, as though wanting to hide the cross from my heathen eyes. I got the feeling I'd annoyed her.

"Sure," I said, mildly annoyed myself. "My people, as you put it, are totally homogenous just like you white folk. We all have the same culture and believe exactly the same things."

"Touché," she said. "I'm sorry."

"No," I said with a sigh. "Don't be. I was raised in a cult, pretty much.

Our god, if we had one, was my grandfather. He preached that the perfect spirit of the Crow had to be preserved, that crows and wolves and men didn't share beds or homes, but each kept to their own. He did pretty awful things to cleave to his vision of how things ought to be. All religion seems to bring people is fear, hatred, and just as dead in the end. I have no use for it."

"No faith in anything greater than yourself?" she said softly. "It sounds lonely."

"I guess I have some kind of faith. I believe the universe is vast and that there are many things I don't understand."

We sat quietly for a little while, her rubbing her crucifix, me trying to figure out why I was so prickly, what felt off about everything. Nerves before battle, perhaps.

"How did *you* find out what Samir intended for you?" Tess asked me after some minutes had passed.

I dragged my gaze back to her face. She watched me intently, almost disturbingly so, but I shoved my feelings away. I was getting pretty good at it.

"I read his diary," I said. "He was pretty clear in his thoughts and feelings on the matter. And he'd done it before, kept a catalog of who and when and what he felt he'd gained from the experience." The experience of killing and eating heart after heart.

I didn't admit that I'd not read as closely as I wished. I'd been in shock, sitting alone in the big library, holding the book I'd pulled off the shelf in my hands, disbelieving that what I was reading was real. I'd slammed through all five stages of grief real quick that day, though I wasn't sure I'd ever hit the acceptance phase. Pretty sure I got stuck on anger.

"You could read his journals?" Tess said.

"They were just there, not hidden or anything. He went away for a few days and I got bored, so I snooped. I stayed away from the older ones, since he had spells on those, but the last couple notebooks were right there for the taking." I knew I was avoiding answering the question she had actually asked, but I didn't feel like broadcasting my language abilities. Even with her injured in bed and her apparent friendliness and sincerity, I couldn't quite bring myself to trust her. Not yet.

I wondered if Samir still kept the journals out. If he still had a library. He'd had a wonderful collection of books, some dating back hundreds of years if not further, beautiful books like the one we'd traded the vampire for. I'd spent hours in that library whenever Samir had to go away for business, often sitting with gloves on in the temperature-controlled room and flipping through old volumes of poetry and lore.

Old books. Like the druid's book. I forced myself to stand up slowly, not leap and run for the door even though adrenaline slammed into my veins.

"I'm going to get some breakfast," I said. My voice even sounded normal. Go me. "Want me to send in anything? Or do you feel up to coming out?"

"The bathroom trip nearly wiped me out," she said with a small smile. "I'm okay. I'll just keep watching this show. Let me know what the plan is, though. I want to help if I can."

"No problem," I lied. "I'll let you know."

I left the room and ducked down the hall out of sight of everyone. Sagging against the wall, I closed my eyes. I knew why the book was familiar, and with that knowledge, other things started to topple into place.

I wanted to be wrong. Because if I was right, we weren't winning at all.

CHAPTER THIRTEEN

I pulled Alek away from the breakfast table with only minor teasing from my friends. Yosemite was outside, standing just beyond the garden in the trees, apparently talking to a birch tree.

Alek set up a ward around us and I laid out my suspicions and my plan.

"It's a lot of guesswork," the druid said, running a hand over his thick red beard.

"Jade has good instincts," Alek said, surprising me with his quiet defense of my theories. I hadn't always been right about things, and he'd been around to witness some of my worst mistakes. Still, his support warmed me better than the morning sun.

"If I'm wrong, we can still get to you in time to help. If I'm right, it will take the pressure off you and allow you to fix the forest and lay Balor back to rest."

"Why Brie?" he asked.

"I saw what she could do with that sword. Also, I trust her not to do something stupid and get in over her head trying to protect me."

"Unlike, say, Harper," Alek said with a rude snort.

"She's got that foxy courage—what can I say?" I smiled at him.

Harper was my best friend, but no way could I trust her to go with this plan if she knew the truth. The very friendship that bound the twins, Harper, and I together would potentially give the game away and get them killed.

If I was right. I really wanted to be wrong, but the pieces fit into a picture we couldn't afford to ignore.

"Ciaran must stay near Brie if she is to fight," Yosemite said.

"If they agree, he can come." I had considered bringing Ciaran into this meeting. I trusted the leprechaun to keep a secret. He and Brie weren't back yet, however, and I couldn't let the plan wait. Our noon meeting was coming, and the three of us had to be in agreement.

"And you are sure they will not see through the ruse?"

I was going to rename this guy Thomas the Doubter. Geez.

"No," I said. "The book is written in Old Irish, Middle Irish, some weird-ass dialect of Latin, and a bunch of words in something the weird part of my brain tells me is called 'Stone.' I doubt it is something anyone besides me could totally parse, but there's enough recognizable there that someone with enough knowledge could maybe make out the meanings." I wondered if humans had been misunderstanding the phrase *written in stone* for centuries, but I shoved that thought aside.

"I cannot say, but that I hope you are wrong," Yosemite said. "These games within games are tiring to even consider." He shook his head and rubbed at the bridge of his nose as though he felt a headache coming on.

"Hope for the best," I said. "Plan for the worst." It was all we could do.

"This plan sucks," Harper said.

We had gathered in the living room like a ragtag band of adventurers. Rosie hovered at the edge, teacup in hand. Max and Aurelio sat on the floor, heads tipped in mirrored gestures of consideration. Harper sat with her feet pulled up in one of the overstuffed chairs, glaring at me. The twins were side by side, Ezee watching Yosemite's face with narrowed dark eyes, Levi sucking speculatively on one of his lip rings. Junebug sat next to her husband, her fingers laced with his. Brie leaned against a wall behind Harper's chair, and Ciaran hovered near her, his red coat bright as fresh blood in the sunlight streaming through the window next to him. Only Tess was missing, but her door was open and I knew she could hear what we said.

I stood at the end of the room, flanked by Alek and Yosemite.

"It's the plan we have," I said. "We have to divide ourselves if we are going to do both rituals. We can't have the magic interfering, and we can't provide one big, juicy target. It's not that bad a plan; come on."

"Whatever. I'm going with you." Harper folded her arms over her knees.

"No," I said, too sharply. I sucked in a breath and forced myself to calm down. "What I'm doing is the more minor thing. Alek, Ciaran, and Brie should be enough. We'll have to be quick and quiet, and we want to distract Clyde with the larger force. That's why the rest of you need to go protect the druid. And Lir. He's the last unicorn, after all."

Cheap shot on my part, but it got Max and Levi both nodding. Harper made a face at me and rolled her eyes.

"Fine," she muttered.

"Great," I said. "Arm up and let's go do this thing. We have to be in place by twilight."

Orders issued, objections quelled, the group broke up into smaller groups. Brie came over to me, her eyes searching my face. When she spoke, however, it was to Yosemite.

"You trust her?" she asked him in Old Irish.

"Yo," I said. "Standing right here, totally understand you."

"I do," Yosemite said, as though I weren't standing right here, totally able to understand them.

"There are many here who think you are worth following, Jade Crow," she said, looking at me now.

It wasn't my imagination or Alek's. Brie was different. She looked a decade younger and her eyes were full of power, her gaze keen as a sword blade. The gentle, helpful magic she infused into her baking was nothing like the hot, sharp power that rippled off her in lazy waves.

"Who are you?" I said, sticking to Old Irish, aware our conversation could be overheard.

"E pluribus unum," she said with a toothy smile that didn't reach her eyes. *Out of many, one.* Like it explained anything. Ha.

"Okay, then," I muttered.

"Brie," Ciaran said, tugging lightly on her sleeve. "Come."

He led her away. Yosemite followed them, leaving Alek and me almost alone at the edge of the room.

"Tell me I'm doing the right thing," I whispered in Russian.

"You are worth following, kitten," he said, wrapping his arms around me.

Not what I'd asked for, but somehow, it was the right thing to say. I squeezed him back and then went to prepare for the worst.

"I'm going with you," Tess said to me as I went to say good-bye to her.

She was up, leaning unsteadily on the bed and trying to pull a sweater over her head. She'd definitely lost weight. Healing was apparently far tougher on her than on me.

"Fat chance," I said. "I mean this in the nicest way, but you aren't strong yet. Worrying about you might get us killed."

"I'm stronger than I look," she said.

"Says the woman who can't pull on a sweater without looking like she's in agony."

"I want to help." She dropped the sweater and glared at me. "Besides," she added, her expression shifting from anger to worry in a blink, "what if Samir comes for me here while you are all out fighting Clyde?"

I'd thought about that. I'd been doing a lot of thinking all morning about Samir, about what I knew of him and how he'd acted toward me so far since I'd revealed myself months ago.

"I don't think it'll happen," I said. "I think he'll sit back, watch to see what Clyde manages with this Fomoire and Balor's Eye crap. Samir likes a show."

She pressed her lips together and nodded. "He does," she admitted. "Clyde might be arrogant and young, but he's dangerous, too."

"So am I." I grinned at her, trying to project more confidence than I felt. Clyde wasn't the only one who could put on a show.

"Still feels wrong to stay and convalesce while everyone else fights," she muttered. She climbed back onto the bed, not quite successfully hiding a pained grimace.

"Someone will need to protect Rosie, Max, and Junebug," I said. I'd used the same argument on Max, only saying *Tess, Rosie, and Junebug* that time. Rosie had forbidden Max to go, much to his anger, but I agreed with her. He was only fifteen. It was hard to remember sometimes; it felt like we'd all been through a lifetime of battles these last few months.

"True," Tess said with a sigh.

I sat on the edge as she arranged herself. The others were almost ready to go, but I had things I wanted to discuss. So many things. There wasn't time for them all.

"You'll be more help later," I said. "After. I think if Clyde fails here, Samir might come himself. Were you serious about us fighting together? You said you know about magic, that you could help teach me."

"I was serious," Tess said. Her eyes fixed on mine, an almost fanatical light burning in their depths.

Doubt whispered in my heart, doubt about my plan, about the connections I was sure I'd made, about Samir's nature and the nature of Clyde's plan. I pushed them away. I had contingencies for being wrong, thin and weak though the beta plan was. I was running out of time, but there

429

was one thing I desperately wanted to know, and I hoped Tess had an answer for me.

"Do you know if Samir lied to me about how we can't be killed unless another sorcerer eats our hearts?" I spat out the question in a rush, thinking about all the times I'd almost died. The times I should have died. Like when I had thrown myself on a freaking bomb only weeks before.

"I think it is true," Tess said after a long moment. "He's lived a very long time, and we don't seem to age much. I've never heard of a sorcerer killed any other way, but we don't exactly appear very often, and we all seem to die only one way most of the time, killed by one man." She looked away from me, one hand rubbing her crucifix, her jaw tight.

"But what sets us apart from human magic-users? Why don't we die? Why do we have power at our fingertips for asking when others must earn it?" I wanted to know what we were. I wanted to know how it all worked, how much of what little Samir had told me was the truth. I'd eaten the hearts of two men, men who had had to train and learn and steal their power from other things. I knew they were different from what I was; I felt their humanity, their mortality. But my knowledge was weak, blind, like knowing the difference between the taste of licorice and the taste of mint. Two different things, but I didn't know why.

At the heart of it, I wanted to know why I was even more different. Why could I see magic? Why did I heal in hours? Why did I know every damn language?

Why had I survived when so many others had not? Why was Wolf with me, and how had she scarred Samir?

I curled my hands into fists, feeling like a small child. All *why* and no answers.

"I don't know," Tess said. "Why is there magic at all? I give those questions up to God. It is more peaceful to accept His will than to doubt."

"Don't you want to know why we are what we are?"

"No," she said, her voice soft, her eyes bright in the sunlight as she stared out the window, not meeting my gaze. "I only want to live, to be free of Samir. To let this cup pass from me."

I knitted my eyebrows together, trying to place where I'd heard those words before. More scripture, perhaps.

"We'll find a way," I said, sounding more confident than I felt. "First, I'm going to go pwn that brat of his."

"Pwn?" Tess said, finally looking at me again. "Like your shop?"

"It's from the Welsh," I joked.

"Wouldn't it be pronounced *poon*, then?" Her expression was skeptical.

"Damn, foiled again," I said.

Alek tapped on the door and stuck his head in. "We are ready," he said, eyes flicking between Tess and me.

I stood up. We were out of time.

Be good, I thought, almost speaking the words aloud.

"Be safe," I said instead. "We'll talk more later."

"Godspeed," Tess said. "Take care, Jade."

CHAPTER FOURTEEN

The ritual had to be performed in a druid's grove, which was apparently specially cultivated and prepared sacred ground. Yosemite had groves spread across the River of No Return Wilderness, but the nearest to us was a four-hour hike from the nearest trailhead.

The woods were eerily silent, though the day was spectacular, a rare sunny fall day full of color and the crisp promise of winter without winter's bite. No birds sang. No deer flicked annoyed tails at us and ran. It was hunting season; the woods and fields should have been thick with rabbit, fox, deer, bear, and many kinds of birds. It was as though the wilderness itself was holding its breath, waiting to see if we could close Balor's Eye and win the day. As we drew near the grove, I kept an eye on the surroundings, picking out a clearing for later.

The supernatural quiet ended abruptly as we crossed into the grove. It was easy to see where the sacred space started and the normal woods ended. The trees here were taller than any around, their leaves still green as though it were early summer, not nearly winter. A burbling creek flowed along one side of the wide circle of green, whispering trees. Algae formed a soft green carpet at the bottom of the stream, giving the water an emerald cast, and Spanish moss hung from the trees as though shrouding this place, curtaining it off from the normal world.

In the trees around us, giant wolves flowed into position. The dying sunlight coming through the leaves cast heavy green shadows over everyone except the unicorn. Lir, his body almost unmarred now, followed Yosemite into the grassy center of the grove. The unicorn seemed to understand what was needed. I'd explained the ritual to Yosemite, and he'd spoken to Lir in the barn before we left. I watched the beautiful creature as he stood, head up, nostrils flared, watching us all with dark eyes that reminded me for a moment of Wolf's, deep black and full of tiny pinpricks of stars, like a night with no moon.

Alek, Brie, Ciaran, and I stopped on the edge of the grove. Alek clasped forearms with Aurelio before the wolf alpha shifted and went to join his pack. Harper, Levi, and Ezee came to me, shifting from their animal forms to human as they approached.

"You aren't going to change your mind, are you?" Harper said, glaring at me.

"Harper," I said, grabbing her into a hug. "Trust me," I whispered, though with everyone around me having super hearing, there was little point. "Please, furball."

"With my life," she said, hugging me back.

Which was why she couldn't come with me. I wanted to tell her the plan, but I knew she'd insist on going where the real action was, insist on helping. I had to keep my friends out of the way if I could. For as long as I could.

"We get hugs?" Levi said, his grin forced.

"Group hug?" I laughed, blinking against the sudden lump in my throat.

I looked at my friends as they finally let me go.

"Good luck," I said. It was totally inadequate, but I felt like I had to say something.

My merry band of four left the grove behind, backtracking to the clearing I'd picked out earlier. I wanted to be close enough that if I was wrong we could get back to them, but far enough away that if I was right, we'd keep the worst of the danger away. Other than the weird lack of wildlife, there was no sign in this part of the forest of Balor's Eye damaging anything. Yet. Hopefully not ever.

Alek walked beside me, retaining his human form for the moment. I slid my hand into his. He'd argued with me this morning about my plan, but I was firm. I couldn't worry about protecting him and doing what I had to do if I didn't have his promise to stay out of fights that weren't his. He was unhappy—I could tell from the way his shoulders hunched and the grip he kept on my fingers—but he would keep his word. Alek was nothing if not honorable, almost to a fault. I loved him for it, needed it from him. He was a reminder that we could and would do what we had to, but that we could still retain some level of goodness, too, a kind of honor in itself.

We stopped at the clearing and I took my supplies out of my backpack, setting up while Brie and Ciaran looked on. They didn't know the whole plan; they still thought I was doing a ritual. Which I was, of a sort.

Unsure if it was safe to talk out there, though it felt like we were alone in this too-quiet wood, I reiterated my instructions.

"Keep anything that shows up off me, but leave the sorcerer to me. If I fall, run to the others."

"I don't much care for that part." Ciaran shook his head, his silver and copper curls bouncing.

"Makes two of us," Alek said with a growl. Yep, he was still mad at me. Awesomesauce.

"I'm fine with it, if anyone is asking," Brie said. She grinned at me, rolling her shoulders before dropping into a hamstring stretch. "Let the sorcerers duel their own."

"I used to like you," Alek told her, transferring his glare.

"So did I," Ciaran said, though he smiled at her, which took much of the sting from his words.

"Jade understands," Brie said.

I wasn't sure I did, but I nodded anyway, my mind already going to what was next. It was a shitty place to be, stuck there with doubts and fears. I wanted to be wrong, but I wanted to be right, too, because it would mean keeping more people safe.

I shook it all off. The sun was setting. Twilight neared. I had to act now, to put on a show for my enemy.

"Places," I said, stepping into mine and gripping my talisman as I summoned my magic.

Alek, Ciaran, and Brie melted into the trees. How half-denuded trees could hide a tall woman with flame-colored hair, a leprechaun in a deep red coat, and a giant white tiger, I don't know. They hid, however. Magic. Fun times.

I started the chant, pitching my voice low and soft, channeling two spells at once. The light dimmed as the sun dropped behind the trees. A breeze picked up, rustled leaves, and then seemed to think better of it. My heartbeat was loud in my ears, pounding in time to my chant. The moments stretched out with no sign of trouble, and for a brief second, I felt something like real hope. Wolf materialized beside me, her lips drawn back in a silent snarl.

Then Tess stabbed me in the back.

Or what she thought was me. Her knife sank into the chunk of wood I'd laid out in the middle of the circle I'd drawn in the clearing. The illusion I'd woven with my magic and a little help from Haruki's memories flared purple and dissipated, the glyph burning away beneath her blade.

I stepped out from the trees where I'd hidden, my steps heavy. It was one thing to suspect, another to see without a doubt that I had been right all along. Instead of vindicated or satisfied, I just felt tired and a deep sense of loss over what might have been.

"I believe my line is *Curse your sudden but inevitable betrayal*," I said, pulling my power into an invisible shield around me.

Tess yanked the knife from the wood and crouched into a fighting stance, her thin face a picture of surprise.

"How did you know?" she asked.

"What, you want me to monologue and give away all my secrets?" I circled to my right, wanting to draw her gaze and attention away from where my companions were hiding. Tess knew they were there—she'd heard the fake plan that morning, just as I'd intended.

"Humor me," she said.

"Humor *me*," I said, my voice sounding bitter to my own ears. "How much of what you said was lies?"

An expression almost like grief flickered over her face and she straightened up, though she kept the knife in front of herself and stayed light on her feet.

"Not much," she said. "I want Samir dead. I will do anything to accomplish that. I'm sorry."

I believed her, damn her. It was what had made it so difficult to convince myself even when all the pieces started to fall into place.

"Clyde gave it away, or at least set the first real doubt," I said. "When he told me you would betray me."

"You believed him?"

"Yes . . . and no. I didn't, of course, not after you got half-dead saving Levi. But what he said was too on point, too perfect. I wasn't supposed to believe him, was I? He was a common enemy, something to put pressure on us with, someone to confirm through denial that you were genuine."

The last rays of the sun lit the trees on fire, and behind Tess I saw movement, something grey and long sliding quietly through the forest. To my left I caught a flash of white in the trees, heading toward whatever lurked there. Tess took the moment of my distraction to attack, her magic flaring cold, warning me.

I poured power into my shield and tried to follow her magic, not her body. She was too fast, warping time around herself so that everything seemed to speed up and then slow down in nauseating waves around me. Her knife bounced off my shield and she retreated as I threw an arc of fire at her, trying to keep it invisible now that I knew she couldn't see my magic.

I'd always envisioned my fire as purple, and when I summoned visible power, it was always purple too. Mostly because I really liked the color purple. Turning off a thing I'd been doing my whole life was difficult, and the streak of flame still had a violet hue to it. She dodged and backed away. We circled each other as something crashed in the trees. This time, I didn't look, but she did, a quick glance and a small smile telling me that she'd been expecting help to arrive for her.

So had I.

"Then there was the book," I said. "And the plan with the Fomoire. From what you'd said about Clyde, from how you didn't know about the unicorns, I knew that you hadn't come up with that part of the plan. So, it was either Clyde or Samir or both. Samir has another copy of the druid's book in his library. I remember seeing it years ago. He wouldn't care about this forest, about the Eye, but he would enjoy something that drew me out, hurt people around me, and distracted me."

"Wouldn't that support me being innocent?" she asked.

"Yes . . . and no. You were too conveniently timed. Plus, I guessed that Clyde was going off the plan, doing showy shit like you said he liked to do. And that Samir didn't tell you the whole of things."

"No," she agreed. "It isn't his way."

"The final piece was how thin you've gotten. You've been healing yourself by speeding up time around you, right? But you can't eat enough to make up for that time, to keep the same appearance."

Her eyes widened and her full mouth curved in a rueful smile. "You learn quickly," she said.

Green light flickered in the woods, and the trees behind Tess started to shake and crash into each other. I needed to stop her, end this, before

Clyde arrived. I knew my friends would buy me some time, but it was dangerous for them to bait the sorcerer and the stone guardians I was laying a bet on that he'd brought with him.

"No," she said, almost to herself. "He can't have you. I need your power."

Talk time was over. Tess disappeared in a blink, but her magic trailed around her, visible as fine pale blue waves, radiating a frosty chill.

Her knife hit my shield from behind, and I threw my weight back as my magic turned the blade. Alek had loaned me a big Bowie knife, since I'd given up Samir's, but judging from how Tess moved, she was accomplished with this hand-to-hand shit in ways I never would be. I couldn't fight her blade to blade.

I leapt to the side, using my magic to carry me feet farther than my legs would have, and threw a wave of fire out from my hands as I twisted. She was too quick for me to aim for, her control of the speed of things around her too good for me to land a blow, so I went for the spray-and-pray method. It was draining and I couldn't tell in the growing gloom if I'd hit. From the singed scent of the air but lack of flaming sorceress, I guessed I'd come close but had no cigar.

A pale blue wave of power zipped in on my right side and I walled it off with fire. She was too close, and I found myself grinning as I poured magic into the flames, extending the wave as far to each side as I could.

She ran through the flame, bursting into view directly in front of me, her momentum too much for me to stop, too quick to dodge. Her hair caught fire but her knife found my stomach.

Pain seared through me, and I lost my grip on my power as I screamed and grabbed at her. I tried to go for my knife, but she clung to me, twisting the blade in my belly. Red spots did a tango across my eyes and my world filled with the scent and sight of Tess on fire, her hair smoldering, her eyes filled with darkness.

I couldn't get away from her, so I clung instead, pushing myself farther onto her blade. Her power swirled around us and the fire in her hair went out in a puff of acrid smoke.

"I'm sorry," she said, her face so close to mine that I felt her breath hot on my cheek.

My fingers didn't want to work; my brain was trying to shut down the pain and run screaming into the dark. Numb cold spread from the wound and up into my chest, pushing the pain away, granting me a small space in which to think, to breathe. My hand closed on my own knife and I dragged it free of the sheath. So slow. Still, she hung on to me until I weakly shoved her back.

She fell away, just a step. Enough. My free hand closed on the blade in my belly, locking it into place as she tried to drag it out, holding her in place as she kept her grip on it.

I jammed my knife up into her sternum, her own scream ringing in my ears as I cut, throwing magic into the blade, going for her heart. I abandoned the knife as she fell backward, following her down to the ground. I knelt over her as she ineffectually tried to pull the buried knife from her chest. Violet claws grew from my fingers, and I plunged my hand into her and ripped out her heart.

Time stopped. The sounds of fighting in the trees died. The air froze and I couldn't breathe for a moment as my body adjusted. Tess's heart in my hand was hot, almost burning me, still beating. Her eyes were open, her pupils huge and black, eclipsing her irises. Speckled with stars.

Her hand, red with my blood—or hers, I couldn't tell—reached up and gripped my own, her silver bracelet shining with its own light, the cross on it a tiny star. She pressed her heart toward me.

"Take," she whispered, the words hardly more than a sigh. "Eat. This is my body, which is given for you. Do this in remembrance of me."

I hesitated, then nodded, biting into her heart, putting out the light in her eyes and drawing it into my own. I'd seen most of the game, played it out almost to the end. As Tess died and became a part of me, her cold power sinking into my own inner ocean of magic, I saw the check and mate.

I'd thought she was lying, that somehow she had managed to deceive Alek, fool his Justice ability. I was wrong, dead fucking wrong.

Tess's memories flowed through me and I saw her choices through her eyes. She was willing to do whatever it took to defeat Samir. She was willing to help me, teach me.

To join her power with mine. Join me.

Literally.

CHAPTER FIFTEEN ▶

Pain flared again, the numbness burning away as time sped back up and the bubble Tess had cast around us died with her. I yanked the knife from my belly before I could think about it too hard and lose my will. Or consciousness.

I poured raw magic into the wound, visualizing it closing, willing my body to heal. The blood stopped gushing, but even getting to my feet was agony. I reached for Tess's cold magic and numbed myself, letting her memories guide me instinctually. It would take practice to learn to do what she had done, but I could mimic what I'd seen, what I'd felt.

The wound throbbed but the worst of the pain faded. Tiger-Alek crashed out of the trees and rolled across the clearing, gaining his feet with a snarl. He spared a glance for me as a huge stone catlike beast followed him, rust-colored smoke spilling from cracks along its body. Blood stained tiger-Alek's white coat, a gash open and oozing along one shoulder.

Trees crashed and shook in the forest, and green light flickered in the twilight between the trunks. I thought I saw two women, both with long flaming hair, dancing out there, swords in hand, fighting the stone snake. The trees and growing darkness made it difficult to tell.

"Clyde," I screamed at the woods. I stumbled forward, every step threatening to break the icy magic I had cloaking my wound. I wrapped my hand around my talisman and gritted my teeth. This battle was only half-won.

He appeared, slender and shining with dark power, springing from the trees. Tentacles of inky light slashed toward me.

"You killed her," he snarled. "She was mine!"

I slashed out with purple fire, burning back the tentacles. Greasy smoke hazed the air, the smell something between a wet campfire and a pile of rotting garbage.

"Come and get her, then," I said through clenched teeth.

His magic was the filth that had tainted the unicorn, the same oily black sludge now turned into slick tentacles that rent the air with acidic smoke. At the corner of my vision, I watched as Alek sprang at the stone beast. The cat was nearly as big as he was, and they rolled back into the trees, a flash of rusty light and white fur.

I wanted to go and help him, but I forced myself to stay focused on Clyde. I'd told Alek not to interfere with my fight with the sorcerers when they showed up, and he'd made me promise to let him and Brie protect me from the guardians that I was sure Clyde would bring with him.

I'd wondered if Clyde would bring along the Fomoire hounds as well, but gambled that he would send those at the druid, seeking to keep them occupied so no one could interfere with him and Tess. The Tess in my thoughts whispered that Clyde had likely hoped I would bring her down, or at least drain her low, so he could take her heart for himself. He would harvest mine for Samir, she thought, and in her memories I saw the heart container, a small silver-threaded bag.

A bag tied now to Clyde's belt. The sorcerer wore a long coat, which he stripped off and dropped to the ground as he gathered more power, circling to my right. Tentacles lashed out from his outstretched hands, and again I threw a wave of magic fire at them, shoving them back.

The red-spot tango was back in my vision, the euphoria I'd felt for a moment as I took Tess's gift to me now drained completely away. I had no time to prepare for the tentacles; he was able to move them independently, sending them at me from both sides. I expended blast after blast of sheer raw power, trying to hang on to reserves, to see a weakness and a way to reach him. I was too hurt to charge him; even sidestepping was enough to cause panic in my body, enough to threaten my balance as my legs tried to give out.

He's so arrogant, mind-Tess whispered to me.

He wanted my heart. He thought he could win, and maybe he could, but maybe I could out-power him. If I hadn't already spent this whole damn week draining myself over and over, if I hadn't been stabbed by Tess, I probably could have. As she'd told me, he was young, inexperienced with doing damage to things that fought back.

He advanced slowly on me, now wielding three tentacles that struck at me from the top and sides.

"Fall already," he snarled at me, his eyes black with his power, filth emanating from him in sickening waves. And I saw my opening.

So, I took it. I fell, dropping to one knee, turning my power from offensive into a shield along my skin, keeping the filth off myself but letting it batter me, drive me to the ground. I used my body to shield my hand from Clyde's line of sight as I picked up Tess's knife, still wet with my blood. Then I waited.

Maybe I really was some kind of Super Saiyan. Glutton for punishment and pain, but rising stronger every time. I almost laughed at the mental image of me with white hair sticking straight up but held it in. That was the delirium talking.

Triumphant, grinning, Clyde ceased his tentacle attacks and closed on me, his eyes flicking around the clearing to make sure we were alone. A terrible battle raged in the trees, but our space was open, only growls and howls and the breaking of branches and shaking of limbs giving any sign that we weren't wholly alone out there.

He stepped in close enough, only a tiger's length away now. I sprang, ignoring the pain in my belly, ignoring the darkness tugging at my vision. I used my magic to shove me forward and flew through the air, slamming into him. We rolled. I stabbed at him, over and over, eyes squeezed shut, mouth closed against the inky, putrid magic leaking from him. He panicked and tried to use his hands, his body, losing his grip on his power.

I sank the knife into him again and again, throwing my own magic along the blade, searing into that darkness, remembering how it had nearly killed the unicorn's wondrous light. Clyde stopped struggling and his screams died. My knife had found his heart.

Rolling off him, I lay on the grass. Stars winked down at me. Wolf appeared, her cold nose sliding under my hand as she crouched beside me. My own breathing was labored, heavy.

Clyde's breath gurgled, erratic. He was still alive. I hadn't taken his heart yet.

Green light spilled from the forest as a keening note, high and pure, rang through the forest. The stone cat and a huge turtle insect plunged into the clearing. Their hides were marked with scores and leaking rusty smoke. Three women followed the turtle, tiger-Alek at their side. They could have been triplets, each with long curling red hair and eyes full of emerald fire.

The light followed, first in streamers and then in a tidal wave, swamping us all. The stone beasts fell apart, their carapaces turning to shimmering mist. The three Bries cried out, their voices singing with glory. Behind them, a small, stout man in red ran toward them. Tiger-Alek roared.

The wave poured over and around me. Faces formed and dissipated before I could make them out. I hadn't realized how hurt I was until the pain just quit, its sudden absence making me gasp. Then the light changed from green to iridescent, and the song, that pure, clear note, became wild with joy.

The soul of the wild. I'd touched a piece of it within Lir. It danced and sang around me, awake and free, cleansing the wood of Clyde's filth, closing Balor's Eye.

Tess, built of green smoke and glimmering fire, appeared beside me.

"Take his heart," she said, her voice many voices, all languages, as though she spoke in tongues. My ears rang with the power in that voice.

I crawled to my knees and looked down at Clyde. He watched me with wide, pale eyes as I formed violet claws with magic around my hand. I ripped his heart out with the ease of pulling a half-embedded stone from sand and held it dripping and beating in my hand.

He shuddered and his eyes bled to black, but there were no stars reflected in them. I started to raise the heart to my already-bloody mouth but stopped.

This would be my fourth heart taken. Each of the others now lived on in me in a way, their experiences now mine, their memories, their abilities, their knowledge. Through me, they survived—even the damned serial killer whose memories I had mostly burned away.

"No," I said. Clyde's power was evil; his knowledge was of evil things, twisted life, ruined spirits. I felt nothing but filth and cruelty from him, in his magic.

I was already killer enough, worried enough that if push came to shove, I'd fall off the cliff of *not quite good* and tumble down into evil in the name of survival.

Mind-Tess railed at me, but the soul of the forest, still glimmering beside me in Tess's likeness, nodded as I met its eyes. I pulled the silver bag from Clyde's belt, ignoring the sweet, familiar feel of Samir's magic. Then I shoved Clyde's heart into the bag and watched his body still and his eyes cloud over as I zipped the bag shut.

The light took his body, the ground beneath me opening up and sucking him in like shimmering green quicksand. The heart in the bag still beat, but Clyde's magic was cut off, dormant, his body just a body without it.

The wild light faded away, but my own magic burned on, my body lighted from within by purple fire as I knelt over the bare ground and let my tears fall.

CHAPTER SIXTEEN ▶

Alek wrapped warm, human arms around me and I opened my eyes. I was no longer glowing and the woods were quite dark. We'd brought flashlights, but they were in a black bag by a tree somewhere.

"The others?" Alek asked.

"The Fomoire are gone," I said, sure of it. "Yosemite finished the ritual."

Alek turned his head even as I spoke, listening to something I couldn't hear. My ears were still ringing from the forest's voice. Ghostly grey and brown wolves appeared and lined the edge of the clearing. They parted and Harper came through, followed by a small herd of unicorns, Lir at their head. The unicorns' coats gleamed like moonlight in the growing gloom.

She limped right up to me as I stood there, my mouth hanging open.

"We won," she said, making it both a statement and a question.

"We won," I confirmed as I tightened my grip on the silver bag.

Harper looked past me. "Who's the kid?"

I turned and saw Ciaran holding a little girl in his arms. She had thick red hair and a confused look on her face. She was tiny, no more than three or four years old. He was whispering quietly to her, the words too low to make out. There was no sign of Brie or her two doppelgangers. He looked up and nodded to us, then disappeared in a puff of gold smoke, taking the odd child with him.

"No idea," I lied. I had a pretty good idea who that girl was, but finding out the truth would have to wait.

"Anyone hurt?" Alek asked.

Ezee and Levi limped out of the trees, both in human form and each favoring a leg. Yosemite followed. He seemed more solid to me, standing even taller. I wondered what the soul of the wild had done or said to him. Whatever it had been, I had a feeling he'd leveled up as a druid.

"We're good," Levi called.

"Is that . . ." Harper said, noticing the body crumpled on the ground behind me.

"Tess," I said. "We need to take her back."

My friends looked at me, then at each other. Wisely, they all just shrugged. I knew I'd have to explain Tess's betrayal—or rather, her not-betrayal. Explain how I'd known that Balor's Eye was just a distraction, that Clyde was after me, so I'd baited him and Tess by separating myself from the ritual, guessing correctly that the sorcerers would come after me. They didn't care if the druid won his fight or not. The deaths of the unicorns had been Clyde playing around, taunting the druid, taunting me. It had helped give away the game in the end.

"Jade," Alek murmured. "She betrayed you."

"She needs to be laid to rest in a graveyard, a Christian one," I said. "She did what she thought was right. I'll explain later." Hopefully, later I'd have figured it all out myself. There was a lot to think through now.

Alek frowned at me but nodded. "I'll carry her," he said.

I'd been mostly healed by the soul of the wild, but it was still a long, slow journey back to the Henhouse. Levi, Ezee, and Harper were all still hurting but refused Yosemite's offer to ask the unicorns to carry them home. The forest spirit had healed them enough that they wanted to make the journey. Harper also pointed out that Max would never forgive her if she got to ride a unicorn when he'd been forced to stay behind.

We ran into Max on the way back. Rosie had realized Tess was missing, and Max was trying to track her. He crumpled when he saw her dead body in Alek's arms. I didn't have the heart to tell him she'd betrayed us. It wasn't wholly true, anyway. We wrapped Tess's body in clean sheets and laid her in the barn.

All I wanted was a hot shower and a million years of sleep. Tomorrow, I would figure out how to break into a graveyard and bury a body. I didn't know any priests, so I asked Yosemite if he would help bury her. He said he knew many Christian prayers and would see if he could find something right to say. Levi overheard us and mentioned he knew a priest and would make a call.

"How tired are you?" I asked Alek after we'd taken a chaste shower together. Mostly chaste. There had been a lot of clinging, as neither of us wanted to break the sheer comfort of skin-on-skin contact.

"What do you need?" he asked, pushing my wet hair back behind my ears as he cupped my face.

I pointed to the silver bag. "Take that; hide it somewhere far away from here or my shop. Don't tell me where it is."

"You didn't kill him," he said.

"I don't want his power. I don't want his filth in me. I know that power is power, magic is magic, that it is all a tool to be used, but this is a tool I don't want. It's an atomic bomb, waiting to destroy me."

"Why have me hide it?" He tipped his head to one side, looking down at me, his expression unreadable.

"I think Samir will come for it." Tess thought he would. I felt her in my head, her memories and thought patterns fresh in my mind. "I think the endgame is coming."

"You do not seem afraid," Alek said. "Why not use the heart as bait?"

"I'm too fucking tired to be scared," I said. "But I'll be scared tomorrow. And honestly? I don't want the temptation. If things go poorly, I don't want to have that thing in reach. I don't want to make that choice."

He bent and kissed me softly, his lips warm and slightly chapped. "I will do this for you," he said. "Go to bed."

That was the best suggestion anyone had made all week, so I did exactly as ordered.

Tess was buried properly; an owl-shifter priest from a church over on the Nez Perce reservation presided. Levi and Ezee had a lot of friends. We still had to sneak into the graveyard, a pioneer cemetery, and borrow a grave, but at least we had a real priest. The ghost of Tess in my head was grateful, her churn of memories stilling and her voice going silent for a while after the prayers were spoken.

Rain started to fall as my friends turned away from the old grave. It was one of the most ancient there, the stone worn down nearly to nothing, the grave barely tended. Yosemite had regrown the grass along the seams of sod where we'd had to displace the earth to lay Tess down. Looking down at the grave, I almost couldn't tell that anyone was buried there at all.

It wasn't right. I shook off Alek's hand as he tried to gently lead me away.

"Wait," I said. "There is something I must do."

I walked around the grave to the headstone and knelt, ignoring the freezing water that seeped immediately into my jeans. I didn't know how to do what I wanted, but I believed I could manage it. Belief would have to be enough.

I called on my magic, thinking of Tess, not as I'd last seen her with blood leaking from her mouth, her chest a gaping wound, her eyes full of the universe. I thought of her smiling, beautiful and delicate, surrounded by my friends. Her memories, what I'd seen of them, told me she had walked a lonely road. While I'd spent my life running from Samir, she had spent hers stalking him, learning what she could while trying to hide in plain sight.

I closed my eyes and sent my magic into the stone, pressing, sculpting, listening to its rhythm and coaxing it beneath my hands. When I finally looked, the light in my talisman revealed new words, carved delicately into the stone, and filled with silver light that only I could see.

RIP Tessa Margaret Haller. She is remembered.

I'd looked up her last words online. They were from the Last Supper, part of the ritual of Communion. She had chosen her sacrifice, believing that I was stronger, that I had a better chance to win against Samir.

She had, in essence, placed her faith in me. Wholly. Irrevocably.

I was going to do my best not to fuck that up. No pressure, right?

After days of neglect and a couple of hexes, my shop was cold and dusty-feeling when I opened it back up two days later. My morning was surprisingly busy for a weekday as regulars came by, asking after my grandmother in a way that had me confused—until Harper showed up and explained she'd spread the story that I'd been out of town most of the last week caring for a sick granny. A little cliché of an excuse, but it seemed to work.

Brie showed up with cupcakes and coffee in the early afternoon. I had changed out all the light bulbs and gotten my computer to boot up finally, wondering just how full my work email was now, and dreading finding out.

She looked her normal self, her hair in two braids coiled on her head, her apron dusted with flour. Crow's-feet once against graced her face, and her body was stouter than it had been when she wielded a sword.

"Ciaran and Iollan send their goodwill and greetings," she said.

Ciaran, his hair more silver than copper now, had dropped by the Henhouse the day before and told me he and the druid were going to go check and make sure Balor's Eye was shut. They promised to be back within a week. I told Ciaran I'd keep an eye on his shop, but him being out of town for periods of time was normal. Everyone would assume he was on a buying trip somewhere.

"So," I said. Lamest opening ever, but how exactly did one go about asking what I wanted to ask? "You look, well, better. Older again." I could add two and two. Or one and three. I wasn't so ignorant of mythology that I hadn't heard of the Morrigan. I mean, she's all over video game lore, too. Goddess of war. Threefold goddess.

"I am not what you think," Brie said, opening the lid of her coffee cup and blowing on it.

"So, you aren't the Morrigan?"

She laughed, the sound rich and multilayered.

"All right," she admitted. "I'm sort of what you think."

"Iollan called you Brigit, though," I said.

"I was three goddesses once, long before, in a time when we walked among men, spoke with them, were revered. But the old ways are lost. We have dwindled. Brigit, Airmid, and Macha, who you call Morrigan, made a pact, we three. We tied ourselves, our memory, our knowledge, to a young druid, one of the last of his kind, and a young Fey, one of the few who remained in this world."

She held up her hand, palm toward me, and a glyph glowed on it briefly.

"A triquetra," I said. The knot was common—an embellishment all over manuscripts, a common piece of tattoo work, too. Yosemite had one right over his heart. Remembering that, I leaned back on my stool and smiled. "Three and one."

"My power is nearly gone. Only our bond holds us together. When I have to use power, I lose myself. I am immortal, in a way, and cannot die, but I become less—we become less."

"A child," I said.

"Ciaran and Iollan guard my memories. They restore me, give me back what I spend, bring me back to life with their belief. There is enough knowledge of the truth of what we were in them to sustain us. For now."

"But people worship old gods, too," I said, still wrapping my head around the idea that I was talking to a freaking goddess. After everything I'd seen this week, it wasn't that tough a stretch, weirdly enough.

"They worship what they think we were. Without knowledge, without truth. The time of gods has come and gone." She shook her head and smiled sadly. Then, rising, she capped her coffee and sighed. "I am sorry I judged you so poorly. It is difficult to hang on to my memories, and the ones that stay are often the most painful. They cloud my judgment sometimes."

"Pretty sure that's normal," I said.

"Perhaps. Well, if you need anything, my door is open to you." She turned to leave, but I hopped off my stool and came around the counter.

"Actually," I said, "there is something I need from you."

Peggy Olsen held book group, which was code for coven meetings, in the basement of the library on Wednesday nights. Brie had been reluctant to tell me, but I swore up and down on all the honor I still hoped I had that I wouldn't kill anyone.

Of course, Peggy Olsen and the twelve women of her coven hadn't heard me make that promise.

I had to wait a week longer than I wanted, because what I needed was on special order and totally out of season, but I slammed my way into book group in spectacular, showy fashion. Purple light danced along my skin, and I'd left my hair loose, expending power so that it floated around me as I kicked in the door and stomped right into the center of the coven meeting, a duffle bag in each hand.

"Stand where you are," I cried out, using more magic to enhance my voice.

The witches froze. Some had been getting coffee from a thermos. There was a long wooden table down the center of the room. On it was a dull ceremonial knife carved from wood. Incense and candles were lit around the room. The witches mostly sat at folding chairs around the table. One looked like she had been taking notes. There wasn't a book in sight. Clearly, they hadn't expected anyone to interrupt them or question their cover story. I felt the hum of warding magic, weak but present, as I crossed the threshold. Whatever they'd warded against hadn't included pissed-off sorceresses, apparently.

I memorized each face, recognizing a few. We lived in a small town, after all.

"What do you want?" Peggy said in a shaking voice, finally summoning the courage to rise to her feet.

"I want to talk to you about magic," I said. "I've been reading up, you see. And you all have been terrible witches."

Gasps ran around the room, the fear and tension rising.

"I'm tired of you hexing me, sending bugs and rats and whatever into my business. Harassing my friends. Basically, being annoying little bitches. You know I could squash you like bugs, bring this whole building down, or burn you all to ash where you stand."

I stopped and looked around at them again, meeting each gaze. Only Peggy looked me in the eye.

"But I won't. Because I'm not evil. If you think I am, you need your prescriptions amended, because you have no fucking clue what evil really is. You are dabbling idiots, mistaking a match flame's worth of power for the sun. But you have laws, rules you have to follow. Rules you've apparently forgotten."

I put down the bags and unzipped them. No one made a move to stop me, which showed serious smarts on their side. I wouldn't have hurt anyone, but I'd practiced holding someone in place with magic all week long. Levi, Ezee, Max, and Harper were pretty sick of it. Alek had just raised a pale eyebrow when I'd asked if he would let me practice on him. He was the only one I'd failed to pin for any length of time.

Ladybugs started to flood out of the bag. I prodded them gently with magic, waking them up. I had gone with those because I figured that if any made it out of the building, they wouldn't infest anyone's kitchen or hurt the landscaping. Wylde was going to be free of aphids next spring for sure.

"I am invoking the threefold law," I said as the little red-and-black bodies took flight, streaming toward the shocked women. "You want to keep being assholes to me? Fine. Everything you do will come back on you threefold. All of you, since I know without a full coven, there is no way you could raise the power Peggy wields. So, think about it before you hex."

Everyone was still frozen in place, staring at me and then at the bugs with shock. Peggy looked like her head was about to implode, her skin turning scarlet.

"Oh, yeah," I said, as I turned to leave. I clicked my fingers, sending a low wave of electricity around the room. Witches started cursing as cell phones in purses made terrible squealing noises and died. Acrid green smoke leaked out of Peggy's sweatshirt pocket. "Hexen," I added.

I used my magic to dramatically slam the door behind me as the women unfroze and angry, scared voices started pestering Peggy with questions. I grinned. That had felt way too good. Hopefully, it would solve my witch problem. I had a feeling it would. Praise Harper and her clever mind.

"Samir will come for me this time," I whispered to Alek as we lay on the blankets piled across my floor that night. "Tess is sure of it."

"Tess is dead," Alek murmured.

"Not in here," I said, tapping my forehead. "I knew him long ago. She knew him lately. He's grown bored, more bored. Without his apprentices to distract him, and with the lure of Clyde's heart, he'll come himself this time."

"Good," Alek said. "We will face him. You are strong, kitten. And you have many allies."

Great. More people to get killed. I shoved the bleak thought away.

"I just hope it is enough."

"We fight with what we have," he murmured. "Not what we wish to have."

"Okay, Obi-Wan." I nipped his chin and settled into his arms.

"I am not quoting *Star Wars*," he said, glaring down at me in mock annoyance.

"No, but you sound wise for your years."

"Protect you, I will," he said. "Love you, I do."

We fell asleep, laughter still on our lips.

CHAPTER SEVENTEEN ▶

Alek knew it was not a dream, because in his dreams, the world still had smells and tastes. The empty street outside Jade's store was quiet, wind blowing but without bringing scent with it, without sound. He couldn't smell the bakery, though its front door was steps away from him.

A figure walked down the empty street toward him, her shape vaguely female but shifting, always shifting. Ears of various shapes and sizes came and went in her white hair; her face grew whiskers, which were then replaced by soft black fur that shifted to an eagle's beak. The Council had come to speak to him. Carlos had told him once of a visit from the Emissary, but Alek had thought such a thing was far beyond any attention he himself merited.

Once, he would have dropped to his knees in awe. Those days felt far away. Instead, he stood and watched the Emissary approach. He had expected this, though he could not guess what the Council would want to show him.

Alek turned his eyes away from the shifting figure and looked up at the dark window above Pwned Comics and Games. In reality, he was up there, his tiger-self curled around Jade's little body, watching over her. His impatience surprised him. This vision might be important.

Its timing was no coincidence, not after such a long silence from the Council. He had started to wonder if he were still a Justice but had pushed away those thoughts, fighting off the dark wave of despair such thinking brought with it.

He could not fight himself forever, he knew. Hard questions would have to be asked, and soon.

Perhaps now.

"Aleksei Kirov," the Emissary said. Her voice was neither male nor female, a blend of tones and pitch. It had the same chill as night winds on the steppe.

Once, he might have shivered. But he was Tiger and had been born to the cold. Here, his heart was colder still, wrapped in a blanket of doubt.

"What do you want?" he said, trying to keep his impatience out of his voice.

"The Hearteater comes for the woman," the Emissary said. "You will give her to him."

He took a physical step back, his tiger rising within, his lips peeling back into a snarl. "No," he said, his voice almost inhuman.

"Look around you."

Alek tore his eyes away from the shifting figure. The buildings now burned, smoke rising, untouched by the odd, steady wind. Bodies littered the street, their blood red like paint, unreal without scent to back it up. Harper lay to his right, her face a beaten mess. She stretched a broken, twisted hand out to him, the look in her eyes one of utter and complete betrayal. Her lips formed words he couldn't make out, the wind taking away any sound she might have made, the vision still silent.

"No," Alek said again. "I will not betray my mate."

"Then they will all die. You will die. Is one life worth so much? You vowed to protect and serve our kind. Would you throw that oath away, throw your life away for a nonshifter? She is not of our kind. She and her battles are not ours to fight."

Alek felt a tightness in his chest. He looked down and watched as a gaping wound opened. There was no pain, just thick spurts of cold ruby blood and a hint of gritty white bone beneath the carved-up flesh. Embedded in his chest just above where the wound gaped, beneath a translucent layer of skin, his silver feather gleamed, infused with power.

He had told Jade once, not so long ago, that he strove for balance. He wanted that feather to weigh more than his soul, when the time came.

"When the time comes," he said softly, speaking mostly to himself, "it will balance."

"You must choose," the Emissary said. "Give up the woman to her kind, and you will save many lives. You are at the crossroads, Aleksei Kirov. You must choose."

Alek willed his fingers to be claws. He sliced his own flesh, digging the feather free. It came out clean and light as down, cool like a snow-flake in his palm.

He raised his gaze to the Emissary and met her yellow, cat-slit eyes.

"I have chosen," he said.

Then he opened his palm and let the feather fall.

ACHIEVEMENT UNLOCKED:

TURN THE PAGE FOR A SNEAK PEEK AT

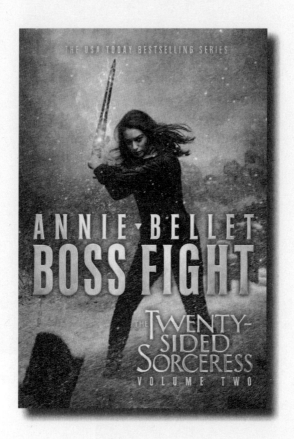

THE USA TODAY BESTSELLING SERIES

ANNIE·BELLET

BOSS FIGHT

THE TWENTY-SIDED SORCERESS

VOLUME TWO

The weather people had been forecasting a blizzard, but the sky was a smoky grey and the town utterly peaceful. Peace might have been nice if I didn't feel like the freaking sword of Damocles was playing hide-and-seek over my head. Alek was scarily full of a desire to keep me in his sights, which didn't help my anxiety levels one bit. I think he would have handcuffed himself to my side if I'd let him. My heart was forecasting doom.

Doom hadn't come. Nothing and nobody had come. Nearly a month had gone by since Samir's last missive to me. The dead apprentice of his, Tess, in my head was so damned sure he was coming for me, and yet . . .

Nobody came. The most eventful thing to happen was Brie's bakery being shut down for health code violations. As the building owner, I'd spent all Friday on the phone begging for a reinspection and silently plotting revenge on the witches. Alek had cautioned that I should be sure they were responsible first. Voice of reason and all. It seemed likely someone had reported the magical cockroach invasion. The roaches were gone. Getting a reinspection was a pain in the ass, though. Neither Brie nor I could even remember the first one. The county bureaucrat might well have been a ninja.

I almost wished for ninjas. It would have given me something to fight against. Instead, I spent four hours on hold and then got told to call back on Monday. Awesomesauce.

I wiped a dust cloth over a shelf that didn't have a speck of dust on it, and wondered where Alek was today. He'd stuck next to me for weeks, hardly leaving my side, and then gone away an hour before, after getting a text message. When I'd asked him where the fire was, he had said only that he'd tell me later.

My door chimed and I turned toward the front of the shop, pulling on magic, almost hoping it was Alek so I could play the annoyed girlfriend. Him leaving like that, given everything going on, it made me even more nervous. I knew the chain around his neck was empty, though he tucked it beneath his shirt, but he'd only shaken his head and told me it was complicated when I asked. We'd come a long way down Trust Lane, but not all the way to Unconditional Trust-ville, I guess.

It wasn't Alek but Brie who came through my door. Or, really, the triple goddesses who masqueraded as a single woman named Brie. She was tall and stacked, with bright red curls always braided up or piled on her head. Today, her hair was neatly pinned back, her cheeks rosy from the chill air. She looked around my game store, peering into the corners, then, satisfied it was empty but for me, she gave me a half-wave and slumped into a chair.

"We're leaving," she said. "We've got to go, tonight. I was hoping you'd keep an eye on the building."

"What?" I pushed my hair out of my face as my guts twisted like rope inside me. "Leaving? For how long? You and Ciaran?"

"We've been called to Ireland," Brie said. Her eyes narrowed and she looked into a middle distance, staring toward the new-release rack but seeing something outside my understanding. She lapsed into Irish. "The Fey are gathering. Ciaran must attend, and where he goes, so go I."

"What about Iollan?" I asked, thinking of the big druid. He and Ezee had seemed to reach a new level in their relationship. Like, having a relationship where they actually mentioned each other to their friends and family.

"Not he," Brie said, her eyes snapping to me as she shook off whatever thoughts had darkened her mood. "The druid cannot return to the Isle. But we must."

"So . . . you'll be back when?"

"I wish I could say."

The door chimed again and Ciaran entered in a sweep of crisp, icy air. The leprechaun wore his usual red coat and had a green army bag, like you'd see in old war movies, slung over one stout shoulder. His red-and-silver hair was tousled and damp, as though he'd showered and hadn't bothered to comb it.

"Brie tell you?" he said, also in Irish.

"She did, though I'm a little confused. Why now? Are you in trouble?" *Trouble I could Fireball, perhaps?* I wanted to add, but made my will save. Or my Wisdom check? Either way.

Ciaran and Brie exchanged a look that didn't help my nerves at all. Then he shrugged one shoulder, the other probably weighted down too much by the rucksack to lift.

"We shall see," he said, lips pressing together at the end. "It has been five hundred years since the last gathering."

"Oh, well, maybe they miss your faces." I tried to smile. "Can I help? Are you magicking yourselves there or something?"

"We have a flight leaving from Seattle tonight. Max is driving us. He'll be walking in here through your back door in a moment." Brie rose, straightening her coat.

Max walked in through the back, setting my wards back there buzzing for a second.

Harper's brother grinned at me. "You really going to leave that door unlocked? Is that safe?"

"Anyone coming to kill me won't care about a ten-dollar lock on a door made of cardboard," I pointed out. "How's it feel to have your license, birthday boy?"

Max had turned sixteen the week before, and the first thing he'd done was go get his license. Levi had gifted the kid a car that was ugly as sin and looked pieced together by a bad game of *Katamari* in a junkyard, but it ran despite being held together with bubblegum and love.

"Car's open if you want to put your stuff in," Max said as Brie and Ciaran both moved toward the back door. "I think they are in a hurry," he added to me as they disappeared down the back hall past the game room.

"Do I get to see the picture?" I resisted the urge to fluff Max's brown hair.

"Oh, God, Harper told you?"

"Dude, really? Of course she told me."

"The camera went weird, I swear. I look like a cross-eyed chipmunk."

"Okay, it can't be that bad."

He shook his head and dragged his wallet out of his down jacket pocket.

It wasn't that bad. It was worse. I'm a terrible person, but I totally laughed. There was no way *not* to laugh. I'm only human. Sort of.

Max yanked his license back and crammed it into his wallet, muttering a bunch of words his mother would have washed his mouth out with soap for if she'd heard him.

"Hey, I'm sorry," I said, trying to stifle the giggles. "It's not so bad."

"Harper said the same thing. Then you know what she said?" Max's lips started to twitch and he was having trouble maintaining the surly-teen-boy act.

"What?"

"'It's just, there's something about your eyes,'" he said in a high, squeaky voice that was supposed to be an imitation of his older sister. "'Something . . . shifty.'" He switched back to his normal voice. "Seriously. Then she laughed so hard, Mom had to tell her to go outside."

"Did you tell her there is a special hell for people who make bad puns?"

Max rolled his eyes, then looked around us at the empty store. "Where is she, anyway?"

"Up at the college, in one of the library silent study rooms. She's got MGL qualifiers to practice for and she says the net up there is better than here. Whole section of this block has turned into an annoying net dead zone. We drop offline all the time." I shrugged. The net was another annoyance; plus, I missed Harper being here, cursing a blue storm. I felt weirdly lonely there in my store, just sitting around dusting things that were already clean and sorting cards already sorted.

Like someone rearranging deck chairs on the *Titanic*.

"Be careful on your drive," I said. I had enough intelligence to know not to question Max's car's ability to even make it to Seattle. His feelings were hurt enough for one day. "The roads and all. You going on to the beach early, then?"

"Yeah, the guys got the house a couple days sooner than we thought." He and some friends had gotten a great deal on a beach house in Washington, it being winter and all. His sixteenth birthday was going a hell of a lot better than mine had.

I was glad he'd be away from Wylde for the week. If shit went down soon, one more person I cared about not in the crosshairs was good. Max had already gotten hurt because of me. I wished I could send them all away. But my friends had made their choice.

I could only hope it was the right one.

I made Ciaran and Brie promise to email me with updates, gave Max a quick hug, and stood in the freezing air to wave them away as Max's patchwork car bumped out of the parking lot and out onto the main road. I watched them disappear down the road and shivered from more than the winter chill. With that damned other shoe waiting to drop, every good-bye right now felt weirdly final.

My shop was so quiet and still when I returned that I almost missed Alek standing like a giant Viking shadow by the center support post. His white-blond hair was messy, the way it looked when he'd been running his hands through it, something he only did when upset or angry. His normally pale blue eyes looked colder than the sky and his mouth was pressed into a tight line.

"What's wrong?" I asked, feeling the metaphorical sword shoe thing lowering over my head.

"Carlos," he said.

"It's Sunday," I said, half to myself. The last few weeks, Carlos, Alek's friend and former mentor among the Justices, had been out of touch.

"He wants to meet. Wants me to meet someone."

"Where? When? Who?" I asked. I pressed my hands against his sides, wanting his heat, wanting to push back the tension and darkness lurking in his face and body.

"New Orleans. As soon as possible. I have no idea," he said. Then he shook his head. "No, I have an idea. I do not like it."

"Does he know about . . ." I looked at the chain disappearing under his collar.

"If I am to meet who I think, yes. He knows I am not a Justice anymore."

Alek's words hung between us, almost tangible, like fog in the air. So. There it was. Finally said.

"What happened, Alek?" I whispered. I had an idea. This, like so much else, was probably my fault. I tried to tell myself that was ego talking, but one couldn't deny the timing or the mounds of circumstantial evidence piling up around us.

"The world changes," he said. His eyes shifted down to my face and he bent, kissing me softly on the forehead. "This is not your fault."

He took a deep breath, his chest swelling big enough that his coat brushed my cheek. I wanted to lay my head against him and tell him everything would work out, but we were beyond lying to each other like that. I hoped.

"Anyway," he said after he let out the breath. "I am not going."

"What? Is this important? Will they try to hurt you?" I added the *try* because there was no way anybody was going to hurt him. Not on my watch.

"It is, and no, I do not think they will. Carlos used our safe code. I do not think he would betray me, not like this. But it doesn't matter. I am not leaving you."

"So, I'll come with you."

"You cannot travel where I would go."

"They have some kind of magical barrier around New Orleans now that keeps out sorceresses?" I tried to smile as I said it, ignoring the painful beating of my heart.

"It is Justice business. I am not sure even I can do what I must, but . . ." He sighed again. "I am not going."

Because of me. The tension in his body wasn't just over worry about the situation. He wanted to go. Something had happened to him. One day, he woke up and wasn't the same. The changes were tiny, things only I had noticed, I thought. The necklace being hidden. His overattentiveness that went beyond worry about Samir. Every time he held me, he had a grip that made me feel like that would be the last time. He was there, almost stifling me, but somehow Alek seemed already gone.

If going, if sorting out this Justice business, would give a piece of him back, I couldn't let him stay. I wanted my Alek back, the man who was always sure of things, who saw the shadows in life and faced them down. Not this Alek who clung to me like the world was ending and I just couldn't see the explosion yet.

"You are going," I said.

"Jade," he started, but I shook my head.

"No. I'm serious. You haven't been you. I don't know what happened, because your stubborn ass won't tell me. But if going to see Carlos and whoever this other mysterious whatever is helps you come to terms with whatever the hell happened? I'm for it."

"I don't know how long I'll be gone," he said, shaking his head slowly, his hair brushing against his cheeks and his expression torn between worry and desire. "What if Samir comes?"

"I've been asking myself that question for twenty-six years," I said as I forced my mouth to form a smile. It kind of hurt, but he needed me to be confident. "He hasn't shown up yet. We're about to get a pile of snow dumped on us. If you are going to leave, you should go. Take care of whatever you need to take care of. Then come home to me."

"I will always come home to you," he said, and I swear to the Universe his eyes looked like he might cry.

The fuck was going on? I shivered again, despite the warm shop, despite his warm arms wrapping around me and pulling me close. Swords. Deck chairs. We were totally screwed—I just didn't know exactly how yet.

"Go," I said to him after he had kissed me hard enough that I wanted him to stay.

Alek pressed his cheek to mine and nodded slowly. When he left, I didn't say good-bye. I refused to, because this felt like good-bye enough.

All I knew was that if the Council of Nine did anything to my lover, I was going to have to go make a whole new cadre of enemies. And if Alek didn't return to me soon, Carlos would be first on my damned list.